THE RED
HAND

An Abaddon Books™ Publication
www.abaddonbooks.com
abaddon@rebellion.co.uk

First published in 2015 by Abaddon Books™,
Rebellion Intellectual Property Limited,
Riverside House, Osney Mead, Oxford, OX2 0ES, UK.

10 9 8 7 6 5 4 3 2 1

Editors: Jonathan Oliver & David Moore
Cover Art: Luke Preece
Design: Simon Parr & Sam Gretton
Marketing and PR: Lydia Gittins
Publishing Manager: Ben Smith
Creative Director and CEO: Jason Kingsley
Chief Technical Officer: Chris Kingsley
Hunter of Sherwood™ created by David Moore
and Toby Venables

ISBN: 978-1-78108-289-8

Printed in the UK

HUNTER OF SHERWOOD

THE RED HAND

A GUY OF GISBURNE NOVEL

TOBY VENABLES

**ABADDON
BOOKS**

WWW.ABADDONBOOKS.COM

For Mum and Dad

I

THE COMING APOCALYPSE

I

Jerusalem
March, 1193

ASIF AL-DIN IBN Salah watched the rat lope along the dark tunnel ahead of the flickering light from his torch.

It was a big rat. A fat rat. As big as the cats that darted about the alleys off the Malquisinat. Those mewling, wide-eyed creatures scavenged a fair living off the so-called 'street of bad cooking' – but they were puny specimens next to this hunched monster. Asif shuddered at the sight of it. For a moment it paused and waved its wet snout in the air like a dog picking up a scent. How such a thing were possible in this foul place, Asif could not guess. The mere thought of the thick stench that lapped about him – and the horrid sheen of the rat's slimy, matted fur – made a sour wave of nausea rise from the pit of his stomach.

He shook it off. Asif needed his wits about him, down here. If the reports were to be believed, there were far worse things than rats.

Intelligence on what had been going on in the forgotten tunnels was garbled – fragmentary at best, and in its details, often bizarre. People had spoken of whole cartloads of provisions – dozens of barrels – disappearing near the sewer's entry points, as if some huge thing had emerged from the subterranean labyrinth under cover of night and swallowed them up. One account – from a terrified Greek merchant who found himself alone one night near the Pool of Siloam – spoke of a man with the blank, expressionless face of a doll rising from under the ground. Another, of a walking statue of a dead Templar. More than once, Asif had heard the claim that the effigy of the Leper King had got up and walked, and was lurking beneath the city, ready to drag unwary Muslims into the depths. One old Jewish scholar muttered a word whose significance Asif had not fully understood, and which all flatly refused to explain to him: *go-lem*.

There was one common feature: Christian knights. What interest Christian knights might have in Jerusalem's sewers was baffling. Asif –

who had been resident in the city for most of his adult life, and helped to keep the peace under Christian rule before he entered the service of the Sultan – knew this city as well as anyone alive. Yet even he was perplexed. Jerusalem was a city of many mysteries – it was, Asif often joked, harder to get to know than a woman. Perhaps, after all, it was nothing. But since the city's recapture by Salah al-Din and the hapless 'crusade' that followed, any Christian military presence here had to be regarded with utmost suspicion.

There was another strange fact that had revealed itself to Asif in these last few hours. He'd known, of course, that rats are ubiquitous in sewers, and when he had first descended into this forgotten netherworld, it had been immediately confirmed. He had tied his clothing tighter about him, and pressed on. But as he had progressed through the cramped tunnels, Asif had seen the quantity of rats dwindle, and for the past quarter hour at least this lone adventurer had been the only beast he had encountered. The absence troubled him. Something had driven them out. It took a lot to drive out rats.

Just one had stayed – and was reaping the benefits.

Asif did not fear rats as some did. Not even in large numbers. But he had no great desire to get closer to this single, grotesquely-swollen creature. It had been well fed of late. It also had no fear of man. Where it was now heading, and what he would find there, filled him with a sense of creeping unease.

And now it was on the move again. He heard its claws scratch on the stone ledge, saw its bald, pink tail whip from side to side. Then, as he swung his torch close to where there should have been only blank wall, a horrid shape loomed from the shadows.

A face. Half human. Less than a yard from his own.

He reeled back, almost stumbling, his free right hand going to his sword. There, in the crumbling ancient wall, was a jagged vertical fissure, and emerging from it, as if prising the stonework apart, were the skeletal fingers of a dead man. His warped skull grinned from the spreading gap, the empty pits of its eyes turned on Asif, while below, part of a leg bone thrust out of the crack as if about to take a step towards him.

Asif heard a harsh curse cut the thick air, only dimly aware that he himself had spoken. In a moment, he understood. He silently berated himself. They were bones, nothing more. Dead, dry, yellowed bones. But these bones, decades old at least – perhaps centuries – had been jammed into this crevice in such a way as to give them the semblance of life. To what end, and by whom, Asif could not guess. He stood for a moment, his heart still thumping in his chest – so hard he could hear it in the flat, eerie silence. A different kind of horror afflicted him now, spawned by his attempts to imagine what could have led to this terrible fate – how one who had once lived and loved could become so pitiful in death, abandoned and forgotten in this awful place.

The flickering light of the flambeau made the shadows about the bony form dance, creating a horrid illusion of convulsive movement. He fleetingly wondered what those long-dead eyes had once looked upon – a wife, a lover; children, perhaps. But whatever this man had been in life, he was now no more than an absurd relic.

As he stood, he felt the queasy pressure of effluent flowing past his calves, and for an instant his concentration faltered. Before entering the tunnels, in anticipation of the rising stink, Asif had stuffed his nostrils with plugs of beeswax mixed with aromatic herbs, and had been breathing through his teeth. But now – thanks, in part, to the panicked panting his skeletal friend had inspired – he was beginning to taste the foul stench. His stomach knotted, almost making him retch. He fought it down, and by way of distraction made himself stare again into the lifeless, hollow eye-sockets of the forgotten man.

He thought of Qasim.

Qasim had never wanted to come down here. But if you were an agent of the Sultan, you went where you were told to go – even if where you were told to go was a sewer. No one relished the idea of wading through shit, no matter how fervently they believed in the mission. To Qasim, however, there was something far worse than that, something that made him even less comfortable with the whole enterprise: wading through the shit of infidels. Especially worrying to him was the prospect of having to traverse the drains beneath the Christian quarter. "It's not just that they are godless," he said. "They are unclean. They eat *pig*..."

Asif sympathised, but – somewhat to his surprise – found his own feelings on the subject to be far more pragmatic. It was crazy to think in terms of degrees of uncleanliness down here. The slurry that now lapped about his ankles was about as unclean as anything could get, and the religious persuasion of the arse it had dropped out of a detail too far removed to trouble him. But no matter how many times he said it, Qasim just shook his head, and shifted uncomfortably, as if somehow troubled that his friend did not share his view.

A week had passed since Qasim had ventured into these gloomy tunnels. There had not been sight or sound of him since.

All at once, Asif was struck by an image of poor, doomed Qasim standing on this same spot, contemplating the same long-dead visage with its mocking grin. Asif's desperate desire to live – to get out of this place – suddenly multiplied a hundredfold.

The flame hissed and crackled on the damp, square stone ceiling of the cramped tunnel, snapping Asif out of his reverie. He turned from his grim companion and focused again on the narrow passage stretching before him, and became aware of a dark intersection ahead.

Something glinted low down in the blank gloom. Two pinpoints of reflected torchlight. He took a step forward. As his eyes adjusted, he saw that the rat had stopped, and was looking back at him, almost as if making sure he was still following. It turned, and scampered around the corner.

Asif set off after it.

He could now clearly see that this tunnel joined another, larger one just a few yards from him. This was, without doubt, the route Qasim would have taken, following the tributary into the wider drain.

From up ahead came an echoing sound of movement. His muscles tensed. Something bigger than a rat. And a dim, reflected light, shifting away to the right. People. He instinctively lowered his torch and thrust it behind him – then cursed as it momentarily cast his vast shadow onto the far wall of the adjoining tunnel. A stupid error. He flattened himself against the slimy wall, praying it had not been seen. There came no shout of alarm. No sudden, urgent movement. Slowly he edged away from the intersection, back against the uneven stones – back to the dead man with his perpetual grin.

Still no sign that he'd been discovered. Asif had been lucky. And it would appear he also, now, had the advantage; he knew they were there, but they, as yet, had no inkling he even existed. A difficult decision needed to be made. He could not risk announcing himself to them as he approached – but in order to avoid it, he would have to extinguish his torch, or leave it behind. Asif stared down at the soupy, lumpy liquid flowing about his feet – only half-aware that, in this light, it seemed to possess a strange blue sheen – and contemplated thrusting the torch into it. It would plunge him into near total darkness. Asif hesitated – then, turning instead to his bony companion, muttered a sheepish apology, and jammed the shaft of the torch into the skull's gaping mouth. Fire was not easy to acquire down here. He would not throw it away unless he had to. Drawing his long, straight-edged sword, he headed on again, towards the new tunnel, the glimmer of his torch dwindling behind him.

ONCE HIS EYES adjusted to the gloom, Asif was surprised at how much he could see. This tunnel had a higher, curved ceiling, constructed from surprisingly large stones. These tunnels were said to be from the time of Herod the Great – which seemed consistent with Asif's observations of the city's structures above ground (he had, over the years, become an obsessive student of its complex, layered architecture). The smaller tunnel he had just left, with its flat slab roof, would have been considerably older.

Sound behaved differently in this tunnel. Shufflings, splashings and strange whispers echoed weirdly along its length, sometimes accompanied by a tuneless humming. They baffled his senses, often seeming to come from behind him, from the walls themselves, or just inches from his ears. The air tasted sharp and acrid.

Then there was the light.

The reason he could see anything at all, he gradually realised, was due to the distant torch flame of his intended prey. It was now a clear glow ahead of him – flickering and moving, sometimes bright, sometimes fading, but always there. Within it – perhaps holding it – and in near constant movement, was what he assumed to be a human figure. And, from time to time, when the figure itself disappeared from view, the light threw into silhouette a huge, unidentifiable shape – uneven, but roughly conical, far taller than a man, and at least five times as wide at its base.

Asif advanced slowly, steadily, at pains to make no sound that peculiar tunnel might carry to his enemy's ears.

The light stopped moving – was raised up so Asif could clearly see its flame, wobbled once, then hung motionless in the air.

There was a thump. The sound of some heavy wooden object being moved into place. A cough. Then the humming resumed.

As he neared – crouched, half-pressed against the left-hand wall, sword ready in his right hand – the hum began to resolve into a tune. A Christian tune. The torch, he now saw, had been stuck in a crack in the wall. The silhouette that had placed it there now had its hands free, and was lifting what looked like a small barrel. Humming quietly to itself, it heaved the cask into place upon a great heap of similar vessels. It was heavy; full. But of what?

Asif was now yards away, moving with painful deliberation, barely breathing. Suddenly the figure turned to face him. Asif froze, praying that he was still undetected in the shadows. The figure strode purposefully towards him. Asif raised his sword, ready to strike. It turned again, and headed to the far side of the heap of barrels, oblivious to his presence, still humming its tune.

Asif simply stood for moment, barely able to believe he had not been discovered. The figure had been a man. For a split second, he had seen him clearly. Lean, European, with a neatly clipped, coppery beard. Beneath his dark cloak was the glint of mail, at his belt a fine sword. A Christian knight.

The sound of his movement receded, and Asif crept towards the great pile of barrels. If he could just identify their contents before the knight returned, it may perhaps reveal his purpose. If not, his goal would be to follow the knight – and try to capture him alive. He hurried the last few yards to the barrels. He risked being heard, but his greater concern now was being seen. He had entered the pool of light spread by the torch upon the tunnel wall.

Reaching for the nearest barrel, he pulled at the wooden bung. It was stuck fast. He tried the one next to it. The same. Then one above. It shifted, and gave. He rocked the barrel, and some of the liquid within slopped out. It was somewhat viscous. Also dark – at least, in this light – but its appearance alone told him little. It struck him, then, that he was currently denied the one sense he most needed – the sense of smell.

Asif was about to remedy this situation when another, far more alarming fact impressed itself upon him. He could no longer hear the knight.

His blood ran cold. He turned. The knight stood glaring at him, eyes reflecting the flame of the torch, filled with a wild hatred.

The knight lunged, grabbing his tunic, teeth clenched, his breath on Asif's face. Both stumbled. The knight let go with one hand, and Asif staggered backwards. His adversary was too close for him to deliver an effective blow with his blade – and suddenly Asif saw a knife flash in the man's fist. With all the force he could muster, he smashed the pommel of his sword down like a hammer upon the knight's temple. The man dropped like a stone, face down in the muck – and did not move.

Asif prodded him with his foot, and turned him onto his back. No response. He appeared not to be breathing. Asif gave thanks to Allah for sparing his life – then kicked the knight in frustration. Why, when you needed someone dead, did it take twenty blows to get the better of them – then, when you needed them alive, they immediately gave up the ghost with one knock to the head? Whatever secrets this man might have divulged were now lost forever.

A glimmer of light on the wall opposite the barrels suddenly caught Asif's eye. The dark, rectangular shape that he had thought was merely shadow was glowing feebly. Flickering. It was the entrance to another, smaller tunnel – and, deep within it, someone was advancing towards him. At some indefinable distance, two points of light bobbed into view, like eyes in the dark. Distant torches.

For Asif, it meant a second chance. But this time, there would be two of them.

He backed into the shadows to the side of the barrel heap, and waited.

II

GALFRID REGARDED THE warm, pungent sludge flowing about his calves and tried not to gag. "'Come to Jerusalem,' you said. 'Good wine. Good food. Lovely climate. Walk in the footsteps of Christ...'" He poked at something lumpy with his pilgrim staff and, with a grimace, decided against further investigation. "Obviously I missed the passage in the scriptures where Jesus went down the sewer..."

The figure advancing ahead of him said nothing. For a moment the taller man stopped, moving his torch to the left and right, his attention focused on the change in the size of the slabs that formed the ceiling of the tunnel. Then, without a word, he moved on.

Galfrid knew they must look an unlikely pair: he, dressed as a Christian pilgrim complete with staff, pilgrim badges and hooded cloak; his master outlandishly clad in the manner of a minstrel or joglar. Nothing could have been less appropriate to his master's temperament. The incongruity had caused Galfrid much hilarity, even in these grim surroundings. But incongruity was the nature of disguise – and disguise had been necessary.

As they walked, Galfrid's gaze came to rest on the long, narrow wooden box slung across his master's back. He chuckled again, and shook his head. It was perhaps just long enough and wide enough to contain two dozen arrows, but he knew it contained nothing of the kind. From one end protruded a curved handle delicately wrought in iron, and along its body was an even row of wooden keys that rattled when the box was bumped. Galfrid reflected on his master's dogged insistence on bringing it down here, and wondered if he was the first man ever to have introduced a hurdy gurdy into a public sewer.

"It's just..." continued Galfrid wistfully, as if his master had deigned to respond, "I thought we might have a chance to actually enjoy some of those things. You know, see the sights. The Holy Sepulchre, maybe..."

He'd tried to sound casual with his example, even though it was perhaps the fifth time he'd mentioned it. Galfrid didn't know why he was bothering – his sad obsession with churches and cathedrals was well known to his master. He looked down again, and immediately recoiled. A dead rat had bobbed to the surface. He felt it bump against his leg and continue on its way. He was coping with the smell – just – but somehow the sight of that was threatening to shatter his resolve.

Galfrid belched, and felt a sudden, urgent need to put thoughts of good food and wine out of his mind. "Is this what they call 'going through the motions'?" he said.

GUY OF GISBURNE had grown so used to the complaints of his grizzled squire that now the comments barely registered. But he also had other, more immediate things on his mind. One wrong turn in these tunnels, and they may never find their way out. Even supposing they kept track of their progress; if they ventured too far to make the return before their torches died... Well, that would be a fresh kind of Hell. And then there was their adversary. He was down here, somewhere. Amongst the rats and the stinking waste. Gisburne was sure of it. But to what purpose?

He heard Galfrid huff again and decided he would benefit from some attention.

"Relax," he said, cheerfully. "Try to enjoy yourself. You've already got further than the Lionheart did."

"Had King Richard succeeded in taking Jerusalem," said Galfrid, no longer bothering to disguise the disgust in his voice, "I somehow doubt that a visit to the sewers would have been his first priority."

"Unless he read that bit of the scriptures you missed," said Gisburne. It showed, at the very least, that he had been listening.

Galfrid gave a snort and muttered under his breath. "At least Christ could've walked *on* it rather than *in* it."

There was one key reason put forward to explain why the Lionheart's conquest of Jerusalem had failed. It was said he had been troubled by reports of growing chaos in his kingdom – of open rebellion by his envious brother John, who wished to take the crown from him. And so, just days from capturing the Holy City – his one avowed object on this crusade – he had turned back towards England. It was an attractive story – and one Gisburne knew, with every fibre of his being, to be false. He knew it because Richard cared nothing for England, and never had. He cared only for battle, for conquest, and for the prizes that came with them. If he could defeat Salah al-Din and return Jerusalem to Christian hands, he would be acknowledged as the greatest warrior in the world – and if he could make himself king of that holy realm, well, all the better. Richard had no interest in sitting on a throne, but every interest in winning it.

Gisburne felt he knew the real reason the Lionheart had turned from Jerusalem: he was afraid he would fail. In Salah al-Din, he had at last encountered a general who was his equal. For the first time in his life, he had been forced to contemplate the possibility of defeat, and all that this entailed. No stronghold had ever been able to withstand his assault. He had cracked every city, every castle that stood against him. But if he were finally to be broken upon Jerusalem's walls, at the hour of Christendom's greatest need, and with the eyes of the world upon him, well... Where would his reputation be then?

So he had not even tried. Somehow, in doing so, he had also made retreat look like concern for his own beloved kingdom. If anyone had a charmed life – an inexhaustible well of good luck – it was surely Richard. At least, so Gisburne had thought until three days ago. Then, from one of the contacts he still had in the city, he learned that Salah al-Din – also doubting his abilities against a formidable opponent – had been one day away from abandoning the city to the surrounding Christian forces. Had Richard only known to wait for one more sunrise, Jerusalem would have been his.

"So," said Galfrid, "how long do you propose we wade about in this garden of earthly delights?" Down here, it became hard to judge the passage of time. The moments seemed painfully long, and they had now been pacing these tunnels for at least an hour – picking their way slowly, carefully. In all that time they had found nothing of note beyond a few ancient bones – both human and animal – some broken barrels, a large quantity of rats – which, happily, dwindled in number as they proceeded – and, most bizarrely, a six-foot brass trumpet with a leather slipper stuffed in the end.

"We go where the trail leads," said Gisburne, without looking back. "Until we find what we're looking for."

Gisburne was well aware that this was primarily *his* mission and not that of their master, Prince John. John had indulged him, nonetheless. In the months leading up to Christmas, there had been another, far more pressing problem, closer to home – a problem that had occupied Gisburne's thoughts utterly. But always, at the back of his mind, he had this other, more personal duty waiting its turn. It was a duty not to a prince, but to a humble squire. To a friend. To Galfrid.

Then, on Christmas Eve, the great problem had been swept aside with startling finality. It had not been without cost. But it had at least left Gisburne free to pursue other aims – even with a void to fill – and he had turned back to this piece of unfinished business with renewed vigour. John, exhilarated by their recent victory, gave his full blessing to the enterprise, and put all available resources at Gisburne's disposal.

It had taken them eight months of dogged investigation to get to this point. Eight months of false leads, blind alleys and disappeared informants. Their adversary was subtle, and at the start, their own methods had been crude. Time and again, as they drew close, their prey would go to ground – vanishing without trace, like a phantom. There were those who believed he was literally that – that he had perished that time in Boulogne, over a year before, and that what now walked the earth was some kind of vengeful spirit. Gisburne had never paid heed to ghost stories. In his experience, the dead stayed dead. But this one was fiendishly clever. And so they had learned, and adapted. With a restraint that had tested their resolve to the limit, they had finally succeeded in keeping themselves invisible to their adversary, resisting opportunities to strike where victory could not be assured, waiting instead for him to reveal his grand plan.

Such restraint did not come easily. Gisburne was a man more used to the battlefield than the chessboard – to attacking hard, or bypassing the fight altogether, when it was to no purpose. During these days, as so often, Gisburne had held fast to the words of his old mentor, Gilbert de Gaillon: "The object of a hunt is simple. Not to attack the beast, but to kill it. You must therefore ask yourself, will attacking now achieve this end – or push it further from your grasp?"

Now, they were tantalisingly close. To what, neither yet knew for sure, but both sensed that the day of discovery – a day they had worked towards with steady determination – was finally upon them. And both were now certain, beyond any doubt, that the one they sought was here, at the heart of this labyrinth. To finally ensnare him – to have him removed forever from the earth... Well, Gisburne knew that, for all his griping and complaining, Galfrid would walk slowly over hot coals in Hell rather than pass up that opportunity.

Gisburne paused and looked about him. "This tunnel joins a larger one up ahead. If I have it right, the Via Dolorosa is now somewhere above us." He turned to Galfrid. "So, in a way, you are walking in the footsteps of Christ. Just... a couple of dozen yards lower."

Galfrid gave a grunt of irritation and passed a hand across the stubble on his head. He had thought, before they ventured down here, that it would at least be cool in the tunnels. In fact, it was sweltering. His head throbbed, the stench seeming to lap against it on every side.

Gisburne moved off again – then stopped so suddenly that Galfrid went into the back of him. Just ahead, projecting a few inches above the surface of the effluent at a point in the tunnel wall where, it appeared, another tunnel entrance had been blocked up, was a rough, horizontal slab of stone.

On the slab was the body of a man.

His throat was cut, the wide gash in the parted, grey flesh grinning open like a lipless mouth. But while the flesh about his neck remained otherwise intact, his face, left arm and left leg had been eaten to the bone. Whatever rats remained hereabouts had evidently made use of him. A sweet, sickly odour rose from what was left.

"Who is he?" said Galfrid in a whisper. "And what in God's name brought him down here?"

"It was more likely in Allah's name," said Gisburne. He crouched over the grim corpse. Fine scale armour glinted upon his torso. From his belt hung an empty sword scabbard and a sheathed knife, both with fittings of gold. "Arab. Well dressed. Well armoured. One of Saladin's. The elite. Whatever it was brought him down here, it certainly wasn't need." He had occasionally heard of beggars and lepers taking refuge with the dead in catacombs, but this man was clearly neither.

"The body hasn't been plundered," observed Galfrid. "Not by humans, at least."

Gisburne glanced again at the exposed skull and suppressed a shudder. "So, whoever killed him..."

"...was not a thief. And also not in need."

Gisburne stood. "I suspect his reasons for being down here may be the same as ours. And that he found what – or who – he was looking for. To his cost."

"Poor bastard," said Galfrid.

Gisburne stared off into the gloom ahead. For a moment, he thought he could detect a faint glow at the edge of his vision – but the effect disappeared as his eyes tried to focus on it.

"The body is only a few days old," he said. "It means we're close."

They followed the flow towards the intersection with the wider tunnel – and within minutes Gisburne understood that his fleeting impression had been correct. Ahead, framed by the distant tunnel's mouth, was the flickering orange light of another flame. It was stationary. As they neared, he could see the pool of light that spread about it, within which was a large, uneven dark shape. Objects of some kind, stacked in a pile. But there was no movement of any kind. No sign of life.

Gisburne drew his sword, and quickened his pace.

They stopped at the edge of the larger tunnel, its ceiling arcing above them, and stared across at the dark, shadowy heap.

"Barrels," said Gisburne.

"Barrels," repeated Galfrid with a nod. "And there was me thinking it was going to be about the trumpet. So, are we too early, or too late?"

The torch upon the opposite wall had been burning no longer than their own. Someone had been here, and could not be far. But which way? Gisburne turned his own torch first to the right, then to the left. "This flows south-east, ultimately to the Kidron Valley. The tunnel we have just travelled comes from the Christian quarter. Across there are tributaries from the Muslim sectors, with the Jewish area up that way."

"Christian, Muslim, heathen or Jew," said Galfrid, his nose wrinkling, "shit still smells like shit."

"Except..." said Gisburne, a frown creasing his brow. "When it doesn't." He sniffed the air. "Do you smell that?"

"Are you joking?" said Galfrid. But beneath the dank, hot reek of stale urine and fermenting excrement, another, sharper smell was rising. Something half familiar.

Galfrid sniffed tentatively. "Vinegar?" he said. At Gisburne's suggestion they had doused their skin with the stuff before coming down here. By this method, Gisburne's old comrade Will Pickle had fended off dysentery throughout William the Good's entire battle campaign against the Byzantines, earning his nickname in the process. He had been convinced its strong, clean smell kept disease-laden odours at bay. Gisburne could think of no better occasion to put that to the test.

He stepped out into the tunnel and stopped, flame held at arm's length, his narrowed eyes scanning the uneven stonework of the clammy ceiling, then every crack and fissure in the crumbling walls. Nothing. Tentatively, he lowered his torch towards the black surface of the lapping effluvium.

Upon it, he now saw, was a curious, iridescent sheen.

Galfrid frowned and stooped to examine the fluid, moving his own flame closer as he did so. Gisburne grabbed the torch. "I suggest we keep our torches above waist height," he said. "Petroleum. Everywhere about us. If that should ignite..."

Galfrid stared, wide-eyed. "...we'll be roasted alive." He raised his torch slowly above his head.

"No rats," said Gisburne in sudden realisation. "That's why there are no rats. But where's it coming from? And why is it here?"

"The barrels?"

Gisburne turned his torch flame upon them. A few had been unstoppered or broken open, but they appeared mostly intact. "There must be more," he said. "Many more. It's covering the whole surface." He looked away to their right, into the deep dark of the arched stone passage. "And it's flowing from... that direction."

He started off into the gloom, but no sooner had they passed the heap of barrels than Gisburne felt Galfrid grip his arm. He turned and immediately saw what had caught the squire's attention. By the left wall, almost obscured by shadow in the cleft between the barrel heap and the stonework and partially submerged, was another body. This time it was clearly fresh, and no Arab.

Gisburne waded over towards it, and was just crouching over the dead man when he became aware of a movement in the deep shadows barely a yard from him. Too late.

The man was on him in an instant. In desperation, Gisburne brought his weapon up. He was aware of a flash of steel – the glint of scale armour, golden in the torchlight. The other's dark face loomed as the attacker swung his sword high – and stopped dead.

For a moment, both stood, transfixed. "Gisburne?" The voice was deep, seeming to echo the length of the tunnel.

Gisburne stared, eyes widening. "Asif?"

Asif – almost a head taller than Gisburne, who was tall himself – threw his big arms around his friend and clapped him on the back heartily, his deep laugh reverberating through Gisburne's chest. Gisburne, stunned, fought to maintain his grip on his torch.

"You two *know* each other?" said Galfrid, incredulous. He looked around, as if reminding himself of their circumstances. "Well what are the odds? Just when I thought the day couldn't get any stranger..."

Asif released Gisburne from his grip and stood back, his hands still on his friend's shoulders.

Gisburne allowed himself a laugh, though the blood was still pumping hard in his veins. "Asif helped keep the peace when I was here... What? Five years ago?"

"Six!" laughed Asif.

"He was also a fabulous archer and a terrible backgammon player. Taught me everything I know."

Asif sighed. "That was before Hattin. Before the crusade."

"Before everything," added Gisburne.

"Time flies when you're having fun," said Asif. And another big laugh welled up in him.

"Looks like you're still in much the same game," said Gisburne. "But in the pay of the Sultan himself, this time, unless I'm mistaken."

Asif cocked his head. "I couldn't possibly say." He looked Gisburne up and down, a bemused frown pressing deep creases into his brow. "But what of you? Are you some kind of... *musician* now?"

If pressed, Gisburne could play two tunes on the hurdy gurdy – one of them badly. "I couldn't possibly say," he said with a smile.

Asif held his gaze in silence for a moment, then smiled. "Well, I think we understand each other."

Galfrid cleared his throat, pointedly.

"Oh – this is Galfrid," said Gisburne.

"Sir Galfrid," said Asif, with a bow of his head.

"My *squire*," added Gisburne.

"But you may call me Sir Galfrid if you wish," said Galfrid with a broad grin. "It has a certain ring to it."

Gisburne turned and nodded towards the body of the dead knight. "Your work?"

Asif looked irritated. "I meant only to stun him. To find out from him what all this is about. But these Europeans from their wet countries – they die too easily." He seemed to remember who he was talking to. "No offence."

"None taken," said Gisburne. He crouched over the body and began to pull back the surcoat, mail and gambeson to reveal part of the man's neck and shoulder. There, over his collar bone, was a tattoo of a skull.

"The Knights of the Apocalypse," said Galfrid, his voice a flat monotone. "We were right..."

This was the final confirmation – the culmination of their months of toil. It would end tonight, here, within this grim labyrinth.

"I have never heard of this order," said Asif.

"They are a recent phenomenon," said Gisburne. "Their ethos insane, their leader a madman. Up above they went dressed as simple pilgrims. Down here, we see them for what they really are – crusaders. Though even that term dignifies their aims. Since King Richard and Saladin reached an accord, there has been peace. But the actions of these men could spark another war – a war that neither side wants."

"Is this what they seek?" asked Asif. "An end to the truce?"

"An end to everything," said Gisburne. "And they must be stopped. At any cost."

"Then we have the same goal," said Asif. "But what are those actions?" He looked at the barrel heap. "What is it they are doing down here? It makes no sense."

Gisburne stared back into the gloom of the tunnel. "This will take us to the answer," he said.

III

THEY MOVED ON together, following the course of the large, central drain – which, Asif informed them, ran the full length of the city, passing directly under its heart. As they advanced, the smell of petroleum grew ever stronger, patches of the stuff on the surface of the city's waste making it ever more slick and viscous. In two side tunnels they had been able to discern the now familiar dark shapes of further piles of barrels. It seemed prudent to assume there were other heaps hidden in these depths, all placed according to some dark strategy. But even they could not be the primary source of the outflow.

Just past the second such tunnel, Asif suddenly raised his hand. All stopped, and stood motionless. It took a moment for the sound to reach Gisburne's ears – distant, echoing, steady and rhythmic. It was half-familiar, but he could not place it, blurred by the distance and the weird qualities of the honeycomb of passages. He could not even be certain from which direction it came. He glanced at the others, then moved off again.

The sound grew in volume as they advanced, its steady rhythm pounding in their ears, beating against Gisburne's nerves. He knew now what it reminded him of, though it made no sense, not in these depths. It was the sound of a tree being felled. And beneath it, now, another sound. A meandering drone that rose and fell. Wordless sounds – but clearly a voice.

Up ahead, to one side of the main drain, they saw dimly flickering light – an entrance to another tunnel, from whose mouth the sounds echoed. But this was no mere tributary. As they neared, they saw it was another large drain at an angle to the first – not constructed in stone or brick, but hewn through the rock. "This could not be of later date than the time of King David," whispered Asif, "and was perhaps much older even than that." A little way along its course, it connected with what appeared to be a natural cave, on the left side of which ran an uneven ledge, almost wide enough, in parts, for two men to walk abreast. They climbed onto it, relieved to be relinquishing contact with the city's stinking discharge.

The curving, rocky passage extended a short distance to another opening, where it appeared to broaden out into an even bigger space – the source of the light, and also of the sounds.

No longer speaking, they exchanged looks, smothered their torches and were plunged into gloom.

They listened to the steady, rhythmic sound in the dark as their eyes adjusted. The glow returned. Faces again became visible. The path once more revealed itself. Then, slowly, they crept forward towards the light.

When finally they peered beyond the mouth of the passage, their jaws dropped at what they saw.

A huge chamber opened up before them – part Roman vault, part cave, walls and ledges of ageless rock merging with soaring, interweaving arches of brick and stone, like the great crypt of some profane cathedral. All around the margins of the chamber, torches were fixed, their flickering yellow flames reflecting weirdly on the vast lake of effluent that the walls encircled. Its undulating surface – slick with an oily sheen – seemed to give back every colour but those which could be deemed natural, the sick stink of it now so heavy with petroleum as to be almost overwhelming.

And there, at the centre of it all, the all-dominating feature that elevated the scene to the status of a nightmare. From the hellish, rainbow-hued sea of ordure, reaching almost to the chamber's roof: a ragged, teetering pyramid of barrels. Hundreds, perhaps thousands of them – Gisburne could not even begin to reckon their number. And within this, a single point of movement – a speck of dogged human purpose. Half way up, perched like an insect on a mound, a knight was breaking open a glugging barrel whilst singing a crusader hymn, each stroke of his axe in time with the music.

Huddled in shadow at the edge of this outlandish scene, the three companions gazed upon the man-made mountain with speechless incredulity. Gisburne had been trained to divine his enemies' motives and capabilities – had thought he alone grasped the extremes to which this one was prepared to go. But nothing had prepared him for this. The mere scale of it baffled comprehension. The effort must have taken months. Simply for the transport of the barrels to have been kept secret, they must have come from dozens of locations. To have been hidden, smuggled, disguised – their contents obscured and mislabelled at every step. It seemed the work of madmen. But its execution was not mad. It was steady. Calculated. Purposeful.

Yet, even as he looked upon it, that purpose utterly eluded him. He could not inhabit the unfathomable minds of his adversaries – could not follow the warped logic that had, over weeks and months, resolutely piled up this catastrophic potential. If all this were to ignite... Gisburne had seen up close what fire could do to stone, how it had been used to break castle walls and crack their towers apart. He had made use of it himself. The piles of barrels were positioned in every part of the labyrinth, and there was no part of the city under which these channels did not run.

The Knights of the Apocalypse meant to destroy Jerusalem.

PETROLEUM WOULD BE released into the sewer from this vast pile, and the smaller heaps set to seep their contents into their respective tunnels. The flames would spread down the main drains and into each of their tributaries, turning them to rivers of flame. The intact barrels in each pile would catch and burn, finally breaking open to fuel the inferno. The ancient stones above would split in the heat. A horde of flaming rats would spew into the streets, setting everything afire. The walls of the Holy Sepulchre, the Dome of the Rock, the Temple Mount – all would crack asunder, the whole of David's Holy City collapsing into the pit of its own flaming ordure.

Jerusalem would become a Hell on earth.

One glance at Asif and Galfrid told him that they had reached the same conclusion. Gisburne turned his attention back to the toiling knight. "We must stop him," he hissed.

"But how?" whispered Asif. The same question was written on Galfrid's face. The knight's exposed position on the mountain of barrels presented a seemingly insoluble problem: how could they get to him before he had the opportunity to cry out and raise the alarm?

Gisburne slung the hurdy gurdy off his back.

"You're going to play him a tune?" breathed a baffled Galfrid.

As his companions watched, Gisburne slid open one end, and from within it pulled out a long, flat drawer into which several parts of some device were neatly set: a steel bow; a slender, steel-reinforced stock; half a dozen tiny crossbow bolts, some shaped like grapples; a length of cord upon a free-spinning reel. Gisburne freed the bow, snapped it into place on the end of the stock, pushed forward a steel lever and – with all his strength – pulled it back to draw the thick string. He plucked up a barbed bolt – but before placing it upon the tiny crossbow, tied the free end of the cord to a loop on its nocked end. Then he checked there were no obstructions to the cord's free movement, and took aim.

It was not quite the purpose for which the bow had been intended.

It had been meant for scaling heights – a development of its maker's earlier experiments. In the event, once here, they had found themselves descending into the depths. There had been no chance to test its accuracy in horizontal flight; Gisburne hoped to God it would serve. There would be only one chance – and even if it found its mark, they would have to move fast.

He held his breath for a moment, then released it slowly as his finger squeezed the trigger. The crossbow leapt in his hands. The bolt flew, the cord whipping after it. The knight gave a stifled cry, crumpled, and slithered part way down the heap.

"He's still alive!" said Asif.

"That's the idea," said Gisburne, and hauled on the cord. It pulled taut, springing up out of the effluent with a spray of stinking liquid. The man gave a hoarse yelp as it yanked the barb in his shoulder, slipped several feet, stopped, then lost his grip completely and tumbled into the greasy muck.

With slow deliberation, Gisburne began to reel him in like a fish.

It was painfully slow – Gisburne did not want to lose him – but the length of time he was beneath the surface of that putrid lake was surely far longer than any could survive. As they pulled him close, he seemed gone. For a moment, all stood in silence. Then a brown, slimy arm shot out of the ordure and grabbed Galfrid's ankle. The squire staggered, was almost dragged in. Asif gripped the arm, lifted the flailing, dripping figure out of the lake in one seemingly effortless movement, and head-butted him into silence.

The knight slumped flat on the ledge, apparently lifeless – then came to in a fit of coughing and retching. Gisburne dragged him further into the chamber, beneath the light of a torch, put a knee on his right arm and leaned over him. "So, shall we keep you, or throw you back?"

The knight blinked back at him, his face contorting into a sneer. "I do not fear pain or death," he rasped.

"I don't need you to fear pain," said Gisburne. "Just to feel it." And he gave the bolt a slow twist. The knight howled in agony.

"The others – they will hear..." hissed Asif.

"I'm relying on it," said Gisburne. Asif cast a bemused look at Galfrid, but the old squire remained silent and inscrutable.

The knight rallied for a moment, his face deathly pale. "I will tell you nothing," he spat.

"I'm asking nothing," said Gisburne, and pushed the bolt sideways.

The knight screamed again.

Asif leaned forward, his tone urgent. "We must get what information we can from him before it's too late."

"We're past that point," said Gisburne. "Draw your sword." Without question, Asif did so. He turned his attention to the dark tunnel.

"D'you suppose I am afraid of you?" coughed the knight with all the contempt he could muster.

Gisburne gripped the man's surcoat in his fists, and pulled him closer. "You should be," he said.

The knight held his gaze – but for a moment his defiance seemed to falter. "Who are you?"

"Guy of Gisburne. The man who broke Castel Mercheval – and your master with it."

Recognition dawned upon the knight's face. "Gisburne..." He slumped back and coughed up blood. Then, inexplicably, he began to laugh. It grew in intensity, in spite of the pain it clearly caused him.

Asif stared at Galfrid in bemusement. This time, Galfrid's face creased into a frown. The wounded knight's left hand gripped Gisburne's robes, and he drew himself up again. It seemed he wished to say something. Gisburne bent lower, and the man spoke, in a rasping whisper. "A red hand is coming..." With that, he began to chuckle. A mad laugh... or an exultant one.

Gisburne stared at him with incomprehension. "What do you mean?" The knight ignored the question, his laughter rising. Gisburne shook him. "*What do you mean?*"

The knight's head jerked sideways with a horrid, convulsive movement, and something splattered across Gisburne's cheek. He blinked, then saw the crossbow bolt sunk deep in the man's temple. The knight fell back, his eyes like glass.

The bolt had come from the dark tunnel. But no sooner had they grasped this fact than their attackers were upon them – three tall figures, striding out of the gloom.

Gisburne leapt up. Two grim-faced figures – Christian knights, their swords raised – were rushing towards him. But it was not these men that commanded his attention. Between them, and a little way behind, was a third – taller, hooded, a crossbow hanging from one hand, a sword in the other, but with a face that glinted weirdly in the torchlight. At first glimpse, it seemed the fresh face of youth – pink cheeked, rosy lipped, albeit with strangely dead eyes. Then one was struck by its lack of expression, its uncanny stillness – the blank, lifeless perfection of a painted effigy.

There was one other detail – so insignificant, that any other would have missed it – but Gisburne's eyes sought it out. The index finger of the hand that held the sword was hooked over the weapon's crossguard. Even in the grip of onrushing threat, Gisburne felt himself shudder. This was the man they had sought these past months.

Tancred de Mercheval. The White Devil.

His bearing, the way he moved; these things were imprinted upon Gisburne's brain. Presumably, the painted visage he now wore was meant to help him pass for a normal man when forced to traverse the streets. It so nearly succeeded – perhaps actually did so when only casually apprehended – but under close scrutiny, its strangeness seemed to grow exponentially. And yet Gisburne knew that what it hid was far, far worse – that behind this strange mask was a face distorted by mutilation, its features destroyed, its scalp denuded of flesh. A living skull.

It was a monster Gisburne himself had helped to create.

He had left the fanatical rebel Templar for dead in the smoking rubble of his own shattered castle over a year ago, his body burned by fire and quicklime. Every day since, Gisburne had cursed that one omission – had regretted that he had not made sure the job was finished, if only for the sake of those Tancred had tortured. For the sake of Galfrid.

Somehow – impossibly – Tancred had risen from that smouldering ruin. And he had not only refused to die, but had returned more dangerous, more twisted than before. There were those who claimed Tancred belonged in Heaven – more still who believed he belonged in Hell. All Gisburne knew for certain was that neither seemed to want him.

The empty holes that were the mask's eyes bored into Gisburne's own. "You..." hissed Tancred. He flung his crossbow aside with a clatter.

Gisburne's was already in his hand – but before he could move, a stocky figure charged past, almost knocking him off his feet.

Galfrid.

He was flying headlong at Tancred, his pilgrim staff swinging wildly, its heavy steel head booming through the air. Galfrid was habitually measured in his actions – it did not benefit either squire or knight to be otherwise. But Gisburne had caught the look in his squire's eye as he passed. It burned with anger and hatred. Such things blinded a man.

The knight to Galfrid's left – entirely overlooked – swung his sword with awesome force, countering the staff long before it had a chance to connect. There was a deafening *crack* as the two weapons met. The staff – notched, but intact – flew from Galfrid's grip, but was evidently far heavier than the knight had anticipated. His own sword was jarred from his hand. He fumbled, grabbing at it, but it eluded his grasp. Galfrid, still in a burning rage, flew at him, grabbing handfuls of surcoat and mail. As they tussled on the narrow walkway, Asif went for the second of the two knights. Gisburne, meanwhile, braced himself to face Tancred. But as he turned his weapon, about to strike, he saw Galfrid suddenly spun by his opponent, and both pitched sideways into the dank lagoon, stinking spray flying up as they hit.

The distraction almost cost Gisburne his life, but he was somehow was aware of Tancred's blade as it sang through the air towards him and instinct took over. He dropped to his knees, Tancred's sword slicing the air inches above his head, then brought his own blade up with all the force he could summon. It was an awkward blow, hastily conceived – but its edge struck Tancred square across the face. Gisburne felt metal hit metal, and fell forward, onto all fours. Tancred staggered back, a silver gash scarring the painted steel of his mask, but the tip of his sword – at the end of its great, uninterrupted arc through the air – caught the top of Asif's skull.

Asif, who had looked like getting the better of his adversary, teetered unsteadily, a bloody flap of flesh and hair hanging where the blade had scalped him to the bone. Then his knees buckled under him and he crashed against the rock wall.

Asif's opponent now advanced on Gisburne. Gisburne, about to clamber to his feet, saw and felt the knight's foot stamp upon his sword blade, pinning it to the rock. His attacker's own blade glinted high above, ready to smash down upon his head. Gisburne gazed up at him, weaponless.

With a roar, the knight struck. In an apparently futile gesture, Gisburne raised his right arm against the flashing steel blade.

The sword stopped dead with a jarring impact. Gisburne's head remained intact. The knight stared at the blade, still resting upon Gisburne's miraculously uninjured forearm, and his brutal features rearranged themselves into an expression of disbelief.

Gisburne grasped the moment. He thrust his forearm up and to the side, and the sword went with it, flipping out of the knight's hands as if plucked from them by a giant's fingers. Before his opponent could recover, he launched himself upward, smashing the top of his head into his attacker's teeth, and slammed him against the rock wall. The knight slumped, insensible. But as Gisburne turned to retrieve his sword, the whole world suddenly seemed to shift around him.

Tancred had plucked the torch from the wall, the deep shadows shifting and dancing as it moved on its course, and now stood before him like a wraith, flame in one hand, sword in the other.

"You fought me with fire once," he said, his voice a dry rasp. "But God's wrath cannot be undone by earthly means. This matter that surrounds us... It is mere distraction. The Devil's work. Corrupt flesh. And Jerusalem is its rotten heart. But it shall be revealed for what it is. It will undergo the judgement of fire."

Then he struck. Against all expectation, he held back with the sword, and instead swung the flame. It smashed against Gisburne's head, sparks flying. He staggered, and tried to back away. But Tancred advanced and set about him, battering him again and again with the burning torch, his eyes fleetingly visible through the dark openings of the mask, blazing in their lidless sockets. Gisburne fell to his knees, clinging this time to the rock wall, but Tancred did not stop. With each blow, sparks flew out across the oily slick, threatening to ignite it. Finally, Gisburne collapsed.

Tancred stopped and stared at the bloodied Gisburne for a moment. He poked at his enemy's forearm with a foot, pushed back the ragged sleeve, and saw the plate metal vambrace that had stopped his knight's sword, and the row of blunt teeth along its lower edge that had trapped its blade. Through his daze, Gisburne thought he heard a chuckle of admiration.

He blinked up at his looming adversary, the expressionless, painted face cocked to one side. "This is not the end I imagined for you," Tancred said. His voice was grotesquely child-like, his tone almost sing-song. Never had he sounded so insane. "I had hoped for something more elaborate. But no matter. An end is an end." He drew himself up to full height again, and sighed deeply, as if with genuine regret. "Time to burn."

And he tossed the torch into the lake.

WITH A GREAT roar, it turned into a lake of fire. In the dazzling light, Gisburne saw Tancred retreating along the tunnel. Then the wave of heat hit, robbing him of his breath. He turned back to the blazing expanse, knowing Galfrid was somewhere in it. He would not leave him. Not this time.

He heard a cry. Splashing at the edge of the ledge was Galfrid, his arm reaching up to Gisburne. As Gisburne watched, flames licked the length of it, then across Galfrid's soaked head. He scrambled towards him, saw the desperation in his face, his mind racing. "Sorry, old man," he said, and shoved the squire back under. Galfrid's expression at that moment was one Gisburne would always remember. A moment later he dragged him back up by his hood and hauled him out, coughing and spluttering, the flames smothered and extinguished.

At his side, seemingly from nowhere, the great figure of Asif loomed, the flap of bloody scalp now bound up with the black material of his turban. Gisburne was never more glad to see him.

"We must leave now if we are to live!" Asif urged. "The smoke and heat will choke us!"

Gisburne began to move, then stopped. He stared through the haze at the mountain of wooden barrels. The fire had not yet spread into the tunnels, but in another few moments, the barrels would burn through and release their load. Galfrid grabbed his arm – "Come on!" – but Gisburne tore it from Galfrid's grip.

There was no time to explain. He ripped the bolt from the dead knight's shoulder, took up his crossbow, cocked the lever to span the bow and loaded the tethered bolt. He did not fuss with it this time – barely paused to take aim.

The bolt flew. It stuck fast in one of the barrels in the lower row. Gisburne pulled on it. It held. He wrapped the cord about the vambrace and gauntlet, and heaved. The barrel stayed where it was. The others now saw his purpose, locked arms around him and added their weight to his.

The barrel still did not move.

Flames licked about them. Gisburne could feel the air being sucked from his lungs. They had their whole combined weight pulling now. The cord was stretched to its limit – was surely about to snap. Then, as they watched, the cord caught fire and began to burn.

Hope was lost. There was nothing left for them to do, no chance of escape. Gisburne supposed there never had been much chance.

Without warning, the barrel popped out from beneath its cousins. They crashed backwards as it bounced once and flew spinning into the burning liquid. Through the smoke and heat haze, Gisburne saw several rows above the empty space shift, and stop. For a moment, nothing moved. Then, in one great rumbling motion, the entire heap collapsed into the lake.

"Brace yourselves!" bellowed Gisburne, and put his arm across his face. A great tidal wave of filth swamped them, knocking them off their feet, and hurled them hard against the rock wall. They clung on as it subsided, threatening to drag them with it.

Gisburne lay huddled for some time before he dared look – and it was only Asif's laughter that persuaded him to do so.

The chamber was filled with thick smoke, the stinking tide of effluent slopping back and forth like a rough sea. But the flames upon its surface had been smothered.

Jerusalem would not burn tonight.

IV

DRIPPING, STINKING – BUT alive – they crawled out of the ragged, square opening in the crooked alleyway off the Street of Herbs and flopped exhausted into the street. At the sight of them, a thickset woman – the only human to witness these weird creatures emerge from the ground – screamed and fled, her basket bowling across the cobbles, strewing a trail of white linen. As they lay panting, Gisburne took advantage of the gift, and, dragging a veil towards him, attempted to wipe his hands clean of the stink of Jerusalem. Only then did he realise that the scabbard at his side was empty. He scrabbled at his belt – an irrational and futile gesture.

"My sword. It's still down there..." He'd lost the crossbow, too. The hurdy gurdy, naturally, was still miraculously attached to him by its strap.

"We are *not* going back for it," wheezed Galfrid.

"Damn it..." spat Gisburne. That sword had been with him since Boulogne.

Asif, still struggling for breath, gave a deep laugh. "Just give thanks that we still have our lives, my friend! A sword... That can be replaced." Then, after a moment, he frowned and added: "What did he mean 'something more elaborate'? What could be more elaborate than the destruction of an entire city?"

"He is a madman," said Gisburne. He disentangled himself from the hurdy gurdy and tipped out a quart of filthy water. "Who knows what he means?"

As Galfrid lay there, he suddenly reached towards Gisburne and took a tight fistful of his tunic. In one hand he still grasped his trusty pilgrim staff, as if battle was not yet over. "Swear to me..." he said, an oddly wild look in his eye, "that next time, you will not let him live. Even if it means leaving me to die." During all the months they had tracked Tancred, Galfrid had gone about the task with apparent ambivalence.

But Gisburne had always suspected that it was an act. A façade intended to keep his darker feelings contained. Now, the façade had collapsed. "Swear it!' he said, and shook Gisburne by his tunic.

"I swear," said Gisburne. Galfrid let his grip loosen and his head droop.

Gisburne sighed heavily. "I failed," he said. "I had him. He was literally in my grasp... And I failed."

At that, Asif gaped. "Failed? *Failed?*" He fell flat on his back with laughter. "You have saved Jerusalem! Would that we could all fail so well!"

"But that madman is free. Still alive..."

"You don't know that," said Asif. "Not for certain."

But Gisburne did. He felt it in his bones. The other knights, he was sure, had perished; the deluge had taken them. But Tancred clung to life.

"I will not make the mistake of assuming it," said Gisburne. "Not this time. But we will track him again. He can't escape us forever."

Asif sat up and threw off his gauntlets. They landed with a splat upon the stones. "Ah, the world is full of madmen," he said dismissively.

Gisburne rubbed his face with the linen and threw it aside. "One of whom, even now, returns to resume his place upon the English throne."

"You mean the Lionheart?" said Asif. "Your King Richard?"

Gisburne simply gave a gloomy nod, and rose upon unsteady legs.

"But you have heard the news, yes?" said Asif.

"Of course," said Gisburne with a frown, hauling Galfrid to his feet. When they had left England at the end of December, there had been no news of Richard for nearly three months. It was known his ship had set sail from the Holy Land in early October. It was reported to have stopped at Cyprus before continuing west, bound for Marseille, and he was expected back in England by Christmas. But the ship never arrived. There was no word, no sign. It was known that there had been violent storms in the Ionian sea, and when Gisburne and Galfrid set out for the east, many were convinced that the King was dead. Prince John's star, it seemed, was in the ascendancy. Then in Acre, Gisburne had learned from a Venetian captain that the King's ship had been blown ashore in Northern Italy and that he had continued overland. It seemed that, against all the odds, the charmed Richard had lived to fight another day after all. "The King makes for England as we speak," said Gisburne.

"No!" said Asif. "He is taken captive – by his most hated enemy..."

Galfrid and Gisburne stared at each other. "Saladin?" said Gisburne.

Asif laughed. "Salah al-Din? Hate Richard? Salah al-Din sent him fruit and horses when he was in need! No – Leopold, Duke of Austria..."

The two Englishmen were stunned into silence by the news. Neither knew what this would mean for the kingdom, nor what they would find when they returned.

As they walked along the dark street, there came a terrible shriek of torment, which was rapidly taken up by other voices. At first, they feared that this was Tancred's doing – that they had failed after all, and that even now, disaster was sweeping the city.

But no, this was something else... Not terror, but grief. Arab women wailed. Ahead of them, a man was beating his chest in anguish, while several more threw their hands up in despair, all of them shouting, many with tears streaming down their faces. Others spilled out of houses and joined the commotion. Gisburne's grasp of the language was not sufficient to make proper sense of what they were saying, but he could pick out a few words: *the end, disaster, death.* He looked at Asif – and saw utter shock writ upon his friend's face. The Arab muttered something under his breath, then turned to Gisburne.

"Salah al-Din is dead," he said.

V

Nottingham
2 May, 1193

MICEL HAD BEEN watching the two men for over an hour. All that time they had been sat in the corner, away from the rest, engrossed in conversation – the big one in the dark coat with his back turned towards the door, the smaller one keeping a sharp eye on the other customers in the alehouse. A few had thrown searching glances at the two strangers when they first entered, but none since had dared risk eye contact.

When he had brought them their ale and their food Micel had also kept his eyes low. But his ears were on stalks. They spoke in English, mostly. But every once in a while, both would slide into the Norman language, or some variant of it. Sometimes, he'd heard them speaking what sounded like priest's Latin. These, Micel did not understand, beyond the odd word. Most frustrating of all was the fact that they made this switch just when the conversation was getting interesting. He never found out what "the remaining forces in Sherwood" were doing, who it was the dark man vowed one day to "bring down," nor the nature of the pair's interest in the movements of the Sheriff, and Nottingham Castle, both of which they discussed at length.

One word leapt out at him, nonetheless.

Hood.

Not "Robin," not "Robin Hood." Just "Hood."

The hushed mention of this name – and the familiar way in which it was spoken – gave him a curious thrill.

There were other subtle eccentricities about them that excited him. They were clearly fighting men. The bigger one had the accoutrements and bearing of a knight – but not quite like any knight Micel had encountered before. This was, after all, hardly the sort of establishment any decent knight would frequent. And this one looked like he had slept rough. His black, hooded surcoat looked to be made of coarse horsehide.

Micel had never seen its like, but it told its own story – of a life lived in extremes. His long coat of mail and the weapons on his belt, well-used though they were, were of the highest quality, and meticulously cared for. Micel had glimpsed the contents of his purse, too – more silver than he or his master would see in a year. In Micel's mind, all these facts pointed to just one possible conclusion. They must themselves be connected with the famed outlaw of whom they spoke. His heart thumped harder at the thought that he was so close to such men. For a long time now, Sherwood had been silent. But Micel had always refused to believe that Hood had simply melted away. Perhaps, after all this time, Hood's men were finally preparing to make their move. And when they did, he would be part of it.

"What is it boy?" said the dark man. Micel looked from face to face, uncertain what to say. The smaller, older man chuckled to himself as he supped. But the dark man frowned, evidently not amused. "Well? Are you going to fetch us more ale or not?"

The boy stood for a moment, literally open-mouthed. But Micel knew, as one always knows, that this was a pivotal moment in his life. He was faced with a choice – turn from the roaring torrent, or plunge over the edge and let it take him where it would. His mouth became dry. His head prickly and hot. Then, as if in a dream, he found himself leaning towards the dark man – so close, he could smell the tang of sweat and horsehide.

"Are you *with Hood?*" he whispered.

GISBURNE RECOILED FROM the words as if stung. "Christ, boy!" he spat. Pairs of eyes flashed in his direction. Blasphemy was a crime, and nowhere disapproved of more than among common folk. While Gisburne had learned to curb his tongue over the years, half a lifetime spent amongst soldiers formed habits that were hard to break. He felt the hot, furtive looks flick hastily away. No one wanted that kind of trouble.

"I thought..." began the boy, flushing red. "I thought you might be" – he lowered his voice – "with... *him*." He swallowed hard as he said it, and looked about him. But all were now intently, deliberately, focused on their ale – and no one else's business but their own.

Gisburne's expression darkened. "And what if we were?" His voice had lowered to a growl.

The boy grew suddenly bolder. "I would join with you."

"Then you would stand against the forces of law," said Gisburne, gravely, "and likely end up hanged."

The boy's jaw clenched. "Better than living as a slave," he said. But even as he spoke the words, his swagger began to falter under the hard, unreadable gaze of the two men.

Gisburne sighed and let his shoulders slump. "What's your name?" The boy hesitated. "Don't worry, we won't eat you. You're too scrawny." Across the table, Galfrid laughed. Gisburne stabbed a piece of pork with his eating knife and shoved it in his mouth.

"M-Micel..." said the boy, raising himself up as he did so, as if in defiance of the sudden, nervous stammer.

"Michel?" said Gisburne with a frown.

"*Mitch*-ell..." repeated the boy, emphasising the hard sound at the heart of it. Gisburne saw Galfrid smile at that. The boy had spirit. And guts. Whether he had brains was another matter. "Micel it is then," Gisburne nodded. "A Saxon name... Precious few of those about these days." Micel gave a snort of disgust, as if it were somehow a sign of all that was wrong with the world.

"Of course you know that, for the most part, even Hood and his men have Norman names?" said Gisburne. "Robert. Thomas. John..."

If Micel did know, he didn't know what to make of it. His eyes flicked to Galfrid and back – at once fearful and hot with rebellion. Gisburne pointed his knife at him, turning its point in a circle. "Of what interest is Hood to a serving boy, anyway?"

Micel's face reddened further – then a boldness took hold of his features once more and he pressed on, his words coming fast, almost without breath. "He is of interest to us all. Hood is a hero. A champion of all true-born Englishmen. He stands for justice. For King Richard, who is our protector and who one day will return to deliver us. For the freedom of honest Saxons – freedom from the Norman yoke!"

There was a moment of silence before both Gisburne and Galfrid burst out laughing – to Micel's obvious bemusement. The speech sounded every bit what it was – something overheard and repeated verbatim; lines that the boy only half understood.

"So, that's the great struggle in this land is it? Between Norman and Saxon? You think real lives can so easily be disentangled?"

The boy stared, and went from foot to foot.

Gisburne broke off a piece of bread and chewed it. "My father was Norman. My mother a Saxon. So what am I? Both? Or neither? Or some third thing, perhaps? And who am I to take up arms against? Myself?" He leaned forward, gesturing with his knife as he spoke. "Tell me, who is this 'true-born Englishman'? What language does he speak? From where does he come, and is his skin dark or fair? Do you see him here? Anywhere? The King himself was not born within these shores. He lives in foreign lands and speaks not your language. Is he such a man?"

Micel's brow was knotted, his lip protruding in indignation. Gisburne continued – more aggressively, now.

"Listen to me closely, boy... Hood cares nothing for you or his fellow Englishmen. And the Lionheart lives only for war. If they are the champions of England and the English, then we are doomed – and if we're foolish enough believe in them then, by God, we deserve to be. They are thieves, squeezing silver from any they can. And do you really believe any of that goes to the poor? Have you, or anyone you know, ever seen any sign of it? Hood would steal from you without conscience. And every other honest working man. King Richard already has, several times over. He called them 'taxes,' but that does nothing to bestow honour upon them. It was money taken straight from their purses and put straight into his, so he could go and make himself king of Jerusalem – because England bored him. Tell me, does that sound heroic?"

Conversation elsewhere had now died completely. Eyes were secretively turned on the trio. Micel himself was redder than the beetroot pickle in the pot upon the table. For a moment, Gisburne thought he would bolt. Instead, he struck back. "It was Prince John made the taxes! King Richard..."

"King Richard buggered off to the Holy Land with three quarters of your wage and left his brother to take the blame for the mess he had left! You speak of things you do not understand, boy." Now, the entire room was plunged into silence, none daring to move, every head turned away.

Micel was shaking. He looked close to tears – a child again. Unable to endure any more, he turned on his heels and fled. Gisburne, fired up and irritable, stabbed at a lump of cheese. Bit by bit, the murmur returned to the alehouse. Galfrid, meanwhile, was giving Gisburne one of his unreadable, inscrutable looks. Gisburne hated them; he felt he was being judged. Though perhaps what annoyed him most was that he actually cared what this irritating squire thought.

Seconds later, Micel returned with the replenished jug of ale. It landed on the table top with far more force than necessary – but the boy lacked the nerve to look Gisburne in the eye as he did it. Without a word, without a sound, he turned and slunk away.

"I don't think you should have said that," said Galfrid.

"The boy needed to be told," said Gisburne irritably, charging his cup from the new jug. "It may save his life." He took a deep swig of his ale.

"Maybe so," said Galfrid. "But he spat in your drink."

Gisburne coughed, flecks of ale spattering the table. A smile spread across Galfrid's face. Gisburne wiped his mouth, then with a shrug clunked his cup against Galfrid's. "I've drunk worse," he said, and gulped at his ale once more. Galfrid gave a snort of laughter, and knocked back his own.

"So..." Galfrid began. "What next for Sir Guy of Gisburne?"

Gisburne sighed and stared into his cup. For once, he had no idea. When they had left for the Holy Land, circumstances had been turning in Prince John's favour. Key enemies had been overcome. John's power base in Nottinghamshire had been consolidated. And with the missing Richard's fate ever more in doubt, even John's enemies had begun to consider the possibility that they may soon owe ultimate allegiance to the Prince.

But, as the poets put it, fortune is fickle. Like the moon, it both waxes and wanes. Gisburne and Galfrid had returned to chaos. So great had been the upheaval, it had proved difficult for the pair to establish a clear sequence of events as they had journeyed north – the garbled accounts muddied by talk of portents, and impending doom. Certain facts were clear: There had been insurrection. The realm had teetered perilously close to open war. So precarious had John's own position become that he had fled to France. Some said he had since returned, but Gisburne himself had heard nothing conclusive. They would report to the Sheriff, Sir William de Wendenal, as Gisburne had agreed they would. But at this moment, he did not even know if his master was alive.

"Back to being a farmer," he said with a shrug. It was half statement, half question. He was not at all sure that the prospect was one he relished. But for now, what else could they do?

Galfrid leaned forward, and allowed himself a smile. "Look," he said, and spread his hands upon the table. For a moment he was silent, as if weighing up his words. "Perhaps it is time to stop all this. To settle."

Gisburne stared, taken aback by the sudden candour. "Settle?"

"You have your father's house. A good sum tucked away. The hard work is done. You have tested the Almighty, and yet you still live. Isn't it time – ?"

"Tancred," said Gisburne. "That work is not done. I thought you of all people wished to see that monster destroyed."

Galfrid sighed. "So did I. But now we are back... Perhaps it's time to let someone else worry about Tancred." He shrugged, and fidgeted with his knife. "The thing is, you are now in the enviable position of having few enemies in England, and none who now would seek you out. You've made sure of that. But if you stay with Prince John..." Galfrid looked as if he did not know how to finish the sentence. But he did not need to.

"You think I will be dragged down with his unpopularity..." said Gisburne grimly. "He's not the villain of the piece, Galfrid."

"Neither was Gilbert de Gaillon," said Galfrid. "But his fall precipitated yours, nonetheless." Galfrid paused a moment for the words to hit home. "God knows I've served the Prince loyally these past years. But I'm saying this for you, now... The Prince's greatest enemy in the realm has been subdued. And you did it. He will surely release you from his service if you request it, and will continue to think well of you." He leaned in again, his customary inscrutable façade now quite fallen away. "But if Richard does return, and you make an enemy of him... That, even Guy of Gisburne cannot survive." He sat back in his seat, and swigged his ale.

Galfrid was right. Galfrid was always right. Even since Christmas, loyalties had shifted. Old scores and resentments had resurfaced. It was by no means certain that those who had once been their allies still remained so. But to just walk away from that... He could not say it did not have its attractions. And perhaps it would not be so bad. Perhaps it really was time he gave up worrying about the world and tended his own garden.

There had been another sign of how things had changed. It was trivial, perhaps, to all but Gisburne, and it stirred mixed emotions in him. The previous day had been May Day. The air was fresh and invigorating, the sun bright and warm on their skin, the rich pastures and woodland they passed through had never looked greener, and the chuckling brooks that wove through them – their banks bursting with birdsong – never more cool and inviting. So idyllic a spring day was it, in fact, that it was hard to believe that strife of any kind ever afflicted this blessed land.

There were other reasons why the mood all about was one of cheer. On this day, everyone, from the lowest peasant to the highest lord, was excused work. It was the nation's holiday – a day of mischief and revelry across all England. As they had made their final approach to Nottingham, Gisburne and Galfrid had seen it in all its forms, from the sober to the wildly anarchic. There was music and dancing everywhere. Wells, barns, and even the humblest of abodes were decorated with bright flowers. There were maypoles, May Queens, and Lords of Misrule in all their incarnations – local peasants crowned king for a day, and whose word was law.

But there was one particular celebration, in a village near Caggworth, that had caught his attention. There, in amongst the usual wild revelries, carried shoulder-high like a hero, was a Lord of Misrule whose form chilled Gisburne to the bone. Dressed head to toe in Lincoln Green, with a long-feathered hat and brandishing a toy bow – with which he shot leather-tipped arrows at the heart of the May Queen – he was, in every detail, and every gesture, a joyous caricature of Robin Hood. Never before had it been made so clear, the extent to which Hood's legend had taken root. Seeing it now, Gisburne despaired for England. It also presented him with a practical problem to which he had no solution. He could fight a man. But how did one fight a legend?

"Anyway," said Galfrid, his tone lightened. "What's the point bringing order to the realm if you never get to enjoy it? You've half a lifetime left you. Make the most of it!"

"Wait a minute," said Gisburne, narrowing his eyes. "Are you talking about yourself now? Is it really you who craves a quiet life?"

Galfrid scowled. "You say that to the man who waded through flaming shit for you..." He spread his hands again. "I just want to see you settle down with a good woman, and – you know – live! And if I get to do the same, well, I'll not complain."

"Ah, this again..." Gisburne stabbed a bit of bread.

"Yes, this again!"

Gisburne grunted. "I don't know any good women." He knew one or two bad ones, but they weren't the marrying kind.

Galfrid sighed heavily. "Yes, you *do*..." he said wearily, as if repeating it for the hundredth time.

"Well," said Gisburne, "as we both know, that situation is no longer so simple..."

"I don't mean Lady Marian," said Galfrid flatly.

Gisburne frowned, and stared at the squire, genuinely perplexed. He knew Galfrid's views on Lady Marian Fitzwalter, even though he had never stated them outright. An unattainable fantasy; a lost cause. Perhaps, in the end, he would be proved right. In truth, the whole matter had become an intolerable agony. He did not wish to think of it – even though, at times, he could think of little else. In spite of it all, however, this irritating little man had now caught his curiosity.

"Who then?"

"You really don't know?"

"I'd hardly ask if I knew, would I?" The squire was testing his patience.

Galfrid shook his head in disbelief. "Not even the faintest clue? Even though it's been staring you in the face for a year?"

"What in God's name are you talking about?"

"Mélisande," blurted Galfrid. "Mélisande de Champagne. There. I've said it."

"Wha..? That's ridiculous!" Gisburne gave a disdainful laugh. But he felt himself redden as he did so. His voice lowered to an urgent whisper. "She is an agent for the King of France..."

"Exactly," said Galfrid. "It's perfect."

"Not that she is not admirable, but what makes you think...?"

"What make me *think?*" Galfrid threw up his hands in exasperation. "Christ, man, a blind beggar could see it. It's like two halves of a wheel that belong together – one fundamental thing out of joint in the universe that is screaming to be put right. So please, if you were to bring just one more bit of order to this chaos, could you not do *something* about it before she goes and marries some fat baron?" He slumped back, almost breathless.

Gisburne stared at him, stunned. "Listen," he said, uncertain whether to appear angry, or mortified, or to simply laugh it off, "this is neither the time nor the place to discuss thi –"

There was a heavy crash as the door behind Gisburne's back was flung open. Both he and the room fell silent. Heavy, jingling footfalls followed. Gisburne did not need to look round to know what they were. Soldiers, heavily armed.

Galfrid glanced unobtrusively over his master's shoulder.

"How many?" Gisburne muttered.

"Three. And at least two more beyond the door."

Gisburne nodded. "Whose? The Sheriff's?"

"Could be." Galfrid narrowed his eyes and took another drink. "Don't recognise their captain, though."

"Nothing to do with us," said Gisburne. "Keep drinking."

"I'm looking for Sir Guy of Gisburne," called the captain of the guard in a booming voice.

"He really needs to learn some discretion," muttered Galfrid.

Gisburne allowed himself to turn and look. There were two men-at-arms, one of whom Gisburne recognised – a guard from the castle garrison. They could only be acting for Wendenal, or for Radulph Murdac, the castle constable. Both loyal to John – in principle, at least. A third man stood in front, his bearded chin jutting out as he scanned the alehouse's interior, his face framed by a mail coif. His manner was aggressive. And superior, like one about to clap irons on a criminal. Gisburne didn't like the look of him.

"Guy of Gisburne," repeated the captain, irritably. "Is he here?"

Gisburne sighed. "Five. We can handle five."

"What did you do to upset him, anyway?" said Galfrid.

Gisburne shrugged. "Exist?" He turned back to his drink. "Don't look. Don't speak." But even as he had been turning away, he had seen one of the guards – the man he knew as Tom – pointing in his direction.

"They're coming over," said Galfrid. "What d'you want to do?"

"Nothing," said Gisburne, and swigged from his cup.

"You are Guy of Gisburne?" said the captain. He did not wait for a reply before adding: "You are to come with us. Your squire, too."

Gisburne wiped his mouth and looked up at him. "You're new, aren't you?"

The captain narrowed his eyes and clenched his jaw.

"You all right, Tom?" said Gisburne to the guard beyond the captain's right shoulder. "How's that mare of yours?"

Tom half smiled, opened his mouth to speak, then met the captain's eye. His eyes dropped to the ground.

"You will come with us," said the captain, then added, as if it were a tooth being drawn from his head: "if you please."

"Not just now," said Gisburne.

The captain pursed his lips, and rested his left hand on the pommel of his sword. It was a fine weapon, meant to impress. But Gisburne judged it had rarely, if ever, been used. "I have orders," he said.

Gisburne sighed. "I'm happy for you. But we have travelled a long way, and I intend to finish my meal."

The captain's fist tightened upon the pommel. The leather of his sword belt creaked. "It is by order of the High Sheriff of Nottinghamshire and Derbyshire."

"He'll wait," said Gisburne.

"It's for the Sheriff to decide what he does," snapped the captain. "He does not wait for..."

"He'll wait for *us*."

The captain's eyes blazed. "You are to come immediately," he said. "I have orders..."

"And we have a jug of ale."

"Also a considerable quantity of cheese," added Galfrid cheerfully, and proffered an absurdly large chunk of the stuff on the point of his knife.

"Now!" insisted the captain. "And by force if necessary..." He gestured to his men. They stepped forward, weapons readied. But reluctance was writ all over their faces.

Gisburne looked him in the eye for a long time. "When we've finished our lunch," he said, and turned away again.

Seeing that no further response would be forthcoming, his patience spent, the captain of the guard placed a rough hand on Gisburne's shoulder.

That was a big mistake.

VI

AN HOUR LATER, Gisburne and Galfrid found themselves standing before Sir Radulph Murdac, the Constable of Nottingham Castle. Flanking them were the guards who had brought them in – dishevelled, tunics awry, their faces cut, lumpy and swollen. It was clear at once who had got the worst of the encounter. In front, the captain – nose so badly broken it was blue, beard sticky with blood, left eye swollen like an overripe plum – swayed precariously. One of his front teeth was missing.

"For God's sake, man," snapped Murdac. "Get those wounds seen to. You're bleeding on my floor." The captain tried to bow, almost fell, then staggered out of the door. Murdac clasped his hands behind him, looked into the faces of his two guests, then, with the deepest of sighs, turned his attention back to the smouldering logs in fireplace – or whatever lay beyond them.

Gisburne felt like a child hauled in front of his father, awaiting inevitable punishment. That did not please him. It recalled vividly the time he had stood before his own father, after daring himself to smash the wasp nest in the horse paddock. This time, he had no idea what it was he was supposed to have done – and he was quivering not with dread, but with burning resentment. His instinct, then and now, was to volunteer nothing. He would wait for the Constable to have his say – if he ever did.

Murdac's hands tapped distractedly behind his back. He simply stared, his expression vacant, as if lost in thought. Gisburne glanced sideways at Galfrid. The squire raised an eyebrow. At first, Gisburne had read Murdac's dark, strange mood as irritation or anger – which, under the circumstances, was to be expected. Now, however, it appeared to be something else altogether. If Gisburne did not know any better, he would say the Constable was troubled. Grieving. No, worse than that. In a state of shock.

"There'd better be a good reason for this," said Gisburne, no longer able to tolerate the empty silence. Murdac did not respond.

This room – with its low, vaulted ceiling, wide fireplace and shadowy recess at the far end – held strong memories for Gisburne. It was the very chamber in which, two years past, Gisburne had first met Wendenal, the High Sheriff of Nottinghamshire, Derbyshire and the Royal Forests. Then, he had been dragged before the Sheriff as a common thief – accused of a crime committed by the man Gisburne had known in the Holy Land as Robert of Locksley, but who now chose to call himself 'Hood.' This chamber, and the encounter that took place within it, had turned his fortunes – had seen him arrive as a beggar and leave as a knight. It was the day he had entered the service of Prince John.

Gisburne allowed the note of impatience in his voice to grow. "Where is William de Wendenal? I know he's in residence."

Murdac turned, his face pale, and looked fleetingly as if he meant to respond to Gisburne's question. But whatever reply rose in him faded before it was uttered. Gisburne tried a softer tone. "We are meant to meet with him today. It was agreed." Murdac nodded slowly, looked into the shadows in the curved recess at the far end of the chamber, as if seeking an answer there, then turned back again. "Yes," he said, without meeting Gisburne's gaze. "Yes, of course it was."

There was no malice in his voice. No resentment or irony. It was a plain statement. And it told Gisburne nothing. Murdac's evasiveness – and the strange look in his eye, which he had only before seen in the faces of men who had suffered some great disaster – were beginning to unnerve him.

"I'm sorry about the guards," Gisburne began. "They were heavy-handed. Their captain..." Murdac raised a hand and waved the issue away. Gisburne continued, more irritably, this time. "If you or the Sheriff wished me to come, you had only to ask..."

"That was my idea." Gisburne knew the voice instantly. From the shadows stepped a familiar figure. Broad-shouldered, not tall; his hair and beard tinged with red. Prince John – Lord of Ireland, Count of Mortain, and, at this moment, the closest England had to a King.

John looked haggard – his cheeks drawn, his eyes shadowed. Gisburne felt a sense of relief at the sight of him, that was almost overwhelming. Ever the pragmatist, he had put aside thought of John's fate. But he understood that his own fate was entwined with John's – that to exist without him now would bring struggle and hardship. And worse besides. Despite his attempts to tread lightly in this world – a strategy which, he had to admit, he was often forced to abandon on a spectacular scale – there were those who would doubtless seize the opportunity to settle scores if he were no longer afforded the Prince's protection.

But this was not the main source of his relief. Nor was it the fact that he regarded John as England's best – perhaps only – hope of reversing the slide into anarchy that had accompanied the rule of its indifferent, absent king. It was simple joy that the man still lived. That one who he respected, and understood, and who understood him – who he even presumed to regard as a friend – was not lost.

"A thoroughly bad idea, I expect," continued John with a weary sigh. "Most people seem to think all my ideas are thoroughly bad – even if they're precisely what Walter de Coutances was saying two weeks before, when they all thought them marvellous."

Gisburne smiled at that. He was glad to see that the Prince's wry humour remained undiminished. In practical terms, John's position now was not so very different from when Gisburne left – he had the same privileges, the same properties – even the same influence, for the most part. Nevertheless, the months in between had clearly taken their toll.

"You seem to relish means of summoning me that put me in mortal danger," said Gisburne as his master stepped down the two steps into the main floor of the chamber.

A flicker of a smile played about John's lips. "It looks to me," he said, scanning the bloody and beaten guards on either side, "as if it was not so much *you* who was in mortal danger..."

He extended his hand – heavy, as always, with as many rings of gold as his fingers would allow. Gisburne took it, bowed his head, and went to drop to one knee. John held fast, preventing him, and gave a shake of his head to indicate that such affectations were not necessary. Only Gisburne was afforded this privilege. Only Gisburne was encouraged – and had the nerve – to speak plainly to him. This, Gisburne did not doubt, was yet another source of resentment for his envious rivals. Secretly, John detested the rituals and etiquette associated with his station – a trait inherited from his father. Mostly it was because he detested those who habitually acted them out. John made the barons and officials go through those rituals anyway. It was a subtle form of revenge.

"My sincere apologies, Sir Guy," said John. He released Gisburne's hand. "I needed you both brought here with all possible speed." He caught sight of a nasty cut on Galfrid's forehead where it had made sudden, violent impact with the captain's front teeth, and grimaced. "For God's sake, Murdac, get these two men a drink," he said with sudden asperity. "They're going to need it." Murdac turned to the cluttered table at the far side of the fireplace and filled two cups of wine from a bronze jug.

"What is this about?" said Gisburne, taking the cup that was offered him. "And where is Sir William?"

At that, John's smile vanished. The colour drained from his face. He seemed suddenly hunched, as if some physical burden had been placed upon his shoulders. The Prince that Gisburne knew was carefree – at least that was how he chose to present himself. His opponents, blind to the Prince's subtle irony, interpreted this breezy nonchalance as lack of concern for the realm and its people. But none could accuse him of arrogant detachment today.

"Drink," said John. Gisburne and Galfrid did so.

John glanced at Murdac. Reading his intention, Murdac, turned to the guards. "Leave us."

They trooped out without hesitation, barely attempting to hide their relief at being freed from that chamber. John waited until the door clanked shut and their heavy footsteps could no longer be heard, then turned back to Gisburne. "Sir William de Wendenal is dead," he said.

Gisburne stared at Galfrid in disbelief.

"The Sheriff? *Dead?*"

"Murdered," said Murdac, his voice flat and emotionless. "On the north road. Yesterday evening. Not five miles from here."

"The Constable is being somewhat restrained in his description," said John. "Having been pulled from his horse, the Sheriff was dragged into the forest, hung from a tree and gutted in the manner of a deer whilst still alive."

Gisburne's mind reeled. Wendenal could be a difficult man, but Gisburne had grown to respect him. That he was gone was shocking enough, but the manner of his passing... "Hood's men?" he ventured.

"Have you known them aspire to anything more than poaching and petty theft of late?" John shook his head. "It's not their style. They're bandits. And he was carrying nothing of value. Nothing to warrant such a risk. The only thing Sir William stood to lose was his life."

"But we always said something like this might come..." protested Gisburne. "Vengeance for the blow that was inflicted upon them."

"That was months past," snapped John with sudden intensity. "And nothing came." John, seeming to regret the burst of temper – temper for which his family were famed – fought to calm himself. "Trust me. They are a spent force. Directionless. Diminished by the harsh winter. I have good information to this effect – or did, until that source was lost. No. This is something else."

Good information. Gisburne supposed he was a fool to think he was John's only agent. From the start, then, the intention would seem to have been murder – and Wendenal was not merely killed, he was defiled. So, it was personal. Revenge. Hatred. Or a message. And there was risk. But John was right. The only man in Hood's gang capable of perpetrating such an act – who would likely find risk an incentive rather than a deterrent –

was Hood himself, and if there was one man who Gisburne knew could not possibly be responsible, it was he.

"How big a risk was this attack?" said Gisburne. Wendenal, formidable though he may have been, was not fool enough to travel the north road alone after dark. "Who was with him?"

Murdac looked to John, and shifted nervously before speaking. "The Sheriff was accompanied by twenty-two men. His personal guard. A dozen knights – the rest, serjeants-at-arms."

Gisburne and Galfrid gaped at each other. *Twenty-two knights and serjeants...* Elite warriors. Such a force could turn a battle. Gisburne's neck grew hot. Such audacity did not sound like a random attack – more like an opening move. "Christ's bones," he said. "What is this? Are we at war?"

"It's quite possible," said John. "Though with what, I am not yet certain."

"There were witnesses?" said Gisburne. "Survivors?"

"Twenty-two of them," said John. "Several were injured, but only incidentally. Sir William was the target."

"Then they can describe the men who..."

"Not *men*," interrupted John. He looked almost embarrassed as he said it. "There was... only one."

"One?" Gisburne stared at him, not fully comprehending. "*One man* did this?"

John hesitated, as if unsure how to answer. He looked to Murdac, appealing for assistance. "We are not yet sure it was a man," said Murdac. "The eyewitness reports are... Confused."

Gisburne looked from John to Murdac and back, appealing for something – anything – to make sense of this. John turned his back to them and stared at the window. "Some said it was a giant. Others that it had the head of a beast. But all are agreed on one thing: that it breathed fire. Their horses recoiled from the flames when the monster charged. Only because of this was it able to take Wendenal unchallenged. There is no doubting their claim. Several were badly burned – men and horses. And there are other reasons for taking their account seriously – reasons I shall get to presently."

Gisburne could feel his temples throb, his heart thump. "But surely there were crossbowmen..." he began.

"And they got off several bolts at close range before it disappeared into the trees," said John. "It was entirely unaffected. No cry. No blood. Nothing."

The four men stood in grim silence. Finally, John turned to face Gisburne again. "It is my wish now that you expend all possible energy in tracking down this... killer. Whoever or whatever it may be."

"I will need to talk to the men of Wendenal's guard," said Gisburne.

"Do anything you see fit," said John. "Whatever you need, I will support it – every power, every resource that I possess is at your disposal. There is no one better equipped for the task – although chasing monsters may seem a peculiar diversion for a man such as you."

"On the contrary," said Gisburne, "I seem to spend most of my service engaged in exactly that enterprise."

"I mentioned other reasons," said John. "Reasons why this must be tackled with urgency. Five days ago, one of my most dedicated supporters, Sir Walter Bardulf, was attacked and killed at his home near Pendleton. His body was... also most foully mistreated. The people there are saying that what slew him was a dragon. Fiery breath, a monstrous head. Scales of red and black that were impervious to arrow and bolt. These claims, I must emphasise, come from those who actually saw it."

"A *dragon?*" Gisburne was aghast. "Surely you can't believe that?"

John held his gaze, saying nothing. Behind the intense, intelligent eyes was something Gisburne had never before seen there. Fear.

"There is more," said John. He took the empty cups from Gisburne and Galfrid and placed them back on the table, amongst an assortment of objects – the wine jug, a water bowl, a wooden board upon which were the crumbled remains of a loaf, some scattered writing materials. Then he picked up what appeared to be a rough, warped square of parchment and held it out to Gisburne. "When I was awoken in the early hours of the morning by the return of Wendenal's guard, I found this placed in my bedchamber."

Gisburne took the parchment. The yellowed, dehydrated skin was uneven and hard, translucent in places, but with scraps of dark flesh still attached upon its rougher surface, and a few dark hairs upon the other – more like something dried before a fire than properly prepared parchment. There was a stink to it that made Gisburne queasy. The wine burned in his stomach. Upon the smoother side was a handprint in what looked like blood, and beneath, in crudely formed letters, a single phrase:

DIES IRAE VENIT

"Hardly a monk's script," said John, "but clear enough."

"'Judgement day is coming,'" said Gisburne.

"To answer your earlier question," said John, "I have never personally encountered a dragon, but I have never heard that the fire-drakes of old were known to write notes." He thought for a moment, then added: "If they did, I somehow imagine it might be in Welsh or Irish, rather than Latin."

Gisburne placed his spread palm over the print. It dwarfed his own hand. "You are certain these matters are connected?" he said.

"The skin was cut from the back of Sir Walter Bardulf, possibly whilst he was still living."

Gisburne shuddered at the information. His instinct was to rid himself of the gruesome artefact as soon as possible, but none looked in any hurry to take it from him. "Could someone within the castle have placed this?"

"We have good reason to believe it came from outside," said Murdac.

"No one saw anything," added John. "But one of the guards was absent from the battlements when due to be relieved by the next watch, and he failed to report for duty today. He was later found in the midden beyond the wall. His skull had been crushed so completely, they say, his face hung about his chest like a burst wineskin." John waited a moment for the information to sink in. "The savagery of the attack is entirely consistent with the deaths of Wendenal and Bardulf."

Gisburne shook his head in disbelief. "But if the returning guard woke you... How did he get here so fast?"

John gave a wan smile and shrugged. "Flew?"

"He could have killed you," said Gisburne. "Cut your throat as you slept."

"Easily," said John.

"But instead he chose to warn you. To inspire dread."

"He. Or she. Or *it*."

Gisburne turned the grisly parchment over in his hands. "But to what end?"

"That is what I wish you to find out," said John, then added, with a casual shrug: "and, ideally, prevent it actually happening."

The Prince gestured to Murdac, who was closest to the cluttered table. "There was also this..." he said. Murdac took up something and handed it to Gisburne – a small, bloody scrap of pale cloth with smudged black markings. "It was nailed to Wendenal's skull," said John. Gisburne showed the scrap to Galfrid – now almost inured to the bizarre turns the case was taking.

"Oilcloth," said Galfrid.

"What of these letters?" said Gisburne.

Galfrid frowned. In a similar, crude hand to the parchment was written: *liv.* "'Live'? Is that some sort of joke?"

Gisburne shook his head, unable to form any conclusion. "You say it was nailed...?"

Murdac looked appalled. "The captain who recovered the body apparently had some difficulty removing it," he said. "Tools were required. But it had to be done. For the sake of Sir William's dignity."

Gisburne could not see how anything could imbue such a circumstance with dignity, least of all that. But he duly noted the key facts.

The knight he had served as squire, Gilbert de Gaillon, had always taught him to pay attention to details. He had directed him particularly to those others overlooked – or those others hoped would be overlooked. "Know your enemy," he would say. "The clothes he wears, the food he eats, his habits, his fears, his vices. If there is something he craves, deny it him. If there is something he detests, put it in his path. If there is any weakness – no matter how small – exploit it. But, most of all, know *why* he fights. What he believes in. How he thinks. To know your enemy, you must become your enemy. Only this way can you anticipate him. In this quest, no detail is too trivial." The advice had stood Gisburne in good stead. But always before there had been something more substantial upon which to hang such details – motives, known history, patterns of behaviour.

"If there's anything else, I need to know it," said Gisburne. "Leave nothing out."

"Sir William's right hand was severed," said John. "Sir Walter's, too. They were not found." He glanced at the dried skin with its palm print of blood. "Hands would appear to be a running theme."

Murdac had picked up the jug as if to pour himself a drink, but then slammed it down before having done so. "Taken!" he said, shaking his head.

"Trophies?" said Gisburne.

Murdac ignored him and turned to the Prince. "I told you, my lord – this is more than murder. It's the stuff of sorcery. You know my view. We should seek the involvement of the church. God knows I'm no credulous peasant, but I've seen this before – and if a curse has been placed... "

John silenced the Constable with a single raised finger. "It is for Sir Guy to determine who is to be involved." His manner indicated that there was to be no further debate. Murdac looked suitably chastened.

"I, too, have seen body parts taken for such purposes," said Gisburne. "But it doesn't take a sorcerer or a demon..." He stopped mid-sentence, his eyes fixed upon the bloody handprint. A memory came to him suddenly, vividly – the dying utterance of an unknown knight in the sewers of Jerusalem. He stared into empty space, trying to understand the connection his mind had already made.

"*A red hand is coming...*" he muttered. Galfrid flinched at the words. Gisburne held up the parchment with its ghastly imprint. "What does that mean – 'a red hand'?"

John cocked his head. "I remember a child's game call 'red hands,'" he said. "I was not allowed to play it. Demeaning to my station." Gisburne remembered it, too – but could recall nothing more than the fact that it involved a lot of vigorous hand slapping. He shook his head.

"*Rubente dextera...*" said Galfrid. All turned to him. "Horace," he said. "One of the odes. It's usually interpreted as *fiery* rather than *red,* but anyway..." He looked up into the far corner of the room, as if some aid to memory were secreted there, and recited: "*Iam satis terris niuis atque dirae grandinis misit Pater et rubente dextera sacras iaculatus arces...*" He translated: "'The Father has sent enough dread hail and snow to earth already, striking sacred hills with fiery hand...'"

"The hand of God..." said Gisburne.

"Of judgement," added Galfrid. Both were now entertaining ideas of apocalypse – although how these could relate to John and his predicament, neither could tell.

"I've heard the Irish also use a symbol of a red hand," said Murdac with a shrug. "Wendenal spoke of it once."

John nodded. "Sir William was one of those who accompanied me when I toured Ireland as its Lord," he explained.

A sudden possibility occurred to Gisburne. "And Walter Bardulf?"

John nodded again, more avidly this time, struck by the same realisation. "Yes... Yes, him too. But that was – what? Eight years ago? Do you think there could be something in that?"

"I don't know," said Gisburne. "It may be nothing, but..." His words faded. He and Galfrid looked at each other again, and Gisburne saw that his squire's thoughts ran along the same lines. "Tell me," he began, turning to the Prince, "Were there any Irish there who might have reason to wish you harm – who you may have crossed or slighted in some way?"

John sighed heavily. "Almost all of them," he said. He went over to the table, and dipped his fingers in the water bowl. "Before you say any more, this will not – must not – bring either my duties or my daily life to a halt. That may be precisely what they want. I will not grant them the satisfaction." Gisburne nodded. John flicked his fingers dry before the fire. "I am due to leave for London before Whitsun. There are matters to be dealt with there – and an important event that I must attend at the Tower." He looked sideways at Gisburne. "An execution, actually."

So preoccupied was Gisburne with thoughts of murder that the significance of these words dawned only gradually.

"Yes," said John, "*that* execution... I didn't think you would have forgotten."

But Gisburne had forgotten. It had seemed so far away for so long. "Upon the feast day of St John," he said. "The twenty-fourth day of June."

"Well, you should know," chuckled John, "since you yourself set the date."

"Continue to make plans for that journey," said Gisburne. "All will proceed as expected. But with one alteration."

"Provided I approve," said John. "What is it?"

Gisburne glanced briefly at Galfrid and Murdac before addressing John in confidential tones. "May I speak with you alone?"

John held Gisburne's gaze for what seemed an age, then nodded at Galfrid and Murdac. A frown creased Galfrid's brow as he turned to leave. Gisburne avoided his gaze.

"One more thing," added John. They paused. "William de Ferrers will now act as Sheriff. He is one of the few I still trust. But please understand – no one outside this room knows of the tragedy save the men who were with him, and they are sworn to secrecy. So it must remain. There are those around us – Hood's men among them – who would happily grasp any opportunity to exploit a weakness."

Both bowed their heads. As they once again turned to quit the chamber, Galfrid cast a final look back at his master before the heavy door crashed shut between them.

VII

WHEN GISBURNE FINALLY emerged, Galfrid was loitering outside, alone, like a guilty schoolboy. "What was that all about?" he asked.

"Nothing you need worry about," replied Gisburne. Galfrid narrowed his eyes. The squire's gaze seemed to penetrate Gisburne's head. Gisburne clenched his fists, and avoided Galfrid's look. He knew he would assume that the private consultation with the Prince had been something to do with the mission that lay ahead. He knew also that, for a while at least, his squire's manner would be grouchy and resentful. Galfrid hated being kept in the dark. But Gisburne could not share everything with him. Not this time. It had been difficult enough to air his concerns before John.

"So," said Galfrid. "Now what?"

"I need to see a Welshman about a dragon," said Gisburne, and marched towards the tower steps.

AS THEY DESCENDED the spiralling stone stair towards the lower chambers – and the mysterious workshop that lay beyond – Gisburne ran over the conversation in his head. He had indeed talked about certain plans for the coming weeks, but nothing particularly crucial. John had stood, patiently listening and answering Gisburne's increasingly unnecessary questions before finally stopping him and saying: "Sir Guy – why don't you just ask me what you really want to ask?"

Gisburne – survivor of Hattin and Thessalonika, nemesis of Tancred de Mercheval, who had breached the White Tower, outwitted Templars and stolen from under the nose of the King of France – blushed. Had it really been so obvious?

"Marian..." he said.

"Marian..." repeated John with a steady nod.

"Has there been any news? Anything at all?"

"Trust me, my friend – I'd have told you before all others." John sighed and shook his head slowly. "There has been nothing since Fountains Abbey. That remains the last place we have a reliable account of her whereabouts. It can be no coincidence that she disappeared at the same time as the monk – and we both know where he was bound."

"There must be some trace. Some trail to follow. Vast as it is, Sherwood cannot simply have swallowed them up..."

"I know that in these matters you remain pragmatic, and that I can speak to you plainly," said John. It was true – in all matters but this. Where Marian was concerned, the realist in him melted away, and what remained clung, child-like, to the frailest hope. "Her father, Sir Robert Fitzwalter, is a wealthy and powerful man," continued John. "But the simple fact is, there has been no ransom demand. No threat. No warning or boast. No word at all."

Gisburne's jaw clenched. "Then, in every likelihood, she is dead," he said.

John sighed again. He paused for some time before he spoke. "I fear it may be worse even than that. It pains me to say so, but all the signs are that she went willingly."

Gisburne's innards burned. He had known it – had, perhaps, always known it. But now, hearing it said aloud, it was made real. And Galfrid had been right: Marian always was the unattainable fantasy, the lost cause. He knew, for his own good, that he should let go. But the choice was not his to make.

He squeezed his fingers into fists, fighting the yawning emptiness that opened deep in his guts, the maddening urge to smash everything in sight to splinters. Part of him longed to exchange this mental agony for physical pain. That, he could understand. But he had no wish to reveal the severity of his feelings to John – although he suspected it must be obvious. Such a thing seemed too much like weakness. A flaw.

It was not that feeling itself was anathema. De Gaillon had always taught him it was right and necessary for a knight – for without it, one risked forgetting that one was human, and why one was fighting at all. That was a road to a greater madness – a madness with which England was already too greatly afflicted. No – such feeling was a weakness only because it threatened to overthrow reason and cloud judgement. It could be used to defeat him. Even when he was in a situation that posed no threat, it went against the grain to give away such secrets.

Only Gisburne knew the true depth of his attachment, and that was how it had to stay. For damned up behind it was all the boiling, venomous fury at the man responsible. And that Gisburne certainly had no desire to release. It was a burning, all-consuming rage which not even Tancred, for all his deranged cruelty, could hope to inspire. It was reserved for one who was the very antithesis of the grim Templar – one who left chaos in his wake, and laughed at it. Who laughed at everything. At pain, at loss, at grief. All these things were a game to him – all the world his gaming board, and all its people his pieces.

This was what had tormented Gisburne for the past two years. The great threat. All Gisburne's rage – all his madness – already had a physical form. It was out there, in the world. And its name was Hood.

"Well, then..." Gisburne's voice was distant, rasping. He had no idea what he was going to say.

John had rescued him. "This part of the story will soon be concluded," he had said, seeming to have read Gisburne's thoughts, "and you will have to think of him no more." He did not need to say the name. "Then it will be a rather different world. A better world. And we shall see what comes of it." Then he had put a hand on Gisburne's shoulder, and no more had been said.

WHEN GISBURNE AND Galfrid had arrived at the subterranean dungeon in which Llewellyn of Newport worked his various miracles, they found him packing. Or unpacking; it was not quite clear which. The workshop – mayhem at the best of times, at least to the untrained eye – was piled high with barrels and chests and containers of all kinds, many of them part-filled with straw which had spilled over the floor, giving it the bizarre impression of a stable. Some chests were apparently in the process of being filled with the various multicoloured bottles, unidentifiable instruments and undreamt-of devices that were the tools of Llewellyn's trade. But as the grey-bearded enginer bustled about – seemingly oblivious to the intrusion of his two visitors – it seemed others were also being emptied according to no discernible pattern. That there *was* a pattern, however, Gisburne had little doubt. The containers were marked with symbols that he recognised as Llewellyn's personal classification system – and which meant nothing to anyone but him.

"If you need anything, you're out of luck," said Llewellyn without once looking up. "Everything is in chaos." He stopped and threw up his hands. "We're on the move again."

"Are we allowed to know where?" said Gisburne.

"You are not."

"Doesn't matter. I already know it's the Tower."

Llewellyn shrugged. "There are worse places to be."

"Like down in the sewer," chimed in Galfrid, fidgeting with a pair of exceptionally long pincers.

"Might as well be a sewer," grumbled Llewellyn. "Damp, stinking hole of a place... And it's the fifth time this year I've had to pack up and move. Fifth! And it's only May." He snatched the pincers from Galfrid and stuffed them in a long, flat chest. "I'm getting too old for this."

"Travel broadens the mind," said Gisburne.

"My mind's broad enough," said Llewellyn. "In fact, if I could narrow it, I would. Wait till you're my age. You'll understand."

"That I should live so long..." smiled Gisburne.

"Given the life you lead, you probably won't."

Gisburne raised his eyebrows and cast a glance at Galfrid. "Well, it's nice to see you, anyway..."

"Speaking of the life you lead," said Llewellyn, "did the items I supplied function as required?"

"Admirably," said Gisburne. "The vambraces saved my life. In fact, those rows of teeth upon the underside..."

"Never mind those," said Llewellyn, irritably. He'd been sceptical about the teeth from the very start – Gisburne's idea, of course. "What of the crossbow? Did the bolts fly true?"

"Yes..."

"And the reel ran smooth? And the cord – strong enough?" Llewellyn looked like a small boy seeking approval for his efforts. Gisburne took both of Llewellyn's hands in his, and shook them gently.

"You want to know the truth?" he said. "That crossbow of yours saved not only us – it saved Jerusalem."

"No details!" protested Llewellyn, breaking away. "Never tell me of your mission. I don't need to know." He calmed, and nodded to himself. "But that is good. Yes, very good. So, where is it?"

Gisburne stared back at him for a moment, then his eyes slid sideways to Galfrid.

"You did bring it back?" said Llewellyn, his eyes narrowing.

"I have the hurdy gurdy..." began Gisburne

"The crossbow, man!" said Llewellyn. "The steel-sprung crossbow!" Llewellyn threw up his hands. "For the love of Christ! I don't just pull these contraptions out of my arse... Do you have any idea of the work that went into tempering that steel spring? How many failed attempts there were? That was one of a kind!"

"Believe me, if I could have brought it back..."

"What pains me most," said Llewellyn, "is that it may now be in the hands of our enemies. Did you think of that?"

Galfrid leaned forward with a conciliatory gesture. "Where it ended up, I think we can safely say, no one else would venture." And he gave a sweet, consoling smile the like of which Gisburne had never seen before.

"Well, that's something..." His manner softened. "Saved Jerusalem, you say?" He grunted, and allowed himself a small, satisfied laugh. "So are there things you need? If so, you'll be in for a wait."

"There will be," said Gisburne. "But as to what they are, even I am not yet sure..." He looked around at the jumble of stacked caskets and chests. "I understand John's entourage is leaving for London in ten days' time," he said.

"I could not possibly confirm or deny that," said Llewellyn, resuming his activities. From the bench he picked up what appeared to be a simple scroll of parchment – except, Gisburne saw, that it had a vicious, eight-inch blade projecting from one end. Llewellyn gave the scroll a firm twist about its centre. There was a click as the blade retreated inside it – then he stowed it safely away in one of his boxes.

"You don't need to," said Gisburne. "But if it's ten days away, why are you packing now?"

"Because I haven't even unpacked from the previous time, that's why! Now do you have any sensible questions?"

Gisburne was in no way certain Llewellyn's answer made sense, but decided to move on. "Actually, yes... What do you know about dragons?"

Llewellyn stopped dead and stared at him. "*That's* a sensible question?"

Gisburne shrugged. "I have a new mission. And I am –"

Llewellyn held up a palm. "Don't tell me! I don't want to know." He began his packing again. "Real dragons or dragons in stories and ballads?"

Gisburne stared in astonishment. Every time he stepped into Llewellyn's domain, there were extraordinary surprises. "You have knowledge of *real* dragons...?"

Llewellyn brushed some stray wisps of straw off his sleeve. "My granny had a scrap of skin that she said was from a dragon. Once belonged to St Patrick, apparently."

"And you believe it was genuine?"

"She bought it from a monk," said Llewellyn. "So, no." He stopped again and stared at Gisburne – a long, searching look. "This is off the beaten track, even for you. Are you asking me all this in my capacity as an enginer, as a student of nature or as a Welshman?"

Gisburne recalled the description of the attack on Wendenal, of the ineffectiveness of the crossbows, the breathing of fire. He had seen many strange sights in his life – some of which he would rather forget – but nothing to persuade him to believe in dragons. And yet... "Perhaps all three," he said.

Llewellyn frowned deeply, turning over in his hands what appeared to be a human thigh bone with steel hooks screwed into it. "You're not asking me how to *kill* a dragon, are you?" Gisburne exhaled – unsure, for the moment, exactly what he was asking.

Llewellyn gestured with the bone, and shrugged. "Well, I have no data. So I couldn't tell you how to kill one anyway."

"Suppose it is not real," said Gisburne. "Suppose someone were merely using the image of a dragon. Why might they choose that *particular* image above all others?"

Llewellyn frowned. "You mean for a flag or something like that?"

"Something like that," said Gisburne.

Llewellyn gave smile and a shrug. "Because they're Welsh?"

"Or Irish..?"

"Irish?" He looked puzzled at the suggestion. "Well, they say the Welsh are just Irish who couldn't swim." Llewellyn chuckled at his own joke. Then he looked at Gisburne again, and narrowed his eyes. "We're not talking about a flag, are we?"

"Suppose it is more than that. Something designed to inspire terror or dread?"

"You mean, something that people *believe* is real?"

Gisburne nodded.

Llewellyn sighed, and perched on a barrel. "This... image, as you call it, means different things to different people. In England, a dragon is a pest. Evil. Something to be destroyed by a brave knight. It is troubling to the established order. But among the Britons and Gaels, well... They have more of a fondness for the scaly beast. In the old tales, the dragon is a noble and benevolent creature. Uther Pendragon, father of the great king Arthur, had one upon his crest – was himself named after it. In Wales, Uther's red dragon has come to represent an entire people." He stopped himself, and waved his hand. "Make of all this what you will... I will say this with certainty: a symbol – and belief in it – is far more potent, and far harder to kill, than any creature of flesh and blood. Take the lion. A fearsome beast. It might kill a dozen men. But put it on a banner that men will follow, and put that banner in the hands of the Lionheart..." He shrugged. "Then, it will conquer nations."

Gisburne leaned forward. "So, you are suggesting that one who would employ the image of a dragon in such a way is most likely a Celt?"

Llewellyn bristled at Gisburne's words. "No, I am not," he snapped. "That, I think, is what *you* have been suggesting... So, the Welsh have a fondness for dragons... So what? We don't own them. It might just as easily be a Saracen. Or a madman. Or one obsessed by the Apocalypse. Or just someone who likes dragons." He stood, rifled amongst the heaped objects on the bench and threw a hammer into a box of tools. It landed with a crash. "And who is this 'Celt' you speak of? What has he to do with me, or

I to do with a distant Irishman or Breton? About as much as you do with a Norseman or Burgundian, I should imagine. Tell me, have you heard of the *Topographia Hibernica*?" Llewellyn did not wait for Gisburne's answer, though the name meant nothing to him. "It is an account of Prince John's expedition to Ireland in 1185. It portrays the Irish as ignorant, hairy savages – and adulterous, incestuous and ugly to boot. Its writer was Gerald de Barri, also known as Giraldus Cambrensis. A Welshman. There's your Celtic solidarity!" He exhaled in exasperation. "I thought Gilbert de Gaillon had taught you better..." The words pierced Gisburne like a blade, and he felt himself redden. "You will not catch your killer with wild guesses and assumptions," grumbled Llewellyn, and he leaned forward and rapped his knuckle on Gisburne's forehead. "The Lord gave you this. Use it!"

So, Llewellyn had known all along. Gisburne wondered if habits were now so ingrained that the old man pretended to understand less than he actually did as a matter of course. He was right – as always. Gisburne was grasping at straws with this lunacy about dragons. But it was practically all he had.

He thought again of the question he had addressed to Prince John. *Are we at war?* The possibility had then seemed startling. But Gisburne was used to war, even in its murkiest forms. Even when it was senseless, he could make some kind of sense of it – could at least build a picture of his enemy, and from that a strategy.

But now? He felt lost. He did not know what to think, or how to act. Every line of thinking seemed to raise a new question to which there was no answer. This enemy was nameless, faceless – existing in an impenetrable fog. It struck out of nowhere and disappeared almost without trace, its nature obscure, its motives uncertain. John was right – this was something new, and it would require new methods. New ways of thinking.

Gisburne reached into his bag. "Can you tell us anything about this?" He handed the scrap of oilcloth to Llewellyn.

The old man turned it over, held it up to the light, sniffed it, rubbed it with his thumb and shrugged. "The staining is blood," he said. "But you probably knew that. And it's been nailed to something. I won't ask what." He thought for a moment. "Do you still have the nail?"

Gisburne glanced at Galfrid, frowned, and shook his head.

"Pity," said Llewellyn.

"What of the fabric?"

"Oilcoth," Llewellyn said. "Too commonplace to make much more of it," then he tossed it back onto the table top. "The black markings are charcoal, though."

Gisburne nodded, then, after a moment's hesitation, drew out the square of human parchment. "What about this?"

Llewellyn reached out to take it, his eyes gleaming with curiosity – but this time his hand stopped halfway. He withdrew it slowly. "You keep that one," he said.

"You know what it is?" said Gisburne.

"What? Yes. Who? No." He raised a palm again. "And please don't tell me – I don't want to know."

"What of these letters?" asked Gisburne. They were the only marks that had any direct connection to the personality of the killer – though it seemed a vain hope that they could yield anything of worth.

Llewellyn turned his attention back to the parchment in Gisburne's hand. He frowned, looked closer, reached for a magnifying lens, then examined it again. So engrossed was he that for a moment his earlier revulsion was entirely forgotten. "The shapes of these letters... Crudely formed though they are, certain characteristics are distinct." He looked up. "Only a monk from an Irish monastery, or one taught by them, would form his letters this way." He thought for a moment. "Or someone trying to deceive you into thinking that."

Gisburne smiled at this small victory. "Thank you," he said, and clapped Llewellyn on the shoulder. Dust and the smell of sulphur rose from the folds of old man's robes.

"That was helpful?" said Llewellyn, bemused.

"More than you know," said Gisburne.

VIII

Pendleton
5 May, 1193

THE SQUAT, ROTTING keep of Sir Walter Bardulf's castle poked up from the slumped, misshapen mound like a broken beehive atop a dungheap.

Sir Walter had evidently not prospered. The castle – if such it could be called – appeared to have hardly changed since the time of the Conqueror, except for the inexorable century of dilapidation. The damp, mossy wood of the mouldering stockade that surrounded the bailey was everywhere crumbling to black shreds, and in at least two places that Gisburne could see had collapsed completely. The castle motte rising above the bailey was lumpy and wrinkled from decades of unchecked subsidence, and the keep that sat hunched upon it – an ancient wooden tower, with sections of wattle and daub – listed alarmingly to the south, its timbers rotting, its plaster cracked and discoloured by age, and in places missing altogether.

"Christ's boots," muttered Galfrid as they approached. "It wouldn't take much to breach these defences."

Gisburne doubted the stockade would even keep a dog out.

THE DAY ITSELF had been dismal. The bright, dry weather of the previous week had turned to flat grey, and as they had approached Pendleton a fine, almost invisible rain had begun to fall – not hard enough to drive them to shelter, yet not light enough to have spared them a soaking. It blew about them in the gusting wind like a clammy mist. The road had been endlessly winding, with numerous muddy side tracks that led nowhere – now, not even the rain seemed to know where it was supposed to be going.

As they had plodded along – Gisburne upon his black stallion Nyght, Galfrid upon a new chestnut mare that he had seen fit to name 'Mare' – Galfrid had mused upon their new enemy. "So, to sum up... We don't know his purpose. We don't know who he is. We don't even know what he is." He sighed in exasperation. "All we have are paltry scraps. Bits of cloth and smears of blood. And what good are they? They're keys without doors."

Gisburne shared Galfrid's frustration. If this was indeed war, it was unlike any he had ever known. When he had stood before the army of Salah al-Din at Hattin, or those rebelling against Richard in Angoulême, or the Byzantines defending their homeland, their motivation had been clear. It had been clear in his mind before he had even left on campaign. But this?

Gilbert de Gaillon had always taught Gisburne that killing was incidental to war. A means, not an end. In the case of the Red Hand, they knew much about the means, but almost nothing about the end. There was no clear motive, no pattern by which he could predict his actions. Not yet. But de Gaillon had also taught him to hold his nerve. To let the other make the mistakes. This was what Gisburne knew he must do. And something else, too – something that he had learned from his last visit to Llewellyn.

He stared at the distant horizon. "We must think in a different way. Relate those paltry scraps one to the other until a pattern begins to emerge. Bring order from the chaos." He smiled. "It's just like building one of those cathedrals you love so much."

"Easier said than done," muttered Galfrid. "Those cathedrals don't build themselves."

"Have you ever been to Monreale, Galfrid? In Sicily? And seen the cathedral there? The mosaics cover almost every part of its interior. Thousands of pieces of coloured glass, placed one after another, like bean seeds in a field – except that these are in acres of gold, and grow into wonders," Gisburne shook his head, marvelling at the memory. "On its own, each fragment means nothing. But put it with others, and together they begin to form a picture. More than that – they bring the past back to life."

"And this is what we are to do?" Galfrid blew out his cheeks. "At least they knew what the picture was."

"Even the artisans of Monreale began with a blank wall."

The squire nodded slowly. "So, how long did this task take them?"

Gisburne shrugged. "Ten years."

Galfrid raised his eyebrows, and nodded again, staring straight ahead. "Better get started, then."

Gisburne knew his analogy was flawed. If this were a mosaic, it was not one they were making from scratch – it was one that had been dismantled, and which they were attempting to recreate having never seen the original. It seemed a hopeless task. Yet at Llewellyn's workshop, he had begun to understand how it must go.

It had been an epiphany, of sorts, sparked by the workshop's strange devices, its parts of mechanisms yet to be realised. Llewellyn worked with the unknown every day. With things never before seen. There was no certainty that what he was creating would work. Sometimes, it never did. But more often, after many attempts, he would achieve his goal, by doggedly testing one part against another, working with what knowledge he did posses – the known principles by which all things functioned. And slowly but surely the parts were put into their proper relationship, and the mechanism came to life. Only then was its purpose made manifest.

This was the method Gisburne knew he must employ, building piece by piece, testing as he went. But not with a device. With a man. Perhaps he should have used that analogy on Galfrid. But he knew the squire liked cathedrals better.

"So," began Gisburne. "What do we know?"

Galfrid sighed. "He kills. He hates Prince John. He's Irish..."

Gisburne raised a finger. "Only what we know, Galfrid. Only what we know..."

"All right, all right... *Probably* Irish?"

"The symbol of the Red Hand was a device originally belonging to the clan of the O'Neills," said Gisburne. "But it has since spread further. It's come to be a symbol around which all the Irish might rally – a symbol of resistance." He glanced at Galfrid. "I've been asking around."

"Very well, then," said Galfrid. "He, she or it employs a symbol widely used amongst the Irish. But then there is the writing, and the fact that the victims both participated in John's Irish campaign."

"Two could be coincidence," said Gisburne.

"We know the Red Hand seeks revenge for something. His letter makes that clear."

"But if it is revenge for something that occurred in Ireland, why wait eight years before striking with such heat?"

Galfrid rubbed his forehead. He could fathom no answer.

"If there is a third death," continued Gisburne, "and they too were with John on the Irish expedition, well..."

"So that is what we must do?" asked Galfrid. "Wait for another death?"

The thought did not please Gisburne. "We must do what we can – and hope a face will begin to appear out of the fog."

Galfrid sighed. "You spoke with Wendenal's guard?" he said.

"All echo John's account," said Gisburne. "These are seasoned soldiers, I trust their judgement of what they saw – or what they believe they saw."

"A scaly giant, with the head of a dragon, impervious to the crossbow and breathing out fire..."

"Not *breathing* fire," said Gisburne. "Several said the flames came not from its mouth, but its fingertips.

"So, not a monster," said Galfrid. "Merely a sorcerer."

"We know how to turn fire to such a purpose – how to use it as a weapon. I have done so, with Llewellyn's help. In the East I witnessed the Byzantines using siphons to spray Greek Fire from their ships. I have heard that there is such a device that could be carried by a man."

"And the crossbow bolts?"

Gisburne recalled how he had stood before Castel Mercheval, a slab of oak slung beneath his surcoat, the bolts from the battlements thudding into him. "They can be stopped – if the armour is thick enough. One witness described the attacker as 'a giant made of iron.' Several reported the clank of metal accompanying his movements."

Galfrid shook his head. "I still don't understand how the Red Hand managed to get away. One man, against more than twenty knights and serjeants..."

"All were startled and confused by what they saw. Their weapons had no effect. By the time they had gathered its wits he was gone with his prey, back into the forest."

"But he was on foot. Why not simply ride him down?"

"He'd chosen the spot with care. The trees and bushes there were thick – impossible for horses. Several rode ahead and searched for a forester's path. Others dismounted and plunged in. But if I were the Red Hand, I would have prepared the route. I would have made sure Wendenal was immediately silenced. Planted traps to trip and confuse them, to obscure my destination and send them in other directions." De Gaillon had hammered that advice into him as a young squire: *Control the battlefield.* "Wendenal's men hadn't a hope. They were in a tangle of brambles, in the dark, with nothing to follow, the sounds of their movements obscuring all others." He shrugged. "It would not have been hard to achieve."

"You talk as if it *was* you doing it," said Galfrid.

Gisburne thought for a moment. "It's what I did in Boulogne," he said.

On that occasion, Gisburne had been hiding out in the Forêt de Boulogne – exhausted, burned and beaten, sleeping rough in a bear cave. Tancred had sent ten knights and six serjeants in after him. Only one had come out alive.

"Well then, he thinks like you," said Galfrid. "That's got to be some help."

Gisburne frowned. It had not occurred to him before now. He thought of the way the Red Hand used fire, how he used armour, and also how he had managed to break into John's private chamber in one of the most secure places in England. All these were things Gisburne himself had done. De Gaillon's words came back to him again: *To know your enemy you must become your enemy.*

Galfrid peered at him "You *not* him, are you?"

Gisburne scowled at Galfrid, not appreciating the joke. "Last time I checked, I had no plans to kill Prince John."

Galfrid snorted. Then, his laugh faded, and for a moment he stared into the distance. "There is one thing that we have not yet mentioned," he said. "*A red hand is coming...*"

To his own surprise, Gisburne shuddered at hearing those words again.

"Can *that* be a coincidence?" said Galfrid.

"I don't know," said Gisburne, gravely. He had tried to dismiss it – to tell himself that the knight was merely taunting him, and that by some fluke he plucked from his mind an image that connected with the fate of Wendenal. But he could not convince himself – could not banish from his head the leering look of satisfaction on the dying man's face.

"He knew," said Galfrid. "About all this. How is that possible?"

He was certain this was not some scheme of Tancred's. Nothing he had seen fitted with the rebel Templar's methods. But, if anything, the alternative was worse. It meant the possibility of collusion between the Knights of the Apocalypse and other groups dedicated to spreading terror in the kingdom.

That was Gisburne's worst nightmare.

As they approached the rickety wooden gatehouse of the stockade about Bardulf's castle, they saw the gates were already open. One was off its hinges, and looked as if it had not moved all winter. The bridge leading to it, spanning the outer ditch, creaked and clunked as they rode across. The dirty water within the ditch – choked with weed and all manner of tumbled rubbish – was topped with green scum and stank like a cesspit.

No one challenged their entry. They rode on through the bailey to the castle motte, a mere diversion for the handful of bedraggled peasants who stopped whatever they were doing and watched them pass in gloomy silence. Some seemed to be doing nothing at all, and simply stood about, looking lost. Several of the buildings within the bailey lay empty and abandoned, their thatch fallen in, rain pooling on their mud floors. From others, grey-faced serfs and skinny, ragged children stared with empty eyes as the passers-by made their steady progress towards the site of the murder.

The crime itself had been committed in what should have been the most secure part of Bardulf's domain. This much they learned from a gangling youth with a crooked nose upon which wobbled a permanent drip, and who appeared to be butchering a dead hound upon a stump. He seemed so terrified by Gisburne's question that all he could do was point.

Still unchallenged, the pair passed through a second unguarded gatehouse heavy with the smell of damp timber, tethered their horses to a rotting rail, and began the slow climb up the precipitous steps to the keep. Gisburne wondered at the stamina of the attacker as they plodded upward, scaling these steps at speed in his thick metal scales. The gates to the upper ward surrounding Bardulf's mouldering ruin of a tower also yawned open – but this time, upon their approach, a guard in ill-fitting livery called out from the rampart, and a slender figure of a man darted forward to intercept them.

He was significantly better dressed than most – better dressed, in fact, than either Gisburne or his squire. Upon his face was an indignant scowl, but as soon as he had proper sight of the visitors and realised Gisburne must be a knight – if a rather unorthodox one – it transformed into the most oleaginous smile Gisburne had ever seen.

"Sires!" He spread his long-fingered hands wide, then bowed low. "Welcome to our castle... Most humbly I greet you." He did not rise, but remained bent almost double, his hands clasped together in a gesture of humility. "Welcome! *Welcome!*" Still in that position, he ushered Gisburne and Galfrid through the gate. Three pasty guards looked down from the ramparts in mute incomprehension. From the sheltered doorway of the gatehouse, a gaunt serving woman – perhaps only twenty, but looking ten years older – watched them pass, her thin hands grasping the shoulders of a spindly little girl of no more than six years.

Gisburne stopped in the muddy castle ward, and looked around. "I am Guy of Gisburne, here on the authority of Prince John."

"Sir Guy of Gisburne!" The man's eyes widened. "Can it really be? Why, your name precedes you, sire! We have heard of your deeds. Even out here..." He gestured about him, his nose involuntarily wrinkling with distaste as he did so. "I have heard what occurred at Clippestone, and may I say..."

"Yes, yes – enough..." said Gisburne, both hands raised. He was never comfortable even with sincere praise; flattery was like sand on a raw nerve.

"Anyway... It is my pleasure to serve you, sire," said the man, and bowed again – so low this time that Gisburne was afraid the man's face was going to hit the floor. "I am Gryffin, sire, humble steward of this castle. What is it you desire? Pray, name it."

It was clear to Gisburne – from the steward's manner, from his dress, from the very air that swirled about him – that Gryffin felt himself too good for this God-forsaken place, that he believed he belonged at court and had styled himself accordingly. Perhaps he even saw in his two visitors an opportunity to further that ambition. But if his efforts were meant to impress, they fell upon stony ground. In fact, they made Gisburne want to kill him on the spot. His smiling obsequiousness felt obscenely at odds with these grim surroundings – not to mention the fact that his lord had recently met a hideous end.

Gisburne gestured for him to get up. "We have heard that your lord, Sir Walter, is dead – and under the most terrible of circumstances," he said.

The steward paled. He looked from face to face, his own distorting into an expression of such tragedy and horror it was worthy of one of the grotesques carved into the capitals of Vézelay. "Gentle lord, it is true..." Gisburne believed he saw the steward force a tear into his eye.

"That is what brings us."

There was another great bow. "We are honoured that you give this matter your personal attention..."

"We wish to discover what we can to help catch his killer."

"Oh, sire," whimpered Gryffin, his eyes widening, his shoulders hunching even more, "would that this were a mere killer. Would that you could have seen –"

"*Mere* killer?" interrupted Gisburne. "I doubt your master would see it that way, since he was the one killed."

"I meant no disrespect," Gryffin reddened and bowed low again. "I meant only –"

"You asked what we desired," snapped Gisburne. "We desire to go about our business. And to have a guide about the keep."

"I myself can –"

"Someone else," insisted Gisburne. He pointed to the silent woman with the child. "You."

The steward, his lips pressed together so hard his mouth almost disappeared, gestured impatiently to the woman. She released the child and scuttled forward, head bowed, as Gryffin passed in the opposite direction, bowing low and backing away.

Gisburne turned and strode off towards the keep, Galfrid at his side, the woman at their heels.

"Shouldn't we question him?" whispered Galfrid. "Find out what he saw?"

"Of course we should," said Gisburne, barely able to keep the resentment out of his voice. "But let's use our own eyes first..."

Any minute spent out of Gryffin's company seemed a minute well-spent.

FOR SOME TIME, Gisburne stood and stared at the thick wooden door of the keep. It was still closed and locked – the key lost since that terrible day, the woman said – and had evidently frustrated the assailant. Not that it mattered much. Next to it, a fresh, ragged hole had been smashed through the wattle and daub wall, as if by a charging bull. This was how the Red Hand had finally gained entry.

There had been other attempts first. The door itself, and much of the plaster around it, were burnt black. The steps below were untouched, as if whatever flames had licked at the door had come straight at it, out of the air. Beneath the charred surface, they could see that the wood had been battered and scored, as if some great thing had smashed at it.

Galfrid raised his eyebrows. "A dragon..." he said.

At the edges of the crow-black, crackled surface, some thin, tarry substance – sticky to the touch – still adhered. Gisburne sniffed the residue on his fingertips. It summoned vivid images: a lake of fire in the sewers of Jerusalem; a burning ship upon the part-frozen Thames; the interior of Llewellyn's workshop. Greek Fire – or something similar.

Gisburne turned to the woman. "Show us where it happened," he said.

She had stood by silently as they carried out their observations. Gisburne wondered what must have been going though her mind – how their strange, uncertain fumblings must look to her. Now, he supposed, she was without purpose, her future uncertain.

Without a word, she led them through the jagged opening and across crunching plaster to a stairway, the air heavy with the smell of mildew and damp plaster. So dark was it, once inside, that both Gisburne and Galfrid stumbled as they ascended the creaking stair.

It led to a cramped upper chamber in the square tower, where Bardulf had evidently attempted to take refuge. A weak light shone through the small window. Despite the boards having recently been scrubbed, a grim ghost of spilt blood still stained half the floor. It stretched before them, describing a weird, semi-human shape – like some lingering spectre of Sir Walter.

"Was there a scrap of fabric anywhere on the body?" demanded Gisburne. "Or somewhere nearby, perhaps, with letters upon it? Marks of some kind?" The servant just stared at him and shrugged, vacantly.

"There was marks on the wall," said a small, reedy voice, "but they was cleaned off." Gisburne turned and saw the little girl framed in the doorway. The woman swiped the child with the flat of her palm, then grabbed her bony arm as if to drag her away.

"Wait!" Gisburne raised his hand. "What marks, girl? Can you remember what they were?" The child looked wide-eyed at Gisburne, then stared up at the servant woman.

"She knows no letters," muttered Galfrid.

Gisburne tried again. "Where were they? These marks? Show us..." She tore free of the grip of the servant and trotted over to a paler section of the stained, mould-flecked plaster wall, near the head end of the blood-ghost.

She extended a skinny arm. "There."

Gisburne and Galfrid examined the wall. Faint, smudged marks were still visible.

"L... I... X..." read Galfrid. "Licks?"

Gisburne slapped the side of his own head. "Idiot! I'm an idiot... L.I.X... L.I.V...They're not words, they're *numbers*. Fifty-nine... fifty-four..."

"Numbers..." repeated Galfrid. "Numbers of what?"

"I don't know," said Gisburne, placing his fingertips on the place where the marks had been made. "But it seems this Red Hand is trying to tell us something."

"Or make us look like idiots," said Galfrid. "What could he possibly want to tell us? And why?"

Gisburne ignored the question, and instead turned to the little girl, kneeling down and taking her by her shoulders. "Thank you," he said. "Thank you very much." And he pressed a silver penny into her hand. Her face lit up – making her, for that moment, the one bright thing in the whole of Sir Walter's bleak domain.

GISBURNE STRODE BACK down to the foot of the castle's wrinkled, rutted mound with renewed vigour.

"So, what now?" said Galfrid.

"To Nottingham," said Gisburne. "But there's someone I need to see first."

"An enginer?" ventured Galfrid. "An alchemist?"

"A priest," said Gisburne, and hauled himself into Nyght's saddle.

IX

Fountains Abbey
7 May, 1193

THE ABBOT HAD the bluest eyes Gisburne had ever seen. "You should know, Sir Guy," he said, testily, "that I have little time and even less sympathy for his Lordship Prince John. That means I have little time for you." He turned and directed his attention back to a half-written parchment on the small table, leaving Gisburne standing. Apart from a wooden chest, a low pallet bed and the chair in which the abbot himself sat, it was the only piece of furniture in the room.

Gisburne had heard that Ralph Haget could be difficult. How Haget had come to learn of Gisburne's connection with the Prince, however, he did not know. He supposed the toadying steward Gryffin must be right: word had spread since Christmas – since Clippestone. How much, he could not be certain. It was inevitable, he supposed, given what had happened, but it did not please him. He had grown used to relative anonymity. To return to England and discover himself with a certain fame... Others dreamed of such things. But to Gisburne it seemed yet another obstacle to getting the job done.

"I am grateful that you agreed to see me..." said Gisburne. "I have only a few questions to ask. It will take very little of your time."

"Your Prince makes no secret of the fact that he hates all things connected with the clergy and God's holy houses," grumbled Haget, still on the same track, as if Gisburne had not spoken at all. "I've heard he'd prefer it if we all shut up shop and crawled back to the Pope. God help us if he should ever become King." He looked aloft, somewhat apologetically, and crossed himself.

"Don't believe all you hear, abbot," said Gisburne – although at least half of it was true.

Haget grunted irascibly. "Hm. Where there's damp, there's usually rot." Haget's own reputation, it seemed, was also deserved. It had been a hard ride from Gisburne's home to Fountains Abbey. He had needed to make the journey in a day, and was hungry, thirsty and exhausted, and knew he stank of horse and the road. But neither food nor drink, nor even somewhere to sit had been offered – nor did it seem likely. It was said Haget's hospitality could be selective, even to other prominent members of the clergy. Gisburne could now personally vouch for it.

RALPH HAGET WAS fifty-three, but looked younger. He was fit and lean, and had a tough, no-nonsense bearing that to Gisburne was familiar; a military man at one time, he was willing to swear. The straight, neat scar on his chin – a wound that could only have been inflicted by a blade – supported this view. Perhaps he could use that insight. He might have to.

Fountains Abbey was the second house of the reforming Cistercian order to have been established in the north. Its relations with the local population had not always been cordial. In 1146, a mob – displeased with its abbot – had burnt all but the church to the ground. Fortunately, the next forty years had seen improvement in the abbey's circumstances, and prosperity had brought major rebuilding and expansion in the grand style.

Gisburne had left Galfrid ogling the abbey buildings, knowing he was always happy with some ecclesiastical architecture to look at. He had been vague about why he wished to come here, but suspected that Galfrid had begun to deduce the reasons anyway. The squire was not a fool. Yet Gisburne found it difficult to share matters that touched upon his personal life. Combat, physical pain, injury, danger – these things were easy to deal with. Affections – those were hard.

This also made his encounter with the already hostile Haget all the more challenging.

"I wish to ask about someone," he began, somewhat awkwardly. "They were in your care. Well, not exactly... But in a manner of speaking –"

"Name?" said Haget, cutting him off.

Gisburne stared at him, momentarily blank.

"This person – he has a name?" expanded Haget, as if speaking to an idiot.

"She..." said Gisburne. "Lady Marian Fitzwalter."

At that, Haget burst into sudden laughter. He rubbed his brow and shook his head in disbelief. "So all this is about a woman? Is this the kind of errand Prince John sends you on?"

Gisburne felt his face redden. "It is not for the Prince that I am here. Not for anyone."

"Well then... Why didn't you say so at the start?" Haget calmed himself and sniffed. "So, I am not talking to John, or John's messenger, but to Guy of Gisburne himself." He nodded. "People talk of you, of the thing you did. You have stirred up a hornet's nest. But I don't trust tittle-tattle. Who is this man I am talking to, and who asks my help?"

Gisburne shrugged, bemused. "Just what you see."

"What I see is a man who is a knight, but who doesn't look like a knight is supposed to look. More like..." Haget did not complete the sentence, but Gisburne knew where it was going.

"A mercenary," he said. The word stuck in his mouth. But he understood Haget's game. He would have to give if he was to receive. "I fought as one. Fought for pay. There were many years like that, before knighthood finally came."

"Finally? Then it was denied you?"

"I was unlucky."

"I don't believe in luck, good or bad. What happened?"

"I was squire to Gilbert de Gaillon. He was killed, disgraced. Because he dared question a man of influence. I was left as a squire without a knight, and no patron would take me on after that. I made my way as best I could."

Haget nodded slowly. "You were not a crusader?"

"No."

"Because you did not believe?"

Gisburne did not believe – not in that way. But that was not the issue. "I was just a man doing a job."

"And are you still?"

"Now I am better able to choose what job I do, and why I do it. A poor man doesn't have the luxury of opinions."

Haget gave a thin smile at that. "Where, then, did you fight?" he said, and leaned towards Gisburne. "Give me one name that I will know. The one that scarred you the most."

Gisburne stared into the stone wall. "Hattin," he said.

Haget's eyes widened at that. When it came to scars, Hattin had left its mark on all of Christendom. For Gisburne, personally, there was perhaps just one other that had struck as deep. It had been fought in a forest in Boulogne, and ended with the destruction by fire of a mad Templar's castle – but that battle had no name.

Haget sat back in his chair, then, and narrowed his blue eyes to slits. "And this man of influence you spoke of," he said, "what was his name?"

Haget knew. Gisburne was sure of it. It was a trap – or a test. But he saw no point in holding back now, even if his words were tantamount to treason. "Richard, Duke of Aquitaine," he said. "Now King Richard – called the Lionheart."

Haget interlinked his fingers. For a moment, Gisburne thought him about to pray. "Well, at least we understand each other a bit better now," he said. "I appreciate a man who speaks plainly." He sat forward, suddenly back to his former bluff self – but with the edges knocked off, this time. "And I know a soldier when I see one, Sir Guy. I was one myself." Gisburne silently congratulated himself. "Fought for King Henry against Louis of France. Gave it up when I was just about your age. I'd seen enough. Done enough." He fixed his ice-blue eyes on Gisburne again. "You know what I mean."

Gisburne did.

"For some, the suffering and bloodshed of others gets easier to bear. Becomes nothing. That's what they always tell you will happen, when, as a young knight, you have that first taste of true slaughter. When it leaves its wretched taste in your mouth." He shrugged. "For me, it was the exact opposite. It started easy, then got worse. And, like you, I was not enamoured of my king. It was 1170 when I left that life behind – the year Thomas Becket was slain in the cathedral. Had I not turned from soldier to monk, I doubtless would have participated in Henry's invasion of Ireland in the year that followed, and witnessed further atrocities."

Gisburne wondered if the fate of Becket had been the last straw – the bloody act that had finally pushed Haget's disgust over the edge. "Many men believe it is possible to be both soldier and monk together," he ventured.

"You mean the Templars, the Hospitallers? So-called warrior monks?" Haget almost spat with indignation, and slapped his hand on his desk so hard it shook. "Warrior monk! What an absurd contradiction! Better to fight for money, as you did. That is more honest." He calmed himself. "I have many friends in those orders. Men who I respect. But I..." He broke off, as if struggling to find the words, or uncertain whether he should be uttering them. Such a view went not only against that of the crusading King and the Pope, but his order's own great champion and revered luminary, St Bernard of Clairvaux – who had himself preached the Second Crusade. Haget took a deep breath. "I am not of the opinion that bloodshed is the solution to our woes. Christ said, 'Love thine enemy.' There is no ambiguity in that phrase. None."

"But it is a hard principle to adhere to when an enemy is bent on destroying everything you hold dear," said Gisburne.

"All war is disaster," said Haget. "Sometimes necessary, but disaster nonetheless." He thought for a moment, then spread his hands before him. "Christ sent out his message using twelve men of simple faith. With frail words, and no more. He believed them adequate. Do you know how the prophet Muhammed spread his doctrine? Through conquest, at the point of a sword, with an army ten thousand strong. We judge them harshly for this – even use it as an excuse to exterminate them – but at least when they fight and kill for their God, they're not making themselves hypocrites."

Gisburne could not fault Haget's logic. And, even if he was at odds with the totality of his view, he admired how the man held firm to it. It put him against the tide of opinion – even put his person in jeopardy. But he had seen war. He was at least better informed than the hotheads who merely sent others to their deaths.

"Tell me," said Haget, after a long pause, "what is this lady to you? Lady Marian?"

"We grew up together," said Gisburne. "Have known each other near our whole lives. I think it was expected, at one time, that we would be promised to one another. That did not happen. But I..."

Haget held up his hand. "But you still have hope." He nodded, his expression suddenly softer – almost fatherly. "Hope is the greatest gift we have. Sometimes the only one. But it is not always easy to bear."

"I need to know how she came here, and the circumstances under which she left," said Gisburne. "Nothing has been heard of her since. It is believed she went into Sherwood, and took up with Hood's gang."

Haget took that in, and sighed gravely. "The Cistercians are a supremely practical order," he said. "We do things. Help people. Contemplation is fine for the soul, but it will not put bread in a poor man's belly. That is what brought me here. Lady Marian, too." He fiddled with the edge of the parchment, suddenly awkward, as if struggling with feelings of guilt. "Many pretend to be good people; some of us – most of us – do good deeds and think good thoughts because we know we should. But there are very few, I have found, who are truly good – good to their souls, without hint of taint or compromise. Who do not have to *try* to be good. But Lady Marian was such a person. Perhaps the purest, kindest person I have ever encountered."

Gisburne knew it too. Many times he had feared for her, believing her nature too trusting. Now those fears had come to fruition. "Go on," he said.

"We see to the needy," explained Haget. "That is part of our mission – a continuation of Christ's own. Lady Marian endeavoured to support this in whatever way she could. Her zeal for the underdog and the neglected members of our community was passionate. As too, unfortunately, was that of Brother Thomas."

"Took..." said Gisburne. He heard hatred in his own voice.

"Thomas Took was a brilliant man. But also deluded, and dangerous. At odds with the world. He had already fallen out with his Dominican brethren at Glastonbury, and came here seeking a return to fundamental

Christian values. I sympathised, and welcomed him – admired him, even. I suppose it was partly vanity. I saw something of myself in his stubborn, rebellious ways. But over time, it became clear that his views were more extreme than I had ever imagined. He had formed certain radical notions on the subject of property that hinted at sympathy for the Albigensian heresy. He had begun to believe that the physical world was inherently corrupt. You must realise that we cannot countenance such a view. What surrounds us is God's creation. To question its nature is to question God himself. 'We are God's handiwork, created in Christ Jesus to do good works which God hath prepared for us to do...'" He shuddered. "He also believed in taking up arms to enforce his view. He'd put all wealthy men to the sword, if he had his way. That was what drew him towards Hood, who he began to revere. And also the insanities of a disgraced Templar named Tancred de Mercheval."

The name – coming from nowhere, entirely without warning – struck Gisburne like a hammerblow. "Tancred?"

"He is no longer of that order," said Haget. "His own philosophy is..."

"I know about his philosophy," snapped Gisburne. "Such as it is."

"They call him the White Devil. He is..." – Haget struggled to find the right word – "pestilence." He sighed deeply. "Why anyone feels the need to idolise such excuses for humanity when there are good men about is beyond me."

"And that is what Took did? Idolise him?"

"And met with him, I believe."

Gisburne's blood turned to ice. First, Tancred's men had seemed to possess knowledge of the Red Hand. Now there was evidence that Hood's men had had contact with Tancred. The nightmare was becoming reality.

"Marian came under the influence of Took. The intensity of their relationship raised eyebrows – though I do not believe there was anything physical in it. If anything, it was worse than that – a meeting of minds." He spread his hands. "For months, Took had been going – for days at a time. Into Sherwood, I now know. Then, one time, he simply did not come back. Lady Marian fell into a state of melancholy. She would speak to no one. Then, a week later, she ceased her visits." Haget place his hands flat upon his table. "And that is as much as I know."

Gisburne sat in stunned silence.

"I am sorry," said Haget. "Truly."

"It's not your fault," said Gisburne.

"I'll pray for your success," said the abbot. "And for her safety. It's the least I can do."

Gisburne nodded, and stared at the floor. "Tell me, Abbot Haget," he said after a while, "what does a red dragon mean to you?"

Haget frowned, and looked hard at Gisburne for a moment, then gazed off into the corner of his cell as if some secret thing lurked there. "'Then appeared another sign in heaven,'" he recited, almost in a whisper, "'a great red dragon with seven heads and ten horns and seven crowns upon its heads. Its tail dashed one third of the stars from the sky, and flung them all to the earth...'" He looked up. "You are familiar with this image?"

Gisburne knew of it – vaguely – but had never exactly been a scholar of the scriptures. "From the Book of Revelation?" he said.

Haget nodded. "That is what a red dragon means to me." Then, just in case Gisburne did not grasp his meaning, he added: "Apocalypse."

X

Nottingham
13 May, 1193

ON THE THURSDAY before Whitsunday, Gisburne and Galfrid stood with their mounts outside the great gate of Nottingham castle watching John's entourage leave for London.

The Prince did not travel light. There were a half-dozen wagons, each with one or two horses tethered behind it, carrying all the necessities and comforts the Prince and his court might desire during their sojourn at the Tower. One was packed with the Prince's furniture, decorative tapestries and his bed. At times – especially during winter – he had even been known to bring his own glass for the windows. One was for food and the means of cooking it. Another was devoted entirely to wine. The Prince did not trust the wine of others. Many took this as evidence of his suspicious nature, and the fact that those immediately about him – who obviously saw him for the villain he was – were constantly bent on his murder. But the fact was, John had grown up with the cheek-sucking, vinegary plonk of his father's court, and simply detested bad wine. Most of the great houses of England were, sadly, not so discerning.

The weather was warm and dry, and they raised a dust as they rumbled past. At the head of the convoy was John's private coach, for which Llewellyn had devised a system whereby the cabin was suspended on thick chains. As John had once told Gisburne, neither the king of France, the Pope nor the Holy Roman Emperor had such a thing. It smoothed out the bumps of the journey and replaced them with a rocking motion which the Prince described as "no worse than a gentle sea voyage". A sea voyage of any kind was absolutely the worst thing Gisburne could imagine, but he smiled and complimented Llewellyn's ingenuity nonetheless.

The coach was adorned with elaborate carvings and brightly decorated in red and gold – but it had also recently been fitted with heavier armour to better proof it against attack. The new additions – stout planks of wood and straps of iron, with thick shutters for the heavily curtained windows – had been painted in accordance with the colours of the coach, but the shade of red was at some variance with the rest, and their general workmanship hurried and crude in comparison. The fastidious John would find that irksome – but on the whole, it was better he remain alive than be killed in a perfectly co-ordinated environment.

Llewellyn's wagon was immediately behind the Prince's, and driven by Llewellyn himself. He never entrusted anyone else with this task, even though it was becoming too great a labour for the old man over such distances. Today, he looked suitably grumpy at the prospect. His eyes flicked to his right and caught Gisburne's, but made no sign of acknowledgment. This was a strict principle of Llewellyn's – one that he adhered to without exception, more for the security of John's agents than his own.

The remainder of the train consisted of at least fifty riders. Many were John's immediate staff of stewards, squires and knights, plus as many petty politicians and bureaucrats as he could stand to have around him (very few of these, and not one clergyman among them). But at least half of them – clustered closely about the royal coach, and forming a distinct body of men – were heavily armed, with scarred, humourless faces and hard eyes that scanned the small crowd that had gathered as the convoy had begun to emerge.

They wore the Prince's bright livery and flew his pennants upon their lances, but Gisburne could tell right away they were not English knights. He knew this look well enough. Norman mercenaries.

The word *mercenary* hardly did them justice. This was no disparate, rag-tag collection of warriors for hire, but a ruthlessly disciplined and organised company. They brought their own command structure, their own internal fealty and cohesion. In case one doubted it, their lances, helms and the mail beneath their identical surcoats were all precisely matching.

They were not merely for display. The lances were plain, ten-foot lengths of ash, knocked and dented along their lengths. The mail hauberks were seasoned by continual use, many with signs of repair. The helms, though polished, were pitted and scored from close combat, in which the wearers had evidently emerged the victors. John could not hope to find tougher or more experienced fighters if he scoured all of England; far less could he hope to trust them with his life. The Norman guard's loyalty, however, was assured – with silver.

In all this, John himself was nowhere to be seen.

Galfrid squinted at the dark windows of the Prince's coach, which were curtained with thick, blackened mail. The curtain parted for a moment, allowing a fleeting glimpse of red bearded face in the shadowy interior before a familiar ringed hand drew it closed once more.

"He's certainly not taking any chances," he said.

"Can you blame him?" said Gisburne.

Galfrid placed a calming hand on his mare's neck as one of the wheels of the wine wagon gave a loud *crack* and a young squire's horse spooked and tossed its head.

"Well, he's heading for the safest place in England," said Galfrid.

"That is good, yes," said Gisburne. "But he has to get there first..." This much, perhaps, went without saying; what did not were Gisburne's doubts about John's safety within the Tower. He chose to leave them unsaid anyway. It had been eighteen months since Gisburne had breached the Tower defences, one icy night in November, and proven that it could be done. Measures had since been put in place, the Tower's weak spots having been revealed. In theory, it should be more secure than it had ever been. But still the thought – the echo – troubled him, for reasons that, as yet, were not even clear in his own mind.

FOUR DAYS BEFORE, as they had neared Nottingham on the final leg of their journey south from Fountains Abbey, Gisburne had expressed a desire to locate the place on the north road where Wendenal had met his end. At first, it had seemed an impossible task; as they travelled the last few miles towards the city, every stretch of thick undergrowth on left or right seemed to suggest it might be the spot.

When finally they found it, there was no doubt.

The verges either side of the track – and especially upon the western side – had been churned and trampled to mud by dozens of hooves. Here and there on the track, the grass was yellowed or scorched black in neatly defined patches. On one magnificent outcrop of cow parsley, a single, prominent head of flowers had been burnt as black as its neighbours were white, and stood out in weird contrast, shrivelled but still fully intact, like the dark skeleton of its former self.

Close to the forest's edge, the low-growing plants – harebells, nettles and wild garlic – had been crushed flat. In one place, the bracken and brambles had been broken and pushed apart where the men had entered. In places, they had been slashed with knives or swords, parts of them still hanging by shreds. And, to the right side of the opening, embedded in the bough of a young oak, was a crossbow bolt.

Then there was the smell. Thick and rank it was, yet also sickly sweet. It was carried on a breeze from the south-west. It could be anything – a dead fox or deer, perhaps – but both knew it was neither.

Even in broad daylight, it had taken them half an hour to find the exact spot – and then only by tracking the knights who had recovered the body.

It was a small, sheltered glade, hidden from almost every approach. This was why the Red Hand had selected it. Little grew here, save a scattering of bluebells and wild garlic. As they approached, their footfalls releasing the sharp, savoury aroma of the bruised garlic stalks, it collided and merged with the sick smell of decay. Flies buzzed energetically – more here than elsewhere.

On the ground beneath a large beech tree was the cause of the stink. It was little more than a shapeless mass – a few shreds of some glistening material now so rotted as to be beyond recognition, the ground stained black in a wide circle around it. Some of the stuff appeared to have been strewn in odd directions. Dragged by animals, Gisburne supposed. They would have made off with most of it soon after it happened. What was left – which was very little – nothing on four feet would now touch.

This was what remained of Sir William de Wendenal. Or at least, the part that was spilled upon the forest floor by his crazed attacker. A damp rope – its frayed end cut by a blade – still dangled from a bough some ten feet above the circle of black.

Gisburne had studied the location, and its approaches, noting how it had required the attacker to double back towards his eventual pursuers. It was the very last thing they would have expected – a bold move on his part. If madness was what afflicted him, there was method in it. And a fierce intelligence. He must not underestimate this one.

For some time, much to Galfrid's irritation, he had scuffed the earth and crumbly leaf litter with his foot.

"What is it?" Galfrid had asked.

"Nothing," replied Gisburne, distractedly. When he was still doing so back on the road, Galfrid had repeated his question. "I had hoped to find the nail," said Gisburne. "The one that pinned the scrap of oilcloth," as he said it, he placed a fingertip on his forehead. He saw Galfrid shudder. Then the squire, too, began rooting around in the dirt.

They never did find it. But, just moments before they had mounted up to continue on to Nottingham, Galfrid's foot had found something pressed into the soft mud, which rose as his foot sank in. Another crossbow bolt. This one had evidently found its mark. But the head was as flat as if it had struck solid stone.

"So, what do we do now?" said Galfrid as the entourage rumbled off eastward towards the Great North Road.

Gisburne, slow to respond, as if avoiding the question, fiddled with his sword, adjusting the belt so it sat more comfortably. It was his father's sword, brought from his home in the village of Gisburne. It felt odd to be wearing it, for this treasured heirloom to have become a mere tool at his side. But it was time. The sword he acquired between Jerusalem and Acre had served its purpose, but already – having only put it to use twice – it was showing signs of poor workmanship. The blade was good – a fine crusader blade, which the seller had scavenged from somewhere – but the re-hilting had clearly been shoddy. The crossguard had begun to rattle, and the leather binding was already peeling away from the grip at that end.

"We do nothing," replied Gisburne, at length.

"Nothing?"

"Until we leave."

"Leave? Leave for where?"

"London."

Galfrid stared at Gisburne, then at the receding convoy, then back at Gisburne again. "Could you not have warned me about this in advance?"

"I'm doing that now."

"But if we're to catch them up..."

"We're not going with them."

"What?"

"We don't leave for another two days."

"Two days?"

"Two days. Relax, Galfrid. There's plenty of time."

"Well, how long are we going for?"

"I don't know." Gisburne shrugged. "Better say a couple of months."

Galfrid gave a peevish frown. "But you could have told –"

"Come on, Galfrid, you've got to two whole days to prepare. I've seen you do it in less than an hour."

"All right, then..." said Galfrid, nodding. He was bemused. But also angry. He sensed some kind of plan – but Gisburne had not chosen to make him part of it. "So why wait? Why not today, as soon as we're ready?"

Gisburne patted Nyght on the side of the neck, and began to lead him away. "No rush."

"But what's it for, this trip?" said Galfrid. "Give me some clue, at least."

Gisburne did not turn around.

"If we're not accompanying him now, when he's most vulnerable, why go at all?" Galfrid called after, making a last bid for some kind of response. But Gisburne, still walking, said nothing.

"I'll just get things ready, then..." said Galfrid feebly, as his master disappeared around the corner.

II

THE GREAT
NORTH ROAD

XI

The Village of Gisburne
June, 1171

GUY WAS LYING awake when he heard his father return. They were the sounds he had been anticipating for over a week: the pounding of hooves from outside, felt as much as heard; the clank of the latch as the front door was opened, its dry hinges whining; the thump and clatter of chattels being dumped upon flagstones. It was done with care, so as not to disturb the slumbering inhabitants – but in the still of the night, every sound seemed loud.

Guy's heart leapt – but he did not move. Instead, he would wait for what he hoped – no, what he knew – was coming. He heard the slow, careful tread of heavy-booted feet approaching his door, a weary sigh and a familiar, stifled cough. Gripping the blankets in his small fists, he kicked his feet beneath the covers and gave a silent laugh of pure joy.

Every one of the thirty nights his father had been away, he had yearned to hear these sounds. Every night for the past eight, he had forced himself to stay awake in expectation of them, not wishing to miss the moment – but on every occasion, sleep had won the battle. He had drifted off into vivid and exhausting dreams of long journeys, in which familiar places suddenly seemed alien and indistinct and he was always getting further and further from home.

Tonight had been no different. The exception had been the dream. In it, he had been at home. It was winter again – something he'd known, rather than seen or felt – and somehow, beyond the ceiling above him, he could see that the dark sky was filled with thousands upon thousands of impossibly bright stars. He marvelled at it. Then, somewhere, there was a tapping – the sound of bony knuckles on wood, steady and deliberate. It came from the wooden shutter at his window. He knew right away that it was Adela.

"Um-brey…" she chanted in her reedy, little-girl voice. She wanted to come in out of the cold. Guy knew that too. She must be frozen, poor little mouse. That was what his mother used to say to her – "poor little mouse". But he felt too afraid to open the window. "Um-brey..." came the sing-song call again. *Tap, tap, tap* went the knuckles against the shutter.

Then he heard her begin to sob – a plaintive, hollow cry he had not heard in a long time – and saw his hand go to the latch.

The shutter was no longer there. Framed within the black space of the window, against a sky that seemed to stretch forever into darkness, was the face of Adela. It seemed to glow like the moon, its light pale and cold, her eyes huge and darkly circled. "Please let me in, Umbrey," she said, and sobbed again.

Guy felt a shuddering horror. Various details inspired it: that she looked so sad. That the window was – he now remembered – twelve feet above the ground. That she was dead.

The face drifted towards him. He was unable to move. *You died...* He wasn't sure if he spoke it or merely thought it. *How can you be here?* The question stirred memories, brought realisations. Adela could not be here. And this was not how his room was meant to be. It was like it was years ago, with the small rickety bed from which his foot once suffered an enormous splinter – so big his father had simply been able to pull it out with thumb and forefinger. His mother had insisted upon a new one then, and they had burned it on the fire that October. As these realisations came, challenging the seeming-reality of the dream, the world had begun to unravel. Its grip on him dissolved. Its images faded. Finally, he had jolted awake – with a deep sense of relief. All around was back just as it was meant to be – the shutter open, the warm night air wafting through, heavy with the scent of honeysuckle, the near-full moon almost perfectly framed at the window's centre. All still. All real. He had lain there for only a few minutes when he had heard his father's horse approach – and the dream was utterly forgotten.

THE LATCH ON the door of the small room – the only such room in the house – clicked. The door was opened with slow, quiet deliberation. A familiar face loomed in the gap.

Guy laughed aloud.

"What are you doing still awake?" whispered his father in quiet outrage. Then his face broke into a smile, and he sat on Guy's bed and ruffled the boy's hair. He smelt of horses and leather and sweat. There was something sweet and reassuring in that smell.

"I missed you," said his father. For an instant, there was such feeling in his voice and face that Guy thought the man he had always regarded as implacable was about to weep. The possibility frightened him. In another moment, it was gone, and his father was laughing again.

"You're back!" Guy said, beaming. Statement of the obvious did not, somehow, seem out of place tonight. He fought the urge to hug his father, however; he thought himself too old for that sort of thing. He wasn't sure if he saw disappointment flicker across his father's face.

"Did you look after everyone for me?" said his father. It was an odd choice of phrase. There was only mother now, unless one counted the horses and the few servants.

"Sol and Luna missed Estoil," he said. Then added, earnestly: "I combed and cleaned them out every day. And took them to the paddock."

His father frowned at him and leaned forward. "You didn't try to ride Sol, did you?"

Guy shook his head vigorously and felt his face redden. That was a lie. The command not to do so had been the last thing his father had said when he left, and yet Guy had made the attempt the very next day, climbing on the gate in the paddock to get himself onto the back of the big destrier. Sol had waited until he was sitting comfortably, then immediately bucked him off, as his father had clearly known he would. Now, Guy just hoped that in the pale light his guilt was not too obvious. As he flushed, he felt his chin itch.

His father grinned, and nodded – either because he believed his son, or was too glad to be home to invite argument. Guy suspected the latter. Then suddenly his father looked closer at him. "What's that?" he said, and raised the boy's chin gently with a rough finger to reveal the vertical red mark there.

Guy had forgotten about the scar. It seemed an age ago it had happened, though was barely more than four weeks.

"I fell against the stone trough in the paddock," said Guy, sheepishly. He chose not to mention that this was when Sol had thrown him, and that he was probably lucky to be alive.

His father frowned, and looked at his face on both sides. "Are you all right?"

"Yes," Guy said; then, looking defiant, added: "I didn't cry."

His father laughed and ruffle his hair. "Brave boy," he said.

"There are wasps up there," said Guy, changing the subject. "Building a nest in the Tall Tree."

"You leave them be," said his father, wagging a finger. "No good comes of messing with those poisonous little bastards."

Guy laughed at that. His father's momentarily stern expression dropped and he chuckled, too.

"Where did you go?" said Guy. He had missed his father too, but now he was more concerned with hearing tales of adventure.

"Your mother didn't tell you?"

"No," said Guy. He expected his father to be annoyed at the answer, but for some reason he simply looked relieved. "She just said it was over the sea."

"That it was," said his father, and sighed deeply.

"What were you doing there?" asked Guy.

His father looked him in the eye in silence, his mouth half open as if he had been about to speak but had suddenly been unable to find the words. He looked absent. Lost. It seemed to Guy his father was suddenly burdened, as if he had recently looked upon something terrible. He could not say quite what it was he saw in his face. But in the pale light of the moon, those features – of this man who had always seemed all-powerful – seemed somehow to have aged, to have gone beyond age, to become something else altogether. A thing without substance. A pale ghost.

WHAT WERE YOU *doing there?* The words rattled round and round in Robert of Gisburne's head, taunting and accusing him. He was exhausted, his body aching and sore and clammy, his clothes stuck to him. The miles, and the days, weighed upon him. He just wanted to sleep and forget, and tomorrow treat the past month as a dream from which he had now awoken. But he knew it would not be that simple. His relief at being home was overwhelming. It felt like deliverance. But something about it terrified him, too.

"It was something for King Henry," he said, finally, and forced a smile. "Something secret. So, you mustn't tell anyone." He leaned in towards his son, his good humour now fully returned. "You swear?"

Guy nodded earnestly, his eyes wide with wonder. "I swear."

Robert had been worried about the boy of late. For the past year he had been running wild, getting into all manner of scrapes and ignoring his parents' commands. No, it had been longer than that. Since little Adela had died of the red fever, in fact – and Robert felt sure it was in some way connected. Brother and sister had always had a close bond. When it had struck – randomly, out of nowhere, a meaningless tragedy – young Guy had reacted not with grief, but with anger. He had wished to blame someone – to call them out and fight them. Finding he could not, he declared that he hated God, then fought with a boy from the village whose family were respected for their piety. He would have damn near killed him if the blacksmith's lad had not pulled them apart.

Robert had meted out punishment as seemed fitting, but in truth had felt ill-equipped to deal with it. His wife Ælfwyn had met the boy's sudden, uncharacteristic aggression with tearful perplexity. They had never been the most devout of couples, but after Adela her relationship with God became all the keener. She began praying for the boy, and, assuming her husband shared her bemusement, urged him to do so, too. He did nothing to contradict her assumption. The real problem was not that Robert failed to understand his son's feelings, but that he felt exactly the same.

"What's that?" said Guy, squinting in the dark.

Robert saw his son's eye caught by something at his side. He immediately knew what. A glint of polished metal – the silver of a pommel atop a black grip.

"A new sword," said Robert. "Given to me by the King himself."

The boy leaned further forward, his hand outstretched. "Can I...?"

"Tomorrow!" insisted his father. "I need to stable Estoil. He needs his sleep. And you need yours." He stood to leave.

"A story, then!" called Guy. "Before you go. From your travels." Robert stopped. His guts tightened. Somehow he managed a good-natured smile. Recounting what had happened was the very last thing he wanted – this night or any other.

"I told you," he said, "it was secret. By order of the King."

"I mean a ghost story!" said Guy. "I haven't heard any for weeks. Mother won't tell me them. You said you'd listen out for new ones."

Robert slumped back down on the bed. "You and your ghost stories," he laughed. "How tales of spooks and ghouls are supposed to help you sleep I can't imagine..."

"Please!" begged Guy.

His father screwed up his face in thought, as if digging deep into his memory. "Well, there was one," he said. "Told me by a pilgrim. But I'm not sure you're ready for it yet..." His father made as if to leave again.

"I am!" said Guy in desperation. "Please..."

His father narrowed his eyes, nodded, and turned back.

"I'll be in trouble with your mother if it gives you nightmares."

"It won't, I promise."

"Well then..." Robert said, nodding slowly. And, in hushed tones, he found himself relating the following story.

THERE WAS ONCE a man named Richard, who went on a pilgrimage. His wife was with child at the time, but Richard's determination to serve his God was such that earthly considerations took second place. And so he said his goodbyes and left her behind in England.

The journey was hard, with many hazards along the way, in the wild mountains most of all. There were thieving bandits, wolves, wild dogs. Every night, one of the pilgrims in Richard's party would keep watch over the others. This particular night, it was Richard's turn to stay awake and warn them of danger.

It was a still night – strangely quiet – and he was almost dozing off when a great clamour jarred him awake. He peered about in alarm, but when he looked about, the deafening tumult had awoken none of his fellows. They lay as if dead in their slumber. Then he looked upon the pilgrim road, and saw, advancing along it, a ghostly procession. Wraiths and phantoms of the dead, blowing tunelessly upon trumpets and banging upon drums – wasted in their flesh, their withered faces drawn into expressions of terrible melancholy. Each one rode upon the back of a beast – not just horses, but sheep, pigs, oxen... the very animals that had been used to pay for each of their funerals. He watched in dumb horror as the ghastly sight swayed past. Then he saw the strangest sight of all. Behind the parade of dead riders was some living thing, rolling along the dusty ground in a leather boot. The pilgrim thought at first it was a skinned hare. Then, to his horror, he realised it was a baby – too tiny to be alive.

"Who are you," he asked, "and why do you roll?"

Peering from its black shroud, the child replied in a thin and dreadful voice. "It is not right that you address me. For I am your child, stillborn and buried without a name."

Struck through with sorrow and remorse, the pilgrim wrapped the creature in his shirt, baptised it and gave it a name. And it gave a great cry of joy, and walked upright into paradise.

The pilgrim kept the old boot. Upon returning home, he asked his wife to bring his boots to him, but she could find only one. To her astonishment, the man then produced the other, and told his tale – whereupon the midwife who had attended her confessed that she had buried the dead child in the boot, unnamed and unbaptised.

THAT STILLBORN CHILD – its face, its voice – haunted Gisburne for months afterwards. It still figured in his nightmares from time to time. But it wasn't just the tale that had affected him so. It was the look on his father's face as he had concluded it – an expression of unutterable sorrow.

For a while after, in his sleep, his father repeatedly muttered a strange word that Guy did not recognise. He thrashed in agitation as he did so, as if recalling some torment. More than once Guy went to him, but neither he nor his mother had ever dared to wake him up. It had passed. Then, when he had nursed the old man on his deathbed, the habit had momentarily returned, and the buried memory was unearthed.

Years later, Gisburne discovered that the word was a name, and that it was Irish.

XII

The road to Berughby
15 May, 1193

GALFRID WAS TO find the answer to his questions at a lonely inn somewhere between Aslockton and Bottesforde.

The squire had been ready soon after dawn. To his great frustration, Gisburne had not gathered himself to leave until long past midday – and the pace from Nottingham had been slow. At times, Galfrid had stared at Gisburne, wondering if something was wrong – if some ailment or injury was troubling him. But Gisburne just looked about, seeming to enjoy the day's fine weather, taking deep breaths of the warm air and the scent of new spring blooms. Out across the cultivated fields, a light haze hung. In the wide open space three small boys with slings were cavorting, charged with keeping pigeons off the bean crop.

Galfrid turned away and eyed a now familiar rectangular box slung behind Gisburne's saddle. "I can't believe you're bringing that."

Gisburne looked at the squire, then at the hurdy gurdy that had somehow survived fire, brimstone, ordure and everything else that Salah al-Din's Jerusalem had thrown at it. "I like it," he said.

Galfrid kept his eyes fixed ahead. "So, what's hidden it it this time? Greek Fire? Poisoned blades? The jewel encrusted arsebone of Saint Jerome?"

"Nothing," said his master. Galfrid stared at him with narrowed eyes. Gisburne caught the look. "Check if you don't believe me."

Galfrid was damned if he was going to do that.

"I just like it," said Gisburne.

Galfrid turned his attention back to the road. "So, is it to be this speed all the way to the Tower?" he said. Part of him relished the prospect. Another part wanted simply to press his horse to a gallop so they could get there and get on with it – whatever 'it' was.

"It's like I said," replied Gisburne, without turning to look at him. "No rush…"

"No rush?" said Galfrid, bemused. "You're always in a rush."

"Not today," said Gisburne.

Galfrid sighed heavily, and looked back out across the fields.

THEY WERE LITTLE more than a dozen miles from Nottingham when Galfrid noticed Gisburne was scanning the horizon ahead. He did so with sudden eagerness, as if expecting trouble. Galfrid followed his gaze. Some way down the road, just coming into view beyond a sheltered copse of trees, was an old inn.

"Are we stopping?" said Galfrid. "Already?" Not that he minded. If Gisburne insisted on taking things easy, then a few extra ales along the way were fine by him. His master grunted, as if only dimly aware of his squire's question, then geed Nyght into a trot.

"Right, then..." said Galfrid, mostly to his horse. "So now we hurry..." And he urged the mare on.

The inn was an odd, rounded building part-covered in ivy, which looked as if it was collapsing in on itself. But the smell of woodsmoke wafted from the chimney, and the alestake outside was decorated with fresh flowers. As they approached, however, his master seemed to be looking elsewhere.

Then he saw it. In the copse of trees, standing motionless and only just visible from the road, was a white horse. On it sat a cloaked and hooded figure, his face entirely obscured. Galfrid felt his muscles tighten. He looked down at the pilgrim staff tucked beneath his saddle bag. There was a sword at his belt too. And a mace tucked away on the saddle's other side. But the staff had become his favoured weapon of late. It gave him additional reach – and the advantage of surprise. That staff hid several surprises. Without stopping, he reached down, loosened the straps, and drew it out.

Gisburne, a good twelve paces ahead of him, had no weapon drawn. The figure on the white horse turned, and walked slowly forward. Gisburne rode straight up to him, still unarmed. Galfrid pulled his horse up beside him, staff gripped and at the ready. He judged that with one good swing he could clout the rider about the head, if need be. That may not unhorse him, but he'd be senseless for a while.

The stranger looked up at his approach, then pulled back his hood. Galfrid gasped in astonishment.

"Good day, squire Galfrid," said Prince John, with a mischievous smile.

GALFRID SHOT A glance at Gisburne, his expression pinched.

"You bastard," he muttered. There was exasperation in it, but also,

Gisburne sensed, relief. He hoped the squire now understood. But even so, he could not resist a laugh at Galfrid's expense.

"Don't blame Sir Guy," smiled John. "I suggested we allow as few people as possible to know of this. He took me at my word, and told precisely no one."

"But I saw you leave Nottingham two days ago..." said Galfrid, in protest.

"You didn't see Prince John," said Gisburne. "Just his entourage. The Prince was never there."

"But I saw..."

"There is a man, who looks very much like me," said John. "Who *is* me, for the moment. Even those travelling with him believe it. Of course, given the risks, he is too wary to leave his carriage. And so the deception is maintained."

Galfrid stared at Gisburne. "It's the bloody skull of St John the Baptist all over again. I can't believe I fell for that a second time."

"Misdirection," said Gisburne. "Let's hope the Red Hand is similarly diverted.

"We maintain an even pace, keeping the royal entourage two days ahead. That is the decoy. If anything happens, we'll know about it. But for now, we are simply a pair of knights and a squire travelling upon the road."

John laughed aloud at that, and slapped the side of his horse affectionately. Gisburne realised that the Prince was actually looking forward to this, even in the face of the present danger. And why should he not? He was free of the court. Free of the bureaucrats and the flatterers. Free of the unwanted attentions of the clergy and the struggles for power. And, most of all perhaps, he was free of what all the naysayers thought of him, be they barons or peasants. For a while, at least, he was not prince or heir – he was just himself. Quite what that was, Gisburne was not entirely sure.

"If this deception is to work," Gisburne said. "We'll have to dispense with calling you *my lord...*"

John shrugged. "You never bothered with the niceties anyway. But it is noted. Address me as 'Sir John.' Or simply 'John.' We're familiar enough for that, I think." Gisburne gave a respectful nod. John turned to the squire. "Galfrid? You are to call me 'John.' Can you do that?"

"Yes, my lor – Sorry, I mean, J – Joh –" But try as he might, Galfrid could not bring himself to address the Prince by his Christian name.

"Galfrid is a squire," said Gisburne, coming to Galfrid's rescue. "It would be more natural for him to afford a knight the courtesy his station demands." He turned and looked Galfrid in the eye. "In fact, to witness it at all would be a novelty..."

"Of course, of course..." said John, nodding earnestly. "'Sire,' then."

"You hear that, Galfrid?" said Gisburne, unable to suppress a smile of satisfaction. "'Sire.'"

"Yes," said Galfrid flatly. "'Sire.'"

Gisburne turned back to John. "One other thing," he said, more tentatively this time. "Your appearance..."

John looked vaguely mortified, and put his hand to his chest. "Is it not fitting to the purpose?" Concerned that the Prince would be unable to resist the fine silks and richly embroidered cloth that he regularly favoured, Gisburne had requested he wear something suitable for a long day's hunting in the saddle. He had specified that they be his oldest riding clothes, and had also instructed John's personal servant and groom to pack his horse accordingly, knowing that this was not something to which a Prince was accustomed. These two trusted individuals were the only ones permitted to know of the change to the plan, and even then only the night before. They now travelled with the impostor in John's ornate carriage.

John, meanwhile, had followed his instructions to the letter, and inhabited his role perfectly – although his oldest clothes, it seemed, were still newer than Gisburne's newest.

"The clothes are excellent," said Gisburne. "Exactly right. But the rings..." He nodded at John's fingers. "They announce you like a fanfare." Gisburne drew his horse alongside John's. John's eyes narrowed as Gisburne held out his hand.

"Isn't this precisely what Hood is supposed to do?"

"I'm saving him the trouble," said Gisburne.

"You are a tyrant," said John, then, pulling off the rings one by one, dropped them into Gisburne's palm. Gisburne tipped them into a pouch, pulled its drawstrings tight and stowed it in the bag upon his belt.

"Am I now fit for the journey?" said John.

Gisburne nodded, and turned Nyght about. "It's five miles to Berughby," he said. "We'll overnight there."

"And tomorrow?" said John.

"The Great North Road," said Gisburne.

XIII

The Great North Road
16 May 1193

THAT DAY THEY had arisen early, and after a leisurely breakfast turned their horses south onto the Great North Road. The three of them were in a bright mood. It was fine weather, the going was good, and all had slept soundly the night before at a crossroads inn near Berughby – the only fleeting interruption to Gisburne's slumber occurring some time in the early hours when John had chosen to piss in a pot less than a yard from his head.

It was still morning when Gisburne turned his horse about and said to Galfrid: "Keep a close eye on the Prince."

"Of course," said Galfrid. He followed on, just behind John, his expectation being that Gisburne would dismount and answer a call of nature at the verge. But at the sound of hooves he turned, and saw that Gisburne was riding away at the gallop, heading along the track towards the village of Ganthorpe. "Right..." he muttered. Gisburne had said the minimum, and then rushed away before Galfrid had time to ask questions; he always did that when he was hiding something.

"Anything wrong?" called the Prince, looking back.

"No," said Galfrid, having not the faintest idea. "Everything's fine."

The wait for Gisburne's return must only have been minutes, but seemed to last forever. He rode up alongside Galfrid without a word, slowing to the others' pace, just as if nothing had happened.

"Everything all right?" said Galfrid.

"Fine," said Gisburne, without making eye contact. He was breathing hard, and Nyght was steaming. Wherever he'd been, he'd ridden hard there and back.

"So what was all that about?"

"All what?"

"One minute you're sticking to the Prince like pitch, not letting him out of your sight, then suddenly you're riding off."

"It's nothing important," said Gisburne. "I'll tell you when it is."

"When it is...?" repeated Galfrid, with a frown.

Then John's voice rang out ahead. "We've passed beyond my lands," he said.

"I DON'T LIKE it," said John. "Feels like leaving home for another country." The lands to the north-east of England were John's domain – a miniature empire, centred on Nottingham, over which he ruled with little interference. It was a sudden reminder to Gisburne that from here, there would be many more threats than the Red Hand.

"London practically *is* another country," muttered Galfrid, coming up alongside.

"More literally than perhaps you realise," said John. "You know that I granted them freedom? In return for the loyal support of the citizens of London when I stood against Longchamp, that time he squirrelled himself away in the Tower. Now they elect their own mayor, and rule themselves. A commune. Neither my father nor my brother would ever have sanctioned such liberty – not for a million silver marks." He thought for a moment. "Well, perhaps my dear brother would. He'd have sold the lot – and for far less – when he was looking to fund his crusade. For a million he'd have let the French tow it to Calais and use it for a midden. Then, with England plunged into poverty, off he would go and squander the lot on conquering the entire known world. How will people remember him, I wonder?"

"Men are rarely remembered as they really were," said Gisburne. "Kings even less so."

John sighed, and nodded sadly, as if contemplating his own fate. "You know, when Saladin died, all he had in his possession was a single piece of gold and 40 pieces of silver – not even enough to pay for a funeral. The ruler of that great empire had given away all the wealth he had to the poor amongst his subjects. Godless he may be, but he could teach many of us something of chivalry and Christian virtues. Of noble kingship."

"He knew how to win battles," said Gisburne. A vivid impression of the disaster at Hattin, where Salah al-Din had crushed the Christian forces, momentarily flared in his memory.

"His people will remember him as a great man," continued John. "Even his enemies respected him. Do you ever wonder how will posterity treat us?"

The words *I try not to* were on the tip of Gisburne's tongue when up ahead, on the road, he spied movement. Two figures on foot, gesticulating wildly. He gestured silently to Galfrid – but the squire had already seen for himself. They drew in front of John, one on each side. Then he, too, caught sight of the figures. "What's this?" he said, and raised himself up in his saddle.

They were dressed as pilgrims. There were no horses to be seen, and they were a long ride from the nearest village. Both were hatless, their clothing awry, and – as Gisburne could now hear – were crying out for help. He could make out the words *robbery* and *outlaws*. To most travellers, this signified honest men in distress. But something about the manner of their dress – and the fact they did not run to seek aid, but remained rooted to the spot, flanked by convenient cover – told Gisburne a different story.

"Christ's boots," he sighed. "Not this again."

"Pilgrims? Robbed?" said John as they neared. "On Whitsunday? This is an outrage. We must help them. Gisburne – you and Galfrid dismount and bring them aid."

Gisburne brought Nyght to a halt. "With respect, my lord, I suggest we spur the horses and pass them at the gallop." In his mind, he added: *...or just trample them into the dirt.*

"You may suggest it, Sir Guy," said John, his tone suddenly testy. "But I insist we offer help." Perhaps, thought Gisburne, it was thought of posterity and honour that had suddenly turned John into a good Samaritan. Perhaps the memory of Thomas Becket haunted him. Either way, the impulse was admirable – but it wasn't the Prince's head at risk.

"These men are no more pilgrims than I," said Gisburne.

John was having none of it. He shook his head. "I'll not have on my conscience the possibility that I left two pious men in distress." And he gestured towards them. "Please..."

A memory forced its way into Gisburne's mind – from almost a dozen years ago, when he was still a squire, but as vivid as if it were unfolding before his eyes. It was of the Prince's brother Richard sending Gisburne's knight and master Gilbert de Gaillon into an ambush. He pushed it aside, reminding himself that the Prince's safety was his primary concern. And this would not have the same conclusion. Gisburne nodded dutifully, and trotted on, Galfrid close behind. "Let's make this quick," he muttered to the squire, and dismounted some ten yards from the two men, who were still wailing about thievery and murder.

No SOONER HAD he got within five yards of the pair than a third leapt out of the bushes, clad all in green, with a part-drawn bow trained on them. He gave a loud laugh. "Take not another step!" he cried, triumphantly, "for I am Robin Hood! Now, hand over your valuables!"

Gisburne looked him up and down, and sighed. "Do you find this works for you?"

The robber's smile faltered for an instant. "Have you not heard of my legend?" He puffed himself up again. "Now, hand it over unless you want to feel my arrow point. My patience wears thin!"

Gisburne stood and stared at him for what seemed an age. The arrow was shaking, the archer's grip awkward, providing an inadequate rest for the shaft. Gisburne shook his head slowly. "You're not Robin Hood."

"I am!" he insisted. There was a hint of panic in his eyes. The two 'pilgrims,' who had merely stood throughout the conversation, began to back away.

"You are not," said Gisburne, and took a step forward. The archer twitched, the arrow shaft clacking against the bowstave.

"How would you know?" he spat.

"Because I've met him," said Gisburne. He heard Galfrid step up beside him. The panic in the archer's eyes was almost frantic. "I've fought him. And Robin Hood would not let me do this…" In one swift movement, Gisburne dropped, grasped a stone, and hurled it at the bowman. It cracked against his forehead and bounced off into the brambles, the feebly loosed arrow whistling above Gisburne's head. The archer howled and staggered, blood coursing down his face. He recovered just in time to see Gisburne boot him in the balls.

The pilgrims did not look likely to be rushing to their comrade's aid, but they were not afforded the chance. Before either could make a move, Galfrid strode forward and smashed the left kneecap of the nearest with his mace. Seeing all was lost, the third made an unexpected lunge between Gisburne and Galfrid and leapt on Nyght's back. In triumph, his pilgrim robes almost falling off him, he kicked his legs against the destrier's flanks, and shouted "Yah! Yah! Yah!"

Nyght moved not an inch. The ineffectual outlaw's expression changed to one of dismay as, with growing desperation, he found himself sat, heading nowhere, spurring the horse uselessly like an idiot.

"Bloody horse won't bloody move!" he cried out to no one, a profuse sweat breaking out on his brow.

Gisburne, walking towards him, raised his right hand, then swept it downwards. Nyght immediately dropped and rolled onto his side, crushing the outlaw's right leg beneath his flank. They probably heard his shriek in Stanford.

For a moment, Gisburne stood over the wailing, sweating outlaw as he made futile efforts to free his leg. He was letting the thief see him – letting him take in his adversary, and wonder at what was to happen next. The man's eyes were wide with fear. "I had my horse taken once before," said Gisburne at last. "Didn't like it. Nor did he. So we came to an agreement – decided we didn't want that to happen again." He turned his head to one side so he could look the man squarely in the face. "Shall I make him roll all the way over on his back?" He turned his finger in a little circle.

"No!" cried the man. "Please!"

After a moment, Gisburne turned away, leaving the man there a little longer.

Galfrid, meanwhile, regarded the writhing figure at his own feet, clutching the shattered knee, huffing through his mouth with such ferocity that he was foaming at the mouth. Galfrid shook his head. "You've heard the phrase 'thick as thieves'?" he said. "It's you they were referring to." And he booted the man in the ribs.

THEY RODE AWAY, leaving the pilgrims with two good legs between them.

"Yes, yes..." said John in response to the silence. "You were right and I was wrong." Gisburne did not feel any reply was needed, and so said nothing. "Still..." John continued. "The man with the bow... Incompetent as he was, he may yet have hit his mark, and taken your life. Did that not give you pause?"

"If I paused for thought every time I stood before someone who might kill me," said Gisburne, looking straight ahead, "I'd be dead already."

John nodded, but the look of concern did not leave his face. "Be careful, Sir Guy," he said. "You're not the Red Hand. Arrows can still kill *you*..."

XIV

Clairmont Castle
16 May, 1193

THE DAY HAD been warm. Now, with the light beginning to fail and the temperature plunging, a heavy mist had risen from the moist, black fenland soil. For a while, the roofs of Clairmont Castle – the highest points for miles, save a few huddled trees – had stood proud of the low swirl, like some great stone ship sat low in a pale ocean. But, bit by bit, that sea had risen to completely envelope them.

All was quiet as Hugh de Mortville strode across the courtyard, his shaggy hound Conan skittering about him. No movement but the guard on the gatehouse and the flap of a lone crow on the manor house chimney, their sounds weirdly muffled by the fog. He rubbed his hands. The cold, damp air now nipped at his fingers, but within he felt a warm glow – a glow of contentment. His belly was still full from the great Whitsun feast, his head pleasantly swimming from the wine that had accompanied it.

There was a satisfaction in his soul, too. He never had been the most sociable sort, but for the feast – held at noon that day, as it was every year – he had opened his doors to all his tenant farmers and their families. It was a chaotic, often raucous affair – so different from the noble gatherings he was occasionally forced to attend. Those, he hated. But the Whitsun feast, a gesture of appreciation to all those who contributed to the wealth of his estate, was a truly joyous occasion. For the week of Whitsuntide that followed, villeins were excused all work. Doubtless the prospect of a holiday helped fuel his tenants' good cheer. Some nobles chose not to observe it – or rather, chose for their villeins not to observe it. De Mortville thought such behaviour reprehensible.

He hoped his own tenants thought him a fair man. In life, he had always striven to be. But he had other, more selfish reasons for sharing the feast, too. Those he welcomed on this day were not jaded nobility, but peasants to whom this was a genuine wonder. Their joy was honest and unrestrained. Lacking any immediate family of his own, their pleasure was also his.

At the main gate, he shared a good-natured joke about the weather with the porter, and the heavy doors beneath the elaborately timbered gatehouse were heaved open. His hound leapt with excitement. As he passed over to the mossy stone bridge that spanned the moat, Conan scampering ahead, he felt the sudden chill from the water and the damp air, and pulled his cloak tighter around him, the stillness of his surroundings a sharp contrast with the day's clamour.

DESPITE ITS NAME, Clairmont was not really a castle. It had been a long time since there had been any threat worth worrying about in these parts. No one passed by the estate of Hugh de Mortville. It was on the way to nowhere, which meant only those with the purpose of visiting its lord were likely to come this way at all. The rest took little interest – if they even knew it existed. Most avoided the Fens altogether, believing them a bleak, savage place.

And that was exactly how Hugh de Mortville liked it.

So he had built for himself not a castle, but a moated manor house. What it lacked in defences, it made up for in comforts. True, it had a wall, and a gatehouse, and beyond that a moat – which in these damp regions needed so little encouragement to fill that it frequently flooded – but at its heart, the long three-storey stone house was not a fortress, but a home. A place not to cower and shiver, but to live – unmolested, in a manner elegant and congenial – in peace and contentment. This, de Mortville was convinced, would be the new way.

It had fireplaces and chimneys. It had large windows filled with glass. It even had piped water which could be heated by fire – contrived, with great difficulty, by an ingenious Welshman of de Mortville's acquaintance. Only at one end, where a stout, square tower topped with battlements made a token stand, did it in any way resemble the castle familiar to his contemporaries. But even this, as with the other supposed defences, was built more for show than protection.

After all, there was nothing to fear way out here. Not any more.

IMMEDIATELY OUTSIDE THE gate, on the left side, was a small collection of sticks – half a dozen or so. These were Conan's sticks, and here was where he left them when the game of throw and fetch with his master was done. Some showed signs of splintering about the middle from the attentions of his teeth, but otherwise had been treated like treasured objects, carefully placed for the next day's play. De Mortville had encouraged the dog in his tidy habit. Hereabouts, trees were few, and good throwing sticks a rare commodity.

He selected one – a good, thick stick, still a little green – and showed it to the hound. Conan leapt, then dropped half flat, front paws splayed before him, tongue lolling, his wide, expectant eyes fixed on his master.

De Mortville smiled and feigned a throw. Conan started, but didn't fall for it. With a laugh, de Mortville swung again and sent it spinning through the foggy air ahead of him, past the end of the bridge. Just a short throw to begin with. Conan, big though he was, was off like a rabbit, diminishing to a grey phantom as he plunged into the enveloping mist.

De Mortville strode after him, humming a tune to himself.

CONAN – AN IRISH Wolfhound – was the second such dog that de Mortville had owned. The first had been a fine silvery-grey bitch with an unpronounceable name that had been presented to Prince John by Irish chieftains back in 1185. It was a great honour, apparently – but John had showed little interest in the dog, and somehow de Mortville had ended up adopting her. Three years later she had died with bad bones, but not before she'd had three pups with one of Eustace Fitz Warren's hounds. One died, one went to Fitz Warren, but the last, and smallest, upon which de Mortville had taken pity, he'd kept. He named the dog 'Conan,' a name he remembered from Ireland which meant 'little wolf' or 'hound' – or so he had been told.

He shuddered to think of that episode in Ireland. John had been no more than eighteen, and many of his closest friends were still young too, egging each other on in their mischief. The Irish chieftains had welcomed them solemnly, warily. In return, John and his entourage had laughed at them, poking fun at their long beards. At the Prince's instigation, Sir John de Rosseley had tugged one of them to see if it was real.

Though de Mortville would like to think he had been above it all, he had laughed along just as enthusiastically. What idiots they had been. The older members of the party – Bardulf, Fitz Warren and the others – had maintained some decorum, but the rest were simply too young, too foolish. They had treated it like a game. No wonder the expedition had been such a disaster.

WITHIN SECONDS, CONAN was back, panting, stick in his jaws. De Mortville fussed him about the ears, grabbed hold of the stick, and for a moment they tussled over ownership of it. That was all part of the game. Conan soon gave it up, and leapt back, looking up at his master in eager anticipation, urging him to throw again.

De Mortville tossed it further and higher this time. Conan disappeared entirely into the fog as De Mortville marched off after him.

This time, Conan dropped the stick at his master's feet with thick, panting breaths. That earned him a reward of a scrap of dried beef. De Mortville glanced back towards Clairmont. Only the gatehouse was visible, rising like a grey ghost in the murk.

He turned back to the path, and his dog. There were places off it that he did not want Conan to go – where he *would* go, if there was a stick to be fetched. Some of these spots had mires so treacherous they would suck man or beast into them in an instant. But de Mortville had learned their location over the years. Even now, in thick fog, he knew precisely where to throw.

Time to give Conan a good run. De Mortville drew back his arm and hurled the stick with all his might. It was swallowed by fog.

Then came the sound. An impossible sound. It was the sound of the stick hitting something made of metal.

It rang out, oddly dulled by the thick air. De Mortville stopped dead, utterly baffled. He knew every inch of this path. Directly ahead was nothing more solid than peaty earth, nothing taller than a blade of grass for a quarter mile or more. No trees. Certainly no rocks. Just flat earth.

Then he noticed the dog.

Conan had not moved an inch. Instead, he was staring into the blank distance, somehow transfixed, his head held low. As de Mortville looked at him, the dog suddenly hunched, his hackles up, a low growling moan in his throat.

"Is someone there?" called de Mortville.

Nothing.

"Gamel?" he called, for some reason thinking it might be the most senior of his farmers, returned to speak with him – even though their business had been concluded earlier that day.

There was another sound – one he could not identify – and Conan broke into a fit of barking that ended in one long, continuous howl.

"If you have business, then announce yourself," shouted de Mortville, his tone more aggressive. "Or I'll set the dog on you!"

Conan snarled and snapped like a wild thing, as if on cue, but did not advance.

Then, from somewhere in the fog, came the distant clank of metal.

It meant nothing to de Mortville – had no connection with anything that made any sense. But somehow, the sound filled him with unutterable dread.

He did not hesitate. With a whistle, he sent Conan back into the gloom, to tackle the intruder. It was a whistle that meant *fetch what's making the noise*. He used it when they were hunting, and Conan always knew what he intended. The dog would try to bring down whatever was out there, and would try to bring it back. Once, with a determination one saw only in dogs, he'd dragged a deer back to his master.

There was a moment of silence. Then a yelp. A heavy thud that shook the ground beneath de Mortville's feet. Then silence again. De Mortville stood, only dimly aware that he was holding his breath, listening for the sounds of the dog – of movement, of dragging. Nothing in the eerie quiet but the lonely, distant cry of a crane.

Then, out of the murk, arcing through the air, something came spinning. For a confused moment, his sense of perspective baffled by the fog, he thought it was the stick. But it was big, and left a scarlet trail in its wake.

It thudded heavily on the wet earth at de Mortville's feet. The lifeless form had had its head smashed so completely it was no longer even recognisable as a dog.

De Mortville felt icy beads of sweat trickle from under his arms. He staggered backwards, in a state of shock. His hand went to his belt – an old impulse – but no sword was there. He never wore a sword around his own home.

Then came the other sound. A rhythmic pounding, like a heartbeat. He felt it shudder in the ground beneath him, as if throbbing in the earth itself. Heavy footfalls. And with them, something bright and sharp – the tuneless clang of metal.

De Mortville turned and ran for the gate as fast as he knew how, the sound thumping closer behind him. He yelled to the guards in the gatehouse; aware, even as he did, that his words were barely making sense. Heads appeared on the battlement. Two silhouetted figures appeared in the open doorway.

"Close the gate!" called de Mortville as his plunging feet crunched along the stone bridge. Two faces – one the captain of his guard – stared in startled paralysis. "*Close it!*"

They began to do so even before he reached the gatehouse. He flung himself through the narrowing gap and put his shoulder to the wood until the doors crashed shut and the bar was dropped into place. De Mortville and his captain stood in the dark space beneath the gatehouse and stared at each other in mute incomprehension.

Then a great impact shook the doors.

It was as if they had been hit by a charging bull. In a moment of confusion, de Mortville wondered if it could be exactly that. But it was no bull that had slaughtered his dog – and no bull that clanked like metal.

Again it struck. The entire gatehouse shuddered. Dust and grit rained down from above. The guards began to back away. The captain thrust a sword into de Mortville's hand. He was grateful for that. Its solid weight focused his mind.

"What is it?" he called up to the rampart. "Can you see it?" He tried to keep the fear out of his voice. But no reply came. He glanced at his captain again – then a third crash almost shook the doors off their black iron hinges.

De Mortville hurried into the courtyard and looked up to the rampart.

"Someone with eyes, tell me," he shouted, his voice charged with anger this time. "What the hell *is* it?"

The guard looked back down at him, his face pale. "It... It's..." he said, shaking his head, as if struggling to make sense of what he had seen.

Before either could speak further, there was a great *whoosh*. The fog about the gatehouse flickered yellow. Through the cracks in the gate, against the darkening Fen, de Mortville saw the bright glow of flames.

"Fire!" yelled the guard upon the battlement. Men ran across the courtyard, fetching pails, scaling the steps two at a time to hurl water down upon the burning gate.

There were chutes either side of the gatehouse to allow the gates to be doused with water from the inside if attacked. They had never been used. Until today, de Mortville had no expectation that they ever would. He heard the hiss and splatter of the water, saw it seeping in under the gates. But no matter how much his men flung down, the flames would not die. De Mortville felt his chest tighten. The whole gatehouse was a framework of wood and plaster. If the flames were allowed to spread, it would be utterly destroyed.

They would have to open the gates.

A dozen armed men had now mustered, and stood before the gate in tight formation, forming a shield between it and their master. They were prepared to make a stand. But against what?

"Lookout?" called de Mortville. "Tell me what you see."

The guard on the battlement disappeared, then appeared again. "Nothing," he said, bemused. "It's gone."

De Mortville wasted no time. "Open them. Quickly."

The porter and gatehouse guards flung the heavy bar upon the ground and heaved the doors inwards. The space beneath the gatehouse filled with thick smoke. Servants of all kinds – every one of them now carrying some vessel – dashed forward in ones and twos and hurled it over the already blackened wood of the castle doors, then beat a hasty retreat, coughing and spluttering as they went. De Mortville and his men stood firm, squinting into the blank fog framed by the gateway, weapons drawn and raised, ready to face whatever might try to follow.

The flames were stubborn. They seemed alive – as if with evil intent. They leapt where one would not expect. Sometimes they burned blue. On several occasions, de Mortville could swear, he saw some portion of the wood completely extinguished, only for the flames to break out upon it yet again. But pail after pail, pot after pot of water was hurled at it until finally, the task was achieved. They stood, surrounded by smoke, the entrance – now a great pool – trodden to black mud. A few smiled as they panted and coughed, hands upon their knees. One man laughed with relief, believing the emergency past.

Then a great, dark shape charged out of the mist.

It was a beast that de Mortville saw thundering across the bridge towards him. Seven feet tall, as wide as two men at the shoulder. Its body glinted with blue-black scales, parts of it splashed with red. Its head bore outlandish, reptilian spikes and fins, its wide mouth grinning with rows of white teeth, its eyes dead black pits.

It was on the knot of servants about the gate before they knew what had happened. They were smashed aside like straw dolls. Bones cracked. Teeth shattered. Air wheezed out of crushed ribs as gore splattered against wood and plaster. A lucky few fled, scrambling and splashing through the mud, their eyes wild.

There had been no time to close the still-smoking gates.

DE MORTVILLE AND his men had fallen back into the courtyard to form a defensive line. Once past the gatehouse, the men on the ramparts, too, would have clear shots. As it pounded towards him, he heard the thunk of crossbows. Two, three, four. One bolt glanced off its target and flew high over the battlement. Another shattered to splinters against the beast. But the beast kept coming.

The men braced themselves. They would give the bastard a fight, if that was what he wanted.

But there was no fight. Before any could land a blow, a plume of flame leapt from the beast's left hand. Men were set afire. There were screams. The smell of burning flesh. De Mortville sensed hysteria spreading behind him. He saw his captain's skull crushed and another man knocked clear off his feet, his bloodied jaw hanging. From the beast's right hand, de Mortville now realised, swung a hammer the size of a small anvil.

Nothing would stop it. In the split second before it was on him, De Mortville turned and fled, stumbling, the clanking giant crashing towards him, closing on him. A crossbow bolt zipped past his head. In some distant part of his mind he was aware that his right foot was burning. The flames roared rhythmically as he ran. Then the leg crumpled and he landed hard, his sword spinning from his hand, the wind knocked out of his lungs. He lay, half numb, dimly aware that those who should protect him were now fleeing in terror.

The pounding footfalls had stopped. De Mortville turned, and stared up at the thing towering over him. The contorted, reptilian face cocked to one side, and seemed to regard him for a moment. Then, with the matter-of-factness of a farrier about to strike a nail, it slowly raised its huge, iron hammer. De Mortville lifted an arm across his face – a futile gesture.

Then black oblivion fell.

XV

Walmesforde
17 May, 1193

THEY HAD JUST entered Walmesford when the news came from Clairmont. Galfrid's bright mood had descended into a sulk, precipitated by the rattling of a loose shoe upon Mare's hoof and another of Gisburne's unexplained diversions off the road. Galfrid had pointedly not mentioned it this time – but as they had come to a halt and dismounted by the inn, John, still testy, had creased his brow and quizzed Gisburne directly about his "private little moments." Gisburne said simply that he had need to keep a check on something. John, dissatisfied with the vagueness of "something," had been about to challenge him further when his words were cut off by a shrill cry in a cracked voice.

"*Murder!*"

That they were outside the alehouse when the young squire galloped in was pure chance – another few minutes, and they might have been gone. But the instant Gisburne saw him, he sensed – whether the squire knew it or not – that the message was meant for them.

The rider was unkempt, his clothes half awry, no hat upon his head. His horse had been pushed so hard it was close to collapse, and even when permitted to stop continued to skip about in state of nervous agitation beyond exhaustion. The squire – young and evidently well-to-do, but apparently near out of his mind with unbearable emotion – slithered from his saddle, his knees buckling as his feet met solid earth. His face was red and swollen, his eyes wide and raw. Gisburne had seen that look before – in battle, or soon after. Those who wore it were destined not to last.

All those gathered there – a rag-tag of travellers – looked up. The natural assumption was that he had been accosted upon his journey – robbed, perhaps injured. A stranger – a dusty wagoner in a wide hat, about to set out in the very direction from which the young squire had come – stepped forward to offer help. Another, old and bearded – a local man, Gisburne thought – took a cup of ale to the lad. He drank half of it down, his hands shaking; the other half cascaded down his front. Paying it no heed, the squire dropped the cup into the dirt, covered his face with quivering fingers and gave such a cry of anguish that Gisburne felt the hairs on his neck bristle.

Then, in fragmentary phrases, he jabbered of some outlandish horror at Clairmont Castle, and Gisburne knew for certain that the Red Hand had not been idle.

"GOD IN HEAVEN," said John. He paled at the boy's words. "Clairmont... That's Hugh de Mortville. He was with me in Ire –"

"Was with you in old days, yes," interrupted Gisburne. His eyes flicked around, checking for any who might have been listening. But all were absorbed by the new arrival. John flushed, and bit his tongue.

"Three makes it no longer a coincidence," muttered Galfrid.

Gisburne pushed forward, Galfrid and John close behind. Men stood back to let them pass, some looking on resentfully. The squire gazed up at the approaching figure with eyes that were suddenly filled with longing – desperate for someone, anyone, to take control of his world, and to make sense of it again.

Gisburne took the squire by the shoulder. "When?" he demanded.

"Last night," panted the boy.

"Were you sent?" said Gisburne. The boy sobbed, and looked as if trying to focus his eyes on some invisible thing – as if the memory were so vivid he could not see past it to the world in front of him. He was losing the lad.

"Sent, boy..." Gisburne shook him hard. The waggoner grunted in disapproval. Gisburne ignored him. "Were you sent?"

The boy started, and looked him in the eye. "No... No... I... I... I mean..."

"You ran away..." said Galfrid in disgust. "What use are vows to serve your lord and to never turn your back on an enemy when – ?"

Gisburne raised a hand to silence him. "You saw it? The thing that attacked him?"

"Yes," whined the boy.

"But what did you see? Tell me exactly."

"A beast... It was horrible. Horrible!"

"What was? What was horrible?"

The boy looked suddenly distraught. "The dog... Oh, God, the dog..."

Galfrid and John exchanged looks of puzzled astonishment.

"Dog? Your master, boy – what of your master?"

But with that, the boy broke down, his face buried in his hands. Gisburne stood back; the squire would be of no more use.

To his surprise, the Prince stepped forward to take his place, a leather flask in his hands. Gisburne caught his arm. John stopped, and looked him in the eye. "Last night I dreamt I met death upon the road. A dead man, but walking. It was just like this."

"Are you surprised, with all that's going on?" said Gisburne dismissively. "It's not some premonition. It's a night in the woods. Those ghost stories. That cursed gallows tree."

"Maybe," said John. Then he knelt, and offered the boy wine from his flask.

Gisburne stood back and left him to it. He regretted his choice of word; he did not believe in curses. Not in ghosts or prophecies. Not any more. But every once in a while he sensed that the child who *had* believed was still there. There was, he knew, only one way to beat these wild notions into submission. "Clairmont," he said, turning to Galfrid. "Do you know it?"

"Of it," said Galfrid.

"I've been there," said John, without looking up.

"Is it easy to find?"

"If you know the way. It's out in the marshes, but find the right road and it takes you to the door."

"How far?"

John shrugged. "Half a day, at a push."

Gisburne withdrew and moved away from the huddle, deep in thought. John, meanwhile, attempted to calm their unexpected guest. The boy drank eagerly. He would never know that he had been comforted by the heir to the English throne.

"WE ARE GOING there?" whispered Galfrid, as they stood apart from the knot of men.

"Yes," said Gisburne. "Immediately. I must see it."

"I would've thought you'd seen enough."

"Not nearly enough. Not until it makes sense. Monreale, Galfrid..."

"But taking John towards his enemy – where we know *him* to have been..."

"He had the chance to kill him before and did not do it."

"But we both know how this game is meant to end," said Galfrid, his tone grave. "Judgement Day. What if he decides that is to be today, and we deliver his prey right into his hands?"

"Then it is our job to stop him."

"Stop him how?"

Gisburne did not have an answer. A party of two dozen elite warriors had failed to stop him. He had smashed his way into two castles, and breached the defences of another without detection. "I must see it," he insisted. "No matter what. But I have an idea. A place he might be safe."

Galfrid hesitated, as if he had wanted to say more but decided against it. He nodded.

Gisburne turned. "We're leaving," he announced to John.

"But Mare's shoe..." said John with a frown.

"Will have to wait," said Gisburne. Then he turned to Galfrid. "All right?"

Galfrid shrugged. "If it flies off, it'll be your head it cracks, not mine."

Gisburne crouched to the level of the squire and lifted his chin with his finger. "Boy – what you saw last night... Would you willingly submit yourself to it again?"

The boy shook his head.

"But do you yet have faith in God, and believe the world a good and just place?"

A tear coursed down the boy's cheek. "Yes..."

Gisburne stood. "Then hang up your sword and join the clergy," he said, and strode to his horse.

"So where is it?" said Galfrid, ushering John before him. "This safe place?"

"You'll see," said Gisburne.

XVI

Burgh St Peter
17 May, 1193

GALFRID GAZED UP into the vast, soaring nave in a state of awe, his crumpled hat clutched in both hands. He had always loved such places – loved them since the age of ten, when his uncle had taken him into the great cathedral church at Ely. But over the years, he had also experienced a growing need for them. They had become places of healing.

He had witnessed many things in his life. Terrible things. The worst that men and women could do to each other. He did not doubt he would witness many more – some before this month was out. Yet when he looked upon such marvels as this, he had faith. Faith in his fellow men. Because if they could achieve this, he reasoned, they could achieve anything – and not all the cruelty and hatred in the world could wipe that out. Had Gisburne been watching the humbled figure there in the abbey church, he might well have declared it the only time he had seen him actually looking like a servant.

THEY HAD MADE Burgh St Peter by mid morning. Mare's shoe had held – how, Galfrid had no idea, but wasn't about to question it – and the road was straight and the going firm. The land had also begun to take on uniquely East Anglian qualities – flatter than a still ocean, empty as a summer sky, but with a quality of bleak melancholy that made it seem somehow... unfinished. Abandoned. Devoid not only of shape, but of purpose. It was a quality that stirred deep unease in most who subjected themselves to it – if one could believe in God here, it seemed to them, then one was indeed a true believer. But to Galfrid, it was like heading home.

The small town was dominated by the great abbey, and the abbey by its church. This was one of the wealthiest monasteries in all England, and over the past seven decades had dedicated itself to converting that wealth into stone. Beyond the thick surrounding walls and stout gatehouse – visible as they approached the abbey precincts – the roof and steeple had pushed ever higher into the endless fenland sky for the greater glory of God.

Abbot Benedict, so Galfrid had been told, was now old and frail, but still a force to be reckoned with. And everywhere that power was evident – in stone, and in the expressions of the monks who admitted them. Gisburne had given them little explanation of his purpose, and insisted on presenting his guest personally to the Abbot and no other. They had not liked that. Gisburne had at no point invoked the name of the Prince, and none had recognised him, but Abbot Benedict certainly would. In fact, Gisburne was relying on it.

The monks had been stern, but efficient. Word was sent, and was swiftly received. Such discipline did not come about of it own accord. But Benedict – once prior of Canterbury and a friend and admirer of Thomas Becket – clearly knew better than to rest on his laurels. Henry II had granted him the abbacy of Burgh St Peter in 1177 – perhaps one of the many ways he sought to make amends for Becket's death.

What Benedict had done since was build. Once within the abbey, the true scale of the new works became clear. On every side, heaped banks of stone rose to steep-pitched roofs, their new tiles gleaming in the sun. At their heart the huge, cloistered courtyard was flanked on three sides by the Abbot's lodging, refectory and chapter house. But the fourth, northern side of the cloister was formed by the thing that commanded Galfrid's attention. It had dominated the sky for the past half mile at least – the great abbey church itself.

The Abbot's lodging rose an entire level higher than the innermost roofs of the cloister – but the nave of the church towered even over that, heaping roof upon roof, row upon row of pilasters and arched windows. Over the crossing, the central tower thrust upward to a steeple of dizzying height, while from the corners of the tower, transepts and conical spires pierced the sky – a forest of slender fingers pointing to God. Galfrid had gazed upon it all in rapt amazement.

"Abbot Benedict is a powerful man," Gisburne had muttered in his ear, as they stood waiting for John to finish relieving himself in the necessarium. "He assisted at Richard's coronation, and is keeper of the great seal."

Galfrid's eyes returned to earth. "Is that in our favour...?" he said with a frown, considering how little love was lost between King and Prince.

"He will take this duty more seriously than anyone in the land," said Gisburne, then added: "And he can call upon more than sixty knights."

Galfrid knew the true cornerstone of Gisburne's plan was that no one

– not even the monks who had greeted them – would know of John's presence here. Since the murder of Becket, it was not to be assumed that the sanctuary of the church guaranteed safety. Given the nature of previous attacks, he was not even certain how many knights it would take to deter the Red Hand. But sixty sounded a fair contingency.

Then John had reappeared, and Gisburne had immediately ushered him into the abbey precincts, accompanied by two rather wary young monks. Both had the bearing of soldiers, and perhaps were set to this task for that very reason.

Galfrid, meanwhile, had been left to explore the great church, allowing himself a private grin of immense proportions.

AND SO HE stood, mouth agape, his neck already aching from the looking, glorying in the paradox this place inspired – being at once bounded and contained, yet feeling himself in infinite space.

Behind him, from outside the west front – as yet, barely begun – he could hear the creak of the great windlass merging with the cries of the masons as stones and timbers were hauled into place. Above him, on teetering, groaning scaffolding of terrifying height, men worked upon the wooden ceiling, creeping like spiders about the vaulted web of stonework.

A fine rain of sawdust fell, the particles turning to golden specks as they drifted through the shafts of sunlight piercing the tall windows. Not far from where he stood, an officious looking monk was sweeping the flagstones with a birch broom, as oblivious to wonders that surrounded him as he was to his own absurdity, the look on his face seeming to express irritation at his never-ending task.

Galfrid gazed up at the new wooden ceiling. The air still smelled of fresh timber. He took a deep breath, gave another sigh of satisfaction, and began to hum quietly to himself. *Te Sanctum Dominum.*

A bony finger jabbed his shoulder blade. "You there!"

Galfrid turned to find the thin-faced monk glaring at him, broom still in hand. "No humming in the abbey church!"

Galfrid stared at the man with a frown, momentarily lost for words. "It's a *Te Sanctum Dominum*," he said eventually, as if this were explanation enough – which to Galfrid, it was.

"I know what it is," snapped the monk. Then he gave a pinched, humourless smile – perhaps intended as some kind of conciliatory gesture. "Not in the church, if you please."

Galfrid frowned deeper, struggling to grasp the man's reasoning. "But it's what *you* sing in here..."

"You may sing what you like outside," said the monk, gesturing irritably.

"*Pro fanum.*"

Galfrid opened his mouth to protest once again, thought better of it, then nodded slowly and shrugged. The monk, victorious, flared his nostrils and stalked off.

Galfrid turned his gaze back to the church's great arches and vaulted ceiling. But it was no good. The spell had been broken. One of the most magnificent and inspirational structures on the face of the earth had been robbed of its magic by a single, self-important idiot – reality and all its woes ushered back in on the end of his broom.

With a heavy sigh, the *swish swish* of the monk's pointless sweeping echoing about him, Galfrid headed for the door. He paused for one long, last look before he exited – and, as he did so, let rip at the top of his lungs with a couple of verses of *The Ballad of the Bibulous Monk and his Ass*.

XVII

Clairmont Castle
17 May, 1193

GISBURNE SQUATTED ON his haunches, staring at the huge footprints pressed into the black fen soil. Cast into deep shadow by the evening sun, they made his own seem like a child's, sunk so far into the ripe-smelling mud they looked to have had the weight of an ox behind them. "A giant made of iron..." muttered Galfrid.

"You're sure they're his?" said Gisburne.

De Mortville's steward nodded, and looked away. He was pale, his features haggard. Though he tried to cover it, his hands were shaking. From the look of him, he had not slept since the attack. "They don't belong to anyone here, that's for certain," he said.

It was sheer chance that these few footprints had been preserved. All others had been obliterated by the frenzied activity since that terrible night. Within the castle, however, signs of his coming were still evident – and all too familiar. The same dark gore staining the ground. The same fierce burning upon the gate. The same sticky residue accompanying it.

There had been the same garbled, incredulous descriptions, too. Most were agreed that it was in the shape of a man – but emphasised *shape,* as if certain the resemblance was only superficial. Several spoke of the clank of metal, and of scales. Descriptions of the head or face – if a face it was – varied most wildly of all. They spoke of spikes, fins, jagged teeth and dead eyes. One man – a cook – made the startling claim that he knew the attacker. When pressed for details, a sweat had broken out on his brow, and he had – with utmost reluctance – whispered the name "Beelzebub." He would not speak more on that subject, and Gisburne had not further pressed the point.

There were some new details. One of these was the hammer. This, Gisburne now knew, was the weapon with which the Red Hand had wrought such catastrophic damage upon his victims. Perhaps not surprisingly, the flames that leapt from the beast's left hand had diverted the attention of witnesses from it – until now. Gisburne, who had seen its terrible, seemingly impossible effects, finally understood them. But he had never seen anyone use such a large, blunt weapon in battle. It was impractical – far too heavy for prolonged use. In fact, the only individual he had ever heard was capable of wielding such a weapon was a god.

A giant. A dragon. A demon. A pagan Norse god... Gisburne fought to banish thoughts of them all from his mind, staring hard at the gigantic footprints, telling himself this man – whoever he was – was as real, and solid, and fallible as he was. He breathed air and drank water, and blood ran in his veins. And he could be stopped, and killed – if only he could determine how.

First, he had to find him – and he had the knack of disappearing like a phantom. According to the steward, after the attack – which, Gisburne calculated, can only have lasted moments – the stunned men had mustered and pursued the fleeing creature, but had soon lost it in darkness and fog. At least one of the squires had fled at that point. They had been dispatched again the following morning, but had found nothing more than wagon tracks and the trail of a fox. All the time he had been telling Gisburne this, he had shaken his head, and cursed his inability to act during those fleeting, terrible moments.

"When it was upon him... I had a sword in my hand. If I had only struck..."

"...you'd be dead like the others," said Gisburne. "And no use to anyone." Gisburne did not blame him. What other action could there have been that had not been taken? None could have anticipated such a horror, and he had seen tougher men stunned into impotence by lesser shocks. "Not everyone is born to fight," he said. "And swords are not the only tools that need wielding. You serve your master well. You are keeping his house and his memory alive." The steward nodded, but looked disconsolate.

What he had done that morning, as the sun had risen on the now lordless castle, was spot the footprints. They were pressed into the mud where the bridge to the castle gate met the far bank of the moat. He then had the presence of mind to surround them with a row of logs from the pile in the yard, so they would be preserved. Even he was not sure exactly why he had done that. He said it somehow had seemed important to him to prove it had not been a ghost, but something of flesh and blood. Gisburne assured him that what he had done was of utmost importance – a thing that all others, thus far, had overlooked.

"You tried to follow these?" said Gisburne. "Back to where they came from?"

The steward nodded. "It's hopeless," he said. "A hundred yards along, the road becomes gritty. Sir Hugh had it made so to keep it in good order."

Gisburne sighed. "So... three... three and a half footprints are what we have."

Galfrid squatted down, raised his eyebrows and cocked his head to one side. "My old uncle was a master when it came to tracking. There was no animal or bird that he could not identify from the prints it made. Not only that – he could tell its age, its size. Whether it was moving swiftly or slowly. Whether it was injured, or healthy. Even whether it carried prey in its mouth. People thought him a wizard. But really, it was just looking."

"So, what would your old uncle see in this footprint?" Gisburne raised a finger. "Only what we know, remember... Only what we see."

Galfrid pulled off his hat and rubbed his palm across his head, as if coaxing his brain into action. "It is large, therefore its owner is likely large."

"We have eyewitness accounts to confirm that."

"It is deep. Exceptionally so – twice as deep as your own, and you are no small or slight man – so we can say he is of very great weight. Even if we account for his height, he must either be excessively fat..."

"Which we know he is not..."

"Or he carries a great weight with him."

Gisburne nodded. "And what makes a man heavy, yet adds little to his bulk?"

Galfrid looked up. "Armour."

"Thick armour," said Gisburne. "Enough to stop crossbow bolts."

"Metal plates. Dragon scales. That clank as he moves..."

"A giant made of iron," said Gisburne.

"But he was running. The toes dig deeper than the rest. To carry such weight – to run with it, and to drag a man of Wendenal's stature..."

"...would require a big man, of prodigious strength. Capable also of wielding a great hammer."

"So, we are certain it is a man, then?" said Galfrid. "What of the dragon's head?"

"A great helm. Made to resemble a beast. To terrify and confuse his victims."

Galfrid's eyes narrowed. "I thought you said *only what we know?*"

"Well, we know it's not a dragon, don't we?" said Gisburne. Then, after a moment's hesitation, as if only then remembering that a third person stood with them, he looked up at the steward. "Don't we...?"

The steward gave a heavy sigh that seemed to shake his whole frame, then drew himself up again as if in defiance of the feeling that was threatening to engulf him. "It matters little to me what you choose to call it. Only how it can be stopped."

Gisburne nodded – even felt himself smiling at the steward's words. "Once again, Master Steward, a wise assessment." He stood. "If one were making armour in order to make oneself invulnerable, a great helm would inevitably be part of it. Such a thing could easily be fashioned to resemble a beast by one with the necessary skills." Galfrid nodded sagely. Gisburne turned again to the steward. "Your master's corpse..." he began. At the image those few words conjured, he saw the man shudder.

"He is laid out in the chapel," said the Steward.

"I would like to see it."

The Steward's expression grew more pained. "If you must."

DESPITE THE STEWARD's persistence in referring to it as *he* – a habit hard to break after years of service – what they stood over upon the stone altar of the still chapel was no longer a man. Quite how it had been manhandled in here, Gisburne could not imagine. It was a thing of stark contrasts. For the most part, despite a few cuts and abrasions consistent with a struggle, the body was intact – that of a man who had suffered no more than a minor altercation. A fight outside a tavern. A fall from a horse.

There were four exceptions to this state. Each of them, Gisburne now recognised, was the mark of the Red Hand. The first was the right leg, which had suffered the attentions of fire. The burning extended little higher than the knee, but below that part had burned with a flame so fierce that the shin was eaten to blackened bone. The second was the head – or what was left of it. Its thick, rank smell filled the air. This, Gisburne supposed, must have been lifted upon a shovel or some other implement as the body itself was carried. He imagined them placing the gory, flattened mass here with a mixture of repulsion and reverence, bits of straw and of gravel still mixed with it from the courtyard, the shovel scraping on the stone as it was withdrawn. This part was no longer recognisable as human. At least, not at first. Though still attached to the body via a battered web of flesh and a few meagre sinews, taken on its own might have been anything – a trampled animal, the waste of a butcher's shop. Then, one noticed human teeth, and – still intact, now fixed in a permanent stare – a single eyeball. Gisburne felt his gorge rise at the sight of it.

The third was the right hand – or, rather, the lack of it – hacked off by the attacker, and, according to the Steward, never found.

But it was the fourth thing – by far the least of them – that captured Gisburne's attention most fully. Upon the chest – passing directly though the breastbone – was a neat hole, barely bigger than that made by a carpenter's awl. Thick blood was caked around it, staining de Mortville's deep blue velvet tunicella black. The puncture might have been made by a bodkin arrow or a slender misericorde, but Gisburne knew it was the result of neither.

"That is where the scrap of cloth was nailed?" he said, extending his finger towards it.

The Steward nodded, appearing as if he wished nothing more fervently than to be able to look away, but was unable to do so.

"And the cloth itself?" said Gisburne. "What of that?"

"Removed," said the Steward. "Discarded. Before I could prevent it." It was clear he regretted the loss, and in observing Gisburne's methods, he was coming to regret it all the more.

"Discarded where?"

"I suppose..." The steward shrugged. "Tossed into the midden."

"Show me where that is," said Gisburne.

MINUTES LATER, GISBURNE was knee-deep in muck – a slimy, layered chronicle of the castle's waste, about which thrummed a thick cloud of black flies. Beneath the surface, some of the matter was now so rotted it had turned to a kind of black soil, which smelled almost like fresh hay. But what lay above it – the addition of more recent weeks, warmed up by today's sun – was not so sweet.

Gisburne had tied a cloth doused in vinegar about his face and now, a look of intense concentration in his eyes, poked about the heap with one of Conan's discarded sticks, turning over gnawed bones, rotting vegetables, mussel shells and things now unidentifiable.

This heap was thoughtfully positioned beneath the northern tower of the eastern wall – downwind of the castle – but even upwind of it, Galfrid caught its pungent reek.

"What is he doing?" said the steward. It was less a question, more an expression of disbelief. He knew well enough what Gisburne was seeking – but he had never seen a knight lower himself to such a task.

"There's nothing he likes better than wading through other people's filth," said Galfrid, deadpan.

The steward stared at him for a moment, then back at the absurd sight of Gisburne, prodding and poking at rubbish with his dog-gnawed stick. Fascinating as this sight was, Galfrid's attention had wandered to the near featureless horizon. The light was failing. Night fell quickly here. Another half hour, and they'd be in pitch darkness.

A cry of triumph made him turn. In the next moment, Gisburne was wading back towards them, cloth pulled from his face, hand held aloft in a gesture of victory, as if he had recovered Escalibor from the waters of the enchanted lake.

It was no sword but a triangular, bloody scrap of weathered oilcloth. He extended his hand to his squire. On it, written in charcoal, Galfrid could clearly make out the figures: *xxxix*. And piercing the fabric was a small spike of iron.

Gisburne drew it out, and held it aloft in triumph. "*This* is what I sought..." he said.

"A nail?" said the bemused Steward.

"A *horseshoe* nail," replied Gisburne. He looked the steward in the eye. "Thank you," he said. Sincere as his expression was, Gisburne's tone carried a finality whose significance the steward did not at first grasp. "You may leave us now," added Gisburne. The steward shuffled, bowed, and edged away.

The moment the steward was out if earshot, Gisburne turned back to his squire, his eyes burning with a new fire. "A man who wields a hammer. Who uses charcoal and fire. And *this*..." He held the nail up between thumb and forefinger.

Suddenly, Galfrid understood. "A *blacksmith*..."

"A blacksmith who has made himself armour. Who has the skill to fashion a helm into the head of a beast. And this oilcloth..." Gisburne held it out again. "Weathered."

"A tent? Cover for a wagon? A sail, maybe?"

"Whichever way you look at it, a traveller. We know he's been on the move these past weeks. And that his appearance, when he strikes, is startling. Terrifying. Yet he moves unseen. Day to day, his appearance is nothing out of the ordinary." Gisburne's words were rapid, tumbling out of him.

"He would need the means to carry this armour. And to live and make his fire. He has help, maybe?"

"No," Gisburne shook his head vigorously. "He works alone." He held up his hands. "I know, I know – I speak from pure instinct now. But I'd stake my life on it, Galfrid. This armour of his... He builds a fortress around himself. I've seen other such men. They are solitary, trusting no other."

Galfrid puffed out his cheeks. "Then he must have a horse as extraordinary as himself. How could any carry such weight?"

"What if it is not a horse?" said Gisburne.

"What else could it be?" said Galfrid.

"No horse was ever seen. He was always on foot."

Galfrid spread his hands apart in exasperation. "But how else could he have got to John's chambers in Nottingham so soon after the slaying in the woods? He got there ahead of Wendenal's guard, even though they were riding full tilt. What other way is there? Wings? Sorcery?"

"Misdirection..." said Gisburne. "Not sorcery. A trick."

"A trick..?"

"What if we're looking at this the wrong way around? What if the parchment had been there all along – if he had placed it there *before* the attack? These are not random actions. He plans ahead. With meticulous precision."

Galfrid rubbed his chin. "Then... His transport would not need to be fast at all." He thought at once of the tracks that de Mortville's men had found – and dismissed – that same morning. "A wagon..."

Gisburne nodded. "A wagon capable of carrying such a man, and his armour, and his tools."

Galfrid stared out across the flat marshy plain, the previous day's fog now completely burned away by the sun. He laughed to himself. "An itinerant blacksmith..."

"Whitesmith, too, perhaps," said Gisburne. "Not a sorceror. Not a dragon. A common tinker."

"A distinctive one, though, if he is indeed a giant."

"Hard to hide on foot, but not so much when hunched upon a wagon. He's invisible, Galfrid. The very antithesis of his monstrous disguise. A thing so ordinary, so banal, it is completely overlooked, even when it's in plain sight."

"My God," said Galfrid. "We might have seen him on the road. At some wayside inn. We would never have known."

"We have to hope he was as oblivious to us," said Gisburne. "That he still believes John to be travelling with his entourage. Nothing suggests otherwise."

"At least we know what we're looking for."

"And if we can tackle him in that guise, while he is divested of his metal skin, we know we can capture or kill him."

"But if we don't?" asked Galfrid. "If chance doesn't put him in our path before he comes looking for John? Before he disappears into the swell of London?"

At that, Gisburne said nothing. His head was held low, his brow furrowed deeply. It was a moment before Galfrid realised his master's attention was focused on the scrap of oilcloth. "These numbers must tell us something..." he muttered.

"Or they're the ramblings of a madman," said Galfrid. "Fifty-four, fifty-nine, thirty-nine..."

"No, the other way" said Gisburne, distractedly.

"What?"

"The order you said is the order we encountered them, not the order in which order they occurred. Thirty-nine was on Whitsunday, and fifty-four – Wendenal – upon Mayday. But Walter Bardulf was the first, five days before that."

"Fine," said Galfrid. "Fifty-nine, fifty-four, thirty-nine... But what does that tell us? We know *who* – after a fashion, at least. But when are we going to know *why?*" He threw up his hands again. But when he looked at Gisburne again, his master's expression had suddenly changed. He was staring into the middle distance, his furrowed brow flattening as his eyes grew wider.

"Galfrid," he said. "When is Whitsunday?"

Galfrid looked back at him, perplexed. "Are you mad? It was yesterday. I know your grasp of time is poor, but even you can't have forgotten *that* day..."

"But how do we *decide* when it is?"

Galfrid shrugged, baffled by the line of questioning. "It's fifty days after Easter."

"And Lent? How long is that?"

"Forty days, from Ash Wednesday to Holy Saturday. But..."

"And Christmastide?"

"Twelve days."

"Exactly." Gisburne's eyes blazed. "We count the days," he said. "Do you see? He's counting..." It was as if, in Galfrid's mind, pieces that had previously been obscure were suddenly shifted into their proper relationship. Thirty-nine had occurred fifteen days after fifty-four, and fifty-four five days after fifty-nine. They were days. Numbers of days. And they were going backwards. Counting down. But to what?

Gisburne's face, momentarily one of triumph, suddenly fell. "What day is this?"

"Monday. The day after Whitsunday."

"No, the *date...*"

"The seventeenth day of May."

Gisburne stood motionless, his hands frozen mid gesture. "By Christ..." his face paled. The fingers of his right hand tightened into a fist about the nail. "It can't be."

Galfrid's mind was racing – calculating. "What? Can't be *what...?*"

Gisburne turned and looked past him, all sense of triumph gone. "We must gather John tomorrow and get him to London with all possible speed. No more delays. No more pretence. And I must speak with Llewellyn."

"Counting to what?" said Galfrid.

But Gisburne, lost in thought, would say no more.

XVIII

The Great North Road
18 May, 1193

THEY STOPPED ONLY once more before London. Three miles from the Templar town of Baldac Mare's shoe had finally given out, and after an hour seeking out the one blacksmith still working during the Whitsun holiday, they had finally fallen into an inn for the night – despite Gisburne's reservations about the place. He did not relish the company of Templars.

For the past few days Gisburne had been possessed by a growing sense of dread. It was not just the attack at Clairmont – although that had snapped him out of any possible complacency. Even before this, he now realised, he had felt things closing in around them. Now he knew their luck, such as it was, was running out – that it had been running out from the moment they had set foot upon the road, like the sands in Llewellyn's cherished hourglass.

Before Baldac, a peculiar event had occurred that had impressed this fact upon him.

They had been approaching a village in the southernmost reaches of Huntingdonshire when Gisburne had left the company and diverted briefly from the road – once again without explanation to the Prince or his squire. This time, however, Galfrid had spied the intricate mark – painted in white on a tree – as he did so.

"So, who is it?" Galfrid had said upon Gisburne's return.

"Who's what?"

"Who is it leaving the messages?"

Gisburne sighed. His squire was no fool. "Llewellyn," he said, with a sigh.

Galfrid nodded, his eyes still fixed ahead. The Prince chuckled with delight. "So, Llewellyn leaves a message, marks the way to the spot with his astrological symbols. You pick it up, and thus are aware if there has been any incident with the wagon train up ahead. Correct?"

"Exactly that," said Gisburne.

"Ingenious!" John laughed again. "And has there been any? Incident, I mean?"

"None," said Gisburne. "But after Clairmont..." He did not complete the sentence. Gisburne had not told John everything about Clairmont. Most, but not all. Not about the numbers, nor the date to which he believed they led. He *would* tell him, but not now. Not while they were still on the road – still vulnerable. His instinct was to keep things contained, and controlled.

It was plain that the Red Hand was moving south. Heading for London, Gisburne was certain. If so, for reasons best known to himself, he had stayed his hand – against John, at least. Or the one he thought to be John. The outrage at Clairmont had just been a reminder – something to tease and spur them on their way. Gisburne did not doubt that by now the train, too, would have heard the news and picked up their pace. He thought again of John's unfortunate decoy, cowering in his carriage, and hoped the man – whoever he may be – was well paid.

"Why didn't you just tell me?" said Galfrid, gloomily.

"You didn't need to know," said Gisburne.

"Don't you trust me?"

"Of course I do," said Gisburne. "I didn't wish to burden you with it." In truth, Galfrid's question stung him – but he wasn't sure if he was feeling slighted, or just plain guilty. He could hear the sullenness in his own voice, and that irritated him, too. "Well, you know now, anyway."

Galfrid sighed and nodded.

It had seemed John might take up the cudgel then – but a sound, coming and going on the wind from the village ahead, prevented him. A moment later, all thoughts of argument were forced from their heads.

THE WHOLE VILLAGE – which Gisburne later learned was named Evretoun – seemed in a state of celebration. The sound of their joyous singing – men, women and children all together – rose and fell on the air long before its source came into sight. When it did, Gisburne saw a great throng of people gathered upon the village green – the whole community, it seemed – their throats filled with song as they prepared for some kind of revelry. At the centre of the green the maypole stood, still adorned with wilted spring flowers – but a little distance from it, something new was being constructed. And it was this that was the focus of the activity. Some women gathered bundles of sticks, which they ferried towards it. Others sat in a circle about a pot and prepared food. The menfolk, meanwhile, were busying themselves at the site of the new structure, chopping, sawing and hammering, children and dogs capering about as they did. And all sang at the top of their lungs, each saw stroke, hammerblow or swing of an axe in time with their jaunty song.

"Can you believe this?" said Gisburne.

"Not entirely," said Galfrid.

"Such joy!" said John surveying the sunny idyll, his eyes glittering with delight. "Now, *this* is what England is all about..." As the tune went round for the third time, they found themselves finally able to make out the words:

Robin's in the green-a
Fa la-la la-la laa!
His bow is ever keen-a
Fa la-la la-la laa!
His merry men are seen-a
Fa la-la la-la laa!
Dancing in the green-a
Fa la-la la-la laa!

Gisburne felt his limbs tense involuntarily. Nyght skipped in response. John looked to him, holding up a reassuring hand. "It's just a song," he said. "Nothing more. Just a song..."

Gisburne knew it was true. In all likelihood they would just as happily be singing about gathering blooms in May, or a shepherd and his sheep. Doubtless many knew little or nothing about the man they called Robin Hood. Yet Gisburne could not remain as sanguine as the Prince. The plain fact remained, *this* was the song they had chosen to express their contentment today – the song that brought them together, and made young and old feel as one. Yes, just a song; but it was never just a song. Behind it lay something far deeper, and more troubling.

THEY CONTINUED TO ride slowly by, a handful of the villagers looking up and cheering or waving as they did so. John could not resist waving back, his smile beaming, his head rocking in time with their music. As they rode on, Gisburne suddenly noted a single point of discord amidst all the merriment. Beneath a tree, sat apart from the rest, three women were sewing, their expressions an odd mix of shock and grief, as if they had recently suffered some great mortification. One had a bruise upon her cheek, and swollen left eye. Over them stood a man with his arms folded and an expression like thunder.

Gisburne felt Nyght quicken slightly. Ahead and opposite the green was an inn, and outside it a broad trough of water. All took the opportunity to dismount and stretch their muscles as their horses drank.

"What do you suppose this is all about, anyway?" mused John, gazing across at the structure – which thus far consisted of little more that a rough-hewn post some twenty yards beyond the maypole. "A wedding, perhaps, or..."

At that moment, a young man came hurrying out of the inn clutching a bucket before him, its contents – apparently ale – slopping about and splattering the dusty road as he did so.

"You there!" called John. The man looked about, as if momentarily convinced John must be addressing someone else. "What is it you celebrate here today?"

He gave a broad, gap-toothed smile. "We caught ourselves a villain! Red-handed." He said. "A scarlet one!"

Gisburne's heart missed a beat at the words. A scarlet villain. Red-handed. Surely that would be too good to be true.

"What manner of man is he?" he said.

"See for yourselves," said the man, indicating ahead, where the road curved away, out of sight. "'E's in the stocks round by the crossroads, awaiting justice." He turned as if to go, then stopped and turned back again with hatred in his eyes. "Just make sure and kick some dirt in his face or whip 'is feet as you pass."

"*Awaiting* justice?" said John. "But the stocks are a punishment in themselves..."

The man laughed. "Well, we wasn't about to let that one wander about free." His expression grew suddenly serious, and he drew himself up. "There was those was for hangin' him there and then. But we says no – it's got to be done proper. So our protector, Lady Isabel de Clare, Countess of Pembroke, God bless 'er" – he crossed himself – "is sending her man to mete out justice to 'im. And that is a meat we shall all savour, and no mistake!" He chuckled at his own joke.

De Clare. Gisburne knew that name well. His father had mentioned it often in his youth. It had been in relation to Lady Isabel's father, Richard de Clare, known to all as 'Strongbow,' who had been a thorn in King Henry's side when Gisburne was a lad of no more than nine or ten. Richard de Clare, so Gisburne had since learned, was Earl of Striguil and Earl of Pembroke – though Henry had stripped him of the latter title. He had ventured to Ireland with great ambitions, and little to hold him back. There he had married Aoife, daughter of Dermot MacMurrough, the deposed King of Leinster. MacMurrough's fee was help in restoring his crown – but before long, de Clare had set his sights on making himself king of that place. His army was formidable, bolstered by a contingent of Welsh longbowmen against whom, it seemed, nothing could stand.

Henry, whose grip on Ireland was tenuous at best, watched matters develop across the Irish Sea with increasing disquiet. There were negotiations with de Clare. For a time Gisburne's own father must also have been caught up in it, for he spoke of it often. Finally, his patience gone, Henry had invaded Ireland – but by then, Gisburne's father had stopped speaking of the matter altogether.

Henry's ultimate solution had been to keep his enemy close. De Clare's daughter Isabel became a legal ward of Henry II, who kept a close watch over her inheritance. She was one of the wealthiest heiresses in the kingdom, owning land in Wales and Ireland and numerous castles on the inlet of Milford Haven, including Pembroke Castle. She had also inherited the titles of Pembroke and Striguil.

Gisburne's father occasionally joked that Isabel would make a fine match for his son. But that was a vain hope. Never one to allow his possessions to lay idle, Henry's heir, Richard the Lionheart, had married off the seventeen-year-old Isabel to William Marshal within a month of his coronation, elevating the landless knight to the nobility and making him one of the richest men in England. William was twenty-six years her senior. Widely considered the epitome of the knightly virtues, the man who would become known simply as 'the Marshal' was also the most humourless, insufferable, self-righteous bore Gisburne had ever had the misfortune to meet. It was said he was the only man ever to unhorse the Lionheart, whilst campaigning for Henry against his rebellious son. He had spared Richard's life, but killed his horse to prove the point. This act secured William an even greater reputation – and the respect of the man he knew would soon be King. On the whole, Gisburne would rather have seen the horse spared – better yet, that King Stephen had carried out his threat to launch the boy William from a trebuchet during the siege of Newbury Castle.

"Of what does this man stand accused?" asked John.

"'E's not standing. 'E's sat on his arse." Gisburne expected the man to guffaw at his own joke – then realised he wasn't aware he'd made one.

"What is his *crime*?" said John, testily.

The man's face darkened. He leaned in, as if divulging something secret. "The scarlet sin. The sin God hates..."

The three travellers looked at each other. Slowly, the scene began to make a kind of sense – the three women separate from the rest, looking themselves like the condemned. But it was customary for them to fare much worse. Gisburne had seen terrible things done to unfaithful wives – flesh branded with hot irons, ears cut off, sometimes noses, too. They were outcast – marked for life – if they survived the ordeal at all. The man, by contrast, was often simply sent packing.

"But it's more than that," continued the man, as if anticipating the questions in their minds. "This one's no mere man. 'E's got the Devil in 'im..." He leaned in even closer as he whispered this, as if doing so would prevent the Devil from hearing. "The scarlet fiend bewitched three of our most respected women. Then, when he was caught in the act, he just laughed. But we was wise to 'im. We heard all about 'im, see. 'E's played this game before, has William Gamewell. So, he sits in them stocks till Lady Isabel's man comes. Then we'll see a celebration – and I reckon half the shires of England will be cheering along wi'us." He laughed again, but there was a wild look in his eye – a look at once defiant and pathetic.

Gisburne looked back across the village green, and finally realised what it was the villagers were building. A pyre. And a stake. They meant to burn their captive – on the very spot where, seventeen days ago, they had celebrated the emergence of new life.

"Isn't all this premature?" said Gisburne. "If the judge has not yet even arrived..."

"Oh, 'e'll be found guilty, all right," said the villager, a sudden note of bitterness in his voice. Gisburne wondered, then, what his relationship was to those three women. "And burning is the only way. The judge will see that! I told you – the Devil is in 'im!" His eyes blazed with their own demonic fire as he spoke. "Burning! That's the only way wi'eretics and perverts – and 'e's both!"

Of course. It made sense now – or as much as it could ever make. There was no discontent in their midst, no straying from the path. The Devil – the outsider – made them do it. And so they could remain in denial about their women's sins. They could focus all their ire on the satanic villain, and, once the problem was burned away, carry on as if nothing had ever happened. Perhaps it was necessary for the cohesion of so small a community. Perhaps it was for the best. But Gisburne wondered how long the illusion would last.

John, meanwhile, had stepped forward, his face flushed with indignation at the man's presumption – but Gisburne gripped his arm. He had heard enough. With a simple nod, he turned away, leading Nyght with one hand and dragging John with the other.

The villager, suddenly remembering his purpose as if awoken from a dream, hugged his pail and scurried away.

IN SILENCE, THE endless round of song echoing at their backs, the travellers continued on their way. Ahead, the road snaked to the left. To their right, almost entirely obscured by the inn, lay the village church. Past the bend, they could see another road forking off to the right, heading south-west, while other, lesser trackways joined the hub at the same point – five in all.

And at the junction of these crossings, set back from the road on a bare patch of earth and positioned so all those passing could clearly see, sat the scarlet fiend himself.

Gisburne stopped. This was no Red Hand – not unless the Red Hand's disguise was more devious than they could ever have imagined. There was no armour. No dragon's head. No fiery breath or feet the size of fish-kettles. William Gamewell was every inch the ordinary man – his frame thin, his limbs wiry, his hair hanging lank and greasy. What set him apart was his face. It was not that there was anything out of the ordinary about the thin nose and thinner mouth – marked and battered though they were by the stones and animal bones and clods of dung that lay about him. Nor were the beady eyes and pock-marked cheeks any different from a thousand other men. It was, rather, the expression that played about these features that was troubling.

It was at once smug and resentful, confrontational and dismissive – even now, confined and humiliated as he was by the stocks, sitting in his own filth. It was an expression that had about it that quality that men most fear in others – that made them step aside for him, and avoid his gaze: it knew no fear, and it did not care. Little wonder that the village thought him possessed by the Devil. In death, Gisburne imagined, he would seem utterly unremarkable. In life, he was trouble incarnate.

"What are you looking at?" he said. His voice was a sneer.

"Nothing," said Gisburne, his eyes remaining fixed on the prisoner.

"Ooh," said the man, in mocking tones. "You're scary. I'd be quaking in my boots – if I still had any fucking boots." He waggled his bare feet stuck out before him. They were filthy and covered in cuts and bruises, his ankles rubbed raw from the wooden boards that held him in check. Gisburne guessed, from the look and smell of him, that he'd been there for two days at least.

"You should learn to have more respect," said John.

"Why?" said Gamewell.

John's eyes flashed with anger – but the reply left him lost for words.

"You don't even know why, do you?" laughed Gamewell.

"I'll not waste words on this vile excuse of a man," said John to Gisburne, and turned away.

"Do what you like," said Gamewell. Then he spat in the dust, and cocked his head back towards the village green. "But d'you hear who they're singing about back there? That outlaw up north. The one they call Hood. Does he show respect? No. He kicks respect in the balls. And he's doing all right. Everybody loves *him*."

"And this is you 'doing all right,' is it?" said Gisburne. Galfrid gave a snort of a laugh at that. "Whilst they're singing they're also building your funeral pyre. That should teach you something."

"Yeah, not getting caught. Not thinking so small. Not letting people live who get in my way." He glared at Gisburne as he said it, as if goading the knight to harm him – daring him to. Then he tore his gaze away and slumped back. "Maybe I'll hook up with that Hood next time. I'm sick of being surrounded by idiots."

"Next time?" repeated Gisburne with an incredulous laugh. "You think there'll *be* a next time?"

"Christ, maybe the villagers are right. Maybe he does have the Devil in him," muttered Galfrid.

"Is that what they said? Well, maybe I like having the Devil in me. But not as much as those three whores liked having it in them..." He gave a hoarse laugh. Gisburne felt himself shudder with revulsion. He could not imagine by what means this man made himself attractive to women – it was if his very flesh was poisonous. "You know why they want to kill me? Why they want me to suffer as I die? Not because I fucked their wives. No. Because their wives *wanted* me to... That's the part they don't want to believe." He chuckled. "What a joke. Do they think I'll beg for mercy? For forgiveness? I won't beg. Oh no..." He leaned forward, his eyes wide, a string of saliva dangling from his mouth. "I'd fuck them all again, and their daughters, even as the flames were licking about me. And you know what? They'd cry out for more."

John turned and went to draw his sword. Gisburne again gripped his arm before it was half free of the scabbard. "For God's sake, let's just get out of here," he said, and pulled at him. But the Prince would not budge.

Gamewell and John stared at each other for what seemed an age. Then, all at once, something seemed to change in Gamewell's face. He frowned, then strained forward as if to peer closer at John, then gave an odd little chuckle. "They say it takes a villain to know a villain," he said. His eyes narrowed, his thin mouth creasing into a reptilian smile. "And I know a true villain when I see one. Well, well, *my lord,*" he sneered. "Fancy humble little me meeting y –"

He never completed the sentence. Without a word, Galfrid stepped forward, swung the head of his pilgrim staff about and brought it up hard under Gamewell's chin. There was a sickening crack. One of Gamewell's teeth arced through the air, accompanied by a spray of blood and spittle, and bounced on the compacted mud of the road. Gamewell's eyes rolled backwards into his skull, and he slumped forward, insensible. In tense silence, all three hastily mounted up, and headed out at the gallop.

For a while, John had ridden ahead. Gisburne wasn't sure if the Prince were doing so for his sake or theirs, but either way he was relieved. The

Prince blew hot and cold, and his anger would pass, but he could live without the distraction of it in the meantime.

"The twenty-fourth day of June," said Galfrid, out of the blue. Gisburne turned and stared at him. "I know that's what he's counting down to. The feast day of St John. I just don't know why. What's so significant about that day?"

Gisburne held his gaze, uncertain where to begin.

"Does the answer lie in London?" Galfrid continued.

"He's not simply following us there. He's making sure. Herding us." It was exactly what Salah al-Din had done at Hattin. He had avoided engaging his enemy, and instead goaded and lured the Christian army towards the battlefield of his choosing. Then he had annihilated it. "That is where the Red Hand chooses to fight his battle. I realise that now. Where it was always going to be fought."

"But do you know why?"

Gisburne looked away. "I have an idea. Part of an idea, anyway." He hardly wished to speak of it. It was incomplete, unclear. And the connection it implied did not please him. But it would not serve them to be in denial. It never served anyone.

"Something is set to happen upon the feast day of St John? Something other, I'm guessing, than the celebration of a saint?"

"It's the reason Prince John is going to London," said Gisburne. "That date is... significant. To one man above all others." Then, after a moment's thought, he added: "And no saint, either. The very opposite."

Galfrid stared at Gisburne for a time, as if reading his thoughts.

Gisburne did not even need to look back at him to know the question on his squire's mind. He was certain, too, that he already knew the answer. But he decided to provide it anyway. It was time to speak the name once again – the name of the man who he had allowed himself to believe was buried.

"Hood," he said.

III

LONDON

XIX

Syracuse, Sicily
May, 1185

SYRACUSE WAS IN uproar. Even now, after the hours of darkness, every street and alley thronged with Norman, Italian and Arab soldiers in the service of the King, their ranks swollen by mercenaries from England, France, Brittany, Brabant and every one of the Angevin counties and dukedoms.

There were tens of thousands of them; far more than the city could reasonably hold. During the day, the fierce heat pressing upon this vast, disparate army – many of whom were unused to the conditions – made men terse and volatile. But if anything, the cooler nights were more hectic. In every thoroughfare a river of sweating bodies jostled and shoved, torch flames glinting on shining faces. Weapons clattered against armour, against cobbles, against each other. There were curses, guffaws and raucous bellowings in every language. Here, the clop of hooves; there, the rumble of cartwheels. Drums were beaten, nails were hammered, oxen lowed and stamped – and on every side the ceaseless sounds of laughter, argument and song, interspersed with the wail of pipes and fiddles, spilled from open doors and side streets.

"Is it much further?" said Baldwin, looking about nervously. Gisburne wove through the heaving crowd ahead of the man-at-arms, edging past two Sicilians who were performing some kind of dance with sticks – to much laughter from their surrounding onlookers.

"Not much," he said above the din. "Just down here, I think." Gisburne knew exactly where he was, but he understood Baldwin's anxiety. Even to one well-versed in the ways of cities, these streets all looked alike.

"I hope we find him," said Baldwin. Gisburne doubted the boy had seen so many people in his entire lifetime, let alone in one place, at one time.

"We'll find him," said Gisburne. "With your help."

Baldwin gave a weak smile, hurrying to keep up, his fingers occasionally nipping at Gisburne's sleeve like a child afraid of losing its parent. Gisburne glanced back at Baldwin's pale, guileless face and judged it time to give the boy a little more reassurance. "When it comes to finding your way back," he said, in somewhat more confidential tones, "here's a tip: just follow the moon."

Baldwin nodded, looked relieved, then laughed. "Like a moth!" he said.

"Yes," said Gisburne with a smile. "Just like a moth."

THE CITY OF Syracuse, perched on the extreme eastern tip of Sicily, was one of the jewels of the Mediterranean. Once revered by the Greeks for its beauty, and a formidable city state in ancient times, it had lost some of its lustre since those great days. Yet its strategic significance, if anything, had grown.

A century had now passed since the Normans – at the peak of their first great wave of conquests – had wrested Sicily from the hands of the Arabs. They made of it a new kingdom, and with characteristic vigour had restored its glory, reasserted its status and expanded its power. Sicily was a stepping stone – a base from which other prizes might be claimed – and its King was not one to pass up such opportunities. North and west of it lay the great Christian kingdoms of Europe and the Holy Roman Empire. To the south and east lay Africa, the spreading empire of the Sultan Salah al-Din, and the beleagured Holy Land, where even now tensions were mounting. None of these, however, were to be the object of the eighty-thousand-strong army.

Most of these men were now crammed into the easternmost quarter of the city, on the island of Ortigia, from which the greater part of over two hundred ships were preparing to depart. For now, the mood was celebratory, the level of anticipation high. Men revelled in the close quarters, the camaraderie, the adventure that was to come. But conditions were already turning squalid. Feeding the vast army and their horses in these cramped conditions was something that their commanders had easily mastered; getting rid of their filth, and their frustrations, was not. If things were not to change soon, that mood – that wildness – would turn on itself. But in two days, when the ships were fully provisioned, the troops would begin to board. Then they would be heading east – to take Byzantium.

Though he admitted it to no one, it was the sea voyage – in the bowels of a pitching tarida, heavy with horses, water, weapons and men – that Gisburne dreaded far more than the battles that were to follow.

Gisburne's new master – the master of all these tens of thousands, now – was William II, the Norman king of Sicily. William the Good, they called him. Gisburne had never seen him, nor did he expect to. It was said the king rarely set foot outside his palace in Palermo, where he enjoyed the finer things in life. In this, he was quite unlike his grim, pragmatic Norman forebears. In just about every other respect, the pleasure-loving king was Norman through and through. Ruthlessly efficient, militarily decisive and energetically devoted to securing his rule, he was as vigorous in diplomacy as he was in war. Like all Normans, he was also driven by an an unquenchable desire to expand his realm, and entirely unhampered by self-doubt – traits inherited, Gilbert de Gaillon said, from the fearless Norse adventurers from whom they were descended. No challenge was too great. Nothing beyond reach. Though master of but one small island, William had engineered a marriage to the daughter of Henry II of England and Eleanor of Aquitaine, and invaded Salah al-Din's empire at Alexandria. Now, he was set to conquer his old rivals, the Byzantines.

And yet, within the kingdom of Sicily itself, William had presided over almost two decades of peace. Under his rule, people of different cultures and faiths were tolerated – even encouraged. Trade boomed. The arts flourished, ultimately finding their most perfect expression in the cathedral at Monreale, a Norman church whose architecture combined Syriac and Italian influences with the work of Byzantine artists and Muslim sculptors. It was, quite literally, a golden age.

But with gold comes envy, and resentment. Subversive elements had arisen within Sicilian society. Meeting in secret, they dedicated themselves to resisting Norman rule, exploiting the oppressed poor to their own ends. Gisburne had heard whispers of them from the moment he landed on the island, but so elusive were they, he had begun to wonder if they were a no more than a myth.

THEY CAME TO the mouth of the cramped, crowded alley. "The moon's been at our back all the way," said Gisburne. "Which tonight means the harbour should be somewhere down... Here."

They turned right into a wider thoroughfare. Along it, and heading in the same direction, carts laden with barrels rumbled – clearly destined for the ships at anchor in the bay. In spite of them, the crowds now thinned enough to allow Baldwin to come up alongside him. Baldwin was at least a foot shorter than he, and half his weight. How he was going to survive what lay ahead, Gisburne could not imagine. "How did you say you knew him again?" said Gisburne.

"In Aquitaine, sir," said Baldwin, enthusiastically. "There was I, fresh from England, knowing no one, lost amongst this great host of dour-faced Flemings and yearning just to hear my own tongue spoken again when a lump of bread is thrust at my chest and a voice says: 'You look like you need a good meal!'" He laughed. "Turned out he was from the next village."

"What was the name of that village again? Yours, I mean." asked Gisburne. In truth, he remembered it perfectly well. He just wanted to keep the lad talking. It would keep his mind off things, at least.

"Anesacre," said Baldwin. Then he shrugged, and cast his eyes down almost sheepishly. "A tiny place. I wouldn't expect anyone to know it. I never met anyone who did. But then, right there, in the middle of Aquitaine..." He chuckled again, and shook his head. "It was like a miracle!"

Gisburne smiled again. "Well, you can be a great help to me, Baldwin from Anesacre. I have only a name. But you... you know what he looks like."

"It's my pleasure, sire," beamed Baldwin. "A privilege."

"It's all right," said Gisburne, raising a hand. "And you don't need to call me 'sire.' I'm not a knight; not even a gentleman. Just a soldier. Like you."

Baldwin frowned at that, as if the ideas behind it were too big for him. "Th-thank you, si –" he began, then corrected himself. "I mean, G... G-G..." So badly did he stutter over the name that finally he just gave up and looked away, red-faced.

Gisburne felt a sudden, sick pang of horror. It rose up in him without warning. He clenched his fists into tight balls and fought it down. It was not for himself or his own fate that he felt it, but that of the boy. He could not imagine how the lad had come to be here, how he had fallen into such a life. Perhaps he was running from something; Gisburne had seen that a hundred times. Part of him wanted to grab the boy by his tunic and implore him to run away home, to meet some plump farm girl, settle down, work hard, live a dull but happy life and have scores of children – to tell him that nothing he could have left behind could be possibly worth this, and that where they were heading was the worst place in the world.

Gisburne at least knew what they were in for. He understood the hardships that lay ahead – knew the challenge of simply surviving day-to-day, before you even got as far as facing an enemy bent on your destruction. But even for him, with all he had seen – and there was much – this was on an unimaginable scale.

It went without saying that it would be bloody and desperate. But it would also unfold in an alien land, and upon a battlefield that would be so vast that even from horseback one could not see to its edge. He pictured the blood-muddied expanse, heaped with fallen bodies – a hellish, tangled marsh of gore the mere crossing of which would destroy the spirit of the strongest of men. And clambering over it, with the roar of fifty thousand throats, eyes wide with hate, their enemy – golden armour glinting, teeth white in the merciless eastern sun, blades flashing like forest of scythes.

Into this scene, the air growing dark with ten thousand arrows, he pictured Baldwin blundering, upon his head an ill-fitting helm, in his hand a sharpened stick. He shuddered and shook his head. Every man here had their own fears and vulnerabilities to deal with, but sometimes it was those of others that proved truly crippling. De Gaillon was right – the best and worst thing to take into battle was an imagination.

Gisburne's eyes scanned the tops of the arched doorways on either side of the cobbled street – then he saw what he was looking for. From the cracked, honey-coloured plaster of one such rounded arch projected an elaborate iron bracket, and beneath it, the size of a suckling pig, hung a wooden effigy of a boar, its back bristling with iron pins, and the whole showing signs of flaking blue paint.

"Here," said Gisburne, and dived into the open doorway.

Inside the heaving, sweaty inn, the sounds suddenly became familiar. By the door, a band of forbidding Brabançon axemen clad in brown leather muttered about a barrel-table, but in every other part the voices were English. Gisburne turned momentarily from the sea of faces in this dark, hectic interior to glance at his companion; Baldwin's expression was one of utter terror.

The men that packed the place were not regular soldiers. They fought not for their own lands, nor for duty, nor honour, nor through obligation. They had come because William the Good was rich, and would pay. And because they had heard Byzantium was abundant with gold, ready for the taking. Such men did not treat this task lightly. They were not ignorant of the hardships of campaigning. Most looked upon William's own soldiers with disdain, and had seen – and survived – far more action than they.

Gisburne no longer had to remind himself that he was looking upon his own kind. To Baldwin, however, this was still an alien world. Gisburne grabbed Baldwin's sleeve, pulling the boy behind him as he plunged into the crowd.

He knew what he was looking for, even if he didn't know a face. A certain build, a broadness of chest – a thickness to the right arm and shoulder. What was distracting him now, however, was the women.

They were grasped or entwined or draped upon the men with varying degrees of reluctance or enthusiasm, or weaving among the jostling, laughing men as they brought more drink or food. Most wore their dark hair down, in brazen fashion. Several allowed their smocks to fall from their olive-skinned shoulders and breasts without shame. A few simply kept on the move as best they could with their heads and eyes cast low, employed purely to fetch and carry. All were continually beset by a ceaseless onslaught of lewd remarks and groping hands, attention that they enjoyed or endured with expressions ranging from delight, to disgust, to total vacancy, genuine or contrived. Gisburne conjured up an image of the tired-looking whores in London, and wondered whether it really was true that foreign women were more beautiful, or whether distance from home merely rendered them so.

In the gloom at the far end of the inn, barely pierced by the flickering lamps and candles, Gisburne could make out a group of cheering, laughing men in a tight circle. Behind them, by the fireplace, more than a dozen tall, tapered staves were stacked against the wall. Longbows.

"This way," Gisburne said, nudging Baldwin. As they picked their way past a pack of crossbowmen, one of their number – a stout man with a prickly beard who had clearly gone too far with the woman upon his lap, or lacked means of payment – was slapped about the chops so hard that it resounded like the crack of a whip. His comrades cheered as he reddened and shrank. The woman looked upon him with a thin, almost reptilian smile of total disdain, and tossed her head of glossy black curls, winning herself at least a dozen new admirers in the process.

The men in the circle were archers. At their centre was a tall man with dark hair and neatly trimmed beard, his shoulders broad, his smile apparently inextinguishable. Gisburne edged into the circle.

On the small table top were spread three cards depicting a maiden, a knight and death. With amazing speed and dexterity he would turn them face down, move them about, then challenge onlookers to find the maiden card. Every time, they failed. Gisburne himself followed the movements intently, certain that he had not once taken his eye off the maiden. But on each occasion, she eluded him. Money was flung down and scooped up. Twice, an entirely new card was made to appear among the three – once a dragon, once a portly abbess – then disappear again without trace. Men cheered and clapped as they drank, several grabbing at the cards from time to time and turning them over to try to discover how it was done. Gisburne noticed the man's right hand was bandaged, and wondered if that had some part to play in the trick.

He turned to see Baldwin frowning as he scanned the company.

"Well, do you see him?" said Gisburne. "Your friend from the north?"

Baldwin looked at every face, his bemusement deepening. "No…"

The magician at the centre of the group suddenly looked up from his tricks, and made eye contact with Gisburne.

"Welcome!" he called out, and extended his hand. "Join us, friends! Always on the lookout for new victims to fleece of their hard-earned pennies!" All about him laughed, which struck Gisburne right away.

Several had, he presumed, already been fleeced by the magician's tricks, or were in the process of being so, yet still they laughed.

"I'm looking for Robert of Locksley," said Gisburne, his voice raised so all present could hear.

"Well, you've found him," said the magician. "I am Robert."

"Then I have a pleasant surprise – this man says he knows you," said Gisburne, gesturing to Baldwin. "Baldwin, from Anesacre." But when he glanced back at him, the young man's face registered nothing but confusion and dismay.

"But this is not..." he began, then his voice faded away to nothing.

Locksley beamed his winning smile. "Tell me, where was it we met? You'll have to remind me – this poor memory is not what it was!" A few around him chuckled. Baldwin simply looked more confused and embarrassed than ever.

"I... I must have been mistaken," he stuttered. "I thought you were someone else."

"I dare say I might be if the situation demanded it," he said. A man next to him guffawed. Locksley extended an arm in welcome. "Join us anyway, lad," he said. "Let's put right this base omission!"

Two of Locksley's comrades grabbed Baldwin and hauled him into their midst, one pressing a charged cup into his hand. Gisburne found one thrust into his, and did not resist. Baldwin looked about, utterly bewildered, and – not knowing what else to do – drank deep from it. The men about him cheered, and slapped his back, and filled his cup again.

Locksley turned back to Gisburne. "And what of you, friend?"

"Gisburne," he said. "Guy of Gisburne."

Locksley grinned broadly, and thrust his hand forward.

Instinctively, Gisburne gripped it – realising only after he made contact that it was the one that bore the bandage. For a moment it seemed pain flickered in Locksley's face and was banished, and Gisburne made to withdraw his hand – but the man responded with a tightening of his grip, and continued the steady shake. As he did so, the bandages shifted, Gisburne now saw that they covered what looked like a burn. It had reduced to a crusty mass the skin and flesh of the first three fingers and most of the palm. It looked, too, as if what tight skin remained had repeatedly cracked and bled, and even now wept into the greying bandages.

"You're injured," said Gisburne.

Locksley let go and held his hand before his face. "A little disagreement with some locals at a tavern in Palermo," he said, examining it as one does some curious artefact. "Three of them. They took rather extreme exception to my presence. So, I made use of the Italian I had learned and told them to kiss my hairy arse." His comrades cackled, nudging each other. "They thrust my right hand in the fire until I could smell the flesh burning. Then they left me there, making to leave. I knifed one and pinned another to a door. The other ran, but not fast enough. I dragged him back and introduced the fire to his face until his brains boiled." He grinned again, and put his hand down. "But it's nothing, really."

"Locals?" said Gisburne with a frown. "Openly attacking soldiers of the King?"

"Openly? No! Dressed up in black hoods that covered their faces." He gave a single, dismissive laugh. "Cowards! Don't ask me what it was about. They were jabbering some bollocks about tyranny and justice..."

"Black hoods?" said Gisburne, his eyes widening. "Christ's boots... The Beati Paoli."

"The Beyati-what?"

Gisburne had heard endless rumours since arriving in Sicily, but this was the first time he'd met anyone who had actually seen them. "Vigilantes. Rebels against Norman rule." Gisburne shrugged. "No one knows exactly what or who they are. You never see a face, just the hood. Sicilians won't speak of them openly. But word is they consider them guardians of justice, champions of the oppressed; you know the kind of thing." He shook his head in dismay and swigged from his ale cup. "It's said they rob from the rich to give to the poor."

Locksley roared with laughter, slapping his thigh. "What an idiotic idea!" Several of the men joined in.

Gisburne raised his cup to him. "Here's to you. You're lucky to be alive."

"Luck?" said Locksley, his laugh dying away. "It wasn't luck."

Gisburne at first thought it was meant as a joke, or perhaps a boast. Various members of the company nearby chuckled at the words. But Locksley's expression, for the first time, seemed deadly serious. Then it melted into laughter again.

Gisburne eyed the injured hand – the hand with which Locksley drew his bowstring. At full draw, that string put enough force behind the arrow for it to pass straight through an armoured man at two hundred yards. And it was those first three fingers that took all that pressure. When released, the string whipped along them – felt like it was damn near taking them off if you didn't do it right. "Can you still...?"

"Yes," snapped Locksley before Gisburne could finish. "I can still shoot. Nothing will stop me doing that." He withdrew the injured hand. It went to a necklace at his throat – a small, discoloured metal disc, threaded on leather.

Gisburne simply nodded, and let it go. When he was ten he had burnt his right foot in a bonfire. The searing pain of it when the wound was fresh, and the feverish days and nightmare-filled nights afterwards when it seemed to throb through his entire being – all that was bad enough. But then, two weeks later, when it seemed to be healing, he had walked on it against his father's advice, and the skin, tight as a drum, had split. He'd had many injuries in his time – several far worse that that – but never had he known such agony. The Beati Paoli had seen Locksley was an archer – even if he had not been carrying a bow, his build told anyone as much – and had known exactly what they were doing to him. Of that, Gisburne had no doubt. They had meant to deprive him of his livelihood and let him live, as a warning to others. But they had not reckoned with the iron will that lay behind it, and now all three were dead. Others who had perhaps been fearful of the Beati Paoli before would now follow Locksley's example. Gisburne began to see how this man had earned his reputation. On the battlefield, such fearless tenacity was worth a king's ransom.

"I've heard you're quite a demon with a bow," said Gisburne.

Locksley shrugged. "I can hit a barn. As long as it doesn't move about too much." There was a guffaw at that.

"Also that your fellow bowmen here would follow you anywhere," said Gisburne. "That they regard you as their leader, even though you have no rank over them."

For an instant Locksley's eyes narrowed almost imperceptibly, as if he suspected some kind of trap. Then, as suddenly as it came, the expression disappeared, to be replaced by Locksley's broad, irresistible smile.

"They're a fine company," he said, "even if we do have to endure the presence of a few Welshmen!" He slapped the back of a fellow who was propped up by the edge of the nearest table. The man – red-faced, and the worse for drink – turned and raised his cup in tribute, almost sliding off his perch as he did so. Locksley grabbed one of the longbows – as tall as he was – and, leaning on it, raised his voice so all could hear. "We're all keen to show these Byzantincs what six feet of English yew can do! Isn't that right, lads?" He banged the bowstave against the floorboards, raising dust. There was a drunken cheer of affirmation. Someone called out "Pleased to meet yew!" and another responded: "*They* won't be!"

Locksley gave a hearty chortle that rose above the clamour. Then he drank his cup dry in one, thumped it down on the table and planted his fists firmly on his hips. On anyone else, the gesture would have looked absurd. Somehow this man Locksley carried it off.

"So, now I know *who* you are," he said, looking Gisburne up and down, "but *what* are you? Yeoman? Serjeant? Knight? Or simply in disguise?"

Gisburne met Locksley's intense gaze. The company hushed a little.

"Your captain," he said.

The hush became total. Locksley stared at him for a moment, then he threw his head back with a great, ringing laugh. The inn once again exploded in joyous uproar as he grabbed Gisburne's hand with both his own, and shook it with all the vigour of a man wringing the neck of a goose.

XX

London
19 May, 1193

"I SAID, WHO *goes there?*" The thin-faced guard peered down from the battlement of the Tower gatehouse. He appeared far too young to be charged with such a responsibility – even his helmet looked too big for him.

"I heard you the first time," said Gisburne, his patience wearing thin. "And I've told you already – it's Prince John of England! The King's bloody brother. Now open the bloody gates."

The guard's head wobbled uncertainly on its thin neck. He looked at the hooded figure to Gisburne's side and back again, then suddenly withdrew.

"God save us..." sighed Gisburne. Behind them, Nyght stamped his hoof on the stone flags of the bridge in sympathy.

The great wooden doors of the Tower gatehouse to which the stone bridge led – spanning an incomplete and waterless moat – were rarely closed between dawn and nightfall. So many came and went in the day-to-day running of the place that, for the most part, it was not practical to close it. There were times, however, when an armed guard at an open gate was not deemed sufficient, or prudent. Times of threat, for example, or when royal persons were in residence.

Today, the gates were closed because Prince John was lately arrived with his entourage. What none guarding the Tower knew was that the supposed royal person they had within their walls was no prince – was not even a noble – and was not named John. Though he wore John's clothes, travelled in John's carriage, and was surrounded by John's servants, his name was Edric, a weaver from Pocklington. But for the sake of the Prince's safety, that had been kept from them, and they quite naturally reasoned that the newcomer at the gates could only be an impostor. The irony was not lost on Gisburne.

"I have spoken with the Lieutenant of the Tower..." called a voice.

Gisburne looked up. There again was the wobbling head of the young guard.

"Good," said Gisburne. "We're getting somewhere..."

"He says you are not Prince John."

Gisburne glowered skyward. "I never said *I* was Prince John," he snapped. "*This* is Prince John!" He gestured to his companion.

"Tell 'im we already got one!" came the gruff voice of a second, unseen guard, followed by a gale of laughter.

"We've already got one!" called the younger, his face as straight as a poker.

"This is preposterous," muttered John. His hand went to his sword hilt. Gisburne saw in his eye the look of a man about to draw his sword and batter the gates. This was unlikely to make much impression on six-inch-thick English oak, but such logic never troubled the legendary Angevin temper. Gisburne calmed him with a gesture of restraint, and called again to the guard.

"Do you know what the Prince looks like, boy?"

The guard nodded. His helmet wobbled.

"And have you seen him inside those walls? Has anyone?"

The guard hesitated, confusion writ upon his face. Clearly, he could not confirm it – although what was going on in the boy's vacillating head, if anything, was hard to judge.

John, who could stand no more, whipped the hood from his head and bellowed up at the boy. "Dammit, if you claim to know his face, then look upon this. *I* am John, your Prince – brother to the King and heir to the English throne."

The guard's eyes widened in panic. "I... I shall speak with the Lieutenant." He withdrew suddenly. There was chatter, and shouting. Another head appeared and disappeared before Gisburne even had time to focus on it.

Gisburne was aware that they must have looked a sorry pair, dusty and dishevelled from the road. The Prince hardly looked the part. But he was exhausted, the day was dragging on, and all he now wished for was to deliver John safe and sound and rejoin Galfrid, who by now would have secured them food and lodgings.

The guard's head appeared again above them. His expression was strained – Gisburne wondered how he came to his current station, and whether he would last the course. The boy swallowed hard, then spoke. "The Lieutenant says the Prince's entourage is within, and that none may –"

"The entourage may be within," seethed John, "but it is also without. It has no Prince, for I am clearly here!" He was visibly shaking.

"God's teeth…" sighed Gisburne, and rubbed his brow. "Have the Prince's closest men come out here," he called. It wasn't the boy's fault – but this absurd puppet show had gone on long enough. "His manservant or his groom – or Llewellyn of Newport. They will confirm it."

Gisburne was suddenly aware that John had drawn his sword, and now thrust it up at the battlement – a singularly unwise act before the gates of the Tower. But trying to relieve the Prince of the weapon in his current state of mind was, perhaps, equally unwise.

"The last time I stood before the gates in this manner," bellowed John, "it was the rat Longchamp, Constable of the Tower, cowering within – and you know what happened to him!"

Gisburne doubted the boy did, but the general point was made.

"Tell you what, boy," Gisburne said, ideas and patience almost spent. "You get the Lieutenant to send for the Prince. Have Prince John come out here in person and clap his eyes on us. If you are right and we are impostors, then we will gladly be condemned to death for high treason and God knows what else. Here. Tonight. We would welcome it. And you would be a hero. But if you are wrong, and you fail to open these gates…" He hesitated.

"I need to speak with…"

"To Hell with that!" snapped Gisburne. "You send your bloody Lieutenant out here so we may speak with him and not his parrot!

Prince John, red-faced with fury, shook his sword aloft. "And be quick about it, boy," he spat, "or by God I'll climb up there and shove this right up…"

There was a *clunk,* and another. The great gates of the Tower of London creaked and clanked, and slowly began to open.

XXI

THEY HAD REACHED Clerkenwell by mid-afternoon, and soon after passed between the wide, open space of Smoothfield – beyond which the River Fleet flowed towards the Thames – and the Priory of St Bartholomew Augustinian. As they passed, Galfrid had craned his head towards its church, and commented wistfully upon its impressive interior – one of the finest in all London, he said – but neither Gisburne nor John were of a mind to stop for sightseeing. Their end was at last in sight.

Ahead, just visible beneath a haze of smoke and dust, lay Aldersgate – one of the seven ancient gates that provided access within the city walls. It was cracked and crumbling and appeared sorely neglected – the walls were built by the Romans, so Galfrid said – but any notion that this was a city in decline was dispelled the moment they passed through.

For miles, as they had drawn closer to the capital – passing fields, pastures, and pleasant, level meadows on the way – they had seen the roads grow busy with traffic of all kinds. There were dusty pilgrims, armoured knights, monks on asses, overladen ox-carts, farmers driving livestock, slogging footsoldiers, rich merchants in carriages, bootless peasants: the Great North Road made no social distinctions. All were steadily funnelled into the great city – distilled and compressed by its streets until each jostled one against the another, closer than any would allow under any other circumstance. It seemed a kind of madness – an impossible trick, folding ever more people into this finite space – space into which far more seemed to flow than ever seemed to leave. Common sense said it must surely reach its limit – a point of crisis, which elsewhere would lead to disaster or panic. Yet this inexorable compression of bodies – each with their own purpose, utterly incompatible with the others – somehow proceeded without incident.

Gisburne believed he understood why. Upon entering the strange, foreign land that was the commune, the streets ceased to be mere conduits or thoroughfares. They were stages, moot halls, pulpits, workshops, eateries, trysting places, animal pens, markets and sports fields – places used not only, nor even mainly, for traversing the city, but for every other thing that life entailed. In winter, the people withdrew to their firesides, but in spring and summer, all life was lived in the streets. In this, one could say it was not so different from any town or village in the land. But so much life was to be found here – on such a vast scale, and in such unimagined variety, from the dandiest earl to the lowest leprotic beggar – that newcomers could do little other than stare in wonder, or horror, or disgust, and forget their own predicaments entirely.

So it was, under such conditions, the trio passed southward down St Martin's Lane, past Stinking Lane – a domain of butchery, which lived up to its name – to the place where the road opened into the broad thoroughfare of Westchepe.

Here, where traffic should have eased, all movement slowed. For here it was that a great proportion of newcomers to the city, perhaps thinking that they were growing used to its wonders after a few hundred yards, stopped and stared, open-mouthed, while horses, carts, nuns, mercenaries and geese attempted to flow around them.

To the west, the Shambles stretched away to Newgate – which, according to the unique logic of London, was older than Aldersgate. East, the road pressed on into the heart of the great city, beyond which lay the Tower. Rising immediately to their left, like a gnarled finger pointing to heaven, was the stone tower of St Martin Le Grand.

It was from here that London's curfew bell was rung. In former times, this had signalled the hour of the evening when all were expected to quit the streets, or face a stiff penalty – one of the ways the Conqueror had sought to control the Saxon populace. His son Henry had overturned the restriction, and for the past century, the bell of St Martin's had announced nothing more than the closing of the city gates for the night. Now, London went about its nocturnal business – which was brisk – entirely unimpeded.

It was the sight that lay immediately opposite as they emerged into Westchepe, however, that inspired awe. The great cathedral of St Paul's – the largest building in London – dominated the view, and overthrew the senses. For over one hundred years it had been under construction, and its stonework was permanently sheathed in a teetering spiderweb of scaffolding, but somehow this only served to emphasise the greatness of its massed stone, and of its ambition.

"Keep moving, Galfrid," said Gisburne. He had seen the squire begin to drift at the sight of the great church. "Plenty of time for that in coming weeks..."

As if in riposte, Galfrid announced that he was taking them away from the main thoroughfares and through certain backstreets that he knew, because it was "quicker".

The earth upon the main streets, exposed to sun and wind, was dry and firm, but on these narrow, winding ways, where the sun rarely penetrated and the air moved not at all, there was a permanent slurry of muck and mud. It stank of dung and decay and stale urine, and sucked noisily at the horses' hooves as if reluctant to let them go. Several times, Gisburne only narrowly avoided dashing his brains out upon the rotting, overhanging buildings, which seemed to be gradually falling in upon them. Dark eyes – strangers to daylight – blinked at their passing from lightless windows. But this way, Galfrid said, would lead them straight to Candlewick Street, and Eastchepe, and – finally – the Tower. Gisburne knew all of this only because Galfrid insisted on giving a running commentary. He seemed determined to display his knowledge of the capital – and, by default, reveal his master's ignorance.

"What do you know about London?" asked Galfrid as they rode out of the thickening crowds past Candlewick Street.

"That it is ruled by no Baron or Earl, but by a thing called a *mayor*. That he is drawn from the merchant classes, and the city enjoys a degree of independence unknown elsewhere. That it lies upon the great river Thames, which brings traders from every nation under heaven. That its bishopric is seated in the great church of St Paul's. That there is a great sale of fine horses held beyond the gates every Friday, that it is noisy, and that it stinks to high heaven."

Galfrid nodded. "Well, I know where to find good food, good drink, and decent lodgings," he said.

Gisburne shrugged, happy to admit defeat. "You have me there."

"Everything is here if you know where to look," said the squire. "Gold from Arabia. From Sabaea, spice and incense. From the Scythians, well-tempered arms of steel. Oil from the rich groves of palm that spring from the fat lands of Babylon. Fine gems from the Nile. From China, crimson silks. French wines – and sable, vair and miniver from the far lands of the Rus."

Gisburne smiled at the unexpected catalogue. "I never had you down as a poet, Galfrid."

"But one has to be... circumspect... when it comes to ale and vittels. There is good reason why all the meat here is chopped beyond recognition, spiced within an inch of its life and smothered with a strong sauce," said Galfrid. "Take my advice. If you want meat, and can't be sure of its provenance, ask for pork. It's the one thing that has a decent chance of being fresh."

"Pork?" Gisburne frowned. "Why pork?"

As if in direct response to his question, a dark, mud-caked creature as big as a barrel darted out from a narrow side street and almost under Nyght's hooves. He danced sideways in alarm, but held his nerve. The pig, meanwhile, gave a piercing squeal, changed direction, and sped off into the shadowy alley opposite, pursued in absurdly comical fashion by a hefty man with outstretched arms, his hose half way down his buttocks. A trio of filthy children dressed in rags ran in his wake, laughing at the tops of their lungs.

"Welcome to London," chortled John.

Gisburne had explicitly requested the Prince remain silent and hooded until they reached the Tower. The hood was already half-pulled back, with John complaining he could not be expected to ride through crowded streets if he could not see what was to either side of him. Gisburne soon realised that his precautions were not only impossible to enforce, but mostly pointless.

"No one notices anyone or anything in London," Galfrid had said as they had approached the city gates. "Unless its a victim ready to be fleeced."

"Then I shall not look like a victim," John had replied, cheerfully. It was as good a strategy as any. He looked calm and confident – clearly relieved to have reached the city. Gisburne's feelings, however, were all the other way. What remained uppermost in his mind was the fact that, whether he looked like one or not, John was the target of a vicious murderer, who even now might be somewhere close by, in these crowds.

Only slowly, by degrees, had Gisburne realised London was the perfect place for the Red Hand to disappear. Part of him had thought it would make his task easier, that the Red Hand would somehow stand out all the more, and that the multitude of witnesses to his potential deeds would surely deter or limit him. Now that he was back in this hectic realm, he understood that this was an illusion. Here, one could hide in plain sight – disappear into the tens of thousands of indifferent, jostling bodies – no matter how outlandish one appeared. Because London had seen it all, and done it all, and cared nothing for what happened in its midst.

"So, you didn't know about the pigs, then..." said Galfrid, deadpan.

Gisburne had known about the pigs – at least, he thought he had. What he had not appreciated was how ubiquitous they were. On the main thoroughfares, on a good day, one could avoid swine entirely. Away from them – and increasingly, the deeper one got into the labyrinth – they seemed to inhabit every yard, and run loose in every alley. They were the perfect city dweller, eating all the rubbish humankind discarded – everything other creatures would not, and more besides. Where they could, they'd even eat the rats. The only problem was preventing them from progressing to bigger fare – cats, dogs, children. In some parts, Galfrid claimed, the hogs had turned completely wild, and there was a bounty for each one killed. Gisburne couldn't help wondering whether the residents of London hadn't simply replaced the customary vermin of the city with a whole new race of rats – half as big as a big man and generating ten times as much reeking shit. But at least, he supposed, these rats could be made into decent sausages.

There was much Gisburne did not know about London. In truth, he had rarely spent longer than a day and a night here, and even then he had remained largely insulated from it. He knew a handful of destinations – the wharves, a few inns, and, of course, the Tower – and the roads that linked them; main thoroughfares, for the most part. He rarely ventured further than his prescribed task required, and returned home as soon as he was able. Perhaps he simply had not encountered its pleasures – but he had never felt greatly moved to seek them out.

He did not like London. He respected it, saw much to admire in it, was even awed by it. But he did not like it. It was a harsh, foreign world, in which the simplest matters became impossible – unless you were a native of the place. He did not like its filth – guts from butchers' shops, excrement of humans and animals, rotting vegetation and all manner of stinking rubbish – which frequently heaped up in the roads with nowhere to go, making everywhere a midden. He did not like the air and the miasmatic sickness that came with it, all of which the inhabitants shrugged off as if illness, parasites and a short life were simply things to be endured – if they noticed them at all.

Least of all did he like the people. Not that in themselves they were bad. Far from it. They were robust, pragmatic, and resourceful – an admirable breed, always ready to regale you with their own unique brand of joke or bawdy song, of which they seemed to have an infinite fund. In business transactions – which they thrust upon every passer by, stranger or not, at any opportunity – they were shrewd and unashamedly relentless. But even this he did not mind. There was also a noisy cheer about them, and while some affected a kind of eye-rolling world-weariness, Gisburne knew this was a pose. Even amongst the lowest of the low in this city, there was a kind of boundless optimism. They would try anything, and see opportunities everywhere, always seeking, always moving.

Ultimately, he came to realise, this was the only way to survive the city. Those who did not – who lacked the strength or the will to do so – were ground to dust by London's merciless mill. They were winnowed chaff, trampled into the dirt by the city's restless feet. It was an environment which, to use an expression of Gilbert de Gaillon's, took no prisoners.

The survivors formed a species entirely their own, uniquely fitted for life in this vast, labyrinthine nest.

These creatures were called *Londoners*.

No, it was not the character of the people that oppressed him. It was their sheer number – the endless, unceasing swell of humanity that flowed along every thoroughfare and alley, pressing at the limits of the cramped courses. The unrelenting, ant-like activity baffled the senses, sapped the will and left one bewildered and exhausted. There was no time for rest, no respite from the faces and voices.

One yearned to hear the simple sound of a bird or a brook – but the only birds that ventured into the interior were harsh-throated crows, and the only running water the waste tipped from windows. There was the lapping tide of the Thames, of course, but to the stranger even this was something alien – overwhelming in scale, and ripe with sewage and the stink of the tanneries. The Seine was a mere ditch in comparison.

Even if such sounds existed here, they would be engulfed. In the streets, the noise of humanity never ceased. None here complained about the relentless din. Most seemed not to notice at all, and merely raised their own voices so as to be heard over it. Gisburne began to believe that some Londoners actually enjoyed it. None would simply converse if they could exclaim loudly, and none would content themselves with exclaiming loudly if they were free to bellow at the top of their lungs – which, of course, they always were. And few exercised their freedoms with greater vigour than the Londoners of the commune.

For the callow visitor from the countryside, these bawled, bloodcurdling conversations seemed like terrifying altercations – to them, entire streets were nothing less than rivers of seething anger, threatening at any moment to burst into savage, unchecked violence. More often than not, visitors left this chaotic nest shaken to the core, and vowing never to return.

Even with his own experience of the city – and no one would call the seasoned knight 'callow' – Gisburne was not immune to its effects. On several occasions, when traversing its thoroughfares, he had felt his hand go to the hilt of his sword at the sound of voices apparently raised in violent outrage – only to witness the supposed combatants breaking into uproarious laughter and slapping each other heartily upon the shoulders.

The city was not without its advantages. Here, one could buy anything, if – as Galfrid had made clear – one knew where to look. There was no pleasure that could not be had for a price. Bawdy houses were everywhere, catering to every taste and pocket, and only outnumbered by the vast array of inns – though the two were not always distinguishable.

It was not only the sheer quantity of inns that made the head spin, but their outlandish appearance. Elsewhere, a stout, gaily decorated stake in the ground announced the presence of an alehouse. In London, as in all matters, things were done differently. Here, the streets were so cramped – many not wide enough for a wagon, some barely even a horse – that alestakes had taken to the air, and now projected out above the doorways, each striving to be more distinct and colourful than their neighbours. From some hung brightly painted boards with garish images of dragons and horses. Others had carved effigies: Gisburne saw hedgehogs, bare-breasted mermaids, two-headed birds and the heads of Saracens. The inns had come to be known by the symbols they bore – the Red Dragon, the White Hart, the Golden Lion – and thus was solved the problem of specifying in which of the twenty inns along Eastchepe one desired to meet.

"The Green Man," Galfrid had said as they reached the far end of that road, and nodded up at the effigy over the door. They were now where Eastchepe met Tower Street, the square turrets of the Tower itself clearly visible ahead. Gisburne looked up at the grotesquely grinning figure over the door, and winced.

"If we must," he said.

"Well, at least you won't forget it," Galfrid said, then turned back the way they had come in search of lodgings. "See you back here!"

Gisburne had heard John chuckling to himself then, and followed the Prince's gaze back up to the effigy over the inn's lopsided door. Above the cracked and greying wood of the lintel, freshly carved and painted green, was a circular mass of interlocking foliage, and at its heart, a jolly but maniacal face. The woodcarver's ambition had been greater than his skill, but his intentions were clear.

Grinning down at them from the inn front – the eyes wild and staring, the smile oddly reminiscent of a voracious predator – had been the cowled visage of Robin Hood.

XXII

GISBURNE SAW JOHN'S face fall as the doors of the Tower gatehouse yawned open.

Framed in the great stone arch were perhaps a dozen men. First came four armed guards bearing spears, and at their centre, a perpetually smiling, bearded man of middle age and generous girth – clearly a person of significance. He chuckled to himself as he approached, hands spread wide in the manner of a genial host welcoming a guest. His appearance was affable enough – his greying hair and beard were full and curly, and somewhat untamed – a look, Gisburne judged, that he had affected for rather too long, as if clinging to his youth. Once, it may have seemed romantic and unconventional, but now, despite his fine clothes and ostentatious Byzantine sword, it merely made him look unkempt and unwashed – like a tramp dressed up as a noble.

Behind him came two grooms, and beyond them, four mounted knights and one magnificent chestnut stallion. It was this beast – or rather the man leading him – that had so caught the Prince's attention.

At first, Gisburne could not place him – but he looked again at John's pained expression, and the fog cleared.

Walter de Coutances, Archbishop of Rouen, Constable of the Tower and justiciar of England in all but name. He had succeeded the detested Longchamp as Richard's right hand in the kingdom, but the two could hardly have been more different. Longchamp had not even had the common sense to hide his weaknesses – the greed, the vanity, the cowardice. De Coutances, ambitious though he undoubtedly was, had none of these flaws. He was shrewd, pragmatic, hardworking and fearless. Even now, Gisburne could see that John feared him. It was de Coutances who had invested Richard Duke of Normandy, who had served as vice chancellor and who stood at the King's side when his great army had journeyed upon its crusade. It was also de Coutances who Richard had dispatched back to England when he had heard of the feud between Longchamp and his brother – a feud behind which, the Lionheart had suspected, lay designs upon his throne.

It had been barely two months since John and de Coutances had last seen each other. Then, John had taken the biggest gamble of his life, and had lost. Believing his brother Richard would now never return from the Holy Land, he had announced him dead, struck an alliance with Philip of France and raised an army in England to secure the throne. De Coutances, however, ever loyal to the rightful king, stood firm against him, besieging Windsor Castle and scattering John's rebels. The Prince had been forced to flee to France, his tail between his legs. The defeat, and the subsequent humiliation – compounded by the widespread belief that he had acted purely out of greed – were still raw.

The big, shaggy-bearded man was first to reach them. "My lord, my lord – welcome," he said with a smile, and bowed low. "I am Sir William Fitz Thomas, Lieutenant of the Tower."

"Ah," said John. "The fabled Lieutenant."

Fitz Thomas spread his hands wide again, this time in a gesture of apology. "Had we only known your plans…" John, however, was already not listening. De Coutances, who was leading his horse forward, had all his attention.

"My Lord Archbishop," said John. He forced a smile, and inclined his head – enough to show respect without in any way implying subordination. "What a pleasant surprise."

De Coutances nodded in acknowledgement. "I take it, then, that the Prince John who claims to be ill and remains mysteriously confined to his carriage is no prince at all?"

"No prince," confirmed John. "And not ill."

"Well, it will be a relief to all to know we do not have dysentery in our midst," said de Coutances.

"I hear it's all the rage in the Holy Land," said John. De Coutances did not laugh. Fitz Thomas snorted uncertainly, and looked from one to the other.

"I had not expected to see you, Walter," said John, "but it is good that you are here. Perhaps now sanity can be restored." And he smiled his most gracious of smiles.

De Coutances did not respond in kind. "Had you not found it necessary to employ such an elaborate deception," he said, "sanity would perhaps not have departed."

Gisburne saw John's muscles tense, heard his knuckles crack.

"The deception was necessary, my lord," said Gisburne. "And entirely my idea."

De Coutances' eyes narrowed. "Gisburne, is it not?" Gisburne lowered his head in acknowledgement. De Coutances nodded. "These are... turbulent times." He shot a glance at John. "It might have been better had you shared this information. But all is now resolved."

"And no harm done," added Fitz Thomas.

"Indeed," said John.

"Well, I'll not keep you. I depart forthwith to join Queen Eleanor in the north – to assist in her efforts to secure the freedom of the King. In my absence, Sir William Fitz Thomas, Lieutenant of the Tower, has full authority over all matters within these walls."

John's fingers once again clenched into fists.

"Under your guidance, of course," added the Archbishop, as if it pained him to admit it.

The fingers relaxed.

With that, De Coutances gripped the pommel of the saddle, put his foot in the stirrup and hauled himself upon his mount. The other four riders formed around him.

"Oh – one thing," called De Coutances from his horse. "Your guard of Norman cavalry..."

"Yes?" said John, as sweetly as he could manage.

"Clearly such a force could not be permitted within the walls of the Tower."

John tried to hide his disappointment. "Well, never mind," he said. "They won't have gone far. I've not paid them yet." And at that he smiled.

"I paid them," said de Coutances, and John's expression soured. "In the absence of a capable Prince, I drew the money myself from the crown and this morning saw them onto a ship bound for Normandy. I'm sure you understand we cannot have such formidable fighting men at a loose end in the capital."

"Well..." said John, his expression pinched, his jaw clenched. "Thank you."

"The money should be reimbursed as soon as you are able. The usual rates of interest apply until that time." And he turned and walked his horse across the bridge, his guard around him.

"You came at just the right moment," said Fitz Thomas, cheerily. "Another minute, and the Archbishop would have been gone!"

"How terrible that would have been," said John with a thin smile. He turned to the receding figure of de Coutances. "Do please pass on my regards to my dear mother."

"I will," called de Coutances brusquely. He gave a brief nod, and was gone.

"Well, your retinue awaits, my lord," said Fitz Thomas with a cheery smile, gesturing inside. "Your chamber is prepared, and I have brought good wine."

"And I suppose I really should relieve my understudy, who has endured the discomfort of being Prince John quite long enough..."

"My deepest apologies again for the misunderstanding earlier," said Fitz Thomas, shaking his head. He chuckled. "I will admit you threw us into quite some confusion." The Lieutenant struck Gisburne as rather too keen to be liked, but his bumbling geniality seemed to work on the Prince.

"Quite understandable," said John, his fury now completely forgotten. "On the whole, it is better to be cautious. As the Archbishop said: turbulent times."

"Indeed! Indeed!" laughed Fitz Thomas.

"I hope the defences have improved in other areas," said Gisburne.

Fitz Thomas' laugh faltered. For a moment, as he looked at Gisburne, the mask of affability seemed to slip, and there was something in his expression akin to indignation. Then the smile returned. "You are familiar with our defences?" he said.

"Sir Guy gave them a thorough testing," said John. "Back when Puintellus was Constable."

"Really!" exclaimed Fitz Thomas. His voice was full of wonder, but his eyes, this time, showed a flicker of resentment. "Would that I had been there to see it. Will you be joining us, Sir Guy?"

"I fear not, Sir William," said Gisburne. "I am required elsewhere..."

"Coward..." whispered John.

"Well, I must not keep you from your duties..."

Gisburne bowed his head. He had no desire to draw this meeting out either.

"Come, Sir William," said John, glancing briefly back at Gisburne. "I shall tell you all about it..." And, leaving his horse to the groom, the Prince ushered Fitz Thomas between the guards and on through the great archway.

Gisburne turned from the Tower, heaved his aching bones into Nyght's saddle, and rode alone to his rendezvous with Galfrid, the Tower's great doors booming shut behind him.

XXIII

GISBURNE WAS FIRST to arrive back at the Green Man. For what seemed an age he sat nursing a mug of ale in the sweaty interior, fighting to keep his eyes open as the hectic life of the inn heaved and jostled and about him. Ripe-smelling bodies barged into him as he sat. Noise butted his ears. The musicians – whose tunes were raw and rhythmic, but fashionably exotic – played loud to be heard above the febrile crowd, and the patrons spoke louder still to be heard above the music. As evening drew on, it began to merge into a meaningless jumble, rattling in Gisburne's head like pebbles in a butter churn.

When Galfrid finally appeared, weaving through the raucous customers, he, too, looked ragged.

"Success?" yelled Gisburne above the racket.

"Yes," said Galfrid. "Eventually."

"Good," said Gisburne. He drained his cup and stood. "Let's go."

Galfrid looked crestfallen. "Really? Aren't we staying for just one?" Only then did Gisburne realise Galfrid had been about to sit. The squire now looked around the place, throbbing with life, as if his one desire was to lose himself in it for a while. Why, Gisburne couldn't imagine, but he was certainly in no mood to humour him.

He wasn't sure the place had ever held much of an appeal, given that it had welcomed him with the grinning mask of Hood, and what little interest it subsequently possessed had rapidly worn thin. With little to do – struggling for something to focus on in the manic blur – his ears had sought out other people's conversations, and in the last half hour he had forced himself to endure the idiotic bile of three men on a neighbouring bench who had, at great length and in great detail, decried the entire Arab race in the most foul terms imaginable. Had he more energy, he might have felt compelled to go over and point out to them that the spices they enjoyed on their meat, the dried fruits they ate from their bowls, the backgammon they played upon the table and the music they stamped at and cheered on with such drunken enthusiasm were all the products of those "filthy Arabs". But what he really wanted to do was just nail their tongues to the table.

Clearly, it was time to leave.

"Let's just get there," he said, and took up a cloth bundle from the table and thrust it into Galfrid's arms. "I saved you some bread and cheese. And a pickle." Galfrid took one more longing look around the low-lit interior before being hustled out into the street by his master. Gisburne was glad to be drawing this long day to a close. All he wanted now was to sleep.

Outside, it had grown surprisingly dark, the streets of London in a strange lull; the day's activities and trades largely gone or winding down, those of the evening starting to take over. Above them, as they untied the horses, the face of Hood – now lit by a burning flambeau in anticipation of the night's custom – looked positively demonic.

"How was your reception at the Tower?" said Galfrid as they moved off. Far behind them, its battlements were just visible, blood red in the setting sun.

"Frosty," said Gisburne. "The tide is not in John's favour."

"Was it ever?"

"So, how did you fare? Better than me, I hope."

Galfrid sighed, and looked shifty. "It wasn't easy. It's still Whitsun week – it seems nearly every bed in London is taken. But I've found something. For tonight." Gisburne wondered at that – *for tonight* – and the fact that Galfrid avoided his gaze as he said it. He was considering whether to query it when the squire spoke again.

"Why did you not trust me to know about Llewellyn leaving messages?" He did not look Gisburne in the eye.

"What?" The question caught Gisburne completely off guard. He wasn't at all sure he wanted to tackle it. Not now, at least. "It wasn't a question of trust," he said. "Of course I trust you."

"And the fact that we would be meeting with Prince John? And that he was not in his carriage as you had led me to believe?"

"Galfrid – such information is a burden."

"You trust me to carry your other burdens. It's my job. Why not these?"

"I told you, it's not about trust. It's just..." He struggled to find the words.

"It's just that if I were captured, I might divulge the information? Under torture?"

So, that was it. Gisburne had been a fool. He had thought he was protecting his squire. Or sometimes just playing a stupid game with him. But he should have guessed that Galfrid's incarceration at Castel Mercheval – and his treatment at the hands of Tancred's vile servant Fell the Maker – would leave marks. Not on his body, perhaps, but marks all the same.

"You think I would break," said Galfrid. "That I would talk."

Gisburne shook his head vigorously. "No! You're the last person who would." But, deep down, he wondered whether he really had harboured such fears. "I'm sorry if it offended you," he said. "Truly. That was never the intention. You know what I'm like. I keep things to myself. It's a hard habit to break."

Galfrid nodded slowly. "I do know it," he said. "But if you think me weak..." He hesitated, as if uncertain whether to continue. His tone strove to remain matter-of-fact. "If you think me weak, then you must say. For if it is the case, I am no longer worthy to serve you. I am here to relieve your burdens, not become one."

Gisburne rode for a moment, feeling the steady rhythm of Nyght's hooves beneath him. Galfrid was not above fishing for compliments on occasion – and, God knows, he probably needed to, given Gisburne's poor record for offering encouragement – but this was not one of those times. This was something else – something more fundamental. Galfrid was not threatening, or making a point, or trying to win some kind of victory over his master. He simply could not bear the idea that he might put his master in danger – that he might somehow fail him. Gisburne felt sick at the thought – panicked by the possibility that Galfrid might leave. The strength of feeling caught him completely by surprise. He had been self-contained and self-reliant for so much of his life. But then, his life had been small – what he could achieve, limited. Now, he was changing things, putting them right. And suddenly it struck him, as never before, that he could not do this alone. "There's no one I trust more in the whole world," he said. "No one."

Galfrid nodded. "Fine," he said.

"And I hope you trust in me too," Gisburne just wanted this over. To go back to normal. To have a decent night's sleep, and to wake up, and for those things he relied on – which were remarkably few – to still be there.

"Now I do," said Galfrid. Then, after a moment, added: "Except when it comes to your piss-poor dress sense."

Gisburne burst into laughter. He laughed until tears rolled down his cheeks. Even Galfrid – capable of maintaining inscrutability in the most extreme of circumstances – could not hold back a chuckle.

For the next half hour they exchanged insults, and recounted some of the more absurd episodes in their history.

As they rode, Galfrid leading the way, the streets grew narrower, darker, more crooked. They were once again in the labyrinth – underfoot, a rich, ripe stew of mud and mire, straw and ash, dung both human and animal, decaying matter of all kinds, rags, bits of bone and collapsed parts of the dilapidated façades. As they proceeded, these gaunt, teetering hives pressed ever closer, as if threatening to bring their seemingly permanent state of collapse to a sudden, shuddering conclusion. Past them slunk strange creatures in human form – some hurrying upon their way, others entirely without direction, looking as if they had only recently emerged from the dank swamp, and might at any moment disappear back into it.

They turned into a long, straight lane, so cramped that both were forced to dismount and lead their reluctant horses, trusting their own boots to the stinking trough of filth. To Gisburne it resembled nothing less than a recently drained river bed, complete with the stink of dead fish.

Up ahead, where the way widened a little, there could now be heard shouts, laughter, raised voices. Some place of nocturnal business, Gisburne supposed. On either side, whores hung out of windows, their obscene mutterings – many barely intelligible – building to a horrid crescendo as knight and squire passed. Gisburne flinched as grubby fingers reached out and stroked his face. He could smell them even above the street's own stench.

"Christ, do we really have to pass through these foul culverts to get where we're going?"

Galfrid looked suddenly shifty again. No sooner had he reached the bawdy house than Gisburne understood why. The squire stopped before its doorway. "Now, before you judge it too harshly..." he began, red-faced.

Gisburne stared at his Galfrid in disbelief, then back again at the awful, mouldering structure. "*These* are our lodgings?" Over the door, fashioned in wood and painted a vivid red, was an enormous and rather badly carved penis.

"Just above," said Galfrid, and gestured to the upper floor of the misshapen pile.

"There are rooms up there?"

"Well, a room," said Galfrid. "Of sorts." Down a narrow alley along one side of the house – if such it could be called – Gisburne now saw there was a rickety wooden stair, its wood green and half rotten. At the top, a creaking door flapped open.

Gisburne had slept in ditches, caves and rat-infested barns in his time. Once, he'd slept in a tree. Right now, he would have traded this for any one of them. His gaze descended once more to the enormous phallus above their heads. He noticed now that its upper side was soiled by a splatter of something that had evidently been tipped from the window immediately above. A slimy tendril of decayed vegetable matter hung from it, swaying limply in the breeze.

"I know, I know," said Galfrid, sheepishly. "So, it's above a knocking shop. But it's the best I could do. It has decent stabling at the back."

"Stabling?" said Gisburne, still aghast. "It sounds like it's got an entire farmyard."

From within, since their arrival, had issued a relentless chorus of bovine grunting, accompanied by a cacophony of moans, cackles, hoots and shrieks, like animals undergoing some kind of torture. As Gisburne stood, it was punctuated by a guttural roar, a piercing squeal like a skewered piglet, then what sounded like someone vomiting from a tremendous height.

"God in heaven," he sighed, his dream of a good night's sleep rapidly evaporating.

"It looked better in daylight," said Galfrid.

"What is the name of this hellhole?"

"It's Master Bigot's place," said Galfrid.

"And the street?" said Gisburne. Galfrid looked back at him, his face a perfect blank. "So Prince John knows where to find us, should he need to...?"

Galfrid shifted on his feet, then muttered something under his breath. Gisburne only half heard. "What did you call it?"

Galfrid sighed heavily. "Gropecunte Lane," he said.

AT THAT MOMENT, a squat man with a head like an inflated pig's bladder barrelled out of the front door, his arm around a young woman in a filthy dress. Her skin was like tanned leather and she had no front teeth, but Gisburne judged her to be little more than seventeen.

"Ah," said Galfrid with a cough. "This is Master Bigot, our host."

Master Bigot's eye's widened at the sight of Gisburne. He let go the girl and, smiling broadly, extended a hand. Gisburne had no wish to take it. "I understand you is stayin' with us," said Master Bigot. "We is 'onoured, Sir... *Sir...?*"

Gisburne nodded, but did not take the bait.

Bigot laughed it off. "And this 'ere's me pride and joy," he said, and put a thick arm around the young woman's shoulder again. "Me lovely daughter Custancia. She's a beauty, ain't she?" She giggled like an idiot, her tongue clacking behind toothless gums, and he gave a gravelly snicker that made Gisburne feel physically sick.

"Like what you see, eh, gentlemen?" leered master Bigot, and gave her a squeeze. "Sixpence buys 'er for your bed, to warm you up whenever you so please." On cue, and with all the passion of a fishwife gutting a haddock, Custancia hitched up her skirt to the knee, pushed her ham-like arms together so her generous breasts bulged still further and gave a gap-toothed but vacuous grin. Bigot leaned forward, confidentially. "There's nothing she won't do."

Gisburne's hand went to the pommel of his sword – and by great effort of will remained there. "You are most generous, Master Bigot," he said. "But I couldn't possibly take your money. We'll just knock the sixpence off the rent." And with that, he turned and walked to the wooden stair.

"Wha – ?" said Master Bigot. "But I..."

"Goodnight, Master Bigot!" called Gisburne. Bigot turned to Galfrid for support – but the squire simply smiled, and turned on his heel to follow his master.

"New lodgings, Galfrid," hissed Gisburne as he climbed the stair, still gripping the sword pommel. "Before I have to kill Master Bigot."

"How long have I got?" asked Galfrid. Gisburne paused at the top of the stairs, before the rickety door. As he did so a great, gruff "Ooooh!" reverberated from below.

"If I stuff my ears with wool, I may just hold out till morning," said Gisburne through clenched teeth.

Galfrid gave a world-weary nod, then turned to get the rest of their baggage. As he passed the still bemused Bigot, the squire raised a finger and poked it at their host's face.

"And if any of your lackwit customers tries to fuck my horse," he said, "I'll cut your balls off."

XXIV

The Tower of London
20 May, 1193

PRINCE JOHN WAS still abed when Gisburne arrived at the Tower next morning.

Never an early riser when left to his own devices – unless there was good hunting to be had – the Prince finally appeared clad in a strange gown suited neither to sleeping nor the rigours of the day. It was, explained John with some pride, for that state in between the two, which, when he was in one of his more indolent moods, could last longer than either.

Gisburne's own night had passed much as expected – slowly – and he had wasted no time in quitting Master Bigot's wretched establishment as soon as he was able. Bigot, to whom Galfrid had unfortunately given the impression that they would be staying an entire month, had ranted at the squire as he saddled the horses in the yard, spittle flying from his fat lips, claiming he had given them a special price only because of the promised length of their stay.

Gisburne, reaching his wits' end at overhearing the outburst, had marched down the stair, put his sword point under Bigot's wobbling, fleshy chin and told him he wouldn't stay a minute longer in his rat-infested shithole even if under threat of death – and if Master Bigot were to threaten him with death, then he would be forced to respond in kind.

Bigot, having involuntarily soiled his drawers, withdrew without further comment.

Galfrid had then set to the task of finding more suitable lodgings – this time benefitting from an early morning start – whilst Gisburne, with a curious sense of *déjà vu,* had once again run the gauntlet of the Tower guard. Eventually, Fitz Thomas was again persuaded to appear, laughing amiably and looking as dishevelled as ever. Rumpled, affable, a little eccentric – but not too much. A friend to his men. A man of the people. "Sir Guy!" he had said. "What a pleasant surprise to see you again!" As far as Gisburne was concerned, it was neither pleasant, nor a surprise.

Prince John showed no irritation at being roused from his bed, but at the mention of the shenanigans at the gate flew into a violent rage. "Who do these bastards think they *are?*" he roared, hurling a stool across his chamber. A leg snapped off as it struck the wall and somersaulted the length of the room. "That smiling snake Fitz Thomas is already dropping dark hints that I should further reduce my retinue – *for the better running of the fortress,* he said. Imbecile! And as for de Coutances... Do you know what he did? He paid off my guard at the agreed fee – the fee that was supposed to secure their services until August. He didn't even haggle! Now I must find the money to pay him for the guard I don't even have. And the damned man talks to me like an equal! No, worse – like *he* is a king! These damned people with their damned sense of entitlement. Maybe Hood did not have such a bad idea, robbing from the rich to give to the poor..." Gisburne did not think it timely to tell him Hood did no such thing. "I'd like to take their unearned wealth and give it to those more deserving! Which would be anyone!"

It took half an hour and three quarters of a flask of wine for him to calm himself – but when he finally succeeded in doing so, the transformation was swift, and total. In moments he reverted entirely to his urbane, sardonic self, as if the other had been some dark interloper.

"Now we are safely in London," said Gisburne, eager to move things on, "I must ask you about the Irish expedition."

"Ah," said John. "That." He took another deep draught of wine. "Not my finest hour." He sniggered at his own words. "No, not even *my* finest hour!"

"All of those so far killed were there with you," said Gisburne. "If we can establish who else was in your party, and ascertain which among them are now in London, we may anticipate the Red Hand's next move."

"And warn them, too, of course," said John. To this, Gisburne said nothing. John thought a moment, then threw up his hands in exasperation. "God's nails, there must have been three hundred knights in all..."

"But the victims belonged to a core group, did they not? Those closest to you personally?"

John nodded. "True enough. But even of those..." He puffed out his cheeks and widened his eyes. "Perhaps I might remember half a dozen or so. Maybe more. But I was not even nineteen, and hardly the most interested in what was going on around me. Too self-absorbed. That was my entire problem."

"If we can establish a list of those men," said Gisburne. "The ones whose loss would hurt you the most..."

"I'll do what I can," said John with a shrug. Then he held a finger aloft. "But there is another way – to be absolutely sure. At Milford, prior to departure for Ireland, the knights accompanying me put their names to a document. Those most favoured – the inner circle, if you will – had their names writ first, and larger than the rest. Of these there were fewer than twenty."

"This document," said Gisburne. "What was its purpose?"

The Prince shrugged. "Pure affectation. An act of youthful exuberance – and idiotic vanity. You will know that prior to their departure from Dives, the Conqueror's knights had their names put upon a scroll to mark the event – so they could show later that they were there. They had a sense they were making history. They were right. We flattered ourselves that our endeavour was of similar import. We were mistaken." He gave a bitter laugh. "The Milford Roll! What fools we were. If we'd only known what a shambles it would become – how much we would later wish to forget it..."

"Can you tell me more of what happened in Ireland?" asked Gisburne.

John winced. "You must understand," he said, "that we were all young. Well, most of us... The older ones tolerated our antics. None wished to upset their Prince – poor little John Lackland, who suddenly had been given a land all his own to play with." He sighed. "Did you know my father wanted to have me made King of Ireland? He even had the crown made. Gold, with peacock feathers – quite a beautiful thing. But the bastard Pope wouldn't allow it. So I was merely to be *Lord* of Ireland – whatever that meant." He gave another humourless laugh. "Even that was a joke."

"You said there were people in Ireland who might wish you harm. I need to know more of that – what offence was caused."

John slumped in his chair. "It began the very first day, when we disembarked at Dublin. We thought it amusing to humiliate our hosts – made fun of their long beards. I had Eustace Fitz Warren tug on one to see if it was real. Not surprisingly, these noble chieftains did not take kindly to being ridiculed, or regarded as barbarians. Over the next few weeks we travelled the land, squandering my father's barrels of silver pennies on our own pleasure while the already tenuous grip my family had upon Ireland slipped steadily away." It was the first time Gisburne had ever heard Prince John refer to his father or brother as family. "I still hold the title, you know," said John, wistfully. He shook his head. "Worthless. Wasted."

"This chieftain – the one you say you humiliated. Can you recall his name?"

John turned up his hands in defeat. "The names were all unfamiliar," he said.

"What of this Milford Roll? This list?" asked Gisburne. "Where may I find it?"

"There is a copy in Nottingham," said John. "I will send for it. Today. It can be with us within the week."

Gisburne nodded his approval.

"I had wondered if perhaps you'd seen it before," said John.

"Me?" Gisburne looked at him, puzzled. "Why?"

"Because it was your father who drew it up, of course."

Gisburne stared at him in mute astonishment.

"You did know he was with us in Ireland...?" added John, and watched as Gisburne's astonishment turned to shock. "Ah. You didn't know..."

"He went to Ireland when I was a boy. Or so I believe. Something for King Henry. I wasn't meant to know."

John nodded. "This was considerably later. When you were in the wilderness..." When he was a mercenary, John meant, but he had the good grace not to say it. "Don't let it trouble you. It means nothing that you didn't know it."

Inconsequential though it seemed, and despite the Prince's reassurance, it did trouble Gisburne. It troubled him that there was something that his father had kept from him. And it troubled him that it was connected, however tangentially, with the Red Hand. It seemed that everywhere around him were connections to that shady figure. Yet, for all that he touched upon things that were so familiar in Gisburne's life, the man itself – at the very heart of it all – remained no more distinct or substantial than a ghost.

These thoughts brought Gisburne back to his key reason for visiting John – something, he sensed, the Prince would not relish.

"There is one other thing I need," he said.

John spread his hands wide. "Name it."

Gisburne turned away from his master. "I need to see him," he said.

"Him?"

"The prisoner."

"Oh," said John, nodding slowly. "*Him*. He has a name, you know."

Gisburne did not respond. If he had a name, a real name, it was surely long forgotten. "I need" – he corrected himself – "*request* permission to see the prisoner. Today."

"Today?" said John. "Is it really that urgent?"

"Perhaps. I don't know."

"You won't try to kill him, will you?"

Gisburne turned to the Prince with a quizzical look. "Why would I do that?"

"You tried it before."

"That was different."

John nodded in acknowledgement. "It was different. But we can't have it happen here. I'm not like my brother. I believe in at least a pretence of due process."

"And you shall have it..."

"Without law," said John, "we are nothing."

"You shall have it," snapped Gisburne. He instantly regretted his irritation, but John remained unruffled.

"Well," he said. "May I at least know why you request this?"

Gisburne took a deep breath and released it slowly. "The Red Hand's actions are in some way connected to the day of the execution. I believe that is when he means to strike against you."

"He?" said John. "It is a man after all, then...?" He waved it away as a bad joke. "You are sure of this?"

"As sure as I can be."

"They are connected?" John stood, and paced, the full import of the possibility now weighing upon him. "How? And why?"

"I don't know. But we perhaps have the means to find out. In a cell in this very castle."

John was silent for a moment. "I seem to recall you questioned him for over a month and discovered nothing," he said. "What makes you think it'll be any different now?"

"Because now I know things he doesn't. You know how he hates anyone knowing more than he. Perhaps it will draw him out."

John nodded slowly. "Perhaps."

"Are you afraid he won't talk?"

"No," said John. "I'm afraid he *will*."

Gisburne stared at his prince, his brow creased into a frown. What in God's name did he mean by that?

John sighed deeply. "He talks the birds down from the trees. Convinces men black is white. Turns brother against brother and son against father..." The Prince thought about those last words for a moment. "Hmm. Bad example..." He gave a sheepish smile, and a shrug. "But you know as well as I do that his words infect like a plague. They spread chaos and doubt; they destroy more surely than fire or tempest. They tear at the very fundamentals that hold this frail universe together."

"Do you seriously believe I am susceptible to his poison?" said Gisburne.

"Do you seriously believe you are not?"

"I've endured it for long enough," said Gisburne. "There's nothing he can tell me that I haven't heard a thousand times."

"Except what you most seek – what he has yet to divulge," said John. And it seemed then that a troubled look came over him. Hastily, he looked away.

"Please," said Gisburne. "I ask little of you. This is my one request."

At length, John nodded. "You do ask little," he said. "And you give much." He frowned, seeming deep in thought, as if his mind were reaching far back into some dark recess. Finally, he looked up. "You may see him."

"Now? Today?"

"Now, and whenever you have need – until St John's Day." He smiled. "After that, his usefulness will be... limited."

"Thank you, my lord," said Gisburne, bowing. "Thank you..."

"Before you get too overwhelmed by my generosity," John said, with a wry smile, "remember that it is *my* life that stands to be saved if you succeed. It's in my interest to accede to your wishes."

"Your safety is my one object," said Gisburne, and bowed his head again.

John smiled again. "You don't have to lie, Sir Guy. You were never so simple a man as to have just one object." His smile faded, and gave way, it seemed to Gisburne, to the same introspective look he had seen moments before.

"But with that safety in mind," said Gisburne, hesitantly, "I would ask..." His voice faded out.

"Yes?"

"I would ask that you do not leave the Tower. If there are goods you wish to buy or people you wish to see, have them come to you."

John affected a wry smile. "So, for the coming month I am to be a prisoner within these walls, too?" he said. "Well, isn't that a turn up! The outlaw and the Prince who caught him, locked in the self-same dungeon."

"In here, we have full command of our surroundings," said Gisburne. "But out there..." He gestured towards the great maze of streets that lay beyond the stone walls.

"Yes, yes, I know," said John. "*Control the battlefield...*" He nodded. "And I will comply with your request. To the letter."

The Prince averted his eyes, then turned away altogether, and did not look back.

"Go now. Speak with him. But whatever he says – whatever revelation spills from those lips – try to keep that one object of yours in mind. Not for my sake, but for your own."

XXV

THERE WERE NO dungeons at the Tower. No cells for prisoners, no chambers of torture. It had not been built as a prison, but as a military stronghold and a palace (in the Norman mind, the two were not only compatible, but identical) – both instrument and symbol of the Conqueror's power over the conquered.

With the exception of one night in November, 1191 – about which the people would never be permitted to know – it had lived up to its reputation as the most secure fortress in the land. But it followed that if it was effective at keeping people out, it could be equally effective at keeping them in. And so, every once in a while, it had found itself pressed into service as a gaol. This honour was reserved for only a very select breed of prisoner – those either of noble birth, or considered so dangerous that no other prison could be trusted to hold them. Frequently both.

Often, these were men who threatened the very stability of the realm – those so significant that they could not simply be got rid of without questions being asked. The natural instinct of any ordinary man would be to put himself as far from such a threat as possible. The solution of a wise monarch, however, was to keep it close, contained, under watch and under guard.

And so it was that, at times, the King and the King's bitterest enemy would reside under the same roof.

The guards – respectful, but efficient – insisted on taking Gisburne's sword and knife from him before he entered. "You too?" he said, John's words still ringing in his ears: *You won't try to kill him, will you?* The first guard looked back at him with a blank expression.

"You think you need to protect him from me?" clarified Gisburne.

"No sire," replied the guard. "This is to protect *you*."

"There is a line drawn upon the ground," said the second guard. "Do not cross it. That is the limit of his chains."

"Do not give him anything, or take anything he offers," added the first. "The door will be locked behind you. Rap on it three times and we will come."

"We'll know it is you, sire," explained the second. "He cannot get within ten feet of that door."

Gisburne nodded. Then they turned the iron key, and shot back the bolts.

THE CELL WAS in one of the newest parts of the castle complex – the stout octagonal tower that overlooked the Thames, at the south-western corner of the new curtain wall built under Longchamp's short-lived custodianship.

Gisburne had noted on past occasions that there was a window in each of the tower's sides, including those overlooking the river. Evidently, most of them had been blocked up, for inside the elegantly vaulted chamber, all was dark but for a small pool of light cast on the stone floor by a single remaining opening – barely more than an arrow slit. Across the floor, a slash of dirty white chalk marked the chains' reach.

As Gisburne's eyes adjusted to the gloom, he began to make out spidery markings upon the walls – dozens, hundreds of lines etched into the surface of the stone. There were crude figures – some on horseback, some bearing swords – bizarre plants and animals, arcane symbols, numbers and letters both familiar and obscure, spirals and straight lines and stars colliding and intersecting and bisecting each other.

Sat against one such wall on the far side of the pool of light, arms on his knees, his head bowed, was a large, ragged figure. A familiar figure. As the door closed and locked behind Gisburne, the man looked up. He sat forward, looming out of the shadows. A broad grin, revealing even white teeth, spread across his face.

"Hello, Guy," said Hood.

Gisburne stared up at the tiny window, then turned once about the room. "Do you know why I am here, Robert?"

Hood looked about the interior. "Well, I should imagine to visit me. Unless there are other attractions in here that have escaped my notice."

Gisburne gave an involuntary snort of a laugh. A response formed in his head. He suppressed it.

"I'd have tidied up if I'd known," said Hood. "What do you think of the place?" He gestured to his weird gallery of carvings.

"Nothing a little whitewash wouldn't fix," said Gisburne. Hood sniggered. *No*, said a voice in Gisburne's head. It was de Gaillon's. *Hold back. Do not engage on his terms...*

He took a deep breath. "And do you know why you're here?"

Hood smiled and screwed up his eyes. "That's a strange question, Guy."

"But can you answer it, Robert?"

Hood laughed. "Why do you keep calling me that?"

"Have you forgotten about Sicily? Byzantium? The Holy Land? Or are you just pretending they didn't happen?"

Hood laughed with gusto and slapped his leg in delight, as if all those memories had flooded back to him in that moment. "D'you remember that Reynald de Châtillon? What a character he was! Did you know Saladin – the Sultan himself – cut off poor Reynald's head with his own sword? Imagine! What a way to go..."

"You were happy to be called Robert then."

Hood sighed. "Yes, but do I *look* like a Robert? I mean, really?"

"You're avoiding my question," said Gisburne. Since the name irked Hood, he continued using it. "Why are you here, Robert?"

Hood gave another laugh – of exasperation this time. "You caught me, Guy. Fair and square. It's just what we do, isn't it?"

"No. It isn't just what we 'do.'"

"Well, it's what I do, old man. What else is there?"

"Order," said Gisburne. "Truth. Compassion. Law."

Hood guffawed, as if Gisburne had told him an outrageous joke. Gisburne waited for the laughter to die before speaking again.

"You are here, Robert, because you violated those things. Broke the law. Killed innocent people. Left chaos in your wake." He suddenly felt like he was his own father, delivering one of those moralising speeches he'd so hated as a child.

"Are you always this serious?" Hood said. "It must be exhausting."

It was. But at least it was sane.

"Do you know what happens on the twenty-fourth day of June?" said Gisburne. "On St John's Day?"

Hood shrugged, picked up a chunk of stale bread from the stone floor and gnawed at it. "It's the day they mean to kill me."

"*Execute* you, Robert. For your crimes. Theft, abduction, assault, murder, treason... It's a long list."

"Don't forget poaching the king's deer," Hood added, cheerfully. There was no remorse. Not even defiance – not in the normal sense. Gisburne doubted Hood even knew what a crime was, beyond some arbitrary rule in the great game.

"Well, let's talk about something else then," said Gisburne. "A friend of yours." For the first time, a look of hesitancy flickered across Hood's features. His hand went to the nondescript, blackened copper disc that hung around his neck – that had been there as long as Gisburne had known him. It was Hood's 'tell' – a mark of uncertainty. It came rarely, but Gisburne had known Hood long enough to have identified it. When Hood had first been thrown in a cell at Nottingham prior to his transfer to the Tower, the guards had wanted to take it off him. Gisburne instructed them otherwise. It was far more use to him where it was.

With a curious feeling of satisfaction that struck him as almost perverse, he turned, so Hood could no longer see his face. "The one known as the Red Hand..."

"Never heard of him. Did you say he was supposed to be a friend?"

"Sorry, I forgot. You don't have friends..."

"Nonsense!" Hood laughed. "You're my friend."

Gisburne ignored the claim. "Perhaps this one is better described as an *associate*. A fellow criminal. I can't believe that a man in your position wouldn't know about him." He looked back at the prisoner.

Hood stroked his chin and made a great show of looking quizzical. "Hmmm. Red Hand... Red Hand... No, don't think I've had the pleasure."

"Well, he knows you," said Gisburne. Again, the flicker of doubt flashed across Hood's face. The fingers toyed with the crude talisman. Gisburne turned away.

"Strange name," said Hood, chewing noisily on the bread. "Will you catch him red-handed?" He chuckled at his own joke.

"I mean to," said Gisburne. The sound of chewing ceased.

"Ah! I see!" said Hood. "You think I know this Red Hand, and so you want me to help capture him..." Gisburne turned back to see Hood grinning and rubbing his hands together with glee. The gesture reminded him of a fly.

"I had thought that," said Gisburne. "But..."

"But..?"

"Now that I'm here, I just don't think you can."

"Don't think I can..?" This time, the laugh that accompanied his reply was devoid of humour.

"It's clear you don't know anything that can help me," said Gisburne. "Nothing of any use. It was a foolish notion." He turned to the door. "I'll leave you to your scratchings."

Gisburne heard the chains tighten behind him. "So you're just going to wait for another knight to have his head stove in, are you?" blurted Hood. "Another number?"

Gisburne stopped dead, his hand still raised to rap upon the door. He turned on Hood. "What do you mean? Another number?"

"Another victim!" laughed Hood.

"No!" said Gisburne. He crossed the line and grabbed Hood by the throat. "You said another *number*... What did you mean by that?"

Hood looked into Gisburne's eyes without blinking, a slow smile spreading across his face. "You're right, Guy," he said, spreading his hands apart. "As always. I know nothing. See nothing. These walls are my world."

Gisburne pushed Hood away. Hood staggered against the wall, and chuckled to himself.

"Sorry, old man," he said. "I suppose you'll just have to wait, after all." He puffed out his cheeks and shook his head. "It certainly will be a shame seeing more good men die needlessly."

Gisburne wanted to knock him down – to dash his brains out against the stone. It was just as John had predicted. But he would not – could not. "Can it be prevented?" he said. He did not look Hood in the eye as he spoke. It felt like an admission of defeat to be asking it outright – a wild swipe with a blunt weapon. First blood to Hood.

"Anything can be prevented," he said.

"Not anything," snapped Gisburne. "Not death."

"Well," said Hood. "Postponed, then." He smiled. "A sense of your strategy would help me make a properly informed judgement. What's going on in that mind of yours?"

Gisburne said nothing. This was not how it was meant to go. And the very last person he wanted in his mind was Hood.

"You do have some idea who he means to strike, I suppose?" Hood continued.

"Yes," said Gisburne. Even as he said it, he knew he was giving up too much.

Hood nodded. "And I suppose you mean to warn them?" said Hood, wearily. At that, Gisburne averted his eyes. Hood laughed. "My God! You don't, do you? You really don't..." And he chuckled with delight.

"There are too many," protested Gisburne. "He has never yet been stopped. It would serve no purpose."

"Wrong!" crowed Hood. "It serves *your* purpose. The Red Hand may be watching. Approach any one of them and you risk him knowing – revealing how much *you* know. You could get them to pack up and leave. Save their lives. But far better to use them as bait. That's what I'd do!"

Gisburne lunged at him in anger. Hood dodged back. Gisburne turned, fists clenched, barely holding himself in check... Hood clapped, his chains rattling. "Well, I am impressed," he sniggered. "You know, Guy, you're far more like me than anyone realises. Even you."

Gisburne had no appetite for games. Nor for the conversation to continue any further. Maybe John was right. Maybe this was a mistake.

"Just tell me how we can stop him," he said.

Hood leaned forward, and raised both wrists, the shackles turned towards his interrogator.

"Take these off," he said. "And together we'll catch him. I won't run. Cross my heart and hope to die..." His chains clanked as he crossed himself. "Come on, Guy! It'd be fun, wouldn't it? You and me against this crazed killer. We'd be the talk of the town!"

Gisburne stared at him – into the unblinking, endless void behind the outlaw's eyes – uncertain whether he was simply playing a game, or actually meant it. Was there even a difference in his mind? "You know I can't do that," he said.

"Well, then," Hood sighed. "I suppose you're on your own, old man. And so are they." He turned, and sat cross-legged upon the ground, and – taking up a small flake of flint – began to scratch a new line upon the wall, humming to himself.

Gisburne rapped on the door with clenched knuckles – so hard it shook on its hinges. There was no sound of movement beyond. He rapped again, harder this time, feeling a sudden urgent need to get out of that mad cell. He went to rap a third time when, finally, the bolts were shot back.

Hood had known that knights were being slain. That they were found with their skulls crushed. And then there was the mention of the numbers... They could be lucky guesses, but some instinct – or was it fear? – told Gisburne otherwise. Somehow, Hood knew.

"No one is to talk to him. Or even nearby," he barked at the guards when the door had once again crashed shut behind him. "Not a word, you hear?" Both nodded.

As he strode away from the prison tower, fingers tightened into fists, he could hear the sound of Hood's laughter echoing from the high window.

XXVI

THEIR NEW LODGINGS were airy and spacious – a long, upstairs room split into two by the intrusion of a large chimney breast, with shuttered windows at either end that looked out front and back. The latched door to the stairway opened into the back half of the space, just beyond the bulge of the chimney breast, and the beamed ceilings were low and sloping on either side. There was little furniture to speak of, beyond the simple beds and single small table, but it was clean and well-kept, and at the back was a generous yard with a good, dry stable fit for three horses. As its owner, the diminutive but punctilious Widow Fleet, had pointed out, it was also ideally located close to the heart of the city and within easy striking distance of the Tower, whilst boasting excellent views across Eastchepe.

"Perfect," said Gisburne. "How much?"

"A shilling a month," said Galfrid. "Which is daylight robbery." He shot a sideways glance at the Widow Fleet. "How this came to be called East*chepe,* I can't imagine..."

The Widow Fleet's face – somewhat reminiscent of a surprised shrew – reddened, but she was not to be defeated. "That comes with all washing done. And all your food for another sixpence..."

"Better value than the last thing we were offered for sixpence," muttered Gisburne. He turned to the good Widow. "Let's say *two* shillings a month for us to be left entirely alone. No food, no washing, and no interruptions." And he gave her his most charming of smiles.

Her eyes widened. She appeared uncertain, at first, how to take the offer. Under Gisburne's unrelenting gaze, she became suddenly coy – even a little flustered. "Of course, sir. As you wish. Most generous! It shall be exactly as you say – though I be mistress of this house, this shall be your domain. Yours alone. You shall be master of it entire. There shall be not one –"

"Thank you, Widow Fleet," interrupted Gisburne. He took a step toward her. She took two steps back.

"If there is anything you require in the meantime..."

"My squire shall see to it, madam," said Gisburne, and continued herding her towards the stair.

Finally getting the message, she bowed and scurried away. She was part way down the stairs when her head appeared once again through the doorway.

"And if anything should fail to please, then..."

"Then I will tell Prince John," said Gisburne. "Who will convey it to his brother the King."

The Widow turned scarlet, looked as if she were about to faint, then rallied and, with a muttered exclamation of "God's teeth," disappeared back around the chimney breast.

"Wait," said Gisburne, before she had even reached the stair. "There is one thing, after all..."

The Widow's face re-emerged, a picture of expectation.

"There is?" said Galfrid.

"Something you might fetch before we get settled..."

Bit by bit, she crept back into the room, like a small creature wary of a predator.

"Well," Galfrid patted his stomach. "Now you come to mention it..."

"Whitewash," said Gisburne.

"Whitewash?" said Galfrid. "I was thinking more of bread and ale..."

"I think this interior could do with a little freshening up. Widow Fleet? What say you?"

"I shall organise it sir! At the first opportunity!"

"Sooner," said Gisburne. "We're going out to get some food." He patted Galfrid's stomach. "Given the ready availability of goods and services in this great city, there's no reason why the painting could not be done by the time we return, is there?"

The Widow looked suddenly flustered again, as if failure to deliver such a service would result in a national scandal. "At such short notice, I..."

"I'll pay double the going rate."

She swallowed hard. "Well, there is Master Birkenschawe, but..."

"Excellent! Then it's decided. Thank you, Widow Fleet."

With an even greater sense of urgency, she picked up her skirts and hurried away. Gisburne heard her retreating down the creaky stair, breathlessly muttering "Whitewash... Whitewash..." over and over.

He turned to his squire. "I have no idea how you found this place," he said with a smile. "But well done, Galfrid. Well done."

Galfrid looked at his master in amazement, as if such words of encouragement were entirely foreign to him. But they were heartfelt. For days, Gisburne had been focused on one immediate goal – the delivery of the Prince to the Tower. The successful completion of that task had – thanks largely to the residents of the royal palace, and the nature of London itself – proved oddly anticlimactic. It had left him drained and frustrated, his brain overloaded. But on this bright new morning, with new rooms secured, he felt, at last, that the real work could begin. It seemed strangely paradoxical, given the grim nature of the task ahead – and of their adversary. Even inappropriate. But he could not deny the heady excitement that now gripped him – a feeling, he only now realised, that had been absent so long, he had ceased even to miss it. For the first time in months – since Jerusalem, in fact – he felt vital, and alive.

"WHITEWASH..?" SAID GALFRID as they stepped out onto Eastchepe.

"That's only half the story. To complete it, I need something else." He looked about him. "Although where to find it in this endless sprawl..."

"I may have an answer," said Galfrid. He took Gisburne's shoulder, and turned him towards the opposite side of the street. "You asked me how I found this place." He pointed. "That's how."

Squatting against a wall, taking in the sun, his eyes flicking left and right as if constantly vigilant, was a young boy of little more than eleven or twelve. His clothes were mostly rags, but amongst his apparel were signs of enterprise. His belt was of new Italian leather and he had slung upon it a fine, sheathed knife. On his head – though too large for it – was a fine wool brimmed cap, and on his feet boots that would cost half a page's annual wage.

"His name is Hamon," said Galfrid. "I spied him on Love Lane trying to relieve a country farmer of a cow without his knowledge. Clearly he was an individual of resource, so I thought I'd put it to constructive use. I'll wager he knows these streets better than anyone."

Gisburne smiled. "Well, let's see what he can do."

"Hamon?" called Galfrid. The boy immediately jumped to his feet. Galfrid tossed him a silver penny. Hamon caught it, bit it, and shoved it into his hose. "You said you could get me anything... Did you mean that?"

"Anyfing sir," said Hamon. "Mirrors. Lemmins. A monkey."

"How about some sticks of charcoal?" said Gisburne.

Hamon grinned like one who had just found the bean in the Christmas cake, then without another word, clutching his cap tight upon his head, pelted off westward along Eastchepe and disappeared into the crowd opposite Crooked Lane.

"I think we may assume that's a 'yes,'" said Gisburne.

XXVII

Eastchepe
24 May, 1193

EXACTLY ONE MONTH before the day of Hood's execution, Hamon brought news that proved his worth beyond a whole stack of pennies.

For the first four days at Widow Fleet's they had done nothing. Of the Red Hand there was no sign. John remained at the Tower; Hood, in his cell. Gisburne and Galfrid simply ate, slept, and grew accustomed to London life.

Thanks to the transformative efforts of Master Birkenschawe – who was still finishing up when Galfrid and Gisburne had returned that day – the place almost glowed. Apparently well used to Widow Fleet's fussing, Master Birkenschawe tolerated it with infinite patience, and just once, when her back was turned, he rolled his eyes at Galfrid and Gisburne. All three smiled as if party to some silent pact.

Though Widow Fleet did not yet know it, this miraculous transformation was to be as short-lived as Gisburne's bright mood. Even as she had regarded the fresh white walls on that first day – smiling and clapping her hands, the paint still glistening wet – Gisburne had taken delivery of a small, dirty sack, which he had placed in the front corner, just past his bed, and beyond Widow Fleet's inquisitive gaze. Then he had ushered her out, with a gentle reminder about the privacy he had bought for his extra shilling.

For some time after, she had remained as good as her word.

Those were strange days. An odd period of peace in this most hectic of climes. It might almost have been a holiday, but neither could relax. Galfrid had the sense that any respite was momentary – merely the calm before the storm. And by only the second day, the combination of enforced leisure and the restless turmoil of London had begun to grate upon his master. And so they waited. For what, neither dared say.

Gisburne was not used to the cerebral life. De Gaillon had always warned of the dangers of action without thought, but thought without action – without the possibility of action as a consequence of it – *that* ground his spirit, leaving him irritable and exhausted.

As if in confirmation of an impending tempest, the days grew thick and airless. Every movement raised a sweat. Nights became unbearably hot. Gisburne took to having the shutters flung open despite the noise of the street, and when sleep eluded him altogether would sit in semi-darkness looking out over London, still waiting, the plaintive sound of his hurdy gurdy drifting on the still, sultry air. Galfrid – too hot and tired either to complain or to bother finding material to stuff his ears – would lay and listen, resigned to it, and once or twice, quite against expectation, found himself lulled into sleep.

On the afternoon of the fifth day, Galfrid returned to their rooms to find Widow Fleet in a flap. As he pushed the front door open, juggling the latch and a weighty sack of comestibles, she was on him like a wasp on jam.

"He's gone mad!" she shrieked, plucking at his sleeve.

"Please, please – calm yourself, Widow Fleet," said Galfrid, sensing even as he said it that his advice was probably arriving thirty years too late.

"Calm myself?" she cried. "How can I calm myself? He's making a mess all over my lovely white walls!"

He had always known that, eventually, she would discover it – and had warned the dismissive Gisburne to that effect. "Oh, hardly a mess..." said Galfrid, sliding past her and backing towards the foot of the stairs. "A few scribblings, that's all... It's just his way."

The charcoal and whitewash, Galfrid had soon discovered, were the means by which Gisburne meant to record key facts pertaining to the Red Hand – numbers, dates, names. Galfrid wondered if it had been inspired by the Red Hand himself, and the marks upon the wall of Bardulf's castle.

It was, without doubt, a perfectly practical solution. Even if Gisburne awoke at night, with some small fragment of information bouncing around in his head, he could immediately add it to one of his lists – no quills, no ink, no scrabbling for parchment. By this method, the wall by his bed had been transformed into a blurry aide mémoire. During the day, and in a mood where he sometimes would not speak for hours, Gisburne would occasionally sit and stare at it, as if doing so for long enough might unlock its secrets.

None of this, of course, meant anything to Widow Fleet.

"A few scribblings?" she hooted. "It's everywhere! Numbers and runes and dancing men and heaven alone knows what!"

Galfrid stifled a chuckle. "Dancing men? I hardly think –"

But she leaned in close to him, eyes as wide as meat platters. "I tell you I'm a-feared of what he's doing up there, Squire Galfrid. It's sorcery, that's what it is..." She threw up her hands. "I'll not have sorcery in this house! I never have, and I never will!"

"Widow Fleet," sighed Galfrid, by now backing up the stairs. "I can assure you it is not sorcery. Just a few marks to help him remember. He's not used to the refinements of city life."

"You tell him," she said, pointing a finger. "I'll not have it!"

Nodding and smiling pleasantly as he ascended, clutching the sack from which a cheese was threatening to escape, Galfrid pushed against the door at the top to find it shut and bolted. Securing the cheese under his chin, he booted the door several times by way of a knock. Almost immediately, it flew open.

"What now?" barked Gisburne, his face like thunder. "Oh, it's you..." He pulled the door wide to admit his squire – and both saw the Widow Fleet launching a fresh assault up the narrow stair.

"You tell him, Squire Galfrid," she yelped. "It won't do!"

"Yes, thank you, goodbye," snapped Gisburne, and attempted to push the door closed before Galfrid was entirely through it. As the squire squeezed by, Galfrid noticed that the fingers of both Gisburne's hands were as black as Nyght's mane.

"You tell him!" said Widow Fleet, trying to force her tiny frame through the door. "My lovely new paint!"

"*My* new paint," corrected Gisburne. "Your walls. My paint. Goodbye." And he slammed the door in her face.

Galfrid opened his mouth to speak, but Gisburne's hand silenced him. For a moment, he looked as if about to speak, but then moved off into the larger of the two rooms that he had claimed as his own, and stood, framed beside the chimney breast, brow knotted, staring intently at the expanse of wall before him.

"She's just a harmless old woman," he said. "And it is her house..."

"You haven't had her squawking in your ear all day..." And with that, he withdrew further into his chamber, and out of sight.

Galfrid stepped forward from the door and dumped the sack on the table, then followed his master. "Well, anyway," he said. "I got us more cheese and a good smoked ham. And wine. And the poulterer on the corner said..." His words stopped dead. He stared. As he had passed around the chimney breast, a ball of cheese still clutched in his hand, the source of Widow Fleet's consternation had been revealed.

Where once had been a few rough scribblings, occupying a small section of the wall, there was now an army of black figures spreading like vermin across the entire expanse. The few simple records had grown and multiplied into a baffling array of spidery figures – words and numbers, lists and scraps of poetry, measurements and passages from the Bible. Some parts had already been struck through, or wiped away entirely to leave a dark smear – the backdrop to a fresh notation. Others had been circumscribed within heavily drawn frames of black, as if to emphasise them. A few were writ straight, but most were askew, or veering at angles as if threatening to slide off the wall altogether.

Most bizarre, however, was – between the words and numbers and smudged fingermarks and handprints – a succession of crude, often half-finished images. Faces. Bits of armour. Weapons of various kinds. Maps. Plans of castles. Animals both real and imaginary. Disembodied heads. A dragon. Sketches of devices, including some kind of siphon. And there, too, were Widow Fleet's "dancing men" – a row of over a dozen small figures, which seemed to process across the foot of the sooty slope. From the heads of perhaps half of these, flying up at an angle like banners, were scrawled names. Among them were the names of the dead, alongside several more that Galfrid did not recognise. One had above it only a single letter: 'G.'

He stared at the apocalyptic frieze. No longer was this simply a record of a few scraps of information – it was more, even, than a chronicle of the Red Hand's crimes, and the clues that might ultimately reveal his identity. It somehow encompassed everything they had encountered on their journey to this point, every thought that had formed in Gisburne's waking head – and perhaps his nightmares as well. And, as with a nightmare, much of it appeared utterly unfathomable.

"Christ's boots..." muttered Galfrid.

"It's my mosaic," said Gisburne, awkwardly, stick of charcoal in hand. "My Monreale. What do you think?"

Galfrid stared, open mouthed. "She was right," said Galfrid. "You have gone mad."

"If I have," said Gisburne, irritably, "then the Widow is to blame..." He gave a brief, dismissive laugh – almost, Galfrid thought, in a kind of embarrassment, as if suddenly aware that he had revealed too much of himself. "I had to *do* something. To form some kind of picture."

"A picture of what, though?" said Galfrid. He could discern no coherence in this crazed disorder.

Gisburne screwed up his eyes. "Something will come. It has to. A pattern of some sort." Galfrid recalled his master saying that Gilbert de Gaillon had been a great one for visualising battle plans. *If you can't see your victory clearly in here,* he would say, tapping his head, *then you'll never take the right steps to achieving it.*

There had been no fresh information with which to work, and there would be no sight of the Milford Roll for another couple of days at least.

They had been waiting – and, although neither wished to say it, that meant another death. But now, Galfrid began to wonder about the unknown names upon the wall – other members of John's retinue in Ireland, he supposed, who, presumably, were also still alive. If that was the case, could not steps have been taken with regard to them?

"Dammit!" said Gisburne, and he hurled the stick of charcoal across the room. It struck the open shutter and broke apart, half of it flying out of the window. From the marks on the shutters and elsewhere, it appeared that a good amount of the stuff may have gone a similar way. Not that its loss mattered much – Hamon had brought enough of the stuff to last years. It had apparently come from an armourer's at the northern end of Coleman Street, though how he had secured it, Gisburne and Galfrid had not asked.

It was as Galfrid stood there, contemplating the frenzied mural with its mystery names, that a new altercation erupted on the street below. "God, what now?" said Gisburne, and moved to the window. Two voices were raised in violent dispute, and getting more heated by the minute: one, a boy's, making insistent entreaties, the other, ever shriller and more outraged, Widow Fleet's.

"That damned woman really does mean to send me mad," said Gisburne, and leaned out of the window to see what was happening below. A second later, he was back. "It's Hamon," he said, his expression concerned. "Were you expecting him?"

"No," said Galfrid. "Not unless..."

Both suddenly made a move for the door.

As Galfrid opened it, Gisburne peered down towards the front door. Widow Fleet was wrestling with the boy, who was insistently – desperately – trying to gain entry, ducking the Widow's swipes.

"Widow Fleet!" yelled Gisburne. "Let the boy in."

"In?" She looked horrified. "This thieving scapegrace?"

"I told 'er it's urgent!" shouted Hamon.

"Immediately," insisted Gisburne. "He has a message for me."

She harumphed and turned back to the boy. "The gentlemen is letting you in this once," she said. "But you keep your pilfering fingers to yourself!"

"Not this once, Widow Fleet," corrected Gisburne, descending the stairs, with Galfrid close behind, "but always. He's in our employ. And there may be others like him in coming days. I tell you this so you may gird your loins accordingly."

Hamon gave the Widow a smirk of victory and slithered past. She flung up her arms in exasperation and bustled off, hands over her face. Hamon was red-faced; he had clearly been running for all he was worth.

"Well?" said Gisburne, squatting down to Hamon's level, his eyes ablaze. He hardly dared to articulate the question they had been waiting a week to ask. "Have you seen him?"

Hamon, still panting, shook his head. "I ain't seen 'im. But someone 'as. I 'eared sumfink. Sumfink like you said about. A terrible attack, last night, wiv flames and a man all done up like a scaly beast."

Gisburne and Galfrid looked at each other. "Where?" said Gisburne

"A castle. Other side of the river. King Stormont, it's called. Belongs to a knight – John de Wassailly or sumfink."

Gisburne's face turned ashen. "John de Rosseley?" he ventured. Galfrid recognised the name as one of those above the dancing men on the wall.

"That's the one," said Hamon.

"Christ..." said Gisburne. He stood upright. "Not Ross..."

"You know him?" said Galfrid.

"The finest knight I ever knew," said Gisburne. There was torment in his eyes. "Christ Almighty... What have I done?"

"What have *you* done?" said Galfrid in bemusement. "You didn't do anything."

Gisburne gave a sharp, anguished laugh. "Exactly! I just let it happen. Sitting here on my stupid arse..." He kicked the stair in fury. It sent such a shudder through the house that Widow Fleet's startled head reappeared from her rooms – just in time to catch a powdering of the plaster dust that rained down.

"What in heaven..?"

"Not now, Widow Fleet!" bellowed Gisburne. She immediately withdrew. "Hood taunted me, you know – told me right to my face it'd be a shame to see more good men killed. And still I couldn't stop it. Too busy playing it like some game..."

"But he's not killed, sire," said Hamon. "That's just the fing! He's alive!"

Gisburne stared at him in astonishment. "You're certain?"

"That's what they said. Alive and well!"

"Who said?" asked Galfrid. "How did you come by this?"

"There's a tavern where a load of Frenchies hang out – knights and toffs and wossnames. Dimplemats."

"Diplomats?"

"That's the one. I know's a lad works the kitchens. Speaks Frenchy. Has to. 'E was there when someone came with the news. There was a French lady at the castle, see. Someone important. It's 'er they was most worried about. But 'e – Sir John – 'e fought the demon off..."

Gisburne looked heavenward. "God bless you, Ross, you old bastard!" He smiled and clapped Hamon on both his shoulders. "You too, Hamon!"

"I ain't no bastard, sir!" said Hamon with a frown.

"No, of course not," said Gisburne. "Apologies to your mother and your father. Here..." – and he pressed another penny into his palm – "You stay here. Don't move. There will be more to come if you help us further."

"Aye, sir," said Hamon. Gisburne, in a state of high excitement, turned and vaulted up the stairs two at a time.

"THIS IS GOOD news," said Galfrid as Gisburne stuffed his scattered gear into a saddlebag. "At least, I think it is..."

"It's the breakthrough we needed," said Gisburne. "We were dreading the next attack, even though we knew we were dependent upon it. But this time – thank God – he missed his mark. No one died."

"It was indeed fortunate," Galfrid said with a nod.

Gisburne looked suddenly shamefaced. "Ross always was blessed with more than his share of luck," he said. "But I'll not trust to it again."

Galfrid shrugged. "Sometimes, it's all there is."

His master nodded, and gave a tight-lipped smiled. "He's not invincible, Galfrid..." he said, with a renewed fire in his eyes. "Here, take this." He thrust a bag of coins into Galfrid's chest. "Tell Hamon he can earn himself all the pennies we have – his friends too. He knows what we're looking for – tell him to get as many others on the lookout as he can. They will be our eyes and ears across the city. No one notices these urchins – they'll be able to go everywhere. Hear everything. Tell Hamon he is to be in charge. That we are making him their captain."

"And you?"

"I'm leaving for King Stormont," said Gisburne. "To meet with the one who faced the Red Hand and survived."

XXVIII

King Stormont Castle
24 May, 1193

KING STORMONT CASTLE was a miracle of modern design. Describing a perfect circle, its crenellated stone walls sat like a crown atop a neat, conical mound on the hill overlooking the hamlet of Brimthorpe. While not as lofty as the castles of old, the mound's sides were steep – their length exaggerated by the deep dry ditch surrounding them.

The circle was broken in only two places. As Gisburne had approached from the north-west along the Kent road, the low evening sun turning the stone to a blaze of gold, a simple, square tower had projected from the curved body of the castle on the western side, like a rectangular jewel set upon a golden ring. This, he guessed, was the chapel.

On the far side of the circular battlement, almost directly opposite, was the gatehouse. Of similar dimensions to the chapel, it opened onto a bridge across the ditch, which led into the bailey. Gisburne entered from a gate in the south-east. Armed guards at the entrance studied him as he passed.

Inside the bailey, surrounded by neat stone walls, was a community that easily rivalled Brimthorpe in size. There were stables, a bakery, kitchens, a brewhouse and a smithy – each of which he identified as much by their smell as their appearance. They all appeared newly built and well maintained. There was also a great hall of adequate proportions, and neat, orderly housing for the workers of the castle's household from the steward down, many of whom now scurried about, fetching and carrying pots and platters – the wreckage of the evening's formal meal in the castle overlooking them. Among the castle's beetling servants – dressed plainly, but all well-presented and scrupulously clean, and all with a clear sense of purpose – Gisburne noted a few in a contrasting, more opulent dress, and apparently less familiar with their surroundings. These were, without doubt, the retainers of de Rosseley's current guest.

As he walked towards the great crowned hill, the space suddenly opened out to reveal something quite at odds with its modest surroundings: a training ground the likes of which Gisburne had rarely seen outside the great castles of Normandy. There were pells and quintains, butts for archery, a field for the joust, jumps, tracks and obstacles to challenge both horses and men, even a pair of wooden towers upon which to test siege and defence tactics – and all set in space sufficient to allow for the hosting of an entire tournament.

Tournaments had long been banned on English soil – one of King Henry's measures to re-establish public order after the horrors of Stephen's reign. Although the pitched battle of the *mêlée* was undoubtedly valuable preparation for knights who had not yet seen battle – and an equally valuable income for many who had – Henry had never been afraid to go against wider opinion. In France and beyond, the *Conflictus Gallicus* had never waned – and expectation was high that if Richard ever returned to these shores, so too would the tournament. It was bloody, it was brutal, and the people loved it.

Gisburne had never participated in one, and now had little desire to; when his knighthood had suddenly been denied him, he had been forced into a different life, with harsher battles. But before that, as a lance-carrying squire, he had supported de Gaillon at the lists on more occasions than he could count. The last time he had met de Rosseley – over seven years ago in France, when he was en route to Sicily, and de Rosseley was heading the opposite way, to England – his old friend had been as infatuated with the tourney as ever. Judging by the ground before him, nothing had changed.

The castle now rose before him, asserting without dominating. Its lines were simple, but beautiful. In size it was generous without being overbearing, its dimensions balanced and pleasing to the eye. Its defensive capability was, nonetheless, formidable – all the more so for not having been overcomplicated. Unlike so many castles in Gisburne's experience – square, dank, draughty dungeons of places, for the most part – it also looked like somewhere one might actually wish to live, and in comfort.

Its crisp stonework was also entirely new. Had Gisburne come this way just five years ago, so a local blacksmith had said, he would have seen nothing here but a dilapidated square keep, a wooden palisade and the bare beginnings of a stone gatehouse. No expense had been spared in bringing it to its current state – though Gisburne had seen far more costly piles which lacked such clarity of vision, and whose meandering building works had plodded along over decades.

All together, the castle created a vivid impression of its young lord.

At the gatehouse, Gisburne dismounted and presented himself to the guards. Their captain was courteous but wary, requesting details of his business. Behind him, members of his guard – fully armoured, some with weapons drawn – kept their eyes on him at all times. Given the outrage of the previous night, he could hardly blame them. This time, he was content to wait whilst his name and mission were conveyed to their master. Within moments, de Rosseley's steward appeared, to escort Gisburne to his master. "Sir John has already retired to his chamber," he said, his angular face giving nothing away, "but I am to take you there directly."

Gisburne nodded and followed behind as a groom led Nyght away to food and water.

Within, the castle opened into a great circular courtyard, now cast into deep shadow by the failing light. What normally would have been a wide open space – room enough to train a horse – was today taken up by two wagons of considerable quality and sophistication. The larger of them – emerald green, picked out in gold – was of such luxury it made Prince John's look like an ox cart. They also had an exotic air about them – curtains and carvings looked, to Gisburne, to be Arab in style, while other touches were distinctly Byzantine. Clearly, de Rosseley's guest was someone of note.

About these, a number of servants moved with seasoned efficiency, securing things for the night, preparing for the morning. One – better dressed than the others, in a finely tailored green tunic, with fastidiously coiffured black hair – bowed low to Gisburne as he passed. His face – or manner – seemed familiar, but Gisburne couldn't place him. Moments later, he was gone.

"Tell me," said Gisburne, as they neared a door on the courtyard's far side, "is Sir John well?" Only now, moments away from the meeting, was he suddenly struck by the need to be prepared for what he would find. He knew only what Hamon had been able to tell him – that de Rosseley was alive, but no more. But was he crippled? Insensible? Either could be possible.

"He is well," said the steward. It was as bland and generic a statement as one could possibly have. They entered the doorway and began to ascend the stone stair.

"I was thinking of the attack made upon him..." pressed Gisburne. "I hope he suffered no ill effects."

The steward nodded. "My lord came through unscathed," he said.

Gisburne breathed a sigh of relief. It seemed a remarkable achievement. Almost inexplicable. *One moment, the Red Hand is an unstoppable force. The next, he's seen off without landing a blow. What made this attack so different?*

The stair led to a curving corridor. The steward stopped at the first door, pushed it open, and stood aside with a bow.

*　　*　　*

AT THE FAR end of the dimly lit chamber, dressed in a nightshirt and shrouded in deep shadow cast by the curtains of his bed, lounged John de Rosseley.

"God's hooks! Guy!" he exclaimed hoarsely, and rose unsteadily to his feet. Gisburne smiled – de Rosseley always had enjoyed his wine.

"Still a blasphemer, eh, Ross?" he said striding towards him.

"Ha!" De Rosseley waved a dismissive hand. "D'you really think I'd have lasted this long if my ways offended the Almighty?"

As Gisburne neared, de Rosseley stepped forward into the light – and Gisburne was shocked at the sight of him.

Guy of Gisburne had no views on God's will, but he meant what he had said to Galfrid. John de Rosseley had been blessed with good fortune all his life – so much so that in battle other men felt their chances of survival increased simply by standing alongside him. He also emanated a boundless optimism that inspired others, in ways Gisburne had never quite managed. Few in his experience had. While there were many knights who were as indefatigable as de Rosseley – and many more who had his irrepressible humour – those who also had the skills to back up the swagger, and to survive, were few indeed. It was a combination Gisburne had seen in only one other man: Robert of Locksley, now known by the name of Robin Hood. They shared many similarities, now Gisburne came to think of it. Irresistible charm, awesome skills, a seemingly inexhaustible energy – not just of body, but of mind. But, for all his bravado, de Rosseley had one quality that nature had seen fit to deny Hood. A sense of honour.

The battered figure that stood before Gisburne now, however, hardly had the look of a lucky man. Nor did it in any way bear out the steward's claim. Barely an inch of his visible flesh was its right colour. His left eye was black and swollen like a rotten apple. His bottom lip was split and crusty, every knuckle barked and ragged. There was a wide gash on his forehead, onto which some greenish-brown, foul-smelling sludge had been smeared. Below the scraped chin, the exposed part of his neck and shoulder showed an emerging bruise of vibrant blues, purples, browns and yellows, hinting at worse beyond. Gisburne was appalled at the severity of them. Never had he seen bruises yellow so fast. De Rosseley's left shoulder was strapped up, and the way his right arm was folded about his side, which he tried to protect from movement, made it clear to Gisburne that some of the bones were broken. He had favoured his left knee as he stood, in a way that betrayed damage to his right. Gisburne supposed he was, at least, lucky to be alive.

De Rosseley, indifferent to his injuries, clapped his arms around Gisburne then stood back to look at him.

"How long has it been? Six years?"

"Nearly eight," said Gisburne. "Though if I'd known you had this fine place I might have come sooner." But he was aware that his own smile had quite fallen away. He looked back to the door where the steward still lingered, and shot him a reproachful glance.

De Rosseley followed his gaze. "Food and drink for our guest," he called. The steward bowed and withdrew. "Sit down, Guy, for God's sake. I'm not royalty."

Gisburne pulled up a wooden chair. De Rosseley eased himself back down onto the bed, now less able to hide his agony. "Christ, Ross," said Gisburne, "what the Hell happened here? That damned steward of yours said you came through last night unscathed..."

"What?" De Rosseley frowned. He looked back at his unexpected guest with genuine bemusement, as if the mention of "last night" meant nothing at all – as if Gisburne were speaking in a completely foreign language. After what seemed an age, the fog lifted. "Oh, *this*..." He gestured vaguely to his injuries. "No, no – I got these last week."

Gisburne stared at him, dumbfounded. "Last *week...?*"

"A tournament," said de Rosseley. He took up a goblet from beside the bed and supped a generous draught. "Cressy or Croissey, or some such place. I forget. I do so many."

"Jesus..." said Gisburne. "You volunteered for that beating? Is is worth it? You look half dead."

He eyed Gisburne up and down again. "Says the man dressed like a scarecrow. What in God's name *is* that monstrous coat anyway?" He leaned forward to see it closer, then coughed, and winced in pain, and lowered himself to the bed once more. "These are the wounds of victory, not defeat. That always makes the pain bearable. And yes, Guy. It is worth it. As you see..." He spread his hands, indicating the stone walls that surrounded them. "Not a bad haul this outing. Captured and ransomed four knights. Won their horses and armour. Two Frenchies, one Austrian, one Byzantine."

Gisburne raised his eyebrows at the last.

"I know," said de Rosseley. "Random. Spectacular horse, though."

"Carry on like this," said Gisburne, "and you'll have to build bigger stables." *If you live long enough*, he thought.

De Rosseley snorted dismissively. "You don't think I'd actually pay to have that horseflesh shipped over here? God, no! Sold them back to their former owners on the spot. Once the knights had been sold back to *their* owners, that is. Brought back a tidy sum in silver." It was becoming clear to Gisburne how his host had acquired the funds for such a magnificent pile. De Rosseley sniggered. "Should've seen their faces. They could've killed me."

"I'm sure that's exactly what they have in mind," said Gisburne. "Watch yourself, Ross. You're not as young as you used to be."

"You're hardly a lad yourself, my friend." De Rosseley smiled, then took another swig and narrowed his eyes. "Prince John's man now, eh?"

Gisburne nodded.

De Rosseley began to laugh, and clutched at his side as he did so. "Guy of Gisburne, a lackey for Lackland! Well, I doff my cap to you, sir. How is the old bugger, anyway?" Gisburne could not suppress a smile at the word *old*. John was all of twenty-six. "Does he still favour silk undergarments and garnish his extremities with gold like a Byzantine whore?"

"As to the latter," said Gisburne, "I could not possibly comment. As to the former, perhaps you would like me to put the question to him when I return to London?"

"Do!" It was issued almost as a challenge. "I've heard he stays in bed all day long and has a bath at least once a week."

Gisburne rolled his eyes. "Stories, Ross – just stories. You know how people are."

De Rosseley sighed. "He never was going to be the popular one of that brood, poor bastard." He forced himself to sit up, and nudged Gisburne on the knee. "From what I've heard, though, you've been doing great things..."

"You heard that?" said Gisburne. He was not used to people having heard things about him. It made him uneasy.

"The capture of Hood. *Everyone* heard about that. Good job, old man! And there's plenty more besides..." Gisburne decided to move the conversation on before de Rosseley had a chance to elaborate.

"It's a different kind of mission that brings me here today," he said. "There is a new menace: the Red Hand. I believe it was he who violated this castle last night."

De Rosseley's brow furrowed. "You pursue him on behalf of Prince John?"

"He has issued a threat against the Prince himself. And he has attacked others. Killed others. The fact is... you are the only one to have survived."

De Rosseley went to speak, but at that moment the door opened and a servant entered with a platter of meat and bread and a jug of wine. De Rosseley sat in silence, his expression grave, until the servant had left the chamber, and the door had once again closed.

"Who has this monster killed?" he said.

"Walter Bardulf was first," said Gisburne.

His host nodded. "I heard about Bardulf."

"Then William de Wendenal," continued Gisburne. "And a week ago, Hugh de Mortville."

"Christ..." said de Rosseley. "Wendenal dead? I thought that stubborn old warhorse was sure to outlive me. And de Mortville? Who did he ever offend?"

"Perhaps no one. But he fell victim to someone's grudge, nonetheless."

"Ireland..." said de Rosseley, nodding. "We were all there. It has to be about Ireland."

"So we believe," said Gisburne.

"Political?"

"It's not yet clear."

"A red hand is a symbol amongst Ulstermen," said de Rosseley. "The Uí Néill clan especially. But others, too. It had some mythic significance. There were stories of an ancient Irish king who sacrificed his own right hand in order to win the crown."

"The victims' right hands were also taken," said Gisburne.

De Rosseley shook his head in disgust. "This killer of knights doesn't act out of duty, or necessity. As you say, a grudge."

"But why now, after all these years?"

"It's not human nature to wait when the blood is up. But perhaps he couldn't act before – somehow did not know who to direct his anger at, or lacked the means."

"Or the slight itself was more recent than we all suppose."

"Or only recently discovered..."

It was immediately clear to Gisburne why de Rosseley was so formidable a fighter. It wasn't just his physical prowess. In just those few minutes he had stripped away all distractions and irrelevancies to identify the key defining factors of his opponent.

"Tell me what happened last night," said Gisburne.

De Rosseley shook his head slowly. "I've witnessed some horrors in my time, and some wonders. But I tell you, Guy, this was the damnedest thing I ever saw." He pressed the fingertips of both hands together. "It was late. Darkness had fallen. I had entertained my lady guest at dinner – a delightful evening. She had retired to her chamber and the household was mostly abed. I was of a mind to make a tour of the battlements, take the air – something I do each night, when it's quiet. The gates were shut for the night; all was well. I had just spoken to the watch and was crossing the empty courtyard when he appeared out of the shadows by the north wall."

"Appeared?"

De Rosseley nodded. "There is no other word for it. No warning. The first anyone knew was when he charged out of those shadows. And I do mean *charged*... right at me. There was no doubting I was his intended target."

"But how did he get in?"

"One of my guards admitted to having seen a large man enter with others of my guest's entourage earlier in the day. He was toting a heavy sack. Several of them carried such burdens – barrels or boxes. My lady does not travel light." He smirked. "The guard assumed the man to be with them. Turns out he wasn't. Must have hidden himself then until nightfall. Close on half a day he waited. It takes a particular type of man to do that." De Rosseley nodded, interlinking the fingers of both hands. "He's a dangerous one, all right."

Gisburne leaned forward eagerly. "So, the guard saw his face?"

"Fleetingly. He was bearded. Unkempt hair. Dark. And he was dressed like a tradesman." De Rosseley shrugged. "That was all he was able to give. I gave him Hell for his assumption – then rewarded him for having the balls to admit he'd seen the man."

"What happened next?"

"It's a jumble of impressions. You know how it is at times like that. There was this... *thing* charging at me, metal plates clanking. I could tell the great weight of the armour by the rise and fall of him. Some kind of heavy weapon was swinging up in his right hand. Huge. Then flames leapt from his left. The brightness of them blinded me for an instant. But they also lit up the grotesque head at the top of him... Nearly filled my breeches at the sight of it."

"You called him a monster..." said Gisburne.

De Rosseley smiled. "Don't let the word fool you," he said. "I know he wants us to think that's what he is – depends on it. To startle, and frighten. But they're just tricks. You've had others describe what they saw?"

Gisburne nodded. "Some called it a dragon."

"Then I'll not insult you by repeating that part. I will only say that no matter what enemy I'm facing, no matter how terrifying their manner or appearance, I keep in mind one thing: *It's still just a man.* When all's said and done, this was just another challenger in armour charging at me. I'd faced that often enough."

"But were you armed?"

De Rosseley shook his head. "No armour. No weapon. Not even a damn knife – I'd left it at the table. Most unlike me, I know."

"Then how the Hell did you survive?"

"More by luck than judgement. But then comes the second, and even more puzzling mystery..."

Gisburne drew closer. He was about to hear something entirely new – perhaps something that might finally tip the balance in his favour.

"The situation was plain. I was injured, unarmed. I knew I couldn't fight him – that if I tried, I'd be dead. I couldn't run. Even if I were at full fitness, fast as he was coming, he'd have been on me before I got three yards." Gisburne nodded in acknowledgement. He had already seen the grim evidence to support De Rosseley's assessment.

"I understood right away that he thought strategically – he got himself into the castle, after all – but there were no tactics. He just *charged*. That's all there was to it. What he lacked in finesse he more than made up for in strength – of his weapons, of his armour, of his person. He was heavy. And fast – over a short distance, at least. But such forward momentum means a loss of manoeuvrability." He wagged a finger. "One must always look for the advantage, no matter how hopeless the situation appears. And in that second when I saw him coming at me, I knew that was mine. So..."

"So?"

"I did nothing. Not until he was almost on me, my eye on that flying hammer of his, hoping to God he didn't fry me in the meantime. Then I let my body fall away to the left of him, like a fainting damsel. I rolled clear as he thundered past." He rubbed his ribs. "Nearly bloody killed me."

"And then you attacked?" asked Gisburne. What now occupied his mind was the possibility that the Red Hand had suffered injury.

De Rosseley shook his head.

"No?"

"I didn't land a single blow."

"But... how did you see him off?"

"I didn't. Someone else did."

"Someone else?" Gisburne was struggling to make sense of this. "Who?"

De Rosseley offered up an odd smile. "I have no idea."

Gisburne sat staring at his host's battered, bruised face and the smile that played about it. He had expected some answer to the Red Hand's apparent invincibility – but now, he did not even know what question to ask. "Believe me, Guy," continued de Rosseley, "I was as baffled as you. But I will tell you what I *saw* happen." He sat himself up straighter, grimacing as he did so. "As I righted myself, my opponent began to turn. I had nothing now, you understand. No weapon to hand and no possibility of one. I could hear the shouts of alarm from the guards in the gatehouse, but they were still precious seconds away. And it was unlikely he would fall for the same trick again." He paused, as if still puzzling over what had happened. "And then... I was suddenly aware of another figure, to the left of me. As slight as my attacker was great, dressed in black from head to toe, as if to merge into the shadows, his head and face completely covered. I swear he had not been there a moment before; it was as if he had just dropped from the battlements like a spider. Then, as the attacker began his second run, the black-clad man darted out, putting himself between the Red Hand and me. It seemed so ridiculous. He barely stood the height of the Red Hand's nipple. I almost laughed out loud."

Something in this description pulled at Gisburne's insides. A pang of familiarity. But it couldn't be... He fought the feeling down. "And then?"

"Our hall-raider thundered forward without hesitation, fully expecting to swat the little man aside. But then the stranger, too, did what he did not expect. He did not stand firm or try to resist, or flee. Like me, he just dropped to the ground – but right before his feet, in a tight ball. Unable to stop, the brute stumbled over the top of him, fell heavily, flat on the ground, all that force and weight now turned against him." He nodded to himself as he saw it play out in his mind. "Then, before he could gather himself, the black figure was up again, and grabbed at the attacker's great hammer – it had come loose in the fall. It was attached to the monster's wrist by a length of thong or rope – but the little fellow was not to be deterred. He swung it all the same, though it seemed the weapon of a Titan in his grip, the great arm of the stunned giant still dangling from the end of it. He dashed the fallen attacker about the head. Once. Twice. Three times. The clang of his helm rang about the stones of the courtyard.

"I wasted no time. My guards were mustered – surrounding him with spears. I called to them to bring oil and a flame. I wanted him to hear me, too – to know what we intended, to feel his own damned fear. But he rallied at that, hauled on the hammer, wrenching it from the stranger's grip, rolled and swiped out at him. The blow struck, and the stranger fell. The Red Hand was once again on his feet, the hammer back in his fist. I ordered my men to hold back – I knew they could not stand against that weapon. Crossbow bolts were loosed from the battlements – but to no effect. Men arrived with the oil. Knowing his situation was hopeless, he loosed a last, great burst of fire and made a run for it. The bulk of my men were between him and the gatehouse, but he headed the opposite way, up onto the battlements. Afterwards, we found a rope he had evidently secreted there earlier that night. Before we could do anything he was down the outside wall, off across the ditch and lost in the dark."

"And the black-clad stranger?" said Gisburne.

De Rosseley shrugged. "Vanished. None saw him go. All eyes were on the Red Hand."

Gisburne had hoped for an answer of some kind – some weapon he could take and put to use. Instead, he had come away with yet more questions. "Were there no casualties among your men?" he said.

"One lost his eyebrows to the flame. Beyond that, none. We were lucky."

Gisburne gazed into his goblet. "Well, here's to the famed de Rosseley luck..." he said, and drank.

"We could have been luckier," said de Rosseley. "We could've caught the bastard. But by the time we rode out, he was long gone. How, I don't know."

Gisburne nodded slowly. "My guess? A wagon hidden off the road to the north of here. He gets himself to it, throws off his disguise and trundles away to London, an unkempt tradesman once more. Unheeded and unhindered."

De Rossely gave a grunt of frustration. "If we'd only known then what to look for..."

"Well, we know it now," said Gisburne, still staring into his wine.

"He's clever," said de Rosseley. "But he's not infallible. His actions are extreme. Risky. He'll make other mistakes."

"I have one month," said Gisburne. "One month for him to make his mistake, or for me to track him down in a city of twenty thousand souls." He raised his goblet again. "Here's to life's mistakes."

"And when that month is up?" said de Rosseley.

Gisburne swigged his wine, but left the question unanswered. Something else, now, was nagging him. The other mystery.

"This stranger all in black..." he said. "Your strange guardian angel. Do you have any idea who it could have been, or what they were doing here?"

De Rosseley was silent for a long time. "I do have one idea," he said. Then he leaned forward, and spoke in a low voice. "Have you heard of the Shadow?"

Gisburne had not.

"They speak of him in France," said de Rosseley. "A dark-clad figure, appearing only at night. Fights like a *hashashin*. Some say he does King Philip's bidding. Others, that he has an agenda all his own. No one has ever seen his face."

Gisburne sighed, and let his head hang. It began to feel like it was filled with lead. "The Shadow. The White Devil. The Red Hand. The Hood... Christ, where will it all end? I seem to remember a time when people could just be themselves, and stand up for what they believed in." He buried his face in his wine goblet once more, thoughts of the dark-clad figure coalescing in his mind. It was all too familiar. But how could that be?

"There is another such character I have heard of recently," said de Rosseley, then leaned in closer still. His voice fell to little more than a whisper. "The Dark Horseman."

Gisburne felt his heart sink. Yet another outlandishly costumed hero, desperate for fame, inspired by exaggerated accounts of the dubious deeds of madmen, charlatans and criminals. It dismayed him that the usually down-to-earth de Rosseley had apparently allowed himself to become enthralled by such men. "And what mischief does this one get up to? To what ridiculous lengths does he go to make himself a subject of ballads?"

"They say," began de Rosseley, "that he made fools of the Templars. Took a great treasure from under their noses. That two crossbow bolts to the heart did not kill him, that he single-handedly destroyed Tancred de Mercheval's greatest knights, and left his castle a pile of smoking rubble..." De Rosseley smiled like a cat, clearly relishing the slow realisation dawning upon Gisburne's face.

"The *Dark Horseman?*" said Gisburne, aghast.

"That's what the French call him," said de Rosseley, sitting back. "What they call *you.*"

Gisburne slumped back in his chair, appalled. De Rosseley chuckled, and clapped his hands together. "Death rides a black horse, my friend!"

"If it's Revelation you speak of," said Gisburne, his voice flat, and emotionless, "Death rides a pale horse. The black horse brings famine."

"Oh, who cares about the details," said De Rosseley, and slapped him on the knee. "Face it, my friend. You are a fucking *legend!*"

Gisburne had faced many monsters in his time. He was about to face another. What he had never anticipated was that he would *become* one. Now, this horrifying thing he had unwittingly created was lumbering off into the world, dragging him and his reputation behind it, entirely beyond his control. That was what a legend was. A legend wasn't real. It was beyond real. It had its own agenda. Now, he realised, he was another step closer to being like Hood. Except that Hood recognised nothing as monstrous. He loved his legend. He sat high upon its grotesque, deformed shoulders as it strode across England, and laughed.

Gisburne clasped his fingers together, and tried to re-establish his focus. "I must return again to this 'Shadow,'" he began. "If you're right – if it was them – what business might they have here?"

De Rosseley shrugged, and looked away into the dark corner of the chamber. "An enemy of this one you call 'Red Hand,' perhaps. Someone like you – but working for a different master." He smiled. "If so, you two should really get together..." He thought for another moment. "But then again, perhaps we're looking at this all wrong. If the Shadow does indeed serve the French King, perhaps they were here not to protect me, but my guest."

Gisburne felt his muscles tense. "Ross – who is this guest?"

"A noble lady," said de Rosseley, evasively. "And, before you say anything, I saw her first..." He shrugged. "Time I started to think about a wife before the last vestiges of sense and vigour are knocked out of me. And one could do a lot worse than the daughter of a French Count."

All at once, Gisburne remembered the half-familiar face in the courtyard, and every tantalising clue fell into place beyond any possible doubt. "Her name, Ross," he said. "Tell me her name..."

Hardly were the words out of his mouth than the door of the chamber clanked and creaked opened behind him. "Ah! It appears I can do even better," said de Rosseley. Gisburne turned and saw, framed in the doorway, three overlapping figures: the steward, the liveried servant from the courtyard, and between them, de Rosseley's esteemed guest. The steward opened the door wide, bowed low and drew back to allow her to enter.

"Gisburne," said de Rosseley, rising from his bed, "allow me to introduce Lady Mélisande de Champagne..."

XXIX

"GOOD EVENING, SIR John," said Mélisande, as her host struggled to remain upright. As if in a dream, Gisburne, too, rose to his feet. She averted her eyes from him entirely as she made her slow approach. "Please, Sir John," she said, lifting the long fingers of her right hand. "Not on my account. You are injured."

De Rosseley sank back to his bed, somewhat abashed but nonetheless grateful for the reprieve.

Gisburne thought he had remembered everything about Mélisande de Champagne – that she was branded in his memory. Only now did he realise he had remembered nothing. All that was familiar about her struck him now as if for first time, just as it had on that frozen street in Paris. That moment, when he had spied her atop a swaying litter as it bobbed above the heads of the teeming, chattering masses like a gilded royal barge, had left him bereft of words. So it was now. A man of action all his life, all he could do was stand and stare.

She was dressed in green, the colour she so often favoured. The silk gown was fitted closely to her slender form, with pendant sleeves that hung almost to the floor, the hems embroidered with fine gold wire. The gossamer-fine veil and wimple were of pure white, topped with a plain circlet of gold, and from the edge of her wimple, a single tendril of red-gold hair fell, just as it had that first time. Then, he had thought it a happy accident. It was, he now realised, a statement.

As she drew closer, he saw that the double belt about her slim waist was in fact a chain of gold, ending in delicate golden tassels. Other than this and the simple circlet upon her head, there were no adornments. No rings, no jewels – not even the sun pendant that she had perpetually worn during their days together. None were necessary.

"Good evening, Sir Guy. What a pleasant surprise to find you here."

Her eyes met his, and as they did so he fancied she allowed a playful smile to flicker across her lips, just for him.

"You know each other?" said de Rosseley before Gisburne could gather his wits to reply, then muttered to his old friend: "Now I understand why they call you the Dark Horse Man!"

But Gisburne was barely even aware of de Rosseley's words. His brain had turned to mud. He was unaccountably hot, his heart thumping so hard in his chest he began to believe those about him might actually hear it.

"We have met," said Mélisande. "Briefly. In Marseille, some eighteen months ago." Her eyes again met Gisburne's, but betrayed nothing of the adventure that had followed that meeting – the flight across France with a stolen relic, capture in the forests of Boulogne, the horrors of Castel Mercheval, and its subsequent ruin. "But perhaps Sir Guy does not remember...?" As she spoke, she offered a shapely white hand – a languorous gesture that barely made it above waist height.

"On the contrary," said Gisburne, his throat dry, "I recall every moment." And, dropping to one knee, he took her hand in his and bowed his head to kiss it. It was not the done thing to make actual contact. But against convention, against common sense, against anything anyone cared to put before him, Gisburne pressed his lips to it anyway, and – quite involuntarily – found he squeezed her smooth palm as he did so. Her skin smelled of rose petals. It made his head swim, memories rioting in his head.

"You look a little flushed, Sir Guy" said Mélisande. "Perhaps it is rather warm in here...?"

"Probably that ridiculous coat or whatever it is..." said de Rosseley. "What is that anyway? Horsehide?"

"It is the skin of my father's destrier," said Gisburne.

"Well, I hope it looked better on the horse," muttered de Rosseley. Mélisande stifled a snigger.

Gisburne stood, staring at the ground, impassive. "Thirty months ago, that horse was all I had in the world," he said. "All I had left of my father. Hood maimed it, left me to finish the beast off myself. This" – he tugged at the front of his coat – "reminds me of that. The day I lost everything, and gained everything. It was also the day I met Prince John and by him was dubbed a knight. A *chevalier.*"

De Rosseley bowed his head and nodded in acknowledgement, and silent apology. He had been a good friend to the old man. At the utterance of the word *chevalier*, Gisburne's mind strayed to the legend of the Dark Horseman – the man who was him and not him, who was named, he supposed, not only for the black horse he rode, but the curious black coat that he wore. To those who knew only the legend – if such it was – it was a costume. An affectation. Something designed to inspire fear. They would never truly understand that it had not been made with any purpose meant for them. He felt the futility of his own quest – his attempts to understand the Red Hand from no more than an approximate image. He knew what he looked like, well enough, but who could say what any of it *meant*?

Gisburne found himself looking into Mélisande's face – those impossibly deep eyes – and saw she too was staring at the ground, apparently miles away, her gaze unfocused. She looked pale – paler than he remembered. For a moment, he even thought she swayed a little. Perhaps de Rosseley's good wine had flowed a little too freely this evening. She inhaled sharply, as if shocked out of her reverie. Gisburne saw her left hand twitch and then tighten into a fist. Then she looked up, an odd smile upon her face.

"I came to ask if you would accompany me on a walk about the battlements, Sir John," she said. "To take the air. But since you are still indisposed from your exertions, perhaps you will not object if I ask Sir Guy to do so in your stead?"

Gisburne could see now that her breathing was uneven, and that she fought to hide it. There were beads of sweat on her smooth brow, and her left hand, still clenched, was shaking.

De Rosseley, who had not seen these things, eyed Gisburne with a look of one who had just been bettered upon the field. "It should be me touring my own castle with my own guest." He sighed, smiled and extended his hand in defeat. "But tonight I must defer to Gisburne, in both capacities. There's no better man in England – though it pains me to say so…"

"Then I bid you good night, Sir John," said Mélisande, looped her arm through Gisburne's and without further ceremony began to usher him to the door. The steward – still waiting, Mélisande's dour servant bolt upright by his side – bowed at her approach and held the door open. "Your chamber is the next along this passage, Sir Guy," he said, with yet another bow. "Your baggage is already within."

Gisburne paused, and turned back to de Rosseley. "See you on the lists," he said. Gisburne had never set foot in the joustyard as a competitor, and was unlikely ever to do so. But the banter had become its own ritual.

"Not if I see you first," said de Rosseley.

XXX

"Sir John's castle really is a wonder," said Mélisande as they walked along the dim passage, her servant padding silently behind them. "Above the kitchens, guardhouse, service rooms and undercroft there are four separate chambers besides the great hall, each with its own fireplace and privy." Gisburne found himself nodding dumbly at her inconsequential chatter. She made a vague gesture. "It is not connected one room to another, but has a continuous corridor built into the circular wall. That means any chamber may be secured or defended independently, without impeding access to the rest. Also, that guests are permitted their own private quarters, and may come and go without disturbing others. My chamber is the furthest along this passage. Sir John chose it for me; it gets the morning sun."

Gisburne had thought that, once alone, they would revert to the close familiarity they had developed in their time together. Somehow, that had not happened. She was, nevertheless, making sure she he knew where her chamber was – or was he reading too much into that? Was it even possible to read too much into Mélisande de Champagne? She was leaning more heavily against him with every step. It felt good – he could not deny that. But it concerned him. Her progress was slow and unsteady. She looked ill.

Suddenly, he saw her face contort in agony. Her eyes rolled back in her head – her body fell limp. Gisburne caught her in his arms. Her servant rushed forward.

"What the Hell is this?" said Gisburne.

"She is... unwell, sire," said the servant. He extended his hands as if to take her from him. His hands were shaking.

"I know that much. But is she injured? Tell me quickly."

The servant hesitated.

"Last night, against the intruder," hissed Gisburne. "Come on, I know what she is..."

It seemed, then, that the servant finally let his steely façade drop. "She took a blow to her left side. Severe. The skin is not broken, but..." he shrugged, then gave a shuddering sigh. Hours of anxiety seemed to show on his face.

Gisburne gently lifted one of her eyelids. Her pupils were large, her skin clammy. "Has she taken anything?" he said. "For the pain?"

"Henbane," said the servant. "And a preparation from her travels in the East. What the Arabs call *afyun* – the tears of the poppy. But its effects are waning."

"Help me get her to her chamber," said Gisburne, glancing back towards de Rosseley's door. "I may know what she is, but Sir John does not – nor the rest of the world, for that matter..."

ONCE SAFELY BEHIND the closed door, Gisburne's mind became pragmatic, efficient. Focused. He was calm. This, at least, he understood.

Placing her upon the bed, he pulled away her veil and wimple. Red-gold hair tumbled free. Her head was hot, her mouth dry. "Pray God it's not a fever," he said as the servant hovered nervously by.

"Should I fetch her maidservants?" he said, wringing his hands.

"No time for that," said Gisburne, unhooking her precious belt and discarding it on the floor. He turned her onto her right side. Upon her dress was an even row of tight lacing stretching the full length of her spine, from her neck to the small of her back. It was baffling to his eyes – providing no clue as to how or where it had been tied. For the first time in his life, he was keenly aware that he was a soldier and not a lady's maid. He hooked his finger through and tugged at it.

"Sire..." the servant grasped Gisburne's wrist. The tone of his voice was firm, his grip surprisingly strong. Gisburne had no doubt he would fight to protect his lady's honour – Mélisande was not one to tolerate milksops.

"It's necessary if she's to breathe," said Gisburne. The grip did not loosen. "Dammit, man," he snapped, "it's not as if I haven't seen her naked before."

The servant gazed again at his mistress, and relented. There was love in his eyes. Gisburne set about the laces again. "What's your name?" he said. It was a moment before the servant realised he was being addressed.

"Bertran, sire."

"You're a good man, Bertran," said Gisburne. Not knowing quite how to respond, Bertran simply gave an embarrassed nod.

Suddenly Mélisande jerked and came to, her breathing coming in short, wheezing gasps. Gisburne pulled again at the lacing, but it resisted him.

"We must cut this," he said. "Hold her still." Bertran did so. Gisburne drew his eating knife, slid the blade behind the lacing and sliced it through. Then again. And a third time. When it was slit almost from waist to shoulder blade, her breathing faltered. He did not trouble with a final cut, but grasped the material and ripped the last of the lacings apart. She gasped as the bindings about her chest were released, shuddered violently, then her eyes swam and she again slumped into Bertran's arms, the full sinuous length of her bare back framed between crumpled hems of green. There was no underdress. Perhaps her injury had made it impossible for her to put it on over her head. Or perhaps it was just Mélisande being Mélisande.

"My lady requested the gown be laced tightly," said Bertran. There was almost apology in his voice. "She said it helped to reduce the pain."

Gisburne nodded. Many a time he'd seen knights strap up their sides and get straight back in the saddle. "But it will not help the wound to heal," he said. "She must breathe freely now." *And keep on breathing,* he thought. Only minutes ago had he found her, and already he was faced with the possibility of losing her all over again. He grasped her shoulders and laid her gently back upon the bed. "Fetch water," he said.

Bertran hurried away to the far end of the chamber as Gisburne peeled the closely fitted silk from her pale body and revealed the wound. The bruise upon her left side stretched all the way from the bottom of her ribs, past her left breast to her underarm. It was edged with purplish red, but at its heart was almost black – a horrid contrast to the pale, perfect flesh that surrounded it. The skin was entirely unbroken, but it was badly swollen. It suddenly struck Gisburne how absurd it was that one of England's greatest knights had been excused his duties as host by a woman who carried a near-identical injury.

"Bones may be broken," said Gisburne as Bertran returned with a dish of water and a cloth.

"What will that mean?" said Bertran.

"Pain. Perhaps for weeks. But she may be lucky." What was on his mind, however, was what other damage had been done and could not be seen. He chose not to speak of it yet. There was little Bertran could do, anyway.

"Surely, given the life your mistress leads," said Gisburne, "you must have seen other situations such as this?"

Bertran cocked his head to one side. "There have been... moments. But she has a talent for inflicting injury rather than suffering it." Gisburne smiled at that. "On the occasions when she has, she has usually insisted on dealing with it herself." Gisburne could imagine the door slamming in Bertran's face. Mélisande was nothing if not independent.

"Not this time," he said. "Lift her feet."

Bertran did so. Gisburne slid the dress entirely from under her and tossed it away, then folded the linen bedsheet over her naked body to preserve at least some dignity, and sat by her.

Bertran proffered the bowl. As Gisburne dipped the cloth into the water, he noted Bertran had strewn dried rose petals into it. He wrung it out, then mopped her brow, and then wrung and mopped again. After the third time, she awoke into a fit of coughing. Her eyes bulged and streamed with tears, purely from the pain. Pain was to be expected, but if it grew worse rather than better, or if she struggled to breathe, or started to run a fever – and especially if she coughed blood – then things would not be so simple. Then, her life would be hanging in the balance. Only the next few hours would tell.

As the coughing ceased, he held her face firmly between his palms and looked into her eyes. They were red and wild, but seemed clear, more focused – if a little indignant. All positive signs. "Can you hear me?" he said. He felt, rather than saw, her nod. "Spit," he said, and held out his palm next to her face. She frowned at the suggestion. "Spit into my hand."

"Not for twenty thousand crowns," she croaked.

She coughed again, and almost doubled up. "Just do it!" he said. Reluctantly, she spat, and slumped back. He spread the saliva across his palm. No blood. That was good.

"Water," she said. "Please..." He put the sopping cloth on her brow again, but she flung it off. "To drink!" she gasped. Bertran was already by her side with a cup and jug. She gulped down three cupfuls in succession before slumping onto the bed once more.

The water seemed to revive her. "Gisburne..." she said with a smile, as if seeing him for the first time. She put a hand on his face. "Have you rescued me again?"

"Hardly," said Gisburne. "From what I've heard, it's you who rescued Sir John."

She let her hand fall back upon the linen sheet that covered her. As her palm brushed across her breast, realisation dawned, and she lifted the sheet to peer beneath.

"I appear to be naked," she said. She looked back again. "Did you do this?"

"It's how I remember you best," said Gisburne.

Mélisande scowled at him. "I only regret that on this occasion I made it easy for you."

Gisburne raised his eyebrows. "Easy?" He mopped her brow again. "When was anything about you ever easy? Last time I saw you like this, I woke up next morning to find you gone."

Mélisande gave a kind of half-shrug, and a smile. "Sorry about that. You know I would love to have stayed. But anyway... Here we both are again."

Gisburne sighed. "And then it turned out you'd helped me get back to England only so Hood could rob me of the stolen relic."

Mélisande reddened, and the smile faded. "Not only," she said. She looked up at Bertran, still loitering awkwardly by, and indicated that he could go. He hesitated.

"I'll stay," said Gisburne. Bertran looked to his mistress.

"Get some sleep, Bertan," she said. "One of us needs to be at full strength when we leave tomorrow."

Bertran bowed, and left them.

"You leave tomorrow?" said Gisburne.

"I must," said Mélisande. Gisburne waited for her to expand upon the answer, but she did not.

"You're lucky to be alive," he said at length. "You know the Red Hand has slaughtered three of England's greatest knights, and threatens to kill more?"

"Red Hand?"

"The mystery raider from last night."

"So, is he the reason you're here?" said Mélisande, feigning disappointment. "Not because of me?"

"Sorry to say, I had no idea you were within these walls."

"And if you had...? Would that have brought you all the quicker, or kept you away?"

Gisburne looked at the stone floor. "What are *you* doing here?" he said.

"I'm just a noble lady seeking a husband."

"So... Are we to expect a betrothal announcement soon?"

Mélisande narrowed her limpid eyes and studied him for a long moment. "Not just yet."

Gisburne struggled once again to conceal his feelings – of joy and relief, this time. "Not your type?"

"Oh, he's definitely my type..." said Mélisande with a sly smile. "If a little... overeager." The smile vanished. "My father thinks it time I gave up my unseemly, wandering ways."

Gisburne nodded blandly. "Does your father know what it is you do?"

"He knows not to ask too many questions," she shot back. It sounded almost like a rebuke – but both knew Gisburne was already too deeply immersed in her secret world for it to have any meaning. She gave a sigh, shuddering as she did so – another twinge of pain, he guessed. Yes, he knew many of her secrets. But there was still much she kept concealed. From him. From everyone. She smiled. "Actually, I think he believes I am having an affair with King Philip. All those trips to court..."

"And are you?"

She gave a snort of derision which ended in a tiny cry of pain. "Now, he really *isn't* my type. Awful teeth." She frowned up at him. "Do you know Philip?"

Gisburne shook his head. "I do not."

"A remarkable man, in many ways. An individual of ferocious energies. But horribly impatient. And fiercely envious. Like a spoilt child, at times."

Gisburne smiled. "That sounds familiar. It could almost describe the Lionheart."

"They always were a little too similar for their crusade to proceed smoothly."

"It seems Richard lost no opportunity to make Philip feel inadequate. Little wonder Philip hates him."

"Hates him?" chuckled Mélisande. "God, no! He *loves* him! Richard epitomises the warrior king he aspires to be, and has all the things he feels he lacks. Strength, stature, leadership..."

"Normandy. Aquitaine..."

"Yes, those too... Of course, Philip already has all of those qualities in abundance, compared with most men."

"Next to Richard, most people feel inadequate," said Gisburne. Then, after a moment's thought added: "Most *men*."

She narrowed her eyes at him again. "Except, perhaps, those who value brains above all else."

He held her gaze for a moment, then tore his eyes away, uncertain if she had meant the words as a compliment. "Richard doesn't lack intelligence," he said. "Good God, you should see him on the battlefield. He's just... Not complicated. He doesn't overthink. Nothing troubles him at night."

"Not even the company of women, I've heard," said Mélisande.

"Not women. Not men. Nothing. It's simply rest before the next day's conquests." Gisburne was convinced that simplicity was the key to Richard's success. People liked their heroes to be simple.

"Well, there we have the difference," said Mélisande. "Philip overthinks everything. He imagines invasions, intrigues, plots to kill him. Everything that might get in his way, everything that could go wrong."

Gisburne nodded slowly and gazed off into some imagined distance, beyond the confines of the stone walls. "You know the best and worst thing one can take into battle?"

Mélisande shook her head.

"An imagination. Best, because you can imagine what might happen next. And worst, because you can imagine what might happen next... Gilbert de Gaillon told me that. Before I discovered it for myself."

"De Gaillon told you so many damn things..." said Mélisande. "He must have been quite a talker."

Gisburne smiled. "Quite the opposite. A man of few words."

"Fewer than you?"

"Even fewer than that."

"Do you have any idea how often you mentioned him in the short time we were together?"

Gisburne nodded and shrugged, sheepishly. "He changed the way I think. Made me what I am."

"At the time you were practically dead in a freezing cave in the Forêt de Boulogne..." she said. "But you even mentioned him in your sleep as I nursed you through that fever."

"And now that situation is reversed..." said Gisburne with a smile, and mopped her brow again. "So I suppose that at least makes us even."

"No. It doesn't." Mélisande's eyes suddenly filled with pain – not physical, this time. "I thought you were going to die in that wretched place."

Gisburne held her sad gaze for a moment, then looked away, dipping the cloth into the water bowl. He could not let her know that he had exactly the same fear.

"So, what exactly is he, this Red Hand?" she said.

"Perhaps the more intriguing question," said Gisburne, "is how you managed to stand up to him when knights of such ability failed..."

"You really need to ask?"

Gisburne smiled. "Not really," he said. "De Rosseley gave me a blow-by-blow account."

"Well then. Why don't *you* tell *me* how I did it?"

Gisburne thought for a moment. "You know those strapping great horses young and foolish knights think are best?"

Mélisande smiled. "All too well."

"That is what the Red Hand is."

"But, as an experienced knight, the horse you choose to ride is different..."

"The horse I choose," said Gisburne, "is strong and fast, but also agile. With spirit and stamina, but also patience. Something suited to the widest range of possible encounters."

"And is that me?"

"That is the Shadow."

She smiled. "You haven't changed," she said.

"Nor you. Except for that new scar on your right thigh." He put his fingertip on the place. "A dagger point, I'd say."

She glared at him again. "A Cordoban monk took it into his head to open my innards with a coustille."

"What did you do to cause such offence?"

"He's lying at the bottom of the Corilha Ravine," she replied. "Perhaps you could ask him." She smiled sweetly. "But what of you?"

He shrugged as if to say "nothing new".

"Nyght?" she said.

"He's well."

"And Galfrid?"

"Also well." He smiled. "I note the order in which you asked those questions. And I approve." She drank more water from the cup. He refilled it.

"So tell me," he said, "did you just happen to be dressed as the Shadow that night, or did you stop to change whilst the Red Hand rampaged?"

Mélisande narrowed her eyes. "Are you teasing me, or testing me?"

"Come on. You had no more idea the Red Hand was coming than anyone else. But you were ready. What were you doing that night? Heading out on some secret foray, or coming back from one?"

"Coming back."

"From...?"

"It's sweet that you ask me that," said Mélisande, and stroked his cheek. "But you must know that I can't possibly tell you."

"Are you sure you couldn't be persuaded?"

"I might. If you told me what you were doing in Jerusalem two months ago dressed as a troubadour."

Gisburne felt his face redden, as if he were standing before her in that ridiculous garb. "You heard about that?"

"Some," she said. "But a girl always likes to hear more. From the horse's mouth, as it were."

"Sadly, I too must decline..."

"Are you sure *you* couldn't be persuaded?" She put her hand to his face again. "I know you, Gisburne. I'm willing to bet that I could have it out of you just like *that*." She snapped her fingers by his ear. The motion of her arm as she did so made her wince with pain. Her face paled and she gripped her side.

"That's a wager I might well let you win," said Gisburne. "But not tonight..."

He lay her back again, and mopped her brow.

"You have known Sir John a long time?" she said, as if conversation might dull the pain. "You seem on familiar terms."

"My father knew him before I," said Gisburne. "They had both served King Henry, though were of quite different generations. Ross – Sir John – was barely five years older than me, but had already forged a formidable reputation." He laughed. "De Gaillon never got to meet him. Not sure he'd have approved. But Ross came to my father's house once when I was returned from Limousin, visiting my parents. I can't have been more than seventeen and still raw from my first battles under Richard. It was a difficult time – away from the demands of conflict and the steady hand of de Gaillon, I wasn't at all sure I'd taken the right course in life. But Ross put me back on track. He didn't set out to, of course. He was just... him. Clear, focused, positive. We talked, rode horses... He was easy company. We've only met a few times since, often with years in between. But on each occasion it's as if no time has passed."

"Such connections are rare. One should make the most of them."

He studied her for a moment, sensing she was talking about something else. Guilt suddenly tumbled in. He sighed and looked away.

"What is it?" she said.

Gisburne felt ashamed. "I could have warned him."

Mélisande frowned. "You knew?"

"I knew he was a potential victim, yes," said Gisburne, his eyes downcast. "And yet I said nothing. I just stood back and waited. Because I wanted to solve the riddle myself..."

Mélisande nodded, beginning to understand. "You did what needed to be done," she said. "And nobody died. What more could he have done anyway, even if he had known?"

Gisburne looked at her, lying there, beaten half to death, then looked away again, unable to meet her gaze.

"But what kind of friend am I to do that?" he said. "What kind of man?"

"Come on..." she said, and took his hand. "It's what I'd have done. Probably Ross, too. Kept a distance so as not to scare the prey. The man catches nothing who keeps returning to the trap."

It sounded like the kind of advice de Gaillon would have given. For that reason alone – never mind the fact that it now issued from Mélisande's lips – it ought to have pacified him. But it did not. He shook his head. "I was a fool," he said. Hood's words were still ringing in his ears, accusing him: *You're far more like me than anyone realises...* Perhaps he was. But that was not what he wanted to be. "If anything had happened to Ross because of my inaction..." He trailed off, shaking his head.

"Sounds like you should be the one marrying him," said Mélisande.

"Even less could I have lived with myself if I had brought disaster down upon you." This time, Mélisande was the one to look away. It suddenly struck him that she was the only one with whom he felt able to share such secrets. And she an agent of the King of France...

"Do you think there's a chance he'll come back? Try again?"

Gisburne shrugged his shoulders. "Nothing has stopped him until now.

We don't know how he will react to failure, what it will drive him to do."
He sighed heavily. "But, honestly, I'd be guessing, whatever I say. This
one is" – he struggled to find the words – "is unlike anything I've seen
before."

Mélisande nodded slowly. He knew without having to ask that she had
nothing to hide – on this subject, at least. "Sir John has doubled the guard
about the castle," she said. "He has them patrolling now – making regular
checks of the perimeter. They'll not make the same mistakes again."

"De Rosseley was just one of the opening moves," said Gisburne. "The
joust before the *mêlée*. Ultimately, the Red Hand has bigger fish to fry."
Here, he expected the obvious question. None came. But she already
knew what master he served – and perhaps much more besides. She lifted
herself shakily upon one elbow to bring her face closer to his, her other
hand clutching the sheet to her breast. For a moment, she simply looked
into his face, as if studying him. She traced one fingertip along his left
eyebrow, past the thin scar that split it, then on down the side of his cheek.

"So, what troubles *you* at night, Guy of Gisburne?" she said. "Aside
from obsessive thoughts of the Red Hand, I mean. What is it you have
thought of these past eighteen months when sleep has eluded you?" He
looked into her eyes. He could not account for why, but they seemed
suddenly to change, to admit him completely. More than that; to reach
out. "Anything?" The last word was little more than a whisper – barely
a breath on her parted lips. The room around him seemed to shift, to
become unstable. Gisburne felt himself growing dizzy, as if falling.

Her harsh cry jolted him back. She stiffened. Clutched her side. The cry
was cut short. What little colour remained in her face suddenly drained
from it, and she slumped into unconsciousness.

Gisburne dipped the damp cloth once more and pressed it against her
brow. Her breathing was agitated – pained – but still strong. If she could
get through the night, she would live. Then – as he gently mopped her
beautiful, pale forehead, droplets of water running into the tendrils of her
hair – he addressed her question. For one thing had always been there,
like a shadow in the background, even when the Red Hand and Hood and
Tancred had seemed to dominate his every waking thought. Something he
had not even admitted to himself – until now.

"You," he said.

XXXI

King Stormont Castle
25 May, 1193

GISBURNE AWOKE FACE down on the Persian rug, his face hot and itchy against its prickly, dusty fibres.

The sun was high in the sky. He sat up hurriedly, sensing it was late. Far later than he had meant to rise. A blanket slid off him as he did so; someone had covered him as he slept.

Everything had changed. Mélisande's bed was now empty, her belongings entirely gone. He felt a sense of panic – which common sense managed to suppress. But the feeling of empty desolation that followed was not so easily subdued.

He struggled to his feet, gripped by a sudden sense of urgency, and mortified at the thought of being discovered in the lady's bedchamber. As he turned, his foot knocked against something. Water slopped and spilled upon the rug. Near where his head had lain was the bowl and cloth, and next to them, tied in a knot, was a scarf of fine green silk.

He felt his heart thump at the sight of it. Snatching it up, without thinking, he brought it to his face. It carried her sweet scent. He drew it away, embarrassed by the impulse despite being completely alone in the chamber.

Perhaps she had left it by mistake. Perhaps she was still here, and it could yet be returned to her. Perhaps he could see her one more time. He gathered himself and hurried to the door, opening it a crack and peering out.

Two things occurred to him as he did so. The knot told him, as clearly as if she had said it herself, that her leaving of it was no accident. And *that* said that she was well. Both facts filled him with joy.

His wider predicament, however, did not.

He was too late. She had gone. Why did it always have to end like this? Why had she not woken him? The strength of his anger startled him. He had no claims over her – he wasn't sure anyone did, if they even could – but the thought did little to console him.

Feeling like an adulterer – and indignant at the injustice of the feeling – he stole along the curved stone corridor to his own chamber. Behind its door, he disordered the bed and made hasty, token adjustments to his appearance.

Moments later, he was striding into the sunlit courtyard. It was now almost empty – just the ruts to show where Mélisande's entourage had been. A handful of the castle's own servants – plainer by far than Mélisande's – went about their daily business, acknowledging Gisburne with a courteous nod as they did so.

"Guy!" called a voice. Gisburne turned and spied de Rosseley upon the eastern battlements, his raised arm silhouetted by the sun.

Gisburne waved, and headed for the stone stair.

"You look like shit," said de Rosseley as his friend approached.

"Good morning to you too, Ross."

"Well, it's true. You've got a face like a boar's ball sack and you look like you slept in your clothes."

"Says the man who resembles a corpse run over by a dozen ox-carts."

"Maybe so," said de Rosseley. "But I'm still the best dressed corpse west of Constantinople."

It was true. He had dressed to make an impression. His tunic was of red with black velvet trim, all embroidered with gold thread. Worn over it, in spite of the heat of the day, was a dazzlingly blue cloak, clasped about the throat with gold. He stood upon the battlement like a heroic captain at the prow of his ship, his hair and his cloak making languid movements in the gentle breeze.

Gisburne followed his gaze out beyond the bailey to the entourage of Mélisande de Champagne, now winding its steady way along the forest road.

"Well, what do you think of her?" said de Rosseley.

Gisburne pondered for a moment, making a mental inventory of Mélisande's qualities. There were too many to count. "Before I answer that," he said, "I have a question for you."

"Yes?"

"Ireland. John's campaign."

"Ah. That. Not exactly a crowning achievement."

"That's almost exactly what Prince John said."

"As well he might," said de Rosseley. "He was the one whose crown was not achieved, after all."

"He characterised it as mainly causing offence to a large number of people."

"That was the one thing we excelled at." It seemed de Rosseley almost blushed at the memory. "Needless to say, your father didn't approve. He was right not to. We were young fools. Did John say that too?"

Gisburne nodded.

"Well, at least he's kept his honesty," sighed de Rosseley. "Though there are times when he might do well to use it more sparingly – especially these days. People see the worst in him as it is. The last thing most of them want is to be told the truth."

"Do you recall anything – anything at all – that may have inspired a grudge?" said Gisburne. "Some particular slight or injustice?"

"That John inflicted? Personally?" De Rosseley puffed out his cheeks. "To be honest, the less contact he had with the locals the better he liked it. He wasn't the sociable, outgoing fellow you see today." A frown crept across his face. "There was one thing," he said. "It wasn't to do with John. Not really. But it was an odd business. An Irish noble – I forget his name – got some mad idea in his head. Ranulph Le Fort caught him creeping in to where we slept, knife in his hand. He challenged him, and the Irishman resisted. Ranulph killed him outright in the fight – those who survived an entanglement with Ranulph were few – but he lost two fingers from his left hand in the process. Poor bastard. The other Irish nobles were keen to smooth the whole thing over. Whether secretly sympathetic or not, they wanted no part of it. Ranulph himself would know more. He kept safe many of the records of that trip. We used to jokingly refer to him as 'the clerk.'"

He sniggered. "Anyone less like a clerk it is hard to imagine. You know, when he lost those fingers, he said the most annoying thing was that he could no longer write. Wrote with his left, you see – didn't care what anyone said about bad luck or the Devil. He'd give them the Devil for saying so! Do you know how awkward it is to write across a page with your left hand? Well, Ranulph did not merely cope with it; he had mastered it. That was the sort of man he was. Then he had to adapt to his right hand anyway." He shook his head. "Your father took over his scribing duties for a time, since he had some experience in that department."

"The Milford Roll," said Gisburne.

"You know of that?" said de Rosseley.

"I hope to have my hands on it soon. But why did my father draw it up, and not Ranulph?"

De Rosseley chuckled to himself. "Ranulph, Thomas of Baylesford and a chap called Fitz Osbert were the very last to arrive at Milford. It was not at all certain they would make it; Ranulph and Baylesford caroused together a great deal in those days, and had evidently led young Fitz Osbert astray. But they did, by the skin of their teeth – and mightily hungover. So, it's thanks to drink that their names appear last on that list."

Gisburne pondered de Rosseley's account. "So what drove this Irish noble to attempt murder?"

De Rosseley shrugged. "Never did find out. It was a bad business, though. Cut your father to the quick. I think he'd come to trust them. He always was the sort to win people over, to give them the benefit of the doubt. I'd wager he was the only one who didn't make an enemy there."

Gisburne looked into the distance. "You know, until recent weeks I didn't even know that my father had been a member of that expedition."

"He didn't tell you?"

Gisburne shook his head.

De Rosseley shrugged. "He was a natural choice. He knew Ireland. He'd been there before – one of the few of us who had."

Suddenly, things began to make a kind of sense. "He never spoke of that trip either," said Gisburne. "But I guessed all the same."

"That one really was meant to be secret. He took such responsibilities seriously."

"But what was its purpose?"

De Rosseley made a show of looking over his shoulder. "I think it's safe to tell you now..." he said. "Richard de Clare, Earl of Striguil and occasionally of Pembroke. Also known as 'Strongbow.' He was building a fine little kingdom for himself in Ireland years ago. Your father was sent to bring him round to King Henry's point of view." He shrugged again. "Didn't work. But it's hardly surprising. De Clare was a hothead. How did you guess, anyway?"

"Before he went away, he would talk of events in Ireland often," said Gisburne. "Then after, not at all." He thought of the image of his father as an agent on a secret mission, and smiled at it. The revelation that they had this in common made him feel closer to the old man than he had in years.

"So," said de Rosseley. "Your turn."

"My turn to what?"

"To answer the question," said de Rosseley. Then, as if addressing someone profoundly deaf, added: "What do you think of the lady Mélisande?"

Knowing he could put it off no longer, Gisburne nodded slowly. "You really want to know?"

"Of course I do. There's no one whose opinion I value more. Except on the subject of clothes." He looked his guest up and down. "You can keep those disturbing thoughts to yourself."

Gisburne looked out across the rolling landscape, images of Mélisande flickering through his mind. His first sight of her in the wintry streets of

Paris – like the miracle of a spring bloom in all that grim, filthy chaos. Their first meeting at her encampment outside Marseille, and her complex game of feigned coyness and coquetry. Unmasking her in a forest in France, her eyes fiery, her hair full and wild. The sad, strong look on her face as she had surrendered herself to Tancred – to save Gisburne's life. That last night in Wissant, knowing they had won, and were alive. Yes, especially that.

He took a deep breath. "I think she's arrogant. Controlling, self-absorbed, impulsive, and unreliable. And probably prohibitively expensive to keep."

De Rosseley stared at him for a moment. "Don't hold back or anything, will you?" He said. "If I didn't know better I'd think you fancied her yourself." De Rosseley always did have a knack for hitting the nail on the head without realising it. Gisburne supposed it was this instinct – or some aspect of it – that had kept him alive all these years.

"You want to know what I think?" said de Rosseley. Gisburne was not at all sure he did. His friend stared out over the trees, towards the hazy cloud of dust raised by the entourage of Mélisande de Champagne. Gisburne was certain there was longing in his eyes.

"I think you're absolutely, totally right."

Gisburne's felt his heart leap in his chest.

"There was something just not right there. Some" – de Rosseley struggled to find the words – "some lack of connection."

"Why, Ross – I never knew you were such a sentimentalist."

"It's like you were talking to her and not talking to her. Like there was someone else in there, hidden behind that façade. Half the time she was in my company, she just looked like she was in pain."

My God, Ross, thought Gisburne. *If you only knew...*

De Rosseley sighed. "I just don't want all that complication, you know?"

"Is this where you tell me you'd rather women were more like horses?" said Gisburne. Last time they'd met, that had almost been de Rosseley's entire opinion on the matter.

"I will say this..." continued de Rosseley. "Grand as this place is – and it is grand, let's not deny the fact – at the end of the day there's only room for one arrogant, controlling, impulsive, self-absorbed person in it."

"You missed out *unreliable.*"

De Rosseley waved the rebuke away, then planted both hands on the stone parapet. "I can't say it doesn't sadden me, though," he said. "I mean – great arse."

Gisburne felt his fists clench. "As I said," he muttered, fighting to keep the indignation out of his voice, "such a sentimentalist."

De Rosseley gave a snort of a laugh and slapped Gisburne on the back, then winced as his own battered bones protested.

"Well, thank you, Guy, for your honesty and plain speaking. You have confirmed what my gut was already telling me, and may well have saved me a lifetime of pain." Gisburne felt a pang of guilt at de Rosseley words, but could not help but be amused that they came from the mouth of one who invited more pain into his life than anyone he knew. "Much as I love being tested to my limits by some worthy opponent – live for it, really – a fellow needs some respite. Not sure I want to fight battles at home as well."

Gisburne smiled to himself. What de Gaillon would think of this small victory, he had no idea. But it was a victory, nonetheless. In his head he uttered a brief apology to the Count of Boulogne's daughter, then looked once more at the train of wagons slowly receding into the distance, wondering when he would see her again. "You'd lose," he said.

XXXII

Eastchepe
25 May, 1193

THE PAGE WAS running. It was one of Hamon's boys who spotted him first; Galfrid saw him nudge his captain in the ribs and nod across the crowd. Galfrid followed the boys' gaze along Eastchepe towards Tower Street, at first seeing nothing beyond a slight disturbance in the throng: sudden movements, hands thrown up, some accompanied by gruff exclamations.

Then he saw the flash of scarlet. Another shove, and it became the red livery of the Prince, almost glowing in the low, early evening sun. Another shout, and from the packed knot of people – through whom he pressed with fearless resolve – the boy emerged, his face as red as his tunic.

His name was Osbert – one of John's messengers. He was ginger haired and ridiculously fresh faced; had his mother given him up as a babe, she would surely still recognise him now. Anyone could see he didn't belong – none more so than the ring of ragged urchins gathered outside the door of Widow Fleet's. As Osbert caught sight of Galfrid and made a determined beeline for him, they eyed him up and down like predators considering their next meal.

"Squire Galfrid!" said the boy, squeezing past the raggedy lads and kneeling in front of their master. He soiled his pristine knee on a scraping of horse dung, and a few of the boys sniggered. Hamon silenced them with a glare.

"What is it, boy?" said Galfrid. Unfazed by either the state of his hose or the half-dozen ragamuffins who now surrounded him, he stood, and – never once taking his eyes off his object – proffered a tiny, even square of white at the end of a poker-straight arm.

"Message for you, sire," he said, in a clear, strong voice. The boy clearly took his duties seriously. Galfrid was sure he would go far.

"For me?" he said with a frown. He took the flimsy scrap – moist from the boy's hot palm – and unfolded it.

It was in English – the language of King Alfred, Harold, and everyone in England below the rank of knight. Yet Galfrid, himself of pure Saxon stock, knew almost no one who wrote in it. A few clerks and poets, perhaps. A handful of monks maintaining age-old chronicles set in motion before the conquest. But, as a rule, those for whom it was their native tongue could neither read nor write and had little use for either skill, and those who could, wrote in Latin or French.

In a close, neat hand it said: *Find me at the Red Dragon*. Nothing else. No name, no other mark of any kind. It offered no clue as to whether this was meant as a code, a riddle, or some veiled reference to their elusive quarry. One quality, nonetheless, rendered it entirely distinct, and told Galfrid all he needed to know – a thing that had nothing whatever to do with the words.

It was written on paper.

Galfrid had not seen paper since Acre, and knew of only one person who used it.

"Hamon," said Galfrid. "Where would I find the Red Dragon?"

"You mean the inn?" said Hamon. "There's a few of 'em. But the closest is dahn there," he pointed east. "On the right, in 'Arp lane."

"Good," said Galfrid. He crumpled the note in his fist and looked down at Osbert, whose intensely serious baby face was still staring up at him. "You get yourself back to the Tower fast as you can," he said. Osbert nodded, and was off like a hare pursued by greyhounds, plunging once more into the bustling crowd.

"The rest of you lads know what you're looking for," said Galfrid as he strode off. "Now hop to it!" Not to be outdone, Hamon's boys dispersed in all directions like wasps from a fallen nest.

THE HEAVING INTERIOR of the Red Dragon was thick with the warm, yeasty smell of stale drink and damp floorboards.

Scanning the room, Galfrid immediately spied a familiar figure sat alone at a rickety table in the far corner, nursing a mug of ale with a dour expression. With a private smile he wove his way through the sweaty patrons and plonked himself down opposite.

"I thought you couldn't come out in daylight," said Galfrid.

Llewellyn of Newport harumphed and scowled at the squire. "Believe me, if I could avoid coming out in the open, I would. It's not good for the business I am in." He sucked at his ale and wiped the back of his hand across his grizzled beard. "But we are a diminishing band at the Tower, so needs must..."

"Diminishing?"

Llewellyn held up his hands. "Don't ask. Suffice to say, Fitz Thomas seeks to gain favour with the King's men by making Prince John's life as difficult as possible." He huffed in irritation. "But at least when he stabs him in the back he does so with a smile on his face, eh?"

Without further comment, he reached down by his side and his hand reappeared grasping a rough-edged scroll tied with a faded ribbon which he slapped upon the table top. The parchment was wrapped about a bar of honey-coloured wood and went down with such a thwack it made Galfrid jump.

"What's that?" he said.

"It's the thing you've been waiting for," said Llewellyn. Then, when Galfrid failed to offer a response, he leaned forward and added: "Take a look."

Galfrid, who knew perfectly well what the scroll was, looked about him at the chattering men packed between the inn's uneven walls.

"Here?"

Llewellyn sighed. "You think any of these imbeciles knows what it is, or what use to make of it?" He did not bother to lower his voice. No one reacted. "How many d'you think can even read it?"

It was a fair point. With a shrug, Galfrid pulled the ribbon free, unrolled the document and spread it flat upon the table.

The Milford Roll was not long – the parchment barely warranted being rolled at all. The majority of it was taken up by a list of a few dozen names written in a small, neat hand across three columns, but at the top, in a distinctly separate section headed by a lofty proclamation in Latin that Galfrid did not bother to read, was a handful of names in much larger and more ostentatious characters. Several, he recognised: Bardulf, Wendenal, de Rosseley – and Gisburne. He raised his eyebrows at that. But of course... 'G.' Gisburne's own father had been one of those dancing men all this time. But the question was, had his master left the name unwritten for the sake of brevity, or did he not wish Galfrid to know? His secrecy had already proved a sore point.

"Well, there it is," said Llewellyn, sitting back. "The Milford Roll – whatever good it may do you."

"We are searching for one large rat in a city of twenty thousand rats," said Galfrid. "Anything that may help transform that quest from the impossible to the merely tortuous is most welcome."

"This rat has a habit of announcing himself," said Llewellyn. His voice seemed suddenly to have lost its edge of gruff, world-weary humour. "It's the other reason I am here. There is news that could not be trusted to a messenger..." He leaned in close, his expression grave, his voice lowered to a husky whisper, only just audible above the din. "You see this name?"

He placed a finger to the scroll.

"Jocelyn de Gaillard..." read Galfrid.

"Not three hours ago he was brutally slain in a manner identical to the others – to the north-east, in Stibenhede, and on property belonging to the Knights Hospitallers, no less. He was of their order. Needless to say, this will not please them." He paused to allow this information to sink in. "I arrived here ahead of the news. It is not yet public, but word moves fast in London – faster than anywhere on earth. It will overtake me – is perhaps doing so as we sit. And already there are wider rumblings. Whispers are abroad of the attack at King Stormont, and rumours of other bizarre killings up and down the land are flying thick and fast. The superstitious speak of devils and monsters – of portents, with worse to follow. The rest sense something is afoot – though whether invasion or rebellion or the judgement of God, none can say. So, the old rivalries and enmities that are constantly on the simmer in this cauldron of a city bubble up to fill the void. Normans blame Saxons. Saxons blame Jews. Jews blame the Hansa merchants. The Hansas blame the worthies of the commune – and the commune blames the crown – or the next nearest thing..."

"John?" said Galfrid.

Llewellyn nodded. "He always was easy to blame, and they know he is here..."

Galfrid shook his head and gave an empty laugh. "What they saw wasn't even him."

"It makes no difference now," said Llewellyn. "It takes little to stir unrest in this city. And believe me, tensions are brewing. You must look to the other names on this list, while some still live..."

Even as he was listening to these words, Galfrid had become dimly aware that the perpetual noise out in the street had grown into a greater commotion. And now, among the shouts, he heard a cry of "murder". Heads in the inn turned. Conversations ceased. Several began to spill out into the street, their drinks abandoned. Galfrid stood, rolling up the scroll and stuffing it into his bag. Llewellyn knocked back his ale and both headed for the door.

Outside, day was turning to night, and the milling crowd – no longer flowing along the street, but surging dangerously this way and that – had begun to turn with it, from dog to wolf. The word "murder" sounded again like a howl, was taken up and repeated until it became a kind of barbaric chant, punctuated by shaken fists. It was uttered with fury, with horror, and with an eager violence. Galfrid could feel the menace beating off the crowd, like heat from a blaze. Within this seething mass arguments were already raging. Fights threatened to break out. Immediately before him, a dark-skinned woman – a Jew, Galfrid thought – was grabbed and pulled to the ground, apparently by a random stranger. No sooner had he done so than he was set upon by two others, and the terrified woman scrambled away, never to be seen again.

Galfrid clutched his bag closer to him. "I think your news has arrived," he said.

XXXIII

SOMETHING WAS HAPPENING south of Eastchepe. Unfamiliar though he was with the ways of cities, Gisburne knew enough of people to recognise a mob when he saw one.

When he had arrived back to the sweltering streets of London, he had found the crowds along Gracechurch Street and Eastchepe already thick, their mood uneasy. There was shouting, mostly incoherent. Some spoke in urgent whispers. Several of those without pressing business had coagulated into groups and shifted edgily, as if looking for trouble, or in fear of it. It happened from time to time, he supposed, when so many souls were stuffed into one place. He had seen it in armies – the mood turning, like milk in the summer sun. What started it was often a mystery – a shift in the weather, stale food, bad news. Sometimes it only took one drop to sour the lot.

Nyght had ridden through it all without flinching. He had seen far worse than this in his time. Threats and shouts meant nothing to him. Weapons, precious little – even fire would not always turn his head. There was only one thing guaranteed to spook him, no matter what the circumstances: the flapping of a chicken. Gisburne had kept this fact close to him. Had his enemies only known to come at him wielding fowl, his career might have been considerably shorter.

When he returned from stabling his horse and found Galfrid not at home, Gisburne stepped back out into the street. This time, he sensed real trouble – not mere restlessness, but true hostility. The crowd's movement had changed. It was now flowing westward, where he could see it joining with others pressing south down Gracechurch Street and on into Bridge Street. This, now, was a rabble with a distinct purpose. They looked angry. Vengeful.

Several clutched the tools of their trade – picks and billhooks, axes and hammers. On any other day on these same streets, any one of them would have passed without comment – as commonplace and innocent as a broom or a milk pail. Now, they were wielded as weapons. Some, like Gisburne, stood and watched in bemusement as the throng pushed by; most were swept up by it, swelling its numbers as it advanced. Almost opposite him, Gisburne spied three familiar faces – women he knew by sight, who he believed to be three generations of the same family. Bemused by the street's traffic, these gentle souls were earnestly questioning passers-by. Within moments, they had shut their doors and joined the rabble, and no more than fifty yards on he saw them shouting oaths and uttering threats with the best of them before the flood finally swallowed them up.

From this, one word rose clear. More than any other, this was the word Gisburne had been listening for these past weeks – the word whose arrival he had anticipated with the same confused mix of emotions he normally felt only before battle.

Murder.

He turned to see his squire's face bobbing towards him in the swell. "Galfrid!" He raised an arm high. Galfrid did likewise, then fought his way across the stream of people.

"What is it?" said Gisburne. "What's going on?"

"I'm not sure," Galfrid looked about him as if still disorientated. "I've just been with Llewellyn," he said. "There's been another one, in Stibenhede. A Hospitaller. And he's on the list."

Gisburne frowned. Stibenhede was north.

Before he could speak, Hamon – heading from the west and struggling against the flow – burst through the crowd and crashed into Gisburne's left side. Gisburne caught him by the shoulders.

"Murder, sire!" Hamon blurted. "'Orrible murder! Like what you said about. They're mad wiv it!"

"Yes boy, we know," said Galfrid still looking at the crowd as if trying to fathom their movements. "Jocelyn de Gaillard. But if that's in Stibenhede, why are…"

"No, not there," interrupted the boy. "Anuvver. On the bridge!" He pointed south, then darted off again, this time following the direction of the crowd – towards London Bridge.

GISBURNE AND GALFRID set off on foot, pushing with the throng towards the river.

It was barely four hundred yards from Widow Fleet's door to the bridge, yet this journey, more than any other they had undertaken in recent weeks, seemed to take an age. But just as the crowd would not be stopped, neither would it be rushed.

When finally the old wooden bridge came into view ahead, Gisburne saw upon it a vast multitude of people, the majority of whom were clamouring towards the bridge's right side, where work on the new stone bridge was in progress.

"What's going on?" shouted Galfrid, struggling to get a clear view above the heads of the crowd. "Can you see it? Is it in the river?"

Gisburne could not see it – nor was he certain that he ever would. It seemed impossible that the old bridge could take any more bodies than were already packed upon it. He was sure that any minute all movement would grind to a halt, stranding them just yards short of their goal. But against expectation, their slow, shuffling progress continued, and as they neared he began to see people upon the wooden bridge pointing, not down, to the water, but across, towards the stout pillars of the new bridge. It was now in its seventeenth year of construction, but as yet stretched barely a third of the river's width, its grey stone arches clad in a ramshackle lattice of timber scaffolding, a soaring span leading nowhere.

The crowd ahead had come to a standstill upon the wooden bridge. None now passed on to the other side. None could. And yet, as if more determined than ever to prove its worth in the presence of its new stone counterpart, the old, rickety structure – some of its lower supports still blackened from the great fire of 1135 – somehow accepted more and yet more of the advancing horde upon it, until finally Gisburne and Galfrid, crushed in upon every side, felt its uneven timbers creak beneath their feet.

With dogged resolve – and little regard for their neighbours – he and Galfrid pushed and edged their way through, towards the rail on the bridge's western side. There were shouts, protests. But Gisburne – still openly wearing his sword against the general prohibition of the city, and with a look of fierce determination on him – attracted no challengers.

Jostling between the horrified onlookers – too rapt in what was before them to notice anything to either side – they at last planted their elbows upon the rail. And then they, too, saw.

LITTLE MORE THAN twenty yards away – close enough for every detail to be clearly visible – hung a body. It was impaled upon a scaffold pole, whose sharpened top protruded from the dead man's upturned mouth like some gruesome, gore-stained tongue. Lips drew back from bloody teeth, and dead eyes stared. The tang of fresh blood, blended with the thick stench of the Thames, wafted on the warm westerly breeze. Beneath him, a cascade of red coloured the complex wooden structure and still dripped into the two dozen yards of grey water that separated them.

Sometimes the mere departure of the spirit renders the dead so alien that their wives and husbands will not recognise them. At other times, even disfigured flesh will cling so doggedly to its animate likeness as to seem uncanny. Gisburne had not looked upon the face of the dead man for a dozen years at least. Yet when he did so – even in this grotesquely deformed state – the man's identity was as clear as if he had stepped from the room only moments before.

"I know him," he said, his voice emotionless. "Mortimer de Vere. A friend to my father."

He was not how his father would have remembered him. The elder knight's right hand was missing – a single, clean cut. His once-fine tunic had been ripped or cut apart to reveal his chest, and carved upon it, like some grim heraldic device, were three crude figures: *xxx*.

"Thirty days..." muttered Gisburne. "Thirty days left."

Close by, a man with a face like a hog, having heard Gisburne utter the name, repeated a hoarse approximation of it, then bellowed something unintelligible. Whatever the exclamation had meant to articulate, its pure rage inflamed the crowd further. They surged forward again, pressing Gisburne against the rail, and the rotting timbers groaned. As he stared down into the dark water far below, Gisburne fancied he could feel the whole bridge swaying under the weight of the bodies upon it.

"We must get out," he said. "Get over there..." They turned to shoulder their way back towards the north bank. No sooner had they quit the rail than new, eager sightseers squeezed into their places.

At the abutment of the new bridge – an area cluttered with stone blocks, timber, tools and stout rope – a party of armed men was barely holding back the jeering crowd. They appeared hastily-equipped, and, though making a decent fist of it, ill-prepared for the task. Gisburne supposed them to be civic militia. If seriously challenged, they would not stand fast.

Parting the rabble like reeds, he advanced on the youngest of the guards. "We must see the body," he said. "Let us past, in the name of the Crown!" And without waiting for a response, he pushed past and onto the bridge's stonework, with Galfrid, chin held high, close behind him. The startled militiamen did nothing to prevent them. Having spied Gisburne's sword, they perhaps took him for a noble – or if they doubted it, had not the nerve to put it to the test. Seeing this incursion, the crowd pushed forward and offered fresh protests, and the guards' attention was then taken up with them once more.

There was an eerie stillness upon the new bridge – a weird sense of separation from the world. Just yards away, all eyes upon this spot, half of

London roared and gestured. But here, on this ghostly stage – thick with white mason's dust – there was not another soul, not another sound.

"We must find out what we can before they come to their senses and try to remove us," said Gisburne. "I have only my sword and John's authority to back me up – and of the two, I think my sword the more reliable."

He scanned the surface of the smooth stone. A dark stain caught his eye. He knelt, tested it with a finger. Blood.

"This pole," called Galfrid. "What do you make of it?"

Gisburne stood, and joined his squire at the parapet. The end of the scaffold pole upon which Mortimer de Vere had been impaled was immediately below them, no more than an arm's length away. Flies buzzed about the body. Gisburne shuddered. The Red Hand had stood where they now did.

"It's been sharpened," he said. "No workman upon this bridge did that. But neither can I believe the Red Hand whittled away at it with a body draped over his shoulder."

"Christ," said Galfrid. "He did it in advance. He came here beforehand and cut the stake in readiness..."

"...making sure it was in just the right place, so his victim would be as visible as possible from the old bridge."

"He's got balls, I'll give him that," said Galfrid. "But when? How?"

"Last night," said Gisburne, as certain as if he had done it himself. "Under cover of darkness."

"And the murder...?"

"I don't believe de Vere was killed here," said Gisburne. "If he had come to the bridge of his own accord, it could only have been by chance, and this killing was not opportunistic. No, the bridge was part of the plan – which means it was done elsewhere." He thought of the sharpened pole, the spot of blood. "He must have waited until work was done for the day. The bridge almost deserted. There would be none to see or stop him. Though how he got the body here in the first place, through crowded streets..." He sighed and turned about. Something nearby – something that had previously seemed of no consequence – caught his eye.

"A barrow!" he said. He strode towards it, and hauled back the crumpled oilcloth that covered the top of the handcart. The wood beneath was stained with blood. "Wheeled through the streets, in plain sight, the body under the cloth. And straight onto this bridge, unchallenged..."

"Just a common workman hunched over a barrow," said Galfrid. "But that would mean he was not in his armour."

The realisation hit Gisburne full force. The Red Hand would have been vulnerable – as vulnerable as any man. For the first time – perhaps the only time. With a roar of frustration, Gisburne swung his boot into the handcart, rocking it onto one wheel, then walked to the bridge's eastern side and leaned on the parapet.

"We could have had him," he said. "With an arrow. With a damned knife!"

"If he made the mistake once, he may do so again," said Galfrid.

"It wasn't a mistake," said Gisburne. "It was calculated. But he's fearless. Cares little for his own safety. And so he will do things people could not possibly expect."

"Like Hood," mused Galfrid.

Gisburne thought on it for a moment. "No, not like Hood," he said. "Hood cares about nothing. But this one... There is something he cares a great deal about. So much so that nothing else matters."

Galfrid looked at the staring faces packing the bridge opposite. "This is hardly an out-of-the-way spot," he said. "Once the body was revealed, the reaction would have been immediate. So, how did he escape?" He turned back to where the half-bridge joined the crowded bank. "Not the same way, surely?"

"It's never the obvious way with him," said Gisburne. "Never the easy way." He peered down past the web of scaffolding on the bridge's eastern side to the lapping water beneath.

"Boat?" said Galfrid, looking over the parapet.

Gisburne nodded. "I'm sure of it." Because that was precisely what he would have done. "But still, *someone* must have seen him."

"I'm guessing he did," said Galfrid, pointing down towards the water's edge.

Near the north bank, in an eddy of swirling tidewater caught against a broken paling, floated a body. By the manner of his dress, he had been a mason. What had happened to the man's head, Gisburne could not tell – but it now flapped in the current like an empty sack.

"You!"

Gisburne looked up to see four armed men approaching – more formidable than the others. At their head was a stout, bow-legged man with a thatch of straight white hair between his hat and the shoulders of his fine robes. He had a gold chain about his neck, and an elaborate staff in his fist. A worthy of the commune, Gisburne had no doubt. His face was pink with fury.

"Our time is up," said Gisburne, and turned back to the parapet.

The stout man huffed to a halt beside him. "What do you think you are doing?" he demanded gruffly, a little too close to Gisburne's ear.

"We're on royal business," said Gisburne.

"Royal!" scoffed the man. He grabbed Gisburne's shoulder and attempted to turn him back around. Gisburne resisted – then turned to face the man of his own volition. He was in no mood for this. "The last person to do that will never remember what happened next," he said.

"Are *you* threatening *me*?" said the man, his tone was incredulous, his cheeks red as a ham. But then he caught sight of the knight's sword, and for a moment his resolve faltered.

"State your business," he barked.

"What's it to do with you, anyway?" said Gisburne. He did not like to be pushed – not when people had not even had the courtesy to introduce themselves.

"In my city, your business is my business," the man said.

Finally, Gisburne understood. Stood before him was none other than Henry Fitz Ailwyn, Mayor of London. Here, he *was* king. Inwardly, Gisburne cursed. Threatening the Mayor was perhaps not the wisest course.

"My business is to bring order," Gisburne said.

"Bring order?" Fitz Ailwyn laughed and looked Gisburne up and down. "You?"

Fitz Ailwyn's captain stepped forward and whispered something in his master's ear. Gisburne did not hear the words, but they knocked some of the haughtiness out of the mayor's expression.

"You are Guy of Gisburne?" he said.

"*Sir* Guy of Gisburne."

"And you serve Prince John?"

"I do."

Fitz Ailwyn huffed. "That is a mixed blessing."

"It is the same Prince John who granted Londoners the freedoms they now enjoy," said Gisburne, holding Fitz Ailwyn's hard gaze. "Who allowed them to have a mayor."

Fitz Ailwyn narrowed his eyes. Gisburne saw the muscles of his jaw clench. Clearly, this was a debt of which he did not wish to be reminded.

"You know what people are saying?" said Fitz Ailwyn. "That these disasters – for all know full well there have been others – arrived with the Prince. That they accompanied his progress from the North. That they are a curse upon him – and now upon us."

"Do you believe that?" said Gisburne.

"It doesn't matter what I believe," hissed Fitz Ailwyn. He gestured wildly towards the old wooden bridge. "They believe it."

Gisburne took a step forward. Fitz Ailwyn's guards gripped their weapons. Gisburne lowered his voice so only Fitz Ailwyn could hear. "I am charged with stopping the man responsible for this outrage – for causing these upheavals among your people. Is that not in your interest? You can help me, or you can leave me be, but whatever you do now will be remembered – if John should become king."

Fitz Ailwyn considered Gisburne's words in silence.

"I am satisfied," he announced. "You may go about your business. But you will vacate the bridge forthwith." He turned to his guard. "See that they do." And with that, he marched off to perform his own examination of the scene. Fitz Ailwyn was every inch the politician, but Gisburne could allow him this one token victory. They were done here.

"He's hedging his bets," muttered Galfrid as they were escorted back towards the north bank. "We can expect no help from him."

"I'll be happy simply to be left alone," said Gisburne.

At the abutment of the bridge a larger contingent of militia had now arrived. Passing them, Gisburne saw three other men with rope and a barrow, come to take the body down.

"Thirty days..." said Gisburne as they headed back up Bridge Street. "There are now exactly thirty days until Hood's execution."

As they walked, the crowds fell away – until, if anything, the streets were emptier than usual. The sun was setting, casting them into deep shadow. A few scattered figures loitered aimlessly – one or two ran past them towards the bridge. Around them now was now the same eerie stillness that Gisburne had felt upon the bridge, as if the infected air of the murder were spreading into the whole city.

"Two in one day," said Galfrid, shaking his head.

"This is how he responds to failure," said Gisburne. "One missed target, and he doubles his efforts."

"In public. And in broad daylight," muttered Galfrid. "Christ..."

"He's showing us what he can do – making sure he has our attention."

"*Our* attention? He's done this because of *us?*"

Gisburne said nothing.

Galfrid nodded in mute acceptance. "Then he knows we are here."

"I am certain of it."

Suddenly, Galfrid stopped and snapped his fingers. "I almost forgot..." he said, and, scrabbling in his bag, pulled out a mottled scroll of parchment. "The Milford Roll," he said, and slapped it into his master's palm. "Arrived just ahead of you."

Gisburne immediately unrolled it and scanned the list of names. There was Bardulf and Wendenal, de Mortville and de Rosseley. And there was de Vere.

"What was the name of the other knight?" he said. "The one who died earlier today?"

"Jocelyn de Gaillard. Why?"

Gisburne saw the name. But that was not all he saw. "We have work to do," said Gisburne, rolling it hastily. "Through the night, if we have to. And then we must go to John without delay."

XXXIV

The Tower of London
26 May, 1193

"THERE ARE FEWER names than I thought," said Gisburne.

"Still more than I remembered..." said John.

There were sixteen names at the top of the Milford Roll – the sixteen who formed the core of Prince John's party in Ireland. Of these, five had lately been brutally slain.

"Galfrid and I have been asking around," said Gisburne. "Trying to establish who among these sixteen are here, now, in London. Based on what we have gleaned – with the addition of information we've had from de Rosseley and Llewellyn – we now have a fair idea. But there are gaps..."

"I'll help where I can," said John. He looked suddenly drawn – as if lacking sleep. Though he fought to maintain normality, his manner was agitated, and anxious.

Gisburne was bone-tired, and he knew Galfrid could not be feeling much better. Half the night they had spent pursuing trails and scraps of information, quizzing Hamon and his boys and sending them on fresh quests, traipsing around endless streets to call upon the sixteen's friends and friends of friends – some of whom, having since changed allegiance, gave them short shrift. Others refused to come to their doors altogether, or had closed their shutters against them. Gisburne was not surprised. London was in an uneasy mood. The hysteria had abated as the crowd dispersed, but strange tensions lingered on the streets. It appeared that many had taken to the perceived safety of their homes a little earlier tonight – while others stalked them far later, and with questionable intent. Gisburne had seen groups of men – one heavily armed, several the worse for drink – roaming the streets like hungry wolves, looking for something upon which to vent their frustration. Later that night, one of Hamon's boys had been brought back beaten to a bloody pulp. The lad, more shaken that he would admit, had dismissed his own injuries, and insisted upon returning to his task. Gisburne forbade it, and sent him to his home – wherever or whatever that was. Hamon took the episode in his stride. It happened, he said.

When it was finally beyond the hour when any could be persuaded to answer their doors, Gisburne and Galfrid had dragged themselves back to Eastchepe. Sleep had not come for Gisburne. His mind had been racing, but for the first time in days, he didn't care. Even the tiresome ritual at the gates of the Tower had not fazed him – despite the guards at first refusing to accept the signed and sealed letter of admission supplied by Prince John. He was exhausted, yes – but he was also, at last, on the scent.

"Taking them in the order they appear on the Roll, then..." said Gisburne, his finger upon the parchment. "Walter Bardulf is our first victim." His finger slid down to the next name. "Eustace Fitz Warren we believe to have been dead some years."

"Correct," said John. "Soon after Ireland. Riding accident. Very sad."

Gisburne struck the name through with a stick of charcoal.

"William de Wendenal – the second victim. Raymond of Colton," Gisburne rubbed his chin. "Of him we could find nothing."

"He took holy orders, I believe," said John. "Holed up in a monastery somewhere in Wales."

"Then we can assume he is safe – at least for now." Gisburne struck him out, too.

"Hugh de Mortville was our third victim. Then we have William Fitz Robert, and Robert Fitz William."

"Fitz Robert died at Hattin," said John. Gisburne crossed off the name.

"And I have it on good authority Robert Fitz William also went to the Holy Land," said Galfrid. "Now settled and with a family in Acre."

He, too, was crossed off.

"John de Rosseley we know about. Jocelyn de Gaillard – he was our fifth victim. Baldwin of Melville..."

"In Cornwall," said Galfrid.

"So, he can also be discounted." Gisburne struck the name through. "Alan Fitz Bruce is, as near as we can tell, in a prison in France."

"Unfortunately, that doesn't come as a surprise," said John.

"Out of harm's way, anyway," said Galfrid. Gisburne struck out the name.

"Mortimer de Vere was victim number six. Robert of Gisburne..." For a moment, Gisburne's hand hesitated. There seemed something terribly wrong about obliterating his own father's name. He forced his hand across the page. "That leaves just three names: Ranulph Le Fort, Thomas of Baylesford and Richard Fitz Osbert." These last three were written in a subtly different hand – evidently added after their late arrival.

"Fitz Osbert died early this year," said Galfrid. "So Llewellyn said. But of the circumstances, he was vague."

"Vague?" said Gisburne.

"The circumstances may not be divulged," interjected John. "He was working for me. Definitely dead, anyway. I can vouch for that."

Gisburne nodded slowly. "On Ranulph Le Fort, I regret we have failed to turn up a single thing."

"I know he fell on hard times," said John. "He always was plagued by ill luck. Last I heard he was in London, but that was nearly a year ago, in connection with Baylesford. They were good friends. Baylesford had given up courtly life altogether and become a merchant, and I seem to recall he put some opportunities Ranulph's way."

"I believe Baylesford to be in London," said Galfrid. "He's not easy to pin down. Always on the move, often at sea. But he owns a house here, by all accounts, and has been seen in the past few weeks. He has a ship at the wharves, too. We'll keep pairs of eyes on them, and if he's here, we'll find him."

"Well, now we have a clearer picture, at least," Gisburne said, his eyes scanning the dwindling list.

"So many of them dead..." said John, shaking his head. "I begin to feel old."

"It's not the number that should concern you," said Gisburne. "It's the rate. Four died in the course of eight years, but in the past two months, that total has risen to nine. And there will be more – unless we stop him."

John sighed and shook his head, as if overwhelmed by the task ahead. He reached for a cup of wine and took a drink. Gisburne saw his hand shaking.

"Are you all right?" Gisburne said.

"Don't worry about me," said John. If it was meant to be reassuring, it failed. He sounded tetchy and anxious – uncharacteristically so. "It's nothing," he added, moderating his tone. "Really."

"There's something else," said Gisburne. He turned the Roll towards the Prince. "Look at the names of the victims – in particular those who have been attacked in or around London. What do you notice?"

"My God," said John. His eyes widened.

Gisburne tapped his finger upon the parchment, following the rhythm of his words. "They were attacked in the precise order their names appear on this list."

Realisation dawned upon the Prince's face. "But that would mean..."

Gisburne nodded. "That the Red Hand has a copy of the Milford Roll."

"But how is that possible?" said John. "A royal document in the hands of a lowly tinker?"

"I don't know," said Gisburne. "He is not what he appears – we know that much. But we also know he plans meticulously, and that orderly mind of his may yet be his undoing." He thought of de Rosseley's words – *One must always look for the advantage* – of the method Mélisande had used to fell the Red Hand. And – as always – he recalled the wisdom of Gilbert de Gaillon: *Your enemy's strength may become his weakness if it can be turned against him.*

"Now we know where he will strike next," said Gisburne. "Or, at least, who." He placed his finger on the next name to appear on the list: Ranulph Le Fort.

John threw up his hands in exasperation. "But Ranulph is the one man we cannot locate."

"He was last heard of in London," said Gisburne. "We have a network established on these streets, and if he is here, we will find him. If that proves impossible – if he is already dead – then we know the Red Hand will turn his attention to Thomas of Baylesford. Either way, our next task is clear. I will track down Ranulph. Galfrid will seek out Baylesford." He thrust his finger at the table top. "Then, by God, we will have him..."

XXXV

"So, what do you want of me?" said Llewellyn, his hands spread wide.

For once, Gisburne did not know. Every other time he had brought himself before England's greatest and least-well-known enginer, he had come with a specific need. To shoot a grapple over a ninety-foot rampart. To hurl fire in the form of a ball. To stop a sword blade without use of a shield.

But today... What was it he wanted?

"Well?" prompted Llewellyn.

Gisburne shuffled on the barrel that served as his seat. "Answers," he said.

Llewellyn stared at him. "Answers... Can you be more specific?"

Gisburne sighed, frustrated by his own lack of clarity – by the words he knew he was about to utter. "Answers to the problem of the Red Hand."

"I'm an enginer," said Llewellyn, "not a mystic. If you want answers, I need questions."

But Gisburne did not know the questions. If he did, they were either too numerous, or too vague to be of use. "The time will come when I must face him," said Gisburne, "either in the streets, or within these walls. It is inevitable. But I must have a strategy – some means of dealing with him. And – though it pains me to say it – I have none." He sighed and rubbed his brow. "We tell ourselves John is now safe within this fortress. But all of us know that even the Tower is not safe against a resourceful man. And this man is resourceful. If we do not intercept him first, then I believe he will come here. I even believe I know when. Somehow, he will gain entry. What happens next – what I must do to stop him – should be straightforward enough. Just like Clippestone. A sufficient number of armed men, correctly deployed. The right bait. Ways left open to admit him. A perimeter that can be rapidly secured. And yet... it is not like Clippestone."

He leaned forward on his seat. "*Control the battlefield.* You know de Gaillon's old adage. Well, I can make all the preparations, set all the traps. That, I know. But this Red Hand is so self-contained, so untouchable, so separated from his surroundings... He walks through all we set before him. He makes his own battlefield – one he brings with him. One we cannot control. I need something to even the field. Something I can use. A sure way to bring him down." He stopped, almost out of breath from his monologue.

Llewellyn nodded slowly. "I see," he said. "You mean weapons. Well, why didn't you just say so?" He placed his hands upon his knees. "I have been considering all that you have told me of him. With regard to this fire siphon of his... Now, that is interesting! We have seen such things in use amongst the Byzantines, but making it operable with one hand only – that is something new. I believe that he may be using the tension of a spring or perhaps even a small bow to exert pressure on the plunger of the siphon. It would not need to be strong or large to achieve this. We know the siphon is attached to his left forearm, and we may imagine that there is a trigger that he can operate with a movement of his hand. It may even be that when he releases pressure on this trigger, the mechanism locks again, leaving some tension in the bow. That would explain how he is able to discharge it several times." He chuckled to himself. "Quite ingenious!"

Gisburne was not entirely sure whether Llewellyn was referring to the Red Hand, or himself. Fascinating though this was, he was not sure how it would help him. "I just need to know how he can be killed," he said. "Or at least, how to avoid being killed myself. De Rosseley's view is that in a sustained fight the Red Hand would tire, but his opponent needs to live long enough to achieve victory. And there is the problem. Crossbows have proved ineffective. His fire prevents anyone from getting close. Even if they do, every weapon is swept aside by his hammer, and no shield or armour can provide adequate protection against it."

"There may be other ways," said Llewellyn, rubbing his beard. "If we think differently. Beyond weapons."

"Beyond weapons?"

"Water will drown him. With that weight of armour, he'd sink like a stone."

Gisburne nodded. "Advantage becomes disadvantage..."

"Exactly."

"But then we have to get him to water..."

Llewellyn shrugged. "Fire will burn him. Those metal plates will deflect a short burst of flame, but set him ablaze and that shell of his would become an oven."

"De Rosseley had that idea, too. Oil and a flame. But they could not apply it in time."

"That is the challenge. To have the means of bringing those elements together quickly. Throwing oil or pitch over him is simple enough – but having it ready, in the right place, at the right time..."

"Greek Fire?" ventured Gisburne. It had worked in the past.

Llewellyn shrugged again. "Possible. But the type I have here must be kept from the air, and thrown in a sealed vessel. Such vessels are too robust to break against a human body – even an armoured one. They're simply not meant for that. They will smash upon the ground, of course, but if he is moving at speed, as all describe him doing..." He shrugged.

"Thinner vessels, then? More fragile?

Llewellyn sighed. "But make them sufficiently fragile and they are no longer safe to carry. One knock and it'd be you going up in flames."

"What about replicating the siphon device he uses?"

"It might be done, if I only had more time, and less limited resources..."

"Am I to have nothing?" said Gisburne throwing up his hands. He had never known Llewellyn to be so defeatist.

"I have only what is here," said Llewellyn irritably. "Take it or leave it."

Gisburne moderated his tone. "I'll take whatever you can give," he said. "Oil, pitch, Greek fire. Anything. We must start somewhere."

Llewellyn nodded, and calmed himself; for a moment, Gisburne thought the old man was going to apologise. Something seemed to occur to him then. He turned towards his impossibly cluttered shelves. "I had been trying to develop a vessel that would burst of its own accord, after a precise interval of time – even in mid-air." He shook his head. "One day, maybe... But there was something I had been experimenting with in that regard. No use to me at the moment – too approximate – though I hope to unlock the secret of their composition."

He delved into a large, lidded, jar and pulled out a fistful of what Gisburne first thought were small candles, a little bigger than a finger, and dull grey in colour. When Llewellyn turned back into the light, Gisburne saw that they appeared to be composed of some papery material, such as wasps used to make their nests, each one twisted into a point at the top.

"I don't know how you might employ them," said Llewellyn, offering one to Gisburne. "A distraction, perhaps. A little surprise." He chuckled. "They will at least be something he does not expect."

Gisburne took it from him. "What are they?"

Llewellyn wandered to the bench and picked up a small earthenware bottle. "They were wrapped with a consignment of silk from the Far East. It came with a Radhanite trader – one of the last of that breed. In the land they were made, so he said, they are regarded as a child's toy."

Gisburne turned the tube over in his fingers, still baffled. Did it make a noise? Did one break it open? Or blow down it?

Llewellyn placed the bottle upon the anvil in the furthest corner of the room, used a candle to light the twisted tip of one of the grey tubes, then dropped it inside the bottle. He turned back to Gisburne. "You may wish to cover your..."

Before he could finish the sentence, the bottle exploded with a deafening thundercrack. Gisburne ducked involuntarily, shards of pottery whizzing past his head, bouncing off jars, ironwork, barrels, and the walls themselves – their strange music mingling with the ringing in his shocked ears.

"That was always the problem," coughed Llewellyn, wafting away the choking, acrid smoke that now filled the room. "Timing."

As Gisburne straightened, he found his hands and knees shaking from the shock. "I'll take them," he said.

Llewellyn stuffed them unceremoniously in Gisburne's bag, as if glad to be shot of them.

Then he cleared his throat, and averted his eyes from Gisburne's as if somehow embarrassed at what he was about to say. "I regret there is one other obstacle," he said. "A more considerable one. As if you do not already have enough..."

Gisburne could not imagine what it could be that he had not already considered. Llewellyn planted himself on a barrel and placed his hands on his knees again, all the while staring at the floor.

"You speak of preparations within the Tower," he said. "Of traps, and armed men. But these walls are not Prince John's. There was a time he could act as its master – *was* its master, to all intents and purposes – but no longer. His guard is dismissed. The Tower's garrison does not answer to his command – and their own commander is not of a mind to co-operate."

"Fitz Thomas..." muttered Gisburne.

Llewellyn nodded. "The balance has shifted," he said. "Oh, it's all done with a smile, of course, as if he is everyone's friend and doing us all favour. And what is so galling is that they all believe it. He has the full trust of de Coutances – and therefore the King. His men worship him. He even has a succession of adoring young ladies visit him here – nobility, every one – who, I can assure you, do not experience the difficulty in gaining access you do."

Gisburne raised his eyebrows. "Adoring young ladies...?"

"It's nothing like that. At least, not in deed. They feel safe in his company. So they fawn and flirt as he regales them with his wit in that eccentric, fatherly way he affects, all the while pretending he is not picturing them naked and debauched. God, give me good honest whoring any day." He huffed in disgust. "But make no mistake – he means only to feather his own nest – rubbing up against the high and mighty, worming his way into their affections and boosting his own sense of self-importance by manipulating those more important than he wherever he can do so without redress. Without tarnishing his image. Just yesterday he booted half of John's retinue out of the Tower precincts. Didn't even ask. Just did it. They're out there now, I suppose, camped on some scrap of ground. God knows where. When challenged, he smiled and said, in that reasonable way he has, that there was little point duplicating services that already existed within the Tower. 'An unnecessary strain upon resources and bad for security,' he said."

Gisburne gaped at Llewellyn in astonishment. "Surely John did not just stand by?"

Llewellyn snorted. "He did not! He raged like you cannot imagine. But I saw Fitz Thomas's face as he did so – when, for a moment, the mask slipped. He enjoyed it. And he knew John could do nothing. There was no one left to do his bidding – he had made sure of it. Except for me, a few pointless hangers-on and a handful of personal servants, you and Galfrid are all he has – all he can rely on. Within these walls, he is no better off than a prisoner. Than Hood. And outside them..."

"Outside them lurks the greatest threat he has yet faced," said Gisburne. The Tower was a trap all right – but it was beginning to feel like it was John who was caught in it. "So, we can rely only on ourselves... Well that's nothing new. But enough of thinking 'beyond weapons.' Just tell me something I can carry in my hands to stop this killer."

Llewellyn sighed heavily. "As you know, plate armour is something with which I have been experimenting. The trick is making the sheets of steel of sufficient size and strength. They must be light enough for a man to carry, yet thick enough to provide adequate defence; soft enough to shape, but hard enough to resist blows and projectiles. Too soft and it can bend or be pierced, too hard and it will split and crack. But none of these issues affect this man. He has covered himself with flat plates, taking such weight upon himself as an ordinary man would not countenance."

"Something must be capable of penetrating them," said Gisburne.

"We already know they have deflected crossbow bolts at close range."

"Might something more powerful be constructed? An arbalest?"

"Again, if I had more time..."

"Is there not something here, like that which you gave me for Jerusalem?"

"Which you left there..." grumbled Llewellyn. "Believe me, if I had such a weapon here I would tell you, and the crossbows in the Tower's armoury are no different from those we know to have failed. And before you waste time looking, you'll not find anything to meet your needs out there, either. The crossbow is frowned upon by the Pope, and meant only for heretics and infidels. Barons may bend the rules, but you'll not find a banned siege weapon knocking about London's streets."

"There must be something..."

"Just one thing, perhaps," said Llewellyn. Gisburne frowned. "Six feet of English yew."

"A longbow?" Gisburne felt his muscles shrink from the idea.

"Little can match it for power," said Llewellyn. "A heavy warbow might have a chance. Straight on, at close range, if the target is not moving..." He turned and rummaged in a small wooden box, then counted out two dozen steel spikes. "These are hardened bodkin points for arrows," he said. "If anything can penetrate that armour, it will be these."

"But you cannot say for sure..."

"No one can say that without seeing the armour."

"By which time, it's too late..."

Llewellyn exhaled sharply in exasperation. "Stop making excuses! You accept defeat before you've even begun! It's not just about the armour. You know as well as I what de Gaillon would say: *every fortress has its weak point* – an overlooked or unguarded spot. The Red Hand has proved that himself time and again."

"You mean an eye-slit in his helm?" said Gisburne. "A gap between the plates?" It seemed a forlorn hope. Not something he wished to stake his life on.

"I heard you were once pretty good with a bow," said Llewellyn.

"A bow's not a knight's weapon," snapped Gisburne. "And no man alive could guide his arrow point to such a target. It would be like..."

"Like trying to hit a silver penny?" ventured Llewellyn.

Gisburne scowled at him.

"I knew of one who could do it," said Llewellyn. "I saw it done."

Gisburne gave a humourless laugh. "Yes, but that man is now in a cell in this very fortress."

"No, no," said Llewellyn, waving his hand dismissively. "Not Hood."

"There's another? Another as good as him?"

"Perhaps better. I saw him. Right here in London. Though whether he's even still alive..."

Gisburne leaned forward. "Tell me everything."

XXXVI

DICKON BEND-THE-BOW WAS perhaps the greatest archer who ever lived.

It was not known from where he had come, only that he had one day emerged from the Forest of Dean and joined with a troupe of travelling jongleurs and gleemen making their steady way to the capital. That they had accepted him so readily said much for the potential they saw. Before the caravan had reached Oxford, his fame was already growing; by London, he was one of the most talked about men in England.

That Gisburne had never heard of him Llewellyn considered of little surprise. At the time – ten years ago – Gisburne had been a world away, running from disgrace and fighting for any master who would pay. And by the time he had returned home, Dickon was all but forgotten.

Yet, for one hot summer in London, as word of Dickon spread across the city like a fire, people had flocked to Smoothfield to see the tricks of archery he performed. He could shoot a songbird from the sky. Hit swinging targets blindfolded, simply by listening. And, from fifty yards or more, he would shoot a silver penny from between the thumb and forefinger of anyone brave enough to stand before his bow. Even as the astonished onlookers applauded the seemingly impossible feat, all wondered about the day he would surely come undone. Perhaps it was partly this that kept them coming back. No one, they said, could keep on tempting fortune so. No matter how skilled he was, one who dwelt perpetually on the edge of disaster as he did must eventually falter and tumble over that precipice. All – in various states of anticipation and apprehension – awaited the day his arrow would strike and maim one of his bold volunteers, and his career and reputation would be finished.

But it never did. His undoing, when it came, took a very different, and even more unexpected form.

"So, where do I find him?" Gisburne had asked. In part, it had been a joke

– something to mock and defuse his sense of frustration. But only in part. Somewhere in him, that frustration was grasping for new possibilities, new strategies, new weapons, no matter how remote or impossible they seemed.

Llewellyn had laughed. "No one knows. Probably he's dead..."

"Probably?"

"Let's just say you'll have to look elsewhere for your answer," said Llewellyn. "It was stupid of me to mention it."

"Tell me anyway."

Then Llewellyn had related the end of Dickon's story, as much as it was known.

One night, so it was recorded, when that glorious summer season was at its peak, a fire had broken out in the entertainers' encampment upon Smoothfield. It had not spread far – most of the wagons were spared or barely scorched – but these were also the early hours, and it had been some time before the sound and smell had alerted the sleeping troupe. By the time they knew what was happening, one wagon – the heart of the blaze – was utterly destroyed. Dickon's wagon. Within its collapsed, blackened frame next morning was found a single charred body. No one knew how or why the conflagration had started. The wagon was near no campfire, and there were many who swore Dickon's lamp had been extinguished for the night before theirs.

"Some, who did not wish to believe him dead, said it was another trick," said Llewellyn. "That he'd had enough of that life and had spirited himself away – though why he should wish to do so at the height of his fame, they were less able to explain. Others said that he had been murdered by an envious rival – and there were indeed those who claimed he'd had a hooded visitor that night. But perhaps, after all, it was just a stupid accident. Such things happen in real life. But everyone had their theory.

"What was yours?" asked Gisburne.

Llewellyn had snorted. "Mine? Mine's worth no more than anyone else's. None of that really matters. I only know he was not seen or heard of ever again."

Llewellyn was right. None of it mattered. Not now. But somehow, Gisburne found he could not let it go. Perhaps it was the very incompleteness of the story that drew him. Thoughts of it were still battering his teeming brain when he again stood before the door of Hood's cell, and the bolts were shot back.

"IT MUST BE very dull for you in here," said Gisburne.

Hood shuffled where he sat, and gave a little shrug. "It has its moments," he said.

"When they bring the bread? When they take out your piss pot? I'm sure you can hardly contain yourself."

Hood smiled. "Well, I have your visits to look forward to, don't I?" He regarded him quizzically. "So, what is it to be today?"

"I would like to make your life – what's left of it, anyway – more interesting."

"Songs?" said Hood, sitting forward. "Magic tricks, perhaps? I am all agog."

"Nothing so trivial. A new game."

Hood rose to his feet, dusted off his hands, his chains rattling, and cocked his head to one side. "This wouldn't be to do with that Red Hand again, would it?" he said.

Gisburne was silent for a moment. He knew that what he wanted would come at a price. So, he would give Hood something. That much, and no more. "There have been more killings," he said. "Right here, in the heart of London."

Hood puffed out his cheeks in an exaggerated expression of surprise. Gisburne tried to fathom whether the surprise was real, but could not. "Well, whatever he's about, it certainly seems like he means some business," said Hood.

Gisburne nodded. "They say he is unstoppable. His notoriety is already outstripping yours. If things continue this way, the Red Hand will be all they talk about."

He saw Hood's expression darken. "Don't try to play me, Guy," he said. "You won't win."

"Won't win? Look around, Robert. You've lost already. You, too, thought yourself unstoppable. I stopped you nonetheless. But there is a way to get back in the game."

"A deal?" Hood's eyes sparkled.

"A challenge. To prove your worth."

"Ah, I see. You want me to do your job for you. To stop the unstoppable Red Hand." He chuckled – without humour, this time. "Well, you stopped me on your own, so you can stop him, can't you?"

"I know you know things. Perhaps enough to bring him down."

"From within these walls? That's not much of a game, Guy."

"But imagine if it was known you had achieved that?" Hood sat motionless for a moment, and Gisburne drew closer. "Your reputation would be greater than ever. And John would look kindly upon such an act. Who knows? Perhaps there would be no need for an execution after all..."

It was a dangerous promise – and one he did not know he could keep.

Hood stared at him for what seemed an age, as if trying to ascertain that Gisburne really meant what he'd said. He began to chuckle again, louder and deeper, until it was a gale of laughter. Gisburne stood and watched in silence. Somehow, such unrestrained merriment seemed obscene in this wretched place. But it was the laugh of a man who felt he had already won. Finally, it subsided, its last echoes dying away as Hood brought himself back under some semblance of control.

"Oh, Guy, Guy, Guy... I've been in prison for six months. How could I possibly know anything?" It was true. The guards swore no word had been uttered within Hood's earshot, and Gisburne believed them. They were good men. "Good that de Rosseley survived, though," he added casually.

At the mention of the name, Gisburne exploded with anger, swiping Hood across the face. Hood staggered and fell, his chains jangling about him.

"How could you know that?" demanded Gisburne. "*How?*"

But Hood simply laughed even more, wiping the blood from his mouth. He rolled over and leaned against the wall. "Are you going to kill me, Guy?" he chortled. "I often used to wonder if you would."

"You're going to die anyway."

"Speak for yourself!" quipped Hood, and spat blood upon the stone.

Gisburne moved away from Hood, and slumped against the far wall, sliding down onto his haunches. For a while they sat in silence, near mirror images of each other.

"I know you know you know who the Red Hand is," said Gisburne. "I also know that were I to beat you to the very threshold of Hell, you would not reveal it. Not unless you wanted to. Instead, let me appeal to you. You have one chance to do some good before you die. To make a mark upon the world outside these miserable walls – to do something memorable." He leaned forward. "I will see that people hear of it."

With one finger, Hood flicked at the dry fragments of bread that lay scattered on the stone beside him. "You know, every day the boy brings the bread and potage. And every day they fish around in the soup and pull the bread to bits before he brings it in." Gisburne sighed. He should have known he would not get a straight answer.

"Why do they bother with that?" continued Hood. He tutted as if horribly inconvenienced, picked up the largest chunk of bread, briefly regarded it in his hand, then broke it in half. For a moment Gisburne had a surreal vision of Hood as Christ at the Last Supper.

"It's to check someone hasn't hidden a knife in it," he said.

"It's unhealthy," said Hood. "Poking about with their dirty blades and filthy fingers... Yeuch!"

Gisburne stared up at the thin slit of light. "Do you know how you are going to die, Robert?" He sensed, rather than saw, Hood's shrug.

"Beheaded, perhaps. Upon Tower Hill. Then my head stuck on a spike on London Bridge. The new one. For all to see."

When Gisburne turned back to look at him, Hood was smiling. His eyes were distant, unfocused. Staring somewhere beyond the walls, to a place that was no place – a circumstance yet to be realised, a time yet to come. At a vision of his own death.

"That's how I see it, anyway," said Hood. "How about you?"

Gisburne marvelled at such unrestrained self-confidence, such magically unburdened ego. It knew no fear, no limits. It trampled everything before it, even in death.

"Beheading is for nobles," said Gisburne. "Not common criminals."

"Do common criminals get locked in the Tower?" said Hood. There was a note of challenge in his voice – one for which Gisburne had no response.

"You are to be hanged," he said. "Not on Tower Hill. Not in public at all, but here, in the Tower precincts. A first, I believe. You should feel honoured by that, at least. Then your body is to be burned, and the ash scattered. No grave, no marker. And for once in your life, there will be no audience to witness the event. No one to weep or wail, no one to appeal or play to, no one to write the ballads or tell the tales when you're gone. No one outside these walls will even know it has happened. One day, years from now, some decrepit drunk slumped outside an inn will say: 'That thief Robin Hood... I once knew a song about that man. Whatever became of him?' And no one will know, nor remember the tune, nor even recognise the name."

Hood sat in silence, staring at the ground, his fingers unconsciously turning the featureless charm about his neck. Gisburne had expected the usual irrepressible chuckle to rise from him, but nothing came. Not for an age. Finally, his hand dropped, and he lifted his head and looked hard at his tormentor.

"You've got it all wrong, Guy," he said. "Reality doesn't drive legend forward. It just gets in the way. Look at our bold Lionhearted king... The less England sees of him, the greater his legend becomes. Should he return, and sit upon his throne and live to a ripe old age growing fat and embittered and discussing taxes and drainage and roads, then the people will see him for what he is. A man. But should he never come back... Well then, his reputation will be unassailable." His face split in an intense smile. "So, you see, Guy – you haven't made people forget me. You've made me immortal."

Gisburne had stood, unflinching, before some of the most dangerous, most brutal men this world had put upon a battlefield. But there was something in Hood's look that was truly terrifying. Something he could not fight, could not grapple with.

"Well, at least I'll not have to think of you any more," he said. And he turned to go.

"Have you thought how you will stop him?" said Hood.

Gisburne turned. "Him?"

"The Red Hand. When you meet him. I'm sure you've been thinking about it."

Gisburne felt an uncanny chill. He stared at him, trying to anticipate the moves he had in his head, but he was unreadable. "I don't need your help, Robert," he said with a sigh. He was suddenly tired – tired of this struggle, these games. "Not unless you're going to tell me who he is."

"I think it's probably better you find that out for yourself."

"Goodbye, Robert..."

"But I'm willing to bet I could bring him down. Armour or not."

Gisburne stopped, but said nothing. He refused to be drawn in this time.

"Oh, you're good with a bow, I know," said Hood. "You should have applied yourself to it."

"I'm a knight," said Gisburne, wearily. "Knights don't shoot arrows."

"No. They just die by them."

Gisburne hesitated again. "Is the Red Hand a knight?" he said.

Hood chuckled. "Nice try! But how would I know? And why would I care? My arrow pierces a knight's heart as easily as a peasant's."

"Not any more."

"Come on, Guy, will you take my bet or not?"

Gisburne simply stared at him. The man really believed there was a chance, even now. In a way, Gisburne admired it. Envied it, even. There was a time when he'd have pitied it, too, but that well had run dry.

He laughed to himself. "Why do you think for one minute that I would let you take up a bow again?"

"Because I'm the best there ever was. You know that. You've seen it."

"I've seen nothing."

"You know my shot would have hit its mark that day at Clippestone," said Hood.

"But it didn't," said Gisburne.

"But it *would* have. You know it, in your heart, don't you?" It seemed to Gisburne that there was a note of pleading in his voice; that Hood was not simply stating a fact – his own version of a fact, at least – but actually seeking approval. "You do believe that I would have won? That I deserved to win?"

If approval was what he sought, then that would be the very thing Gisburne would deny him. He turned to Hood. "You did not win," he said. "And you'll not hold a bow again, Robert. Not ever. Think on that a while. You have twenty-nine days to do so."

Hood did not look away. His eyes blazed with a cold fire. "You think you can stop him, Guy? This Red Hand? I would like to see how that turns out, I really would."

Gisburne felt anger boil up in him. "I know another who can," he spat. "Better than you. And respected, too, all over London – not some damned criminal." He didn't know why he said it. It just tumbled out of him. There was no point to the response. No strategy. Everything of worth had already been said; he was simply kicking out – wanting to make Hood *feel* something: anger, pain. "If I needed a bowman," he continued, "one I could depend on, it's him I'd call for. Not you. I don't need you."

"Another?" said Hood, staring. Gisburne's childish outburst had hit home. Hood's black eyes were filled with a monstrous outrage. "Who?"

Gisburne felt a crude sense of satisfaction. "What's the matter?" he said. "Can't believe there was ever anyone better than you?"

"Who?" said Hood.

"Dickon," spat Gisburne. "His name is Dickon. Perhaps you've heard of him?"

At this, Gisburne half expected Hood to do what he always did: to roar with laughter. For him to clap his hands and throw back his head and hurl at his tormentor the fact that the Dickon of whom he spoke – of whom no one had heard for ten years – was long dead.

What passed across Hood's face upon hearing that name, however, was the very last thing Gisburne had expected to see there – something that, in all these years, he had never before seen upon those features.

It was a look of terror.

IV

DICKON

XXXVII

Clippestone Royal Palace, Sherwood Forest
24 December, 1192

GUY OF GISBURNE stared out across the hazy, hectic field and dared to contemplate victory.

Exhausted from lack of sleep and chilled to the bone, one side of his face burning in the heat from the brazier on the royal stand, he blinked against the freezing wind and the drifting, greasy smoke of the cooking fires, knowing that somewhere within the seething multitude – into the jaws of his painstakingly prepared trap – walked Hood.

He pulled at the mail coif about his head, the metal made hot as a cooking pot by the brazier's flames and looked out from his vantage point on the *berfrois*. Below him, five trumpeters – their hands clamped over the mouthpieces to prevent the metal freezing to their lips – waited to sound the fanfare. Royal pennants whipped above in the gusting breeze. Shouts and chatter and jaunty Yuletide music wafted all about. His brain felt cooked, his limbs frozen, but he no longer cared. At last, on this bright December day, he dared to believe what for so long he had chosen to deny. Today would see the greatest triumph of his career. He would write the ending of Hood's story.

"Well, what a merry ballad this will make," said a quiet voice behind him, and he turned. Prince John was in his richest robes of blue velvet trimmed with white fur, a gold-hilted dagger at his belt, his many rings worn over black gloved hands. "Men shall sing of you and of this day, Guy of Gisburne," he said, beaming. "Mark my words."

Gisburne felt a hand upon his back as John ascended the two steps to his raised dais, and seated himself upon its gilded throne with a sigh of satisfaction. A special place had been made upon the *berfrois* so the brazier could be positioned immediately before him without impeding his view – or setting fire to the stand. Now he sat toasting his extended fingers in comfort, while on the tiered benches to either side the invited barons, noble ladies and high-ranking clergy sat on steadily numbing buttocks, their extremities turning to ice – another of John's minor acts of revenge upon them.

"Join me, Sir Guy," called John, and gestured to the seat next to him. The heads of several gathered nobles turned. The bishop scowled. This was revenge too – publicly favouring so lowly a knight as Gisburne over these high-born buffoons. Gisburne hesitated. Until now, he had been in the shadows, working for the Prince behind the scenes, in secret. John read his thoughts. He leaned forward. "Time to give credit where it is due," he said.

Gisburne, feeling a fraud in the ceremonial knight's mail that had never once been worn for combat – even though he had been in combat more often than any man here – climbed the wooden steps under the steady gaze of the most powerful men in the kingdom, and took his place at the Prince's right hand.

ARCHERS HAD COME from all over Nottinghamshire, Derbyshire and the northern counties to compete for the prize. Perhaps further afield even than that. Undoubtedly, however, it was the chance to see the palace itself that had so swelled the numbers.

Clippestone was a royal residence of unrivalled size and splendour; its stables alone had stalls for over two hundred horses. Yet in the three whole months Richard had spent in England since his coronation – mostly under sufferance – he had never once set eyes on it. Gisburne wondered whether he even knew of its existence, tucked away here. Perhaps it was just as well; he doubtless would have sold it.

John, meanwhile, was not one to look a gift horse in the mouth – especially when it could facilitate endless hours of hunting. Today, it would play host to the greatest hunt of all – the culmination of a quest that had absorbed them for the past year: the capture of the man who Gisburne had once called Robert of Locksley, known to the world as Robin Hood. For this great purpose, Clippestone's location in the heart of Sherwood Forest could hardly have been more fitting.

"We should have some fine sport today!" announced the Prince, and raised a steaming goblet of mulled wine. Several barons and worthies seated nearby smiled and nodded at his words – a little too eagerly, Gisburne felt. But only he knew what John really meant.

"Let's just hope the bastard turns up," muttered John into his cup.

But of course he would. That was the beauty of Gisburne's plan. Anyone else would have seen it for the trap it was, and and steered a wide berth. But not Hood. He would see it was a trap and come anyway. And others of his band of merry men would come with him, blindly putting their lives at risk for their leader. Their presence served no purpose; Hood stood a far better chance of evading capture alone. But he required an audience. Someone to tell the tale, write the ballad.

Gisburne stared out across the teeming crowd once again, his eyes straining to pick out a face – that face. Gilbert de Gaillon would have slapped him down for such impatience. *You're letting your enemy take control,* he would have said. *Granting him power over you. Do not allow it. You control the battlefield. Now stand back. Let him commit. Try to force it, and your prey will flee.*

He looked away from the throng, and surveyed the faces in the stand instead. "The bishop doesn't look too happy," he muttered.

"The bishop never looks happy," John snorted. "Who will rid us of these troublesome priests..." Gisburne looked at John in alarm. John raised his eyebrows. "It was a joke." After the murder of Thomas Becket, however, the joke did not amuse. "Oh, come along, Sir Guy," said John, dismissively. "Enjoy yourself. I command you..."

"I think enjoyment is the problem," said Gisburne. "I sense the bishop disapproves of such activity on the Eve of Christmas."

John shrugged. "Well, of course he does. He wants everyone to be as miserable as him. But wasn't it God put joy in our hearts? Christ knows it wasn't the bishop..."

"I fancy it's not our hearts he's thinking of, but our stomachs. It's supposed to be a day for fasting."

John clutched at his chest with faux mortification. "Are you accusing me of fostering irreligious behaviour, Sir Guy? Look around. Do you see any prohibited food being consumed? You do not. We are observing the holy writ – to the letter. It doesn't mean we have to mope about like condemned men."

"What of the geese you have roasting on spits between the Two Oaks?" Gisburne nodded towards the trails of smoke. "There looked to be at least fifty of them."

"Seventy," said John with a smile of satisfaction. "But you will find they are *barnacle* geese. A creature of the sea – and according to the church's own rules, regarded as a fish. Therefore, entirely acceptable fare for a fast day."

Gisburne nodded slowly, almost allowing himself a smile at John's ingenuity. John caught the bishop's eye, and gave him a broad smile, and a regal nod. The bishop dutifully nodded back – with as much reticence as he could muster. Amongst this joyful throng, his red face stood out like an angry boil.

"Yes, that's right..." muttered John, still smiling at the pontiff. "Don't, whatever you do, miss an opportunity to spread your resentment and your misery." He tore his look away. "He has his secret supply of veal and sausage tucked away somewhere, you can be sure of it..." He sighed deeply. "Well, we have a fine gathering, and a fine day. And it is my birthday. A day of celebration – with more to celebrate come nightfall. The others can keep their gold and their riding cloaks – you will be giving me the best birthday present of the lot." He turned back to Gisburne and clapped him on the shoulder again – more in the manner of a friend than a prince. "So *enjoy yourself*. I insist!"

Gisburne took a breath of the icy air, laden with the aroma of roasting meat, and lifted his eyes away from the crowd, to the tops of the tallest trees at the edge of the forest. Dotted about their topmost branches, as if waiting for something, was the largest gathering of crows he had ever seen.

THAT SAME MORNING, just after dawn, Gisburne had ridden out on Nyght. At that hour the royal palace itself – which never truly slept – was already coming alive. In two hours' time, the great open space in which the competition would take place – known as the 'tournament field,' although no tournament had ever taken place there – would begin to buzz with stewards and servants, cooks and pages. In four, the entire field would be swarming with every kind of curiosity seeker from the peasantry up, all eager to take whatever free handouts John had to offer and, Gisburne did not doubt, revel in the sight of a common archer taking a valuable prize off the Prince.

There was no real need for Gisburne's tour. All preparations for the day's bold plan had been gone over time and again, and he had barely shut his eyes the previous night for thinking about the day that was to follow. This moment, with only Nyght for company – this quiet, idyllic moment – was to be one of respite. Of prayer, almost. The calm before the storm.

Gisburne had arisen as soon as there was light in the sky. He left Galfrid snoring and crept out alone through the freezing, foggy air to the vast stable block. With the earthy, sweet smell of the stable filling his nostrils, he combed Nyght's sleek black coat until it shone, pausing to crush the few stubborn beads of caked mud still stuck in the long hairs of his tail. He ran his hand down the back of each leg, checking for any lumps or tender spots, then lifted the hooves to his knee and scraped the mud and muck from around the shoes. On went the blanket, its creases smoothed, ready for the saddle. It was only a few weeks old, still with the smell of fresh leather. It had been made for him by a half-blind saddlemaker in

Beestone whose work was revered by those in the know. What most also knew, but had the courtesy not to acknowledge, was that it was actually his daughter who now did the lion's share of the work.

It took some time to seat it right, but he did not rush. He relished the work; over the years, fighting as a rootless mercenary, he had grown accustomed to doing things for himself. In truth, terrible though those years had been, he missed this part – the steady ritual, the pleasure of losing oneself in simple tasks. So often these days they had to prepare in haste. But this morning, he would take things at his own pace, and do them in his own way. Nyght tolerated it with the patience of Job – a quality he reserved exclusively for Gisburne and Galfrid.

Finally, he led him out. On the stable door a spider's web sparkled like a fine jewel of glass. In the yard, the ruts had tiny puddles of thin, opaque ice, under which the water seemed somehow to have disappeared. They cracked like empty eggshells under Gisburne's booted feet.

Then man and horse headed out to greet the dawn.

When he had looked out from his small, icy window, his first impression had been that snow had fallen during the night. In fact, it was merely a hard frost – but the transformation, if anything, was more complete. Crystals of ice clung to every surface, turning every tree, leaf and blade of grass to a white ghost. The timbers of the *berfrois* – not yet adorned with pennants and coverings – shimmered like the frozen bones of some Leviathan. In the air, meanwhile, hung a low, thick mist which the sun struggled to penetrate.

The air was so cold, it stung his eyes. Icy tears ran down his cheeks, and he could feel his jaw siezing. Within half an hour, his toes and fingertips were numb. But it was a joy. As Gisburne rode, breath coming in thick, foggy clouds, he watched crystals of ice form on the fine black fur at the edges of Nyght's ears, until they were completely fringed with white.

Then he had returned to the palace where Galfrid was already awake, and prepared for battle.

"It's time," said John, and plucked a fleck of goose down from his hose. At his signal, the five heralds raised their instruments in perfect unison, and blasted out a fanfare. The Prince stood and straightened his robes. All faces turned toward him.

"My lords, ladies..." He glanced towards the bishop, then evidently decided to depart from the prepared formalities. He cast his arms wide. "My fellow Englishmen!" There were a few hurrahs at that.

For Christ's sake, keep it simple, thought Gisburne.

John cleared his throat. "I shall be brief," he said. Another isolated cheer.

"You all hear more than enough pontificating in your daily lives." He could not resist a fleeting glance at the bishop as he said it. At this, there were cackles of laughter. The crowd began to warm. Gisburne doubted more than one man in ten knew what *pontificating* meant, but they got the gist. The bishop, meanwhile – who had entirely missed the Prince's look – managed to confirm prevailing opinion by remaining grumpily oblivious.

"We are here today, by the grace of God, in celebration. Tomorrow we celebrate the birth of Our Lord Jesus Christ." There was a murmur of appreciation. "Today..."

Please God don't mention that it's your birthday, thought Gisburne. *They'll think your comparing yourself to Christ...*

"Today, we celebrate *your* skills. *Your* dedication. *Your* tenacity..." The murmur, which had ebbed, surged again, and grew to a swell of excited chatter.

"There is food. There is drink. There is good sport. And most of all, for one champion archer among you – no matter how humble his birth – a great prize..." John spread his fingers in a languid gesture to his left. Before it was even completed, two pages hurried forth bearing a long, red velvet bolster trimmed with gold upon a polished oak board. They tilted it towards the throng as far as they dared. There was a collective gasp.

Sat in a groove on the cushion was what first appeared to be a solid, metallic rod. As the pages moved, it shifted slightly, glinting in the pale winter sun. "A yard of pennies!" announced John proudly, gesturing again at the row of stacked silver coins. "An arrow's length!" Most arrows were shorter than a yard, but it had a good ring to it – and it made John appear generous. "You wonder how many that is? I'll tell you. It is one thousand, three hundred. I counted them myself!"

"I bet you bloody did!" came a muted voice from the back. John chose to ignore it, and the laughter that followed.

The pennies had been Gisburne's idea. At first, John had been determined to have a solid silver arrow made, and had even consulted with Llewellyn about the possibility of casting such a thing from a real arrow. Galfrid had grumbled at the prospect. "A silver arrow's a fine trophy for a knight or a noble," he muttered to his master. "But what good is it to a peasant farmer or Yeoman? Better to give them cows or sheep."

Galfrid was right; it should be something they could use. Something familiar, yet still impressive. Finally, he had convinced John with what seemed the perfect compromise. Everyone knew the value of a penny – of ten pennies. All could, therefore, imagine the worth of a hundred – a thousand. For most here, the prize was a fortune – more than their labouring would earn in five years. Enough to buy ten cows, or two war horses, or a fine suit of mail. To buy a house.

Enough for Hood to distribute amongst all his men, and ensure unswerving loyalty through another hard winter.

"Before this day is out," continued John, "one of you shall leave with three and three-quarter pounds of silver in his poke!" He took up a goblet and raised it high. "Here's to you all, archers of Sherwood! Eat! Drink! And may your arrows fly true!" A great cheer welled up from the core of the bowmen as John drank. Some of his men, positioned about the crowd, hurrahed and clapped heartily. It spread and multiplied until it was a single roar.

THE CONTEST BEGAN with all comers lined up to shoot at garlands of holly pinned upon the butts – the turf-covered mounds at the end of the range. Archers were permitted a single arrow, and shot one after another, in quick succession, from a distance of only sixty yards. Those who failed to get their arrow within the garland were immediately eliminated from the rest of the contest. This, John explained with a smile, was to "sort the sheep from the goats". Many there were these days – especially after the rise of Hood – who fancied themselves bowmen.

Most of these, it soon became clear, were goats. Doubtless a good number could hit a tree or barn door from thirty yards – but from twice that, in front of a roaring crowd, many of them wilted.

It was a good-natured affair, accompanied by much raucous laughter. Those with genuine skills – the archers who would fight out the true battle later, when competition intensified – sailed through with ease. But this round was not about them. For now, the entertainment consisted chiefly of laughing at the expense of the incompetent – those whose nerve did not hold out, or whose skills were so pitifully poor that Gisburne had serious reason to wonder if they had even seen a real bow before today, let alone drawn one. Arrows went backwards, sideways, flew alarmingly into the crowd – most, fortunately, with less force than a child's toy. One man almost took his own ear off, his arrow skidding along the half-frozen ground all the way to the targets, whilst another – with a bow that looked to have been made that morning from a still-green branch – drew his weapon with a great flourish only for it to snap completely in two. The crowd cheered and fell about. He turned with a wide grin and bowed deeply, as if his object had been entirely achieved.

And perhaps it had. After the initial elimination, all who had taken part were given food and drink for their trouble – a thank you from John. And then Gisburne understood. The contest had been free to enter for anyone with a bow. He judged that at least half had come here – with bows they had dusted off, borrowed, or made that morning – with the intention not of winning, nor even really taking part, but purely of taking advantage of the Prince's hospitality.

John had not only accepted these fakers and hangers-on – he had been relying on them. Now, there was a great gathering of well-fed and grateful men, and a crowd whose mood had been transformed to one of irresistible cheer by their antics. Whether they would still think well of their Prince come the next morning's hangover remained to be seen. But here, now, were gathered the merriest men in all Sherwood. It was one of those times when Gisburne found himself marvelling at John's subtlety – when he saw in him his father's shrewd wisdom, coupled with a generosity that seemed not to belong in the house of Anjou at all.

John cared about England. Not just the crown, or the wealth, but the nation itself. But none would see it. For John also had a face and manner which instilled unease and mistrust in nearly all who encountered him. Apart from occasional ill-luck, this was John's only curse. England's unquestioning adulation all fell upon his brother Richard – lucky, handsome, brave Richard, who cared for England not one jot.

NEXT, THE ARCHERS who had gone through – numbering perhaps fifty – were directed to a grove of trees on the far side of the range. The trees had been screened off by a huge expanse of oilcloth, painted to resemble an orchard. At another signal from John, and another blast from the heralds, the cloth was dropped, to a great "Ahhh!" from the gathered crowd. The skeletal, leafless winter branches – some still pale and glittering with frost – were festooned with gaily coloured ribbons, and between them, out of reach, all manner of prizes hung. There were hams, pouches of coins, good knives, flasks of ale and every kind of trinket, just waiting to be shot down and claimed by those with the skill.

Favours, ribbons and bits of bark rained down as arrows hit – and missed – their marks. Men of all ages, some flushed with concentration, others near insensible with laughter, dashed and scurried about to claim their prizes. Those arrows that missed flew in all directions; it seemed little consideration had been given to what they might strike once past their intended targets. That no one went the way of old King Harold, or the Conqueror's heir, William Rufus, was a miracle.

As the jolly crew returned to the main field – few of whom had come away empty handed – Gisburne scanned the scene once more, checking the distribution of his men, looking for faces, anomalies, patterns. He had failed to spot any familiar face or frame during the elimination round, which disturbed him. But out there, somewhere, was Hood; he knew it as surely as he knew the sun would rise and set. Galfrid, too – competing as one of the archers so he might mix with them, converse with them, listen to their gossip. Galfrid had seen Hood but once, and only briefly. Hood had seen him too – but Hood had a face that stuck in the mind, while Galfrid's blended in. Gisburne gambled that Hood would not recall Galfrid's face even if he saw it. Not until it was too late.

The moment's diversion with John had passed; Gisburne was a soldier again, and there was a job to be done. But this was not shoeing a horse or making a barrel. If this went wrong, men would die. That was the soldier's lot. There was satisfaction to be had at the end of it, nevertheless – or so he hoped.

There was perhaps one other source of simple pleasure today. One face now missing from the scene. Marian. She would soon be here, he knew. Prince John had invited her personally, and that could not be ignored. Not even by Marian.

His heart leapt at the thought of her arrival. But he dreaded it, too. It was not simply that she did not return his stronger affections; he had almost grown used to that. Her company had become more difficult of late. She had become restless. Occasionally, she had flown into a temper such as he had never seen. Always it was to do with some issue of injustice – or what she perceived to be injustice. Lately it had focused almost entirely on Hood and his exploits. She seemed entirely swayed by popular opinion on the subject, believing the ballads and the extraordinary tales as if they were gospel. How and where she had picked these up, he could not guess, but more than once he had caught her humming some scurrilous, outlawish ditty under her breath.

From time to time she disappeared altogether, giving her chaperones the slip. Hours later, she would reappear, as if nothing whatever were wrong – and when challenged, was as sullen and spiky as ever. Suspecting she had been keeping bad company, Gisburne had, on one occasion, followed her. She had put a shawl about her head and made her way to a noisy inn upon the west road, where she had sat for the best part of the evening over a single mug of ale. There had been no great revelation, no secret assignation, no consorting with dangerous outlaws. She simply sat, and sang along with the songs that filled the place. Songs of Robin Hood and his Merry Men. And, for the first time in months, she appeared to be happy. Then, as the tavern began to grow quiet again, she had slipped away under the crescent moon, back towards Nottingham Castle, where she had presented herself at the gates and demanded entry.

It should have been reassuring, Gisburne supposed – that she was not in thrall to Hood or one of his men, and was not involved in clandestine trysts. Yet somehow, the alternative was more disturbing. It meant that she was not being lured away from normal life, but repelled by it. Had she really become so discontented with her daily existence that her only pleasure was to pretend it did not exist, and that she was someone else? An infatuation could be overcome – but not discontent.

FINALLY, THE MAIN competition got underway. With everyone merry – bellies full, drink flowing, a good portion of them clutching their prizes – it became serious. Upon the butts were placed wooden boards, painted with concentric squares, at which the remaining competitors shot in pairs from a distance of a hundred and eighty yards, each with three arrows. This was another quick elimination, in which the weaker of each pair was instantly put out of the contest – to a chorus of cheers, boos and cries of sympathy. By this means, the numbers would be rapidly reduced by half, leaving twenty-four to fight the final battle.

"God, if I could have a thousand such men!" said John as the victors' arrows drove into the targets. "What could stand against them?"

AS THE LAST pairs were being called by name, Gisburne spied Galfrid – now out of the competition, but clutching a capon tied about with green ribbon – edging through the crowd. Gisburne moved down to the left corner of the stand.

Galfrid did not look him in the eye, did not acknowledge him in any way. As he passed, and continued on towards the ale trestles, he said simply: "Simon-Over-Lee. Black hood."

But Gisburne had already seen him. The hood entirely obscured the wearer's features, but Gisburne did not need to see a face to know. He recognised the posture, the shape, the way he moved. How he had missed him until now, he could not imagine. Nearby were two other figures, eyes darting about shiftily – one, he recognised. A tall man, red-bearded. That had to be John Lyttel.

Trumpets sounded. "Next to shoot," called the announcer, "Rainald the Fletcher..." There was a drunken cheer from a group of men within the throng. "And Simon-Over-Lee." No cheers accompanied the second name.

Gisburne did not let his eye leave the black hood until its owner stood before the butts to take his turn. And when he drew, there was no doubt.

Gisburne descended from the stand and exchanged curt words with the captain of the guard. At his command, a company of armed men in plain clothing were deployed, spreading about the nucleus of competing archers like a net. But it would not close until the very last. Gisburne moved forward, towards the crowd.

Rainald was good. Every arrow – shot with steady deliberation – struck squarely in the target's centre. He stepped away from the line with a nod of satisfaction, bow raised in triumph, his comrades cheering his certain victory. Had he been pitted against almost any other opponent that day, his place in the final would have been assured.

Simon-Over-Lee loosed his arrows in rapid succession. There was no hesitation, no thought, yet his draw of the great Welsh longbow – as tall as its owner – was stronger than any upon the field. So fast was it that one half expected the arrows to go askew and miss the mark entirely. But when the crowd looked, hardly realising what had happened, they gasped. All three were clustered dead centre of the middle square – so close one could not get a knife blade between them. "Simon-Over-Lee wins!" cried the announcer. In the throng, new bets were made – others renegotiated.

THE REMAINING ARCHERS would now compete for points in groups of six, with the four victors shooting against each other for the championship. John Lyttel and the other had now disappeared into the crowd, but Gisburne didn't care about them. Hood was the prize. His black cowl was still visible atop his tall frame. Even if he broke through the net of the captain's men, there were crossbowmen positioned every twelve yards around the edges of the tournament field, archers atop the stand, and mounted men behind the copse ready to ride him down. There would be no escape.

With de Gaillon's words ringing in his head – Gisburne hung back, stopping at the rail mid-way between the royal stand and the shooting line. John had also insisted on him holding back until Hood had won or lost. He would have his sport this day, come what may. Just beyond the rail, the five heralds were now positioned, blowing fanfares to mark the victory of the bowman in each group.

Gisburne lost count of the number of fanfares. They began to rattle his brain. At the sound of the cry "Simon-Over-Lee wins!" he felt his teeth clench and his muscles tense more than he knew possible.

Two dozen became four: Robert Willeson, Lambert of Bowland, Osbert Le Falconer, Simon-Over-Lee. The shooting line drew back to two hundred and twenty yards. The entire field, now, was in a state of high excitement. There was hush as each man took the line.

Robert Willeson was first out. Osbert Le Falconer – who seemed to sustain some injury to his right hand with his first shot – fell next. Now it came down to two.

Lambert of Bowland hardly looked the part. Balding, stout, barrel-chested and fifty if he was a day, he was the last man one would have picked out as a champion. He breathed hard, as if moving a great weight. His technique was minimal, seeming to involve the least part of his body. This extended even to his expression, which never changed. But with steady deliberation – in marked contrast to his opponent – he matched Simon-Over-Lee shot for shot. Gisburne thought he saw tension creep into the hooded man's draw. All it would take was one error, and he, too, would fall. But he did not fold. Try as they might, the judges could not separate them. The hushed crowd cheered with each loosed arrow.

All shafts spent, a new fanfare sounded. All looked about, uncertain what the outcome of the contest. As the murmur grew, the crowd was parted by liveried guards, and Gisburne saw Prince John making his way towards the butts.

This was not part of the plan.

John stepped out between the archers and the targets, accompanied only by three pages – two bearing the cushion bearing the yard of silver pennies, a third carrying a small iron pail which smoked in the cold air.

"Friends!" called John, his hands raised. All hushed. "So great is the skill displayed upon this field today, it seems we have a tie for first place! So, we have devised the ultimate test..."

The crowd buzzed with excitement at the prospect. All Gisburne saw, however, was the Prince standing unprotected in front of dozens of lethally-armed strangers.

BY ORDER, THE archers had not brought arrows to the field. Arrows were provided by the Prince, and each batch bore a unique mark so as to clearly identify the man who had shot them. In reality, there was little need for the arrows to be identified thus in the early stages of the contest – but Prince John had an ulterior motive. He allowed those competing to keep the arrows they had been given, another part of his great bounty. The arrows themselves were blunts – or what Gisburne had known as *half-blunts* when he was a boy. Like all blunts they had a bulbous wooden head, and were favoured for practice shooting or for hunting small animals and birds, because they killed the animal without damaging their flesh. But the half-blunts also had a short iron point, to ensure they would embed in the targets. They may not have been meant for killing, but they could still fell a deer – or a man. Should they later be used for any such nefarious purpose, it was understood that John had a list of names and marks, and that the owner of the arrows would be held to account, whether personally responsible for the deed or not.

How this would help John if some madman decided here and now to send an arrow through his chest, however, Gisburne did not know.

John turned, and took up a coin from the cushion. He held it aloft, catching the light. "A single silver penny!"

There was a murmur as the third page took a stick from the pail and dabbed a spot of pitch upon centre of the target. It grew into a rumble of excitement as John pressed the penny into it, realisation dawning. Meanwhile, at the shooting line, two squires darted forward and, on bended knees, presented the two remaining competitors each with a new arrow. Broadheads. Killing arrows.

Christ, John, thought Gisburne. *Say your bloody piece and get off...*

"One arrow apiece!" called the Prince. "The victor shall be the archer who is first to split the coin; the first to miss forfeits the competition!"

There were gasps, exclamations, applause. Most were clearly marvelling at the impossibility of the task – from here, the tiny coin was barely even visible. Only a few had perhaps realised that John was encouraging them to direct their arrows at an image of the king.

John withdrew from the range, and Gisburne breathed once more. "Lambert of Bowland shall shoot first!" called the announcer.

The old man took his position on the line, and squinted at the distant speck. The crowd fell so silent, Gisburne swore he could hear the archer's whistly, nasal breaths. He nocked his arrow, stared at it upon the stave for a moment, then marked his target again. For what seemed an age he scrutinised it, then, in one move, he drew. The arrow flew, and struck dead centre. The crowd gasped. A page dashed out to inspect the target.

"The coin is struck!" called the boy. There was uproar. Several dashed forward to congratulate Lambert, and were held back. Lambert himself remained implacable – but already the crowd was celebrating his win. They almost drowned out the reedy voice of the page as he added: "But it is not split!" The tumult died away, and all looked at each other in astonished bemusement. It was not over.

Simon-Over-Lee stepped up to the line, head bowed. For the last time they fell into awe-struck silence, wondering what – if anything – could be done to better such a shot.

Gisburne knew what Simon-Over-Lee meant to do before he made his move. It was a sudden memory of Hattin that triggered the realisation – of an act so audacious, so challenging, that it could only have been attempted by the man he had known as Locksley. And yet, it had been Gisburne himself who had suggested it. At the nadir of the battle upon that dusty, parched outcrop, with the Christian army near annihilated by Salah al-Din's vast army, Locksley had been seeking a target for his last arrow – a final act of defiance in the face of certain death. And Gisburne, beyond desperation, but suddenly gripped by a mad idea, had pointed a shaking hand at the yellow tent of the Sultan – at Salah al-Din himself.

Now, as Simon-Over-Lee laid his last arrow upon the bowstave, ready to take his shot, Gisburne saw the archer's obscured face turn briefly beneath the shadowy cowl – towards the royal stand, and back again.

And he knew.

Gisburne vaulted over the rail, knocking a herald flying as he did so, and sprinted towards the shooting line. All that followed seemed to unfold as if the whole world were grinding to a halt. He saw Simon-Over-Lee begin to draw his bow.

Running headlong, he pushed past men and women, barging them out of his way with little regard for their fate. They tumbled, faces contorted with near-comical outrage. He leapt over flailing limbs. If he fell now, it would all be over.

In the closing moments he was suddenly aware that all eyes were on him. There were shouts of alarm. A hand clawed at his face and bloodied it – whether by accident or design, he never knew. He was dimly aware of men closing in from other, more distant parts of the crowd – his men.

In the confused mêlée, the archer was momentarily blocked from view. When he appeared again, his bow was more than half drawn, his body turning towards Gisburne – towards the Prince.

As he turned, his face was revealed. Gisburne met his gaze. Simon-Over-Lee. Robert of Locksley. Robin Hood. Astonishment flickered on that face as his arrow point swung around. It became a smile.

With little thought for his own safety, Gisburne flung himself at Hood. His forehead hit something solid, which cracked under the impact. The arrow flew, whooshing past his right ear, its fletching grazing his temple. As they both hit the ground, Gisburne on top of Hood, something snapped, and the wind was knocked out of him. They rolled on the hard, frozen ground, and as he turned over Gisburne looked back to see John staring – astounded, but very much alive – and a vertical rent in the cloth pavilion where the arrow had passed.

He had to be pulled off Hood. Afterwards, when Gisburne thought back on it, that whole part was a blur. He had never had much time for the notion of demons, and possession. It seemed to him that the plain folly or insanity of men was more than enough to account for the evils in the world. But, now and again, even he had seen madness that seemed to come from nowhere – without warning, and for no discernible reason. And then, every once in a while, he wondered.

This was such an occasion. But this time, the possessed man was him.

There was one memory that remained vivid in his mind. As he had been dragged off the bloody but still laughing Hood, he had looked up and seen Marian. How and when she had arrived, he had not been aware – he knew only that her expression would live with him forever.

She regarded him with horror, outrage. Revulsion. He felt the door slam on years of intimacy and affection. As the guards closed in around Hood and bound him, she turned and quit the stand, then plunged into the pressing crowd, as if unable to bear another moment in this place, in this company.

In his daze, he felt the hands of his comrades – the very same ones that had pulled him away from Hood – shake him, and slap him on the back. There were cheers. For a moment, he thought they would even lift him onto their shoulders. In the open pavilion, John smiled a broad smile and clapped his hands.

On this day, Gisburne had achieved his highest ambition – a thing beyond the capabilities of any other knight in the realm. He had engineered the capture of the most dangerous man in England. He had saved the life of the heir to the English throne. He had put right the wrong that had gnawed at him every day for the past two years – that had threatened the very future of the kingdom. He had done all this, because he believed – no, he *knew* – that it was right. This was his greatest victory.

And it felt like disaster.

XXXVIII

London
June, 1193

"I HAVE SOMETHING!" bawled Galfrid as he bounded up the stairs. With a cackle of delight he ducked his head under the low beam and booted open the unlatched door. Three times now he had cracked the top of his head on that beam when ascending the steps – twice when he was in a hurry. The last time, he'd struck it with such force that his knees had buckled and he'd slithered all the way to the foot of the twisting staircase. For a good few minutes afterwards, he had lain there in a heap, just gathering his wits, eyes watering, glad that on this particular occasion Gisburne was not in the house.

This time, however, he knew Gisburne to be at home. He'd spied him up there from the rain-soaked street, his profile framed in the open window, sitting, staring. Galfrid knew why, and he knew at what. He seemed to be doing a lot of that these days. Too much. It frustrated Galfrid; it certainly wasn't helping them towards their goal, and it was tying his master in knots. But try as he might, whether through subtle manipulation or bluff cajolery, Galfrid seemed unable to break the fixation. He might pull him out of it for a few hours – a day – but it would always draw him back, and he would see Gisburne closing in on himself again. Sometimes he would awake in the night to find Gisburne playing the hurdy gurdy by the open window – tunes Galfrid no longer recognised. Even the hooting interjections of Widow Fleet – of late in a perpetual state of war with her neighbour Osekin, whose pig continually invaded her yard – could not get through to him. And then there was the peculiar direction that Gisburne's inquiries had begun to take.

Today, however, Galfrid was triumphant. He had new information – something definite, this time. Piddling though it was in the scheme of things, after days of fruitless searches through sodden, muddy streets it felt like the retaking of Jerusalem.

"I have something," he repeated, throwing off his bag and flinging his sopping wet cap upon the table. Gisburne sat in exactly the same attitude Galfrid had seen from the street, chin on his fist, elbow on his knee, staring at his wall in intense concentration. With his other hand he turned one of Llewellyn's bodkin points over and over. He did not turn. He did not speak.

Galfrid shook the drips off his head and stepped into the front room. "New information..." he said.

"What?" Gisburne stirred. His eyes flicked sideways, but still his head did not turn. "Oh. Good." Then, his brow knotted, he was once again lost in his tangled, private world.

Not all the rain London could tip upon Galfrid's head had dampened his spirit today, but Gisburne had pissed the spark out with three words. He wiped a hand over his wet face and sniffed. He'd seen Gisburne like this a few times of late, but even so, this was a bad one. He fought the urge to kick the stool from under him, or throw the doorstop at his head. "Well, don't you want to know what it is?" he said.

Gisburne snapped out of his reverie, dragging his attention from the wall. "Yes, of course," he said.

The mad mural – Gisburne's grubby, soot-black Monreale – had, in the past two weeks, grown and spread like a grimy weed, finally claiming every inch of wall. When that had run out, it had begun to creep across the ceiling – had even colonised parts of the floor. To what end, Galfrid could no longer guess. For as it had developed, so it had degenerated. Here and there, elements of it were still coherent – words, plans, devices – but the greater part had been drawn over and wiped out and drawn over again so many times that the overall impression was of something slowly disappearing into a smudged, foggy blur.

"Baylesford," said Galfrid. "He's been seen. Two days ago, on Catte Street."

"You're sure?" said Gisburne.

"There's no doubt this time. The witness – a wool merchant by name of Adelard – has known him for years. Even sailed with him on a couple of occasions. Gave a full and detailed description."

"Good," said Gisburne, nodding. He sounded like he meant it this time, as if he was returning to the real world. "This is good."

"There's something else..." Galfrid paused. He had Gisburne's full attention now. "When Baylesford saw our witness, he ran."

"Ran..?"

"Adelard said when Baylesford clapped eyes on him from across the street, he gave a brief smile of recognition – looked for all the world like he was about to greet his old friend – then his face fell, and he was off like a startled deer."

"Has Baylesford any reason to fear this man? To wish to avoid him?"

"None that he knows. Things have only ever been cordial between them. But there is one other possibility... That Baylesford was running *because* he was recognised – that he wishes to avoid being found."

Gisburne rose to his feet, considering these words. "My God," he said. "He knows. He knows he is a target, and has gone to ground..."

"Perhaps Ranulph Le Fort too," said Galfrid. "If they've heard of the murders, it would not take much for them to have drawn their own conclusions. Little wonder they have been so elusive." He sighed heavily. "Unfortunately, it makes our task all the more difficult."

"But also the Red Hand's," said Gisburne. And he smiled.

There had been no murders for over two weeks – not since the startling double event of the twenty-fifth day of May. Gisburne had theorised that the Red Hand had originally meant to spread the killings – that had the attack on de Rosseley proved successful, the murders of Jocelyn de Gaillard and Mortimer de Vere would have been days apart at the very least, maintaining a steady pressure on his pursuers. Now it seemed there may be other reasons why he had been quiet – and not of his own making.

His late silence had done nothing to quell the fear he had inspired, nor dampened the city's morbid fascination. If anything, it had fuelled them. All knew that he was out there, somewhere, unapprehended, free to act, preparing to do so – and every day that passed without event only made some new horror more likely. Imaginations rioted. There was a void to be filled, and every wild dream, prejudice and dread flooded in to fill it.

Some took the opportunity to blame the Jews. Others, the church. Many there were that talked of the Red Hand as a demon – even a harbinger of impending Apocalypse. But for some, he was an avenging angel, bringing judgement upon John and his cronies, upon authority, upon the city itself. Priests in the pulpit invoked his name. One claimed outright he had come as punishment for their failure to wrest Jerusalem from Saracen hands. Few who listened could see reason to doubt his words. As moods turned and tensions grew, Gisburne and Galfrid were forced to face the possibility that some fanatics might even feel driven to protect him.

As if to confirm the arrival of some dark force, the long-augured storms had finally fallen upon the city. At midday on the first of June, day had turned to night, blinding lights flickered from the boiling, black clouds, and the sky cracked open. For days now it had rumbled on with no sign of respite and bringing no relief, and for days they had stuck doggedly to their task, wading through thick air and thicker mud.

*   *   *

GALFRID KNEW GISBURNE'S search for Ranulph had yielded nothing. What he did not know was how much was due to lack of information, and how much with his master's dangerously diverted attention. "So," he said, striving to maintain as casual a tone as possible, "how did you get on today? Found anything to rival my revelation?"

"Actually, yes," said Gisburne. He tossed the bodkin point in the air and caught it. "Except..." His brow creased. He shook his head. "I'm not sure what to make of it yet."

"Well," said Galfrid, "I'm listening." He had not expected this answer.

Gisburne looked suddenly shifty – almost embarrassed. His hand closed about the arrowhead. "It's nothing, really."

"Ah," said Galfrid. "Dickon..."

Galfrid had watched as Gisburne's curiosity about this man had turned into obsession. Why, he did not understand. He had told himself that his master had his reasons – that perhaps there was some obscure connection that Gisburne had not shared with him. He had a frustrating habit of not sharing information, after all. But, generous though he tried to be, he was struggling to find justification – and Gisburne, he sensed, knew it.

Galfrid sighed heavily. He had no desire to hear about Dickon Bend-the-Bow. But, as he turned to leave, Gisburne suddenly began to blurt out his story, as if desperate to be heard – or for someone to bring clarity to all he was about to describe.

"I spoke today with someone who knew him," he said. "More than knew him. A whore named Osanna, who frequented Dickon's caravan during the summer he spent in London. She's a sad wreck now, destroyed by drink, but probably quite a beauty in her day. It took two weeks of enquiry to get to her. She was with Dickon the very night he disappeared. And she told me something. A secret she'd kept to herself for years in the vague hope he might return. Now, she'd tell it to you for half a cup of ale, except no one's interested – or they weren't, until I found her..."

In spite of himself, Galfrid turned back to face Gisburne. His master's eyes were glinting. "Three men called upon Dickon that evening. Many sought audience with him at that time – women especially. But this was different. Two were serjeants or knights – she could not tell which, and anyway only glimpsed them beyond the wagon cover. The third was clearly a knight – and a noble one. She remembered his name: Sir Geoffrey of Lemsforde. He insisted on speaking with Dickon in private, inside the wagon. She was never meant to hear their hushed conversation. No one was. Dickon presumed her passed out in his bed; Lemsforde probably did not even know she was there. The knight said he came as a representative of King Henry – that Dickon's abilities had been noted, and that he wished to offer him an opportunity. That opportunity was never spoken outright, but it's clear what was meant."

"An agent," muttered Galfrid. "Acting for the King."

Gisburne nodded eagerly, and sat forward. "But Dickon politely declined – a response that must have taken Lemsforde aback, given that it was, in effect, a summons from the monarch. But who can blame Dickon? He had fame, women, people throwing silver at him night after night, and at no danger to himself. Then Osanna heard Sir Geoffrey ask him if they had met somewhere before. Dickon said not. And with that, they parted ways. But what she could see and others could not was that this question had disturbed him. She afterwards questioned him on it. He flung her out of his wagon in a rage. She found some other corner to sleep in that night – unaware, then, that his rejection had probably saved her life."

"And you believe this testimony reliable?" said Galfrid.

"I do. It tallies with all I've heard."

"A fine story. But where does all this lead?"

"There's more..." said Gisburne. "The next morning she returned to find Dickon's wagon destroyed and the camp in uproar."

"You think Sir Geoffrey may have been responsible – because Dickon had refused the King's offer?"

"It's a possibility I briefly considered," said Gisburne. "There was a hooded visitor to Dickon's wagon later that night who no one has yet been able to identify. But there was another mystery. When she arrived, the wreck was still hot. She was among the first to pick through it. She saw the charred remains, and, distraught, had an idea to find some keepsake of him. An arrowhead came to mind, she said, and even in her distress, she considered gathering several, to sell as trophies. But she could find nothing. Everything was destroyed."

"So, he's dead after all," shrugged Galfrid.

Gisburne raised the bodkin point between thumb and forefinger, and stared at it. "The odd thing was the arrows."

"You said there *were* no arrows."

"That was the odd thing. The arrowheads were of steel. According to Osanna they should have found at least two dozen of them in that burnt wreck. But they found not one."

"So?"

"Obviously, someone took them."

Galfrid frowned. This just seemed to be going from one pointless observation to another. "Why would anyone take Dickon's arrows?"

"They wouldn't," said Gisburne, "unless they were Dickon himself. He did not die that night. Someone else – the hooded man, perhaps – died in his place, and Dickon took his bow and arrows and fled. Or perhaps he became an agent of the Crown after all, and is still operating in that capacity – in secret." Gisburne sat back, at last satisfied.

Galfrid regarded him for a moment, uncertain quite how to respond. "That's it?"

"Isn't that enough? I know it's not Sir Ranulph, but..."

"No, it's not Sir Ranulph," muttered Galfrid.

"But Dickon is alive."

"So what?" said Galfrid, throwing up his hands, his patience spent. "What has been the point in all this – in chasing this ghost? Even if he were alive, do you seriously believe he could help you?"

"It's not that," said Gisburne.

"You know what drives me mad? Not only is this a wild goose chase, you don't even *need* his skills. You're as good an archer as any I've ever met."

"It's not that," Gisburne snapped.

They stared at each other in silence. "Fine," said Galfrid. "Explain it to me then. Make it make sense. Or can you not bring yourself to? Like you couldn't tell me about John's decoy, or Llewellyn's messages, or the fact that your own father had been with the Prince in Ireland?"

Gisburne's jaw clenched, as if holding in his answer. Galfrid took a step towards him.

"Those street urchins are out there, day and night. They have Baylesford's description now – to the last detail – and they will find him. But it's not his name next on your precious list; it's Le Fort's. You're the one who worked that out – *you* – and now you have abandoned him. The man's life is at stake, yet all you can do is worry over someone who has no connection with the task, who is in all probability already dead."

"But he *is* connected," insisted Gisburne. "And he's not dead. Haven't you been listening?"

"That was ten years ago! No one's seen or heard of him since! And what if they had anyway? What difference can any of this possibly make?"

"Because he's connected with Hood," barked Gisburne. "Hood knows of him. Is afraid of him. Right here, right now. Hood knows he is alive, and he blanches at his name!"

So, that was it. Hood. At last, Galfrid began to understand. His heart felt like lead. He exhaled heavily. "Hood dies in fewer than a dozen days, God willing," he said. "But others stand to die before that. Those deaths, I should like to prevent. Wouldn't you?"

Gisburne stared at him, mute – as if robbed not only of words, but of the will to speak.

Galfrid could take no more. He puffed out his cheeks. "I'm going to get some food," he said, then grabbed his bag and hat and headed out, down the stairs and back into the rain-lashed street – knowing full well that within minutes of his leaving, Gisburne's mind would once again turn away from Ranulph Le Fort, and back to the fabled bowman.

XXXIX

Crippelsgate
14 June, 1193

ON THE FOURTEENTH day of June, the Red Hand's interlude came to an abrupt end.

On that day, Gisburne and Galfrid were sat in a tavern in the shadow of the church of St-Giles-without-Crippelsgate. By the look on his face, Galfrid had not seen its like before. There were cloths covering the long tables. On either side were not benches, but chairs. And around them on every side sat the fashionable, the noble, the well-heeled.

Galfrid shifted uncomfortably. "What is this all about?

"I told you," said Gisburne. "Food."

"But we have food. There's half a gallon of hogget stew left. And bread that was fresh this morning. And some of those German pickles you like."

"*Good* food."

Galfrid's face hardened. "Are saying my cooking's not up to scratch?"

That was not at all what Gisburne was saying. "Galfrid, please," he said, holding up both hands. "Just accept this... in the spirit it is meant." He had intended this meal as an apology, but Galfrid, as always, was not making it easy for him. "Your food is fine. Excellent, in fact. I just thought..." He gestured to his surroundings, hoping they spoke for him.

Finally, Galfrid seemed to understand. He nodded, even threatened to smile. "Well then..." he said. "I suppose the hogget will keep." With that, he drew out his eating knife – a pitted and discoloured old blade with a plain wood handle and a point that had at some stage been snapped off and crudely sharpened back. He went to stab it into the table, but Gisburne thrust his outstretched hand, narrowly avoiding a skewering in the process.

"Please," he said. "Not here..."

A foreign noble with the longest nose Gisburne had ever seen and a beard like a nun's chuff shot them a sour look. Galfrid looked around, then carefully placed his battered old knife upon the table before him.

Wine was brought. Cups charged. A bowl of steaming broth arrived, followed by a salad of fragrant herbs, bread and cheese, and a dish of soft, spiced figs. They were immediately joined by a broad platter of hot *ravieles* – thin dough parcels of egg, cheese and saffron covered in butter with yet more grated cheese on top. Their lugubrious server – immaculately dressed in dark blue and white livery – named each dish in a monotone, managing to maintain an air of perfect civility whilst simultaneously regarding them as if they were a pair of animals wandered in from a provincial farmyard.

"I have heard this is some of the best food in London," said Gisburne, after the servant had sloped off. Galfrid at first prodded the *ravieles* uncertainly, then spiked a parcel on his knife, sniffed it, and shoved it in his mouth. His face broke into a smile. From there on, there was no looking back.

For some time they ate in silence.

"It was not intentional, you know," said Gisburne after the wine had been flowing a while, "me not telling you about my father in Ireland."

"It's your choice," said Galfrid between mouthfuls. "And not my place to criticise."

"You were right to criticise. The fact is, I did not know myself, until these past weeks. All that time he had kept it from me. I suppose I just wanted the secret to be mine for a while."

Galfrid nodded slowly. "It doesn't matter," he said. "Really."

At that moment, another dish landed upon the table – some kind of gargantuan fowl with onions in a deep red sauce. The aroma of garlic and wine made Gisburne immediately salivate.

"What's this?" he said.

"A new dish from France," said the server wearily. "Cock in wine." Then he added, deadpan: "And I've heard all the jokes." He plodded off, leaving Gisburne and Galfrid staring down at the dish in wonder, and not a little trepidation. "Cock in wine..." repeated Galfrid.

It was clear from the legs alone that in life it had been a cockerel of considerable dimensions. That did not bode so well – but at least, if it turned out to be like boiled wood, thought Gisburne, they could lap up the sauce. When they went at it with their knives, however, they found the meat so tender it fell off the bone. Gisburne spiked a piece awkwardly. Galfrid, giving up on that approach, attacked it with a spoon. Both ate. The soft, gamey meat merged with the flavour of rich, reduced wine, onions, butter and tiny pieces of smoked pork. Galfrid raised his eyebrows. "This is not something I thought I'd find myself saying," he said, "but that is without doubt the best cock I've ever tasted."

They demolished the dish without further comment, and were taking on the sauce with what remained of the bread when the clamour burst upon them.

To his dying day, Gisburne would never know how Hamon found them there. But he was glad he did. Whether Hamon was as glad, having run the gauntlet of the tavern's fanatically officious staff, was perhaps another matter.

It began with a banging at the door. Then shouting. The mud-splattered figure of Hamon briefly appeared, then – protesting in the most colourful of terms – was dragged back by his ragged tunic. There was a tussle, a crash, a number of firm entreaties that were flatly ignored. Somehow he broke through again, and made it half way to Gisburne and Galfrid before his pursuers caught hold and wrestled him to the tavern floor.

Gisburne stood, sending his wine cup bowling off the table, its contents spraying over a pair of excessively loud Flemish merchants. One jumped to his feet in reflex as the wine hit his face – and his belly almost upended their own table, sending a dish of spiced pork smashing to the floor, shards of bouncing pottery and splatters of sauce peppering the thrashing blue and white bodies of the servers. But before Gisburne could even make a move – and with a determination that made the Tower guard look positively easygoing – they had hauled the struggling Hamon up by his arms and legs, like a sheep for the shearing, and were heading for the door ready to fling him out.

Hamon had uttered nothing coherent to his masters during that chaotic encounter, but he had delivered his message, nonetheless – the message that both hardly dared hope would arrive. For as he had been dragged away, he had raised his right hand in a peculiar gesture, in which the thumb and first two fingers were extended. This signal had been established so he might deliver this most grave piece of news without having to speak the words aloud. It related to the Red Hand, and it said simply: *We have found him.*

With the tavern now in uproar, Gisburne and Galfrid scrambled for the door. Outside, Hamon lay sprawled in the muck.

"Are you all right, boy?" said Galfrid, hauling him to his feet.

"I've 'ad worse," said Hamon. Then he turned back to the door of the tavern and slung a clod of dung at it. "Stuck-up bastards!" he shouted.

"Let's all get out of here," said Gisburne. "Before they realise we haven't paid the bill."

As THEY HURRIED round to the yard where Nyght and Mare were waiting, Hamon – still breathless – apprised them of the situation.

"It was my mate Tom," he said. "'E seen this bloke who fitted your description: a tinker, bearded and big, but all 'unched so as to 'ide it. He followed 'im, and he stopped 'is wagon outside an 'ouse in Jewen Street, and then 'e 'eard 'im ask for Ranulph Le Fort."

"Christ," said Gisburne. "He's found Ranulph. Is there more?"

"The people of the next door 'ouse was Jews. They's all Jews down there. They turned 'im away, said 'e'd come to the wrong place. And off 'e went."

"Did Tom follow?"

"'E 'ad to leave him to come and tell me. But this were just minutes ago. Just as long ago as it took to run from Jewen Street."

"Come on, then!" said Gisburne, and hauled himself into Nyght's saddle.

XL

THERE WAS NOTHING Londoners feared more than fire. Though there were few alive to remember it, all here had parents or grandparents who had told them of the Great Fire of 1135. It was this fire that had damaged London Bridge, and which destroyed most of the properties between St Paul's and St Clement Danes.

As Gisburne and Galfrid rode through narrowing streets, Hamon running ahead of them, limbs flailing, they saw ahead of them a rising column of black smoke. A sense of panic gripped Gisburne; they knew the Red Hand used fire, but this could destroy the city.

Though the rain had held off all day, the streets were thick with mud – heavy going for boy and horse. At times it seemed Hamon had the advantage, disappearing entirely out of view as he pressed ahead and darted off down the next alley. It only served to emphasise how painfully slow was the horses' progress.

They had no trouble identifying the house on Jewen Street. Smoke was billowing from an upper story window, and the orange light of flames flickered inside. All around, local people milled and shouted – many in a tongue Gisburne did not understand – rushing with pails and pots of water in an attempt to fight the flames. Without hesitation, they plunged into the front door of the burning building, emerging moments later, coughing and choking. It seemed the height of selflessness. But if this house burned, their houses burned. As Gisburne dismounted, a woman next to him put her hands over her ears and simply wailed in anguish.

Hamon, meanwhile, was already talking avidly to a spindly lad who was watching out front – Tom.

"Is this it? The house where he knocked?" said Gisburne. "You're sure of it?"

Tom nodded with awesome vigour. Hamon put a hand on the lad's shoulder and turned to his masters.

"'E says 'e 'eard a fearsome shoutin' and crashin' inside before the fire started," said Hamon. "But 'e ain't seen no one come out since. 'E thinks the Red 'And must still be inside."

Gisburne and Galfrid exchanged looks. "Get your staff," said Gisburne. He pulled his sword – his father's sword – from beneath Nyght's saddle, where it had been discreetly stowed, and threw its strap over his shoulder. "Mark the front," he said. "I'll take the back. You boys watch the streets – and holler if you see anything."

Gisburne ran off with heavy, mud-caked feet down the thickly mired alley running down the side of the next house, his palm on his sword pommel. As he went, leaving the immediate turmoil behind, he felt a thrill rise up in him. If this were true – if it were as Hamon said... For the first time, they were close. Better than close. They had him trapped.

At the end of the alley was a low, rotting gate, leading to a lane running along the backs of the houses. It was stuck fast in the mud; Gisburne vaulted over. A clutch of scrawny chickens flew up in the next yard as he did so, setting off other animals in the process. A large dog barked nearby. A smaller yapped from a distance, the sound muffled by the damp and mud. In a small enclosed yard, a single cow lowed gruffly. Gisburne slithered along the lane, back towards the burning house, the cries at the front somehow distant. The back door, he now saw, had been smashed so completely that it was now almost non-existent. Upon its hanging top hinge, only a splinter of wood remained. Gisburne drew his sword.

As he approached the yard, his attention momentarily diverted by the deep, foot-sucking mud, he seemed to see, from the corner of his eye, a large shape drop from one of the back windows. There was a heavy thud and a clank of metal, then silence.

He stood, motionless, seeing nothing – thinking, for a moment, his mind must be playing tricks. Then, beyond the low woodpile, a great figure rose up.

He had heard the descriptions a dozen times, had pictured the thing every hour of every day. But now it stood before him – solid, real, spattered with mud and gore – he felt his mouth turn dry and his damp limbs shudder.

The man was big, but it was his armour made him monstrous. Battered, spiked projections on the helm gave the impression of height, while its nightmarish face recalled the most grotesque carvings on the cathedral of Autun, a demon ready to consume lost souls. The rest of the armour – irregular plates ranging in size from palm to platter – seemed something animal: part reptilian, part insect. Its scales were almost black, but with a sheen of blue, like the carapace of a beetle. Gisburne had seen that before – cooked metal plunged into oil to keep it from rusting. Simple pragmatism, but the effect was pure evil. From one great, clawed arm, partially obscured by the heaped logs, hung the huge hammer. Upon the other was a long, copper cylinder.

For a moment they faced each other, its dead, empty eyes on him. It took three heavy steps around the woodpile. Gisburne could hear it breathing. Then, with a roar, it charged.

To stand firm was folly. That much, Gisburne knew. He feigned a swerve as the Red Hand closed, then flung himself to the opposite way. He heard flames roar as he rolled – felt their heat in the air. He righted himself, waited for the hammer to come as he knew it would, prepared to dodge it.

But it did not come. The Red Hand did not turn or stop. Caked in mud and muck, Gisburne scrambled to his feet as the great figure pounded off into the lane. The Red Hand had already pushed his luck to the limit with this attack. His only object now was escape.

Gisburne smiled. In leaving him alive, the Red Hand had made his greatest error. He had no mail to protect him – nothing but his horsehide coat, his sword and his eating knife. But he could still run – all day if he had to. Now he would see how long the Red Hand could last.

He sped off in pursuit, closing on the lumbering giant. The hammer smashed through a side gate, and the Red Hand headed off down another alley. Then another – twisting and turning through the tangled maze of back ways and tracks. He knew exactly where he was going – and he was fast for a big man. Gisburne's wet surcoat flapped and wrapped about his legs with every step, and the past weeks of inactivity suddenly seemed to weigh upon him – on his lungs, on his limbs. But in this task, unencumbered as he was, he knew he was still the stronger – until the Red Hand chose to stop, and face him.

As he drew closer, his pumping feet heavy with mud, his mind raced, calculating his options, his eyes scanning the back of his adversary for gaps, weak points. When he took him down, it had to be complete; if any fight was left in the big man – any at all – Gisburne would not survive.

And then it hit him with the force of revelation. The Red Hand did not know he was being pursued. His visibility – and his hearing too – were limited by his great helm. And now, he was leading Gisburne back to his wagon. He thought of de Rosseley's advice – how stamina would be what the Red Hand lacked. If he only hung back now, and kept pace, the Red Hand would be bringing defeat upon himself with every step.

But then, as they turned down a narrow gap between two dilapidated buildings, labouring through the slimy, near-black mud, he saw it. With each increasingly heavy stride, the bottom edge of the Red Hand's helm rose momentarily where neck and shoulder met. A gap – appearing and disappearing with the rhythm of his great stride. He could not let such an opportunity pass. The timing would have to be perfect. He would have only one chance – and if he missed, he would alert the Red Hand to his presence. Gisburne raised his sword across his shoulder.

As the Red Hand cleared the two buildings, he turned a sharp right – and Gisburne's opportunity disappeared up a low bank and through a gap in the crumbling wall. Gisburne fought to make the turn, skidded and slithered on the bank. He recovered and leapt through the gap, to find himself in a wide trackway with scruffy yards on either side – and in the middle of it the Red Hand standing, facing him.

Whether he had heard him stumble on the bank, or glimpsed him as he turned, Gisburne would never know. But it mattered little now. The Red Hand would not run any more – not until he had put his pursuer down for good. If this great hulk charged at him, as he surely meant to, there would be little Gisburne could do. He could dodge him once – maybe twice. So he did the one thing he knew the Red Hand would not expect. He ran at him.

The hammer swung – but too slow. The weapon's great head boomed past Gisburne's head as his right shoulder smashed into the Red Hand's sternum, all his weight and momentum behind the blow. It was like running into a stone wall. But he heard the great man groan, and stagger back, and as he did so, Gisburne swung his whole body round, arms fully extended, sword gripped in both fists. He turned almost full circle, the tip of his blade shrieking as it swung through its great arc.

Detached, almost curious, Gisburne watched as the Red Hand raised his left arm – not, he realised, to protect himself, but to release a burst of Greek Fire. The Red Hand's flank was hung with thick plates of steel; Gisburne entirely unprotected. The flame would strike him full in the face from less than a yard.

As his sword completed its circuit, he brought it down low, striking the Red Hand's left knee with such force Gisburne feared the precious sword would warp. The blade turned as it met metal, bent about the knee joint and sprung back, whipping out of Gisburne's wet grip, somersaulting twice and sticking in the mud four yards distant. Gisburne's unchecked momentum sent him teetering off balance. His feet slid sideways in the slimy mire, and he crashed to the ground. But as he did so, he heard a roar from within the metal mask – a roar of pain.

Strike a knee joint side on with enough force and it will make the bones shudder no matter what armour is laid against it. Gisburne – helpless, face down upon the ground – was aware of a moment of complete stillness –

then felt the ground quiver beneath him as the Red Hand's huge frame slammed upon it.

He scrambled for his sword. With the Red Hand down, he had a chance. He could find a gap, and thrust his sword point into it. But even as his hand closed about the grip, the giant was up again. A piercing, half-human squeal cut the air, and Gisburne whirled round in confusion. The huge figure was loping unevenly towards him – hammer already swinging. Gisburne had only a second to judge its trajectory – but such a weapon cannot be made to change direction. He dropped and rolled again, out of its path – and was suddenly aware of another dark shape hurtling towards him. The ghastly squeal sounded again – now right by his face. Other harsh cries seemed to echo distantly. Then the hammer struck.

Flesh and bone burst apart with a sickening crunch. Gisburne felt hot blood gush over him – buckets of it – and a pig, still twitching, its head obliterated by the hammer blow, collapsed over his chest. The blood splattered into his eyes, momentarily blinding him. Shocked, horrified, drenched in gore, Gisburne thrust the pig off him and scrambled backward in the mud, trying to blink the blood away. It rolled over like a bristly barrel, its legs convulsing as if still believing they could deliver it from harm. Behind him now, he heard a grunt. Snorting. The sticky patter of feet in mud. Ahead of him, through the stinging red mist, he could make out the looming figure of the Red Hand. But he was backing away.

Gisburne turned just as the feral, mud-caked hogs fell upon him.

They had smelled the blood. There was little they wouldn't eat, but this had sent them into a frenzy. Grunting and squealing, they pulled at his coat and thrust their wet snouts at him. He swung and stabbed at them, and for a moment they drew back. He struggled to his knees, then the biggest of them – warty and bristled like a boar – went for him, barging into his chest.

He fell backwards – felt one bite his boot, its teeth near breaking his toes. A trotter stamped into his side as the boar-hog came straight for his throat. His foot could take its chances, but his throat he meant to keep. He lashed at the hog with his blade, catching it square across the head and cleaving its skull an inch deep. The squeal that came from it was like nothing he had ever heard – a sound no one should hear. Such a blow would have felled a man, but the great bristled beast did not drop. It bucked and shrieked, spraying blood as it bit wildly at its fellows, its brains scrambled. The squealing grew into a hellish cacophony as each turned on the other and Gisburne, for the moment, was forgotten. He crawled backwards, watching in horror as the pack feasted on the steaming flesh of its fallen comrades.

When finally he staggered to his feet, the Red Hand was gone. Gisburne turned this way and that, looking out across the impossible labyrinth of yards, paths and alleys, straining desperately to see some familiar shape, some pattern of tracks in the mud. But there was nothing. He glanced back at the pigs, still occupied with their meal. From nowhere, unbidden, a vision of the tavern and their dish with its deep red sauce entered his head, and he shuddered. As he turned to go, intent on putting as much distance between himself and them as possible, something in the mud caught his eye. He stooped, and picked it up. A thick, blue-black plate of metal, its leather bindings cut through – a piece of the Red Hand's armoured shell.

XLI

It AMAZED GISBURNE to discover just how far they had run. As he picked his way back through the maze, he found he was grateful for that column of smoke. Yet it seemed, as he neared, that it was now thinning. When finally he arrived, he saw the fire had been entirely quenched by the swift actions of the people. All that remained now was to enter the house, and see what new chaos the Red Hand had left in his wake.

Looking around, he caught sight of Galfrid further up the street, deep in conversation with a well-groomed young man of the neighbourhood. The young man had his arm around an older woman – clearly a servant – who was weeping. Gisburne raised his hand and called his squire's name. As he did so, a woman nearby turned and screamed. Gisburne drew his sword, and swung around. Another joined her. Several men cried out, now – some cursing harshly. Gisburne looked this way and that, but could see no threat. Turning back, he saw Galfrid's horrified expression – then he realised they were screaming at him.

Blood. He had some blood on him. Of course.

"It's all right!" he called, sheathing his sword and raising his hands in a gesture of submission as he strode past. "I'm all right..."

"Christ's bollocks," said Galfrid as he approached. "What happened to you?"

"Don't ask. Let's just say I may be off ham for a while."

"Are you hurt?"

"No," said Gisburne. He wiggled his toes in his boot, and winced with at the sharp pain it induced. "It's not my blood."

Galfrid's eyes widened. "His?"

"Sadly, no. Just an animal. How bad does it look?"

"About as bad as it possibly could."

Gisburne felt his scalp, slimy with mud – or what he had supposed was mud.

"Is it in my hair?"

Galfrid nodded, his eyes still roving about Gisburne in disbelief. "It's like you dived in and went for a swim in it."

Gisburne sighed. "I almost had him, Galfrid," he said. "I was so close... But I injured him. And he left something..." He reached inside his surcoat and pulled out the metal plate.

Galfrid looked at it, and puffed out his cheeks. "D'you really think anything could get through that?"

"We can at least find out now," said Gisburne. As he pocketed the plate, he noticed the young man to whom Galfrid had been speaking lurking a little way from him, still comforting the weeping woman. Galfrid followed Gisburne's gaze.

"This is Isaac," said Galfrid. "Most of the people have been reluctant to speak with me, but Isaac is different." Galfrid smiled at him. "This is his house. And Ranulph Le Fort is" – he corrected himself – "*was* a guest in it."

"Dead?" said Gisburne.

Galfrid nodded.

Isaac was well-dressed, his black hair neatly cropped – a man of decent means. Yet his face had an unhealthy pallor and was oddly lacking expression. Gisburne noted his hands were shaking. His home had almost been destroyed, and a man murdered; it was no surprise he was in a state of shock. As Gisburne stepped towards him, Isaac spoke some gentle words to the woman. She inclined her head, wiped her tears, and left them.

"My housekeeper," said Isaac. "I've known her since I was a boy. When I came back and saw the flames, I thought..."

Gisburne nodded. "Ranulph was alone in the house?"

"So it would seem."

"You knew him well?"

"I knew him," said Isaac. "He was a good friend over many years. Not just to me, but to the Jewish people. Even during hard times."

Gisburne nodded again. By all accounts, Sir Ranulph had championed all manner of causes, but he had not heard of this one.

"How did you know him?" he said.

Isaac blinked, and frowned. "Does it matter now?"

Gisburne decided to leave that line of questioning for later. "Did he know the nature of the thing that threatened him? And did he say anything of it to you?"

"He knew something came for him. And, yes, he spoke of it. Only in the vaguest terms, but then..."

"But then..?"

"All of London is talking of the Red Hand."

Gisburne looked up at the front of the house. Upon the door was scratched an *x*.

"We need to look inside," he said.

"Maybe you should get cleaned up a bit," said Galfrid, looking him up and down again. When Gisburne glanced around, he saw that almost all gathered outside the house were now staring at him, their expressions ranging from dread to disgust.

"The house first," said Gisburne. He turned to Isaac. "May we?"

"Please," said Isaac. He smiled, and gestured to his door as if welcoming them in for wine. Then he looked up to the blackened window and it seemed the heart was once again torn out of him.

Before they took a step, a commotion down the street made them turn. A delegation was approaching – clearly the leaders of the community – at their head a grizzled, bearded man with an expression like a wet tombstone. Gisburne sensed danger. The man was small, his best years long past, but people shrank from his approach nonetheless. Isaac sighed. "It is Elazar," he said. "Nothing happens around here without his say-so."

"Another outrage committed against our people!" Elazar bawled as he drew near. He stopped suddenly before the bloody figure of Gisburne and gazed in disbelief.

"*Adoni shelei...*" he muttered, looking him up and down. "What horror is this?"

"It's all right," Gisburne said. "It's not my blood."

Elazar stared, as if appalled that that the creature before him had deigned to speak. "Who are you?" he barked. "What are you doing here? And why are you covered in... in..." Words failed the old man at this point. Given recent events, Gisburne supposed there was little he wasn't covered in.

"We are here on royal authority," he said, "charged with investigating this attack."

Elazar stared for a moment, seemingly incredulous – then burst into laughter. Several about him joined in. "Royal authority?" chuckled the old man. Gisburne was the first to admit he hardly appeared the part. He stood and endured the laughter until finally it died away – and a sudden change came over Elazar's face. A dark fury. "Do you want to know what I think of 'royal authority'?" he said. A tall, muscular man to Elazar's side muttered something and put a hand on the patriarch's arm, but Elazar shook it off, took a step forward and stared up at Gisburne with hard unblinking eyes. "At the coronation of Richard, Jewish leaders – all respected citizens – came bearing gifts to show their respect for their new

King. They found themselves barred from the ceremony, and were stripped and beaten. Word went around that the new King meant to kill us all." He shrugged. "It wasn't true, of course. But a mob went on the rampage anyway – all believing they acted on 'royal authority.' Across London, Jews were massacred. In other cities, too. Their businesses smashed, their houses burned. Some were baptised against their will; others set on fire in the street. I saw this with my own eyes – saw as my own wife was dragged from the house..." Elazar's voice broke, and he gathered himself. "The new King condemned these terrible acts. Punishments were meted out – generally against those who had mistakenly destroyed Christian households. But most were never held to account. My wife's murderers, whoever they were, went back to their lives. No doubt they live them still, somewhere in this very city. So, you will forgive me if I meet the notion of *royal authority* with some scepticism."

Gisburne lowered his head, and nodded slowly. "It is not Richard who is my master," he said, "but his brother John, who made this city a commune. And my task is to bring a murderer to justice."

"And you think you can do that?" scowled Elazar. "That you can begin to understand *this*..." He pointed a gnarled finger at the *x* scratched upon the door, then turned back to the gathered crowd. "You see?" he cried. "The cross upon the door! The mark of the anti-semite!" There were angry mutterings. "I know how things are in my own city. How easily they shift. Are we simply to stand by and watch while it happens again?" The mutterings grew to angry shouts. Gisburne noted that Elazar was not speaking to his people in their own language. This display was clearly for his benefit.

"It was not an attack against Jews," Gisburne said, raising his voice above the clamour. They hushed. "There are other hatreds in the world, though you may not believe it."

"What do you know of that?" snapped Elazar. "It is beyond the understanding of one such as you."

"Since you have not once clapped eyes on me till today," said Gisburne irritably, "you can have little idea of the limits or otherwise of my understanding. But I will tell you this..." He drew closer to Elazar, and lowered his voice so the crowd could not hear. "Half of London is looking for something – anything – upon which to vent its rage. If you persist in claiming that it was an attack against Jews, you will succeed only in whipping up mindless acts of revenge – and in doing so, supplying all the excuses your enemies need to fuel another massacre." He drew away again, and addressed the crowd in a clear voice. "This attack was not upon your people, but upon a Christian knight. It's he who lies slain in that house."

There were murmurs, exclamations. Elazar glowered at him, but before he could respond, Isaac stepped forward and addressed the people in their own language. There were more dark mutterings as he did so.

Isaac turned to Gisburne. "I told him what you say is true," he said. "That the dead man is not a Jew. That I gave him sanctuary here."

Elazar glared at Isaac. "So. You brought this upon us."

"I helped a man," said Isaac. "One who had need."

"A gentile," said Elazar.

"A *man*," insisted Isaac. An anger burned in his eyes, of a quite different order from Elazar's. "This is my house, and I am master of it. I alone paid the price. And I would gladly do so again." He stepped forward. "'Thou shalt not stand idly in thy neighbour's blood.'" Several mumbled and nodded at Isaac's words.

Elazar clearly did not like having the scriptures quoted at him. But he could not argue – not with this. Not when the crowd swayed towards Isaac. Instead, he looked the blood-drenched Gisburne up and down once again.

"So whose blood is this?" he said.

"Not a neighbour's," said Gisburne. "At least, not a human one."

Elazar appeared bemused by his words. "What then?"

"A pig's," said Gisburne.

The circle around him visibly widened.

XLII

INSIDE, THE HOUSE reeked of damp and smoke. It was a neat house, well-cared-for. But for the track of muddy footprints going in and out of the front door, one would hardly know anything had happened.

As they followed the muddy trail to the stairs, that impression began to change. At the foot of them, Isaac stopped. He turned, his face suddenly very pale. "Forgive me," he said. "I do not wish to go up there..."

Gisburne patted the man's shoulder, and sent him on his way. Then knight and squire turned to climb the steps into darkness.

THE WHOLE INTERIOR of the room was blackened. A choking haze hung in the air, thick with the smell of burnt meat. Water dripped from the ceiling and formed dark pools on the floor, mixing with some other greasy substance, now beginning to solidify in grey lumps. Fat from the body. Nothing remained of the mattress or the hangings about the walls and bed. The fire had been fierce – but the charred beams and posts had not fully caught before the neighbours had got to them. Gisburne supposed it was at least one reason to be thankful for days of English damp and rain.

On the bed – or rather, collapsed within it, huddled on the floor inside what was left of the frame – was a body. Its head was smashed, the rest burned almost beyond recognition. The right hand had been taken, the arm now a smoking stump. The left hand was drawn into a claw, but in horrid contrast to the rest, the gold rings on its fingers shone as bright as ever.

"This is what comes of playing with fire," said Galfrid.

But as he stared at the body, Gisburne wondered at the words. Like Galfrid, he had at first assumed that the fire was accidental – or, at least, a consequence of the Red Hand's attack. Now, he was not so sure.

"Why was Ranulph burned after he was dead?" he said. Galfrid looked again. "His head was smashed, he fell upon the bed, *then* he was burned. Why?"

Galfrid looked around for further clues, and shrugged. "Perhaps the bed was afire before the Red Hand struck the fatal blow."

"Perhaps," said Gisburne. He moved around the bed. It was built into the fabric of the room, its head part of the wall, the corners at its foot formed by stout posts between floor and ceiling. About one of these, he now saw, was wrapped a thick chain, which in turn was attached to a low wooden chest bound around with iron. The lock had been hammered – no, not merely hammered, but beaten out of shape. Yet it had not yielded. As if out of frustration, one end of the casket had also been battered. The iron bands were scored and warped, the wood split and flattened. Still it had refused to give up its secrets. Gisburne was in no doubt that this was also the work of the Red Hand's hammer.

"He tried to break this open," said Gisburne. "Tried and failed."

"Robbery?" said Galfrid, casting his eyes over the chest. "That's something new. Perhaps he has something in common with Hood after all."

"Clearly it contains something of value to him." Gisburne poked the chain with his toe. "Or he believed it did."

"Gold? Silver?"

"Something he sorely wanted... How many blows do you think he delivered before giving up? Twenty? Thirty?"

"Thirty at least," said Galfrid.

Gisburne turned and looked at his squire. "Would you stand there and deliver thirty blows to a chest in a room that was on fire? Less than a yard from the blaze?"

Galfrid looked at the destroyed bed, at the blackened chest, then back at Gisburne.

"This was no accident," said Gisburne. "I think when he failed to get what he wanted from this chest he deliberately set the place afire – perhaps to destroy this box and what it contained."

"Why destroy something of value?" said Galfrid. "To stop someone else having it?"

"Or *seeing* it," said Gisburne. "You remember Ranulph was the record keeper on the Irish expedition?" He lifted the corner of the chest with his foot and let it fall back on the boards. "It's not silver or gold in here..."

Gisburne and Galfrid looked at each other, both knowing what the other was thinking. "Get back down there," Gisburne said. "Tell Isaac we'll need this chest. And tell him to light a fire in the back yard. A big one, that will make as much smoke as possible – enough to keep the

Red Hand convinced that this house is burning to the ground." Galfrid nodded and hurried back down the stairs.

Gisburne turned back to the body with a grim sense of victory. The Red Hand had eluded him today – but now they had the chest and whatever secret it contained, and the Red Hand did not know it. He allowed himself a smile as his eyes roved over the blackened corpse.

Then he saw it – the thing that had been staring him in the face from the moment they had entered the room – and his jaw dropped.

GALFRID FOUND ISAAC sitting on the step outside. He had vomited, and his limbs were shaking – the shock starting to bite. But at least some of his colour had returned.

A large crowd had now gathered before the house – some of them concerned neighbours, but many simply curious. Of Elazar, there was now no sign. Galfrid ignored them all, and, squatting beside Isaac, explained what had to be done in slow and measured tones: the need to remove the chest, the importance of securing the house until they could do so, the building of the fire. Isaac nodded steadily as he spoke. Galfrid sensed he would feel better for having something to do.

Eventually Isaac stood, smoothed his tunic and, with renewed vigour, looked about for friends and neighbours to help him put the plan into action. As he did so, something within the crowd caught his eye. Galfrid saw his expression change again – to shock, and then deep despair. He gave an almost imperceptible shake of his head, then, with clenched fists, turned and moved swiftly away.

Galfrid followed the direction of his gaze. At first he saw nothing out of the ordinary. But then, within the throng, he noted a hooded man clutching a bag of newly bought provisions to his chest. What marked him out was his expression. It mirrored Isaac's precisely – as if he, too, had just lost someone in the fire. But instead of pushing forward to find out more, he turned and hurried away. Galfrid watched until he had disappeared completely into the crowd.

"Let's go." Gisburne's voice snapped him out of his reverie. His master had emerged from the house, and was now looking about with a new sense of purpose. He noted Isaac talking animatedly with three men by the gate, then turned again, scanning the crowd.

"Hamon?"

As if by magic, Hamon appeared with their horses

"Sire?"

As Galfrid took the horses from the boy, Gisburne spoke to him in urgent, hushed tones. "The man who we entered the house with," he said.

"You see him? Don't let him see you're looking. His name is Isaac. Put a lad on him. I want to know everywhere he goes."

Hamon nodded, and was off.

"You're having Isaac followed," said Galfrid. "Why?"

"All in good time," said Gisburne. "We must find a blacksmith." He thought for a moment. "Two blacksmiths... I want that chest brought to our lodgings and opened before the killer realises his attempt failed."

"Failed?" Galfrid was bemused by Gisburne's choice of words. "Ranulph Le Fort lies dead up there!" He tried to put aside thoughts of Dickon, of how Gisburne's obsession had made him neglect the search for the man who was now murdered. Neither he nor his raging indigestion could face that.

"But he's not dead," said Gisburne.

"What?" Galfrid gaped at him. "You saw that roasted lump. It's as dead as my lunch."

"Yes," said Gisburne. "But that is not Ranulph Le Fort."

XLIII

Eastchepe
15 June, 1193

"CHECK EVERYTHING – NO matter how trivial it may seem," said Gisburne. "The answer may lie in a single figure. A single name..."

Galfrid gazed across the room and felt his heart sink. The contents of the newly opened chest were spread over every inch of floor. Gisburne's deduction had been correct. It did not contain treasure – at least, not of the conventional kind. Indeed, if there *was* anything of value amongst the piles of documents, it was proving hard to find. In addition to records of tax, copies of charters and accounts of legal proceedings, there were letters, lists, bills of sale and purchase, maps, scraps of poetry, random parts of the Gospels, descriptions of animals and plants and what appeared to be an Arab treatise on warfare. A proportion of these documents also related to the Irish expedition, and it was these that they had first endeavoured to separate out, and which now occupied the space immediately between them. One was a less ostentatious copy of the Milford Roll. Ranulph, it seemed, had kept everything.

And yet, where was Ranulph himself?

"We have heard that Ranulph Le Fort had two fingers missing from his left hand," Gisburne had explained as they had ridden away from Jewen Street. "The burnt body in the room did not. Unless he had managed to grow them again, it could not be Ranulph."

"But Isaac said..."

"Isaac is simply protecting his friend," Gisburne had said. "He wants everyone to believe Ranulph killed. What better disguise than death? No one hunts a dead man."

As to the mystery of the charred corpse, both had hoped the chest might furnish something of worth. Clearly, its contents were thought to be dangerous by the killer. But why? It seemed to offer no clues – only more questions.

GISBURNE HAD BEEN testy prior to the chest's arrival. He had paced the room, trying to rid himself of energy that Galfrid knew no amount of pacing would dissipate. What his master needed was to get himself on a horse, to put both it and himself through their paces with lance and sword for a day, to collapse exhausted into a bath and then sleep for a full night. But for now, this room was his prison cell.

The one thing that had dragged him from it during the tense wait was the Widow Fleet. The moment Galfrid heard her shrill tones from the back yard, he feared the worst. In an attempt to calm the situation, he had discretely closed the back shutter against it, even though he suspected Widow Fleet's voice could penetrate eight feet of stone. At any rate, it was too late.

"What in God's name is going on now?" thundered Gisburne.

"Oh, it's nothing," said Galfrid. "Looks like the Widow's got into another argument with Osekin about that pig of his." Galfrid had spoken as dismissively as possible, but no sooner had he said it than Gisburne was storming down the stairs. He followed hard upon his master's heels, swearing under his breath.

Osekin, it transpired, had heard of Widow Fleet's new whitewash and set about painting his own back wall. To Widow Fleet, who only that morning had headed off another attempt by Osekin's pig to decimate her vegetable patch, this was the last straw.

"You shouldn't be whitewashing your walls!" she howled at her neighbour as Gisburne entered the yard. "You should be mending this excuse for a fence!" And, glaring at the rooting pig, she gave the rickety structure a sound kick. "Oh, tell him, please, Sir Guy!" she pleaded.

Osekin looked upon Gisburne approaching, and for reasons best known to himself saw in him a kindred spirit. "Ah!" he said with a genial smile. "I was just explaining to the Widow Fleet how it is in the nature of the animal..."

"Is this your pig?" demanded Gisburne, pointing at the creature.

"Yes, but..."

Gisburne grabbed the whitewash brush, slapped a white cross upon the pig's dark, bristly back, then plopped the brush back in the pail, splashing the paint down Osekin's left leg in the process.

"Hoi – what's that all about?" said Osekin.

"So I have something to aim at," said Gisburne.

"Aim...?" Osekin went as pale as his new walls.

Gisburne took a step closer. "I don't care about fences, or whitewash, or whether this pig is yours or someone else's or has had itself elected

Pope. But next time I see that pig in this yard, I'll hang it up and use it for target practice." He turned from the shocked Osekin as if to go, then suddenly turned on him again. "And if you trouble Widow Fleet with this one more time, I'll shove its head up your arse. Then I'll shove *your* head up *its* arse. Clear?" And with that, he turned and stalked off.

"He's a bit off pigs at the moment," said Galfrid.

Widow Fleet had beamed, gazing after the departing Gisburne as if he were her personal hero.

"LOOK AT THIS..." said Galfrid. It had been sitting in front of them for the best part of an hour, a scrappily written record of some aspect of Ranulph's finances. Galfrid could make little of it, except that those finances were far from healthy. But the parchment upon which they were written was a fine one, and when Galfrid finally thought to turn it over, it revealed an older and far more significant text – one that connected directly with the story related by de Rosseley. He passed it to Gisburne.

It was an order from John that money be paid to Ranulph in compensation for the loss of two of his fingers during a fight with a chieftain named Faelan Ua Dubhghail. It was mentioned that Faelan died during the fight, leaving a wife and two sons: his heir Ailin, aged twenty-four summers and Niall, aged thirteen. Out of this estate was to be paid compensation to Ranulph of six hundred deniers or one good war horse. The attack was described as unprovoked and to have been undertaken 'in a manner most sly.' But nowhere was it suggested why Ua Dubhghail wished to risk everything by killing one of John's men that night.

"This must be in my father's hand," said Gisburne. "Ranulph could not write immediately after the attack." He held it out to Galfrid. "Would that he had written a little more clearly. Can you make out the wife's name?"

Galfrid could not, except that it began with an *L*.

Gisburne sighed. "The key must lie within this document," he said "It's the one thing that seems to connect with what we know so far."

"Could our killer be one of those two boys? The younger would be a man now."

"If so," said Gisburne, "then we have before us the Red Hand's true name."

"If he suspected the existence of such a document, that alone would be reason enough for him to wish it destroyed," said Galfrid.

Gisburne stared hard at the page, as if daring it to speak further to him. "But we cannot know for sure. And what could do we do with this information even if we knew? How does this help us?" He flung it down in exasperation, his hopes dashed. "The document confirms one thing, at least," he said at length, and turned to his squire. "Ranulph Le Fort did indeed have two fingers missing from his left hand."

"So whose body was it in the burnt house?"

Gisburne placed the tips of his fingers together and rubbed the forefingers against the bridge of his nose. "I have been thinking on that... We know that Ranulph was often in debt. Yet the body had gold rings on its fingers – not a sign of a man in need. More like... a merchant displaying his wealth." He looked up. "I believe we may have found Thomas of Baylesford."

Gisburne stood, and turned about the room, paying little attention to the documents that crumpled beneath his feet. "We know the two men had been friends – that Thomas had gone into hiding, apparently aware that his life was under threat. Perhaps aware that Ranulph's was, too. I believe Thomas went to find Ranulph. Perhaps to warn him. Perhaps thinking there would be safety in numbers. But if Thomas could find him, then the Red Hand could too. And he did. Unfortunately for Thomas, it was he who was alone in that room the day the Red Hand came to call."

In the space of a minute, Galfrid's entire world had shifted. He had of late been guilty of indignation at Gisburne's failure to find Ranulph. Now, it seemed it was instead Baylesford who had perished, and who had done so because he had realised he was being sought – not only by the Red Hand, but by Galfrid too.

"The question is," said Gisburne, "what became of Ranulph?"

And all at once, it came to Galfrid. "I think I saw him..." he said. And he told Gisburne of the man in the crowd whose look had so puzzled him. To this he added one detail, that until now had seemed of little significance. "At the time, believing Ranulph dead, I thought nothing of it. Just a curiosity. But the hand with which he clutched his wares – his left – it had fingers missing."

"You saw him clearly?" asked Gisburne.

"Clear as day."

"You would recognise him?"

"I believe so."

Gisburne smiled. "We are getting somewhere. At last. Nine days, Galfrid. Nine days until Hood's execution... In that time we must find Ranulph and make our final preparations. He is now the only one left who knows what really happened in Ireland. But we have a couple of advantages, at least. The Red Hand is injured, and he does not know we have the contents of the chest. If we can only fathom what they mean..."

"We have two more," said Galfrid. "The killer thinks Ranulph already dead. And we have this..." he held up the armour plate. He had meant this as a positive gesture – one of defiance. But at the sight of the blue-black scale, Gisburne's face fell.

Instinctively, Galfrid understood: it reminded his master of the impossibility of the task ahead – of the moment when he knew he must face him for the final time.

XLIV

Hamstede Heath
16 June, 1193

THE NOTE SAID simply *Hamstede Heath. Noon,* in Galfrid's hand. It did not specify which part of Hamstede Heath nor for what purpose. He had found it pinned to his coat when he woke up that morning, and his squire gone. But why was he now communicating with him via scraps of parchment?

It was good to get out of the city – to leave behind its spreading madness. As the ever-present press of humanity was left behind and gave way to trees and heathland, he felt a pleasant calm descend – of a kind he had not felt in weeks. The space widened out into a broad meadow edged with trees, punctuated only by the rotting stumps of a trio of felled oaks, and a new concern took over. How was he ever to find Galfrid in this vast expanse?

In the event, his ever-resourceful squire found him. Within minutes, Gisburne heard the sound of hooves, and there was Galfrid upon Mare, beetling towards him across the spongy meadow, his trusty pilgrim staff strapped across his back. Gisburne met him half way, a stone's throw from the oak stumps.

"So, what's this all about?" said Gisburne by way of a greeting. He noticed, now, that what Galfrid carried across his was back not his pilgrim staff at all – that was tucked in its customary location on his saddle – but a stout longbow. By his side hung a sack whose object Gisburne could not guess.

"Training," said Galfrid. Gisburne laughed, then saw Galfrid did not mean it as a joke. "That's what a squire does, isn't it?" Galfrid said. "Helps his knight to prepare? To remain at his peak?"

"Are you asking or telling?" said Gisburne, still smiling.

"The point is," said Galfrid, "you've been sitting on your arse for the best part of four weeks."

Gisburne recoiled. "I've traipsed about every whore-strewn street in London! And two days ago I fought the Red Hand himself. I hardly think that qualifies..."

"Yes, but I bet you felt it afterwards," interrupted Galfrid. "In your legs, in that dodgy shoulder of yours. Can't have that with the challenges coming up. Training's what you need."

And with that Galfrid dismounted, and lifted the sack from his saddle, then looked across towards the stumps.

"Perfect distance, I reckon," he said. "Yes, just here will do just fine."

"Fine for what?" Gisburne was already beginning to tire of this game.

"To get back to what you're good at..."

"And what is that?"

Galfrid took the the huge bowstave off his back, put one end upon his boot so it would not sink into the soft earth, bent the bow with supreme effort, and strung it. He held it out towards Gisburne, a smile on his face.

Gisburne studied it. "Where did you get this?"

"I liberated it," said Galfrid.

"Liberated it?"

"From the Tower armoury."

Gisburne's eyes widened. "You stole from the Tower? From under Fitz Thomas's nose?" He could not resist a smile. "How in God's name did you get it past the guards at the gate?" He looked at the thing – it was taller than Galfrid himself. Not the easiest object to conceal.

"The Welshman had a potion to render both me and the bow invisible," said Galfrid. He remained utterly deadpan as Gisburne stared back at him.

"How remarkable that Llewellyn never mentioned this potion before," he said, his voice heavy with sarcasm.

"He lost it for a time," said Galfrid, "on account of it being invisible." Then he sighed. "All right, I walked out. With the bow in plain sight, over my shoulder. And I gave the guards a hearty greeting as I did so – made sure every one of them saw me. So they thought nothing of the bow." At this he almost allowed himself a smile of his own. "The first rule of being successful as a thief is not to look like one."

"I dare say you could give Hood and his rabble a run for their money."

"The Welshman did help with its procurement from the armoury," said Galfrid. "He also fixed these up for you." Unwrapping the bundled sack, he revealed a quiver full of arrows, and drew one out. It bore one of the bodkin points that Llewellyn had given him. Gisburne had not even noticed they had gone. "Those fletched in red are bodkins, those that are plain are blunts for practice."

"Practice?" said Gisburne, looking from Galfrid to the stumps and back. Then he noticed the curious harness upon the quiver. He lifted the strap, puzzling over its arrangement. "And what is this?"

"That was my idea." Galfrid beamed. "You wear it not at your waist, but across your back." He slung it over his shoulder to demonstrate. "You can draw an arrow and lay it more swiftly upon the bow, in one smooth action. Even if you are on the move."

Gisburne nodded in approval. "Ingenious." His attention went back to the bow, and he turned the yew shaft around in his hands, testing the string. It was a good bow. The right size for him, but also the heaviest bow he'd ever seen – at the very limit of his pulling power, he would guess. Doubtless Galfrid had selected it for precisely those reasons. Then his smile fell away, and he thrust it towards the squire. "But I don't want it."

Galfrid, who had taken the bow back purely in reflex, stared at him in amazement, then pushed it towards his master once again.

"You have need of a powerful weapon," he said.

But Gisburne did not take it. "And it is appreciated. But it's not enough." With firm hand, he again pushed it away.

"It's the best England has. Your best chance."

"I don't trust to chance," snapped Gisburne.

The bow came back again. "Then what do you trust to? Even the slimmest chance is better than none. You taught me that. And don't give me all that *a bow is not a knight's weapon* shit!"

Galfrid had anticipated exactly what Gisburne had been about to say. Now, thrown back at him like this, the words seemed idiotic, arrogant. Not like his own words at all. "I have not shot a bow since Boulogne," he said, avoiding Galfrid's gaze. "That skill is gone."

"Bollocks. It never leaves you," urged Galfrid. "And we both know how this is going to go. You will come up against this man again. But you cannot let him get too near."

"Don't you think I know that?" snapped Gisburne. "I'm the one who's seen him up close, remember."

"The bow is your best chance." He thrust it hard against Gisburne's chest. This time, Gisburne took it, flung it upon the ground and turned back to his horse.

In a burst of anger Galfrid snatched it up, and lunged towards his master. "What is it with you? Are you really so pig-headedly proud? Do you *want* to be killed? Or is there some other fear brewing in there? The fear that using the bow somehow makes you more like Hood?" He roared the last, with such heat that he startled a cloud of crows from the nearby treetops.

Gisburne stood silent, motionless, listening to the mocking laughter of the black birds as they wheeled overhead. The words had hit home. Until now, Gisburne had known only that he felt a deep reluctance to rely on the bow. He had not interrogated that feeling. Perhaps he had not wanted to. But, as he so often did, Galfrid had pinned it.

The squire took a step towards his master, his expression suddenly changed. "I just don't want you to die."

Gisburne turned, grabbed the bow with one hand and a blunt with the other, then turned and in one swift movement loosed an arrow into the air. There was an explosion of black feathers and a crow fell spinning to the earth.

"Satisfied?" he said, and stalked off back to his horse.

GALFRID STOOD LONG after the sound of Nyght's hooves had faded, staring at the crumpled black bird, its feathers fluttering in the gusting wind. Its breast glistened with wet blood. The arrow itself had bounced off. He would retrieve it later.

His attention wandered to the forest's edge. Gisburne, always self-contained, had of late become an enigma. A Gordian knot of tangled problems. Clearly, the past weeks, and those to come, weighed heavy upon him. But something else was gnawing at his soul. Galfrid did not know quite what – but he had his suspicions. Dickon. Dickon the distraction. Dickon the irrelevance. For good or ill, Galfrid sensed that until Gisburne solved the unsolvable enigma of Dickon Bend-the-Bow, he would never be himself. And if he was not himself, how could he hope to stop their most determined adversary? He had pursued Dickon in the hope that it might help; instead, it was in danger of bringing about his downfall.

A sudden sound made him start. The flap of wing, close by. At first he could see nothing. Then it came again. The crow shifted on the ground – twitched and flapped with sudden ferocious energy. Galfrid stood, transfixed.

Then, as he watched, it flopped, sat upright, shook its ragged feathers and – to his utter astonishment – flew away.

XLV

THAT NIGHT, GISBURNE had a strange dream. A man burning – but not the one he thought. Though the face was indistinct, he knew it to be Thomas of Baylesford, and fought to get to him, his limbs heavy as lead. But then, somehow, it was Hood's face laughing up at him from the flames, even as his flesh sizzled and blistered and fell away from his bones. And in his hand, refusing to be consumed by the fire, was an arrow. No, not an arrow – a rose.

He awoke suddenly, in a sweat. The dream swirled in his head – some impressions from it still vivid, others already fading. Within the confusion, Osanna's words came back to him – words that had been clattering around in his head as he slept. Something she'd said about Dickon. *Sweet little rose – that's what he called me.* Gisburne sat bolt upright in the dark room, and laughed, loud and deep. In the still of the night, it shook the rafters.

"I'm such a fool!" he said, only dimly aware that he had said it aloud. Then he leapt out of bed and hauled on his boots, hurrying past the chimney breast in a series of awkward hops until he had reached Galfrid's chamber.

The drowsy squire stirred and propped himself up on one elbow.

"I'm such a fool!" laughed Gisburne, and clapped him heartily upon the shoulders. "The answer was right there!"

"Wha – ?" croaked Galfrid. But before he could articulate anything more, Gisburne, with another great guffaw, had grabbed the longbow from the corner of the room, taken up the quiver of arrows and – still in his nightshirt – was clumping away down the stairs.

GISBURNE STOOD IN the dark silence of the back yard, a bodkin point arrow resting upon the bow. He laughed to himself – then chuckled more at the impression he would have given anyone watching. They would have thought him a madman. But he did not care. So many nights he had sat awake striving to puzzle out the mystery, with no relish for the day to come. But tonight, he was eager for the dawn.

At the far end of the yard came a snuffling. Osekin's pig was pushing its snout through the loose pickets of the fence, making a bid for Widow Fleet's emerging turnip tops. Gisburne raised the bow, took aim, and began to draw. As if somehow aware, the pig fell suddenly silent and stood stock still, the white cross upon its back gleaming in the moonlight. Using all his strength, Gisburne drew the arrow to almost its full length. "Not today, Sir Pig," he whispered, then turned and loosed the shaft into the drying post at the end of the yard.

It split the four-inch thick post asunder and continued into the night, the thunderclap of its impact sending Osekin's pig scrambling for refuge and setting dogs barking all across London.

XLVI

The Tower of London
17 June, 1193

ONCE MORE, GISBURNE stood before Hood in his cell. This time, it was Gisburne who was laughing. "Dickon..." he said. "*Dickon!*"

That same look of fear flickered in Hood's face.

"All this time I was searching for this phantom in the hope that he might in some way help me understand you," said Gisburne, pacing and turning about the cell as if he were the one caged. "But he *was* you. *You* are Dickon!"

Hood merely looked confused, as if he was being spoken to by an idiot. "I don't know what you're talking about, old man..." But his fingers fidgeted with the necklace at his throat.

In a fury, Gisburne grabbed Hood's shackled wrists and hauled him to his feet.

"Of course you do! You know it all. But your lies are catching up with you. And I vow to hasten them upon their course... Geoffrey of Lemsforde called upon you with two of his captains to recruit you for Henry's secret service. But you declined. Why? Osanna said he seemed to recognise you. But where from? An army from which you deserted? Another life with which you grew bored – which you also left in flames? Not until later did Lemsforde recall where you had met. He came back alone to confront you. A fatal mistake – for him. You set afire the wagon, took your bow and arrows, and were gone." Gisburne stood for a moment, his face inches from Hood's. Hood's eyes remained as empty of expression as a snake's. Gisburne pushed him away in disgust. Hood fell back hard against the wall, then – chuckling quietly as if this were all part of some child's game – slid down until he was sitting on the floor. Gisburne turned away, exasperated, and paced the cell. "And then what?" he muttered. "Who did you become next? Robert of Locksley? Or was there another before that – before we met in Syracuse?"

"Ah, Syracuse!" smiled Hood, and slapped his knee. "Those were good times, weren't they? Do you remember that Scottish archer with the one eye that looked way off to the left?" He laughed at the memory, shaking his head. "I wonder whatever became of him?"

"He died, Robert," said Gisburne. "Saving your neck. He scalped a Turcopole who was about to skewer your guts with his lance, then took one of our own incendiary arrows in his back. You left him burning."

Hood frowned at Gisburne's words, as if trying to recall a lost dream, and failing.

Gisburne sighed heavily. "Well, there's no one to save your neck this time," he said. "And you are the one who will burn." For all that Hood had done – all the chaos and misery and false hope he had spread – it nonetheless tore at Gisburne. Hood had still been a friend, of sorts. Gisburne was not like him: he could hide his emotions, yes, but not turn them off. In a perverse way, the thought reassured him. "Your execution is now one week away. Your last chance to reveal the truth."

Hood looked back at him with a vacant expression. "Truth?" he said. He uttered the word as if it were in an unknown tongue.

"What does it matter anyway?" said Gisburne in defeat. "It can't change anything. Thessalonika. Hattin. Rose."

Hood perked up at the name. "Rose? Is Rose coming? How wonderful!" He grinned at the prospect, rubbing his hands in glee, his chains rattling, then looked suddenly perturbed. "I really should tidy up in here..."

"She's dead, too, Robert. You killed her. Don't you even remember that? That poor whore in Jerusalem whose life you snuffed out? And I helped you bury her. Dear God..."

"No, no... Rose is coming. To see me. You really should meet her, Guy. You'd like her."

And with that, he began to sing softly:

"There is no rose of such virtue
As is the rose that buried you
Alleluia!"

The song dissolved into another insane chuckle.

Gisburne did not believe Hood's mad act – not for one minute. Finally, he was done with him. "No more..." he said, and turned to the door. "You'll not see me again, Robert."

But before he could reach it, from the gloom behind him came a peculiar, sing-song voice. "Mis-di-rection!"

Gisburne stopped in his tracks. He turned. "What did you say?"

Hood spread his hands. "Magic tricks. Remember those? I remember them. People always loved my magic tricks."

"I've no time for your mindless riddles," said Gisburne. He turned again and hammered his fist on the door. "Guard!"

"You see, the essence of a magic trick," persisted Hood, wagging a raised finger, "is that the most important thing of all is happening while everyone is busy looking somewhere else."

Then he cocked his head and looked Gisburne straight in the eye. His eyes were burning with a strange intensity. It was not madness, but a fierce and unfathomable intelligence. As it bored into him, Gisburne felt the hairs on the back of his neck stand up.

"I've already wasted precious time looking in the wrong place," he said. "And seen a life lost because of it. Why are you telling me this now?"

"Because I want to help you," said Hood, his voice barely more than a whisper.

Gisburne stared at Hood for a moment. His gaze did not falter. In his eyes there was no madness. "How does this help me?"

"Because it's what you most need to know." He grinned. "The answers to your questions are far closer than you think." And he tapped the side of his head.

Gisburne took a step towards him. "What do you mean?"

The thick iron bolt was shot back, and the door creaked open. Two helmeted and armoured guards stood framed within the space it left. Hood raised his eyebrows. "Goodbye, Guy," he said.

"What does that mean," demanded Gisburne, "'closer than you think'?"

But Hood simply sat, and smiled, and bowed his head, and sang quietly to himself.

XLVII

Jewen Street
22 June, 1193

FOUR DAYS PASSED. On three of them, the streets erupted into violent confrontation. None really knew who they were fighting, nor why – but fear fuelled their anger, and opened the door to their prejudices. Two Jews were beaten and left for dead. A burning brand was hurled into an inn where two of the perpetrators were known to drink. It was swiftly extinguished – but still the city smouldered. A red hand print appeared on the stones of St Paul's. It proved to be paint, not blood – but Gisburne did not doubt that blood would follow.

He and Galfrid, meanwhile, puzzled further over the document. Gisburne quizzed de Rosseley and Prince John about the names it contained – but the questions yielded nothing. And, at Gisburne's insistence, Galfrid did not search for Ranulph.

"But you said we must find him," Galfrid had said.

"It is in hand," said Gisburne, but would say no more. Instead, he had instructed Galfrid to keep up casual contact with Isaac – both to keep him safe, and to make sure he kept him abreast of their investigations. That, Galfrid had done.

Gisburne, meanwhile, practised with the bow. They rode and sparred upon Hamstede Heath, and Gisburne had taken to wearing his mailcoat again – not just for this training, but all day. To get used to its weight again, he said – but these days it seemed wise to go protected. Galfrid had followed suit; they were now on a war footing.

On the evening of the twenty-second day of June, with Hood's execution date two days away, Galfrid found himself in an inn just off Jewen Street, sat opposite his master.

"So, what are we doing here?" said Galfrid.

"The weapons," said Gisburne, "did you pack them?"

"They're with the horses. But why?"

"We're going to an inn."

"An inn." Galfrid looked around him. "Am I missing something?"

"A different inn. One frequented by our friend Isaac."

"But Isaac is at home this night. He has friends dining with him – to celebrate the last lick of paint going back on his walls."

"Exactly!" said Gisburne, and his eyes gleamed.

Galfrid sighed. "Do you keep me in the dark on purpose," he said, "or is it an illness?"

Gisburne leaned forward, and spoke so they might not be overheard. "These past few nights our friend Isaac has been visiting an inn near the wharves at Douegate. Not a very safe place for a London Jew to venture – and certainly not a place of which Elazar would approve. Why do you think he does that?"

"Perhaps he just likes that kind of inn," said Galfrid.

"It's not *that* kind of inn. And anyway, does he look like the sort?"

Galfrid shrugged as if to say: "You never can tell."

"But there's another thing..." said Gisburne. "Yesterday – quite independently, it would seem – that same place was visited by another friend of ours."

Galfrid couldn't think of any friends; and if Gisburne meant enemies, the list was too long to even contemplate.

"Bearded," explained Gisburne. "Extremely tall. Likes to put on armour and bash people's brains in..."

"He was there?"

"And gone again before we could make anything of it. But his being there at all tells us much."

"You don't suspect some connection between the Red Hand and Isaac?"

"But there already is a connection."

"Ranulph?" said Galfrid.

"Ranulph," said Gisburne. "Consider this: the Red Hand strikes at Isaac's house. Ranulph runs. He hides out, but also gets word to Isaac to reassure him he is safe. Isaac, who is now regularly apprised of our efforts, arranges to meet him so he can pass on that information."

"You think Ranulph is at that inn?"

"He has not been seen," said Gisburne. "Not once. But I would stake my life on it. The place is a haunt of Hansa merchants. They are a closed community, untouchable by the authorities. I doubt there's a better place to hide in all London."

"I've heard tell that Baylesford had dealings with the Hansa. And his ship lies at dock a mere stone's throw away. Perhaps Ranulph means to leave on it."

"If he hasn't already," said Gisburne. "But we find out tonight, come hell or high water." He sat back and drained his cup.

"So, to go back to my original question," said Galfrid, "if our business is at an inn down near the wharves, why are we *here*?"

"We're *here* to make sure that Isaac is not *there*."

"Well, I saw him not half an hour ago," said Galfrid, "welcoming his guests. Settling in for the evening."

Gisburne smiled. "Then we are free to go." A commotion near the door made both turn, and Galfrid glimpsed the flailing limbs of a familiar gangling figure fighting to get past the mistress of the establishment. "And, if I'm not mistaken, here comes our guide..."

XLVIII

Douegate
22 June, 1193

THE EXTERIOR OF the Hansa's tavern was black as a crow's belly. It stood in a dark, cobbled street just where the River Wallbrooke flowed into the Thames, and was built of the thickest timbers Gisburne had ever seen – some carved with the shapes of outlandish maritime creatures. From within came the muffled drone of dark, unfamiliar music. But for a single white gull, the street itself was utterly deserted, as if everyone in London knew something about it that Gisburne and his squire did not.

"If fighting breaks out," said Gisburne as they tied the horses, "the one thing we absolutely *must not allow to happen* is for it to spill into the street."

Galfrid nodded slowly as Gisburne strapped his sword to his left side, then drew his seax from his saddle and concealed it beneath his horsehide coat at his right. "And do you think fighting is likely to break out?" he said. Somehow, Gisburne had managed to make it sound like a certainty.

Gisburne chose to ignore the question. He tightened his belt a notch, adjusted his purse and eating knife, and straightened the mail beneath his black coat. "Inside, the fight is contained. Quarters are too close for swords to be drawn. But outside..." His voice trailed off. He took a deep breath as they turned and stood before the low, black door.

"Well, I've heard German hospitality can be generous," said Galfrid. "That King Richard has been afforded certain luxuries whilst in prison." He shrugged. "Maybe they'll extend us a warm welcome."

Gisburne pushed the heavy door open.

THE GLOOMY, COBBLED interior was a mere two steps down from the level of the street. Yet, as they had ducked their heads beneath the monstrous lintel and stepped in, it had felt as if they were descending into some hidden subterranean realm – a place of dwarf blacksmiths and gold-hoarding dragons.

To say it was austere was an understatement. As near as Gisburne could tell, every surface was stained or painted black, making those that were lit just as dark as those in shadow. The black benches and tables were tall, and angular, and oddly skeletal in character, and across them stretched a sea of shaven heads and grim faces, weirdly illuminated by the thick candles that were dotted about the benches. Every pair of glinting eyes was on them.

As they stepped forward, the thrum of chatter hushed, but even when it was clear to Gisburne that he and Galfrid were the topic of conversation, it did not cease. It did not need to. There was no English, no French spoken here, and of German, Gisburne grasped but one word in twenty. Nothing about their surroundings – not the clothes, nor the furniture, nor even the smell of the food or ale – had the familiarity of home.

They heard the door clank shut behind them. Gisburne turned to see a thickset man with a forked beard leaning against it, toying casually with a thin, black-handled blade. There was no going back now. Next to him, on the inside of the door, a disc of bronze imprinted with a two-headed eagle marked the place as Hansa territory.

"We're not in England any more," muttered Gisburne. Then he turned and smiled pleasantly, as, one by one, the faces turned away, back to their own business.

At the farthest wall of the tavern's deep innards, Gisburne spied a hawk-faced man whose chair was raised higher than the rest, his table heavy with silver platters. The chair in which he sat was practically a throne, the backrest – higher than his head – carved into the shape of the same two-headed eagle that adorned the door. As he sat and picked at his meal with long pale fingers, he conversed with a broad-shouldered, shaven-headed man who stood at his right hand, his eyes fixed on the newcomers.

Gisburne nudged Galfrid. "What do you think?" he said. "The king of this place?"

"At the very least," said Galfrid.

"Well, then. No point wasting time." And he strode towards the Hansa king. At his approach, the man sat forward and placed his fingers together, but before Gisburne could set foot on the low dais, his crony – almost a head taller than Gisburne – stepped forward and stopped him with a firm hand against his chest.

"Otto," said the Hansa king, and waved his hand. Otto withdrew. He sat back again. "I am Günther von Köln," he said. "You are welcome here. May I ask your business?"

Gisburne bowed his head in acknowledgement. He had no idea of this man's status. He had given himself no title – was not an earl or baron, nor commander of an army – yet here he clearly held sway.

"I come not to trade," said Gisburne, "but in search of two men. One whose life I believe is in danger, named Ranulph Le Fort."

"Never heard of him," said Günther. The response was too swift, too neat for Gisburne to believe it. He decided, for now, to move on.

"The other is the man who threatens him. The killer who is now abroad in this city, known as the Red Hand. I am tasked with hunting him down. I believe he may have been here."

Günther's eyes narrowed. "You think this a den of murderers?"

"He would not have seemed a villain," said Gisburne. "But his appearance is distinct. He is large. Larger even than him." He gestured to Otto. "Shaggy haired, and bearded. Perhaps dressed like a tinker. And his accent would be Irish."

The German nodded slowly, reaching for his goblet. "Perhaps you can tell me on whose behalf you perform this deed. It may help me to understand why I should help you."

"Prince John of England," said Gisburne, "whose life is also threatened."

Günther almost choked on his wine. "*This* is supposed to persuade me?" He began to laugh. Several nearby chuckled with him.

Gisburne, however, had another weapon. "If his name means nothing to you," he said, "then do it for the sake of Thomas of Baylesford – a fellow merchant cruelly slain by the fiend."

At this, Günther's expression became deadly serious – but his eyes showed no surprise. That told Gisburne everything. He could not possibly be aware that it was Baylesford who had perished in the house on Jewen Street, unless he had been told by the only ones who knew – Isaac or Ranulph. Günther sat for a moment, staring at Gisburne, his eyes unblinking. "There was such a man as you describe," he said at length. "He came looking for Baylesford. He said Baylesford owned a ship and he wished to charter it. His reason did not convince me. I said I could not help him. Then he enquired about hiring a ship from the Hansa – for a great purpose, he said. That it would help him be rid of someone who I would also be glad to get rid of. When he told me the man's name, I admit I was tempted. But I don't hand over ships to people I don't trust, and I don't trust anyone without money up front. Especially in these troubled times." He shrugged. "So, I sent him packing." He thought for a moment. "That is the phrase, is it not? 'Sent him packing'?"

Gisburne looked at Galfrid with a frown. "Was he planning his escape?" said Galfrid

Gisburne turned back to their host. "When did he require this ship?"

"The twenty-third day of June," said Günther. "Tomorrow."

The day before Hood's execution. The day before Gisburne had supposed he would strike. Did he really plan to depart then? It seemed to make no sense. "Where was it bound?" said Gisburne.

"He did not say."

"But surely the crew..."

"He desired no crew," said Günther. "Just the ship. From the western end of the wharves, by the bridge. He was quite specific."

"No crew...? Did he mean to supply his own?"

"I saw none. But, either way, he was not getting his hands on one of my ships."

Galfrid frowned. "Without a crew he'd be lucky to get as far as Wapping Marsh."

"You understand my reticence," said Günther. "And since it has transpired he is also the murderer, my instincts would seem to have been proven correct."

"Why do you think he brought this request to you?"

Günther shrugged again. "You know what we are – how we operate. We have no restrictions placed upon us. We go where we choose, trade as we choose. No tolls, no taxes. Such was the dispensation granted us by the old King, may God rest his soul. A great man. Forward thinking. We shall have to see how this new one is, should he ever come back. We also have a reputation for – how shall I say it? – keeping ourselves to ourselves. Not entirely unfounded – we bother no one if no one bothers us. And of late, I will admit, we have withdrawn a little further from public life. These streets are now not so friendly to foreigners. Too many unruly elements looking for excuses to get even more unruly. Anyway, all these attributes of ours he perhaps saw as advantages in his... quest."

"One thing puzzles me," said Gisburne. Günther reached for a walnut, and cocked his head on one side. "You haven't yet asked who I am."

"Oh, I know who you are," he said. "You are Guy of Gisburne."

This, Gisburne had not expected. "How did you know that?"

"It is my business to know in my city."

"Your city?" Gisburne laughed. "You know, you're the third person this month who has told me this city is theirs. You people really should get together."

Günther laughed without humour, and cracked the walnut between his palms. "There is another reason for me knowing about you..." He began to pick out the bits from the shattered shell. "I have heard of the exploits of the famous Dark Horseman on his black charger," he said. "At Castel Mercheval and beyond. It is quite a thrill to finally meet him." He smiled and popped a shard of walnut into his mouth. The cronies on either side chuckled.

Gisburne's own smile fell away. "I'm not what people think I am," he said.

"Oh, on the contrary," said Günther, looking him up and down, "you are exactly as I expected." The cronies chuckled harder. Günther flicked at the wreckage of the walnut for a few moments, then added: "I understand you knew my brother."

This caught Gisburne completely off guard. His mind raced, trying to recall all the Germans he had ever encountered in his life. Of this rich and varied parade, not one came to mind as significant. Seeing his struggle, Günther leaned forward to fill the gap in his memory. "His name was Ulrich," he said, "and he died at Castel Mercheval. By your hand." The smile withered on his lips. "You see, it was *you* the Red Hand offered to rid me of..."

IN ALL HIS years, in spite of all the battles he had fought and all the enemies he had made, Gisburne had never yet stood face-to-face with a relative of one he had killed. There had been no hysterical parents, no devastated wives. No embittered siblings or offspring bent on revenge. Now, the fact struck him as extraordinary. Had it been merely luck that had spared him this? And was it that same capricious agency that had put Ulrich's brother before him today? He cared nothing for this man Günther. But somehow, that was not the point. There were certain thoughts one did not wish to entertain in battle – that were kept at bay behind the thickest wall one could build – and now he felt those defences crumble. For the first time he wondered not only what number he had killed in his time on earth, but how many holes he had left in families.

With a soldier's instincts, Gisburne readied himself for whatever violence Günther meant to unleash. Perhaps for the first time in his life, he found he could not blame him for it.

Günther rose to his feet. "Fortunately, it was not a sufficiently tempting offer," he said. "My brother was unwise in his choice of masters. He paid the price for that folly. Now our business is done." He turned to Otto. "Give these men whatever they want. Show them some German hospitality..." Otto bowed as Günther left the dais, passed behind a tapestry curtain and disappeared through a concealed doorway.

FOR SOME TIME, Gisburne and Galfrid – stunned at the bizarre turn of events – had sat where Otto placed them, staring at the beer, bread and sausage upon the table. The food looked good, but neither was in much of a mood to eat. Galfrid picked at it as Gisburne – idly spinning his eating knife upon the table top – kept his eye fixed on the far end of the room. There, Günther sat and drank and talked as if nothing out of the ordinary had occurred.

"What now?" said Galfrid.

Gisburne had been anticipating the question for the past half hour, but was still no closer to an answer. In that time, the crowd had thickened in the tavern. A few moments before, Günther had reappeared from the back room behind the tapestry and resumed his place, not once looking across at Gisburne as he did so. It was meant to appear casual – as if to avoid drawing attention to the room. But the whole time Günther had been absent, Otto had positioned himself before the door, guarding it.

And suddenly the course ahead became clear.

"I want to get a look in that room," said Gisburne.

Galfrid stared at him. "Seriously?"

"We know Baylesford went looking for Ranulph. I think he was trying to get his old friend to come back with him to a place of safety. A place where Baylesford had friends. Powerful, secretive friends. Before they could move, the Red Hand struck. But Ranulph already knew where to go – and he's been here ever since." He turned to Galfrid. "I think Ranulph Le Fort is in that room."

Galfrid looked pained. "You're not going to... Are you...?"

"I just need a distraction," said Gisburne. "Enough to get me in there. If I can just stand before him, I can convince him we mean to help. That he can help us."

"And if he's not in there?"

Gisburne shrugged. "Then I'll just say I got lost on the way to the privy."

Before Galfrid could say any more, Gisburne was on his feet and starting to weave through the crowd towards the small group of musicians – and closer to the concealed door. As he did so, he saw Günther's eyes on him, and immediately turned and engaged the nearest drinker in conversation.

"The privy," he said. "This way?"

The German – a stern-faced man with drooping black moustaches and a jaw like the prow of a boat – stared back at him blankly, clearly comprehending not a word Gisburne said.

"The privy," repeated Gisburne. "For a piss. Here?" He mimed the act. At that the man burst into laughter. All of his front teeth were missing. He nodded and pointed across towards the other side of the room. When Gisburne glanced back towards Günther, he could no longer see him. Clapping his new German friend upon the shoulder, he looked across to Galfrid – who gave an almost imperceptible nod in response.

As a server brought more beer to the table, Galfrid dipped a sausage in mustard, took a great bite, then violently spat it out on the waiter's shoes. "Christ! Are you trying to poison me?" he howled. "If that's German hospitality I'd hate to be around when you're pissed off!" The waiter shouted something incomprehensible – but clearly angry, in any language. Several patrons nearby were immediately on their feet. Galfrid was momentarily obscured from view. Gisburne could just hear his voice, raised in indignant protest. Otto stepped forward from his post, sensing trouble.

With all eyes turned to the apparently suicidal little English squire, Gisburne inched his way to the tapestry. He slipped his hand behind it, pulled its edge forward from the wall, and peered behind. The door was half open, a light flickering within. A shadow passed across it. Gisburne drew the tapestry further back – then a rough hand dragged him back by the neck of his coat.

"What the Hell are you doing?" growled Günther, and swung him around, away from the door. As Gisburne wheeled around, he caught Galfrid's eye again, and shot an urgent, wide-eyed look at the squire.

Galfrid saw it and, misinterpreting Gisburne's intention completely, upped the diversion by head-butting the waiter.

All Hell broke loose. Otto waded into the fray. Gisburne broke away from Günther and piled in to save his squire, just as Otto heaved the flailing figure of Galfrid from the crush like wet-nurse lifting a babe from its bath.

"*Genug!*"

With a single word, Günther brought the brawl to a shuddering stop. Fuming, he advanced on Gisburne, who struggled against restraining hands. All cleared a path for the German; Gisburne had rarely seen such deference, even for a prince.

"My brother may have been a misguided fool," hissed Günther. "But he was still my brother. I give you one chance to leave here with your life. But should you ever set foot in here again, it will be immediately forfeit."

And without further comment, Gisburne and Galfrid were thrown into the street.

THEY HAD RIDDEN no more than a dozen yards when Gisburne stopped, panic writ upon his face. He patted his belt urgently.

"What is it?" asked Galfrid.

"I have to go back," said Gisburne.

Galfrid stared at him in disbelief. "You *what?*"

"My eating knife," he said. "I left it on the table."

"I'll get you another..."

Gisburne shook his head. "No – no, you don't understand. I have to go back." He dismounted.

"They'll kill you."

"I won't give them the chance," said Gisburne and began to creep back towards the tavern door.

Galfrid also dismounted, though whether he meant to stop his master or help him, he wasn't sure. "But what's your plan?"

"I walk in, grab the knife. Walk out. Possibly run out."

"And me?"

"Just be ready with the horses." Gisburne was already back at the door.

Galfrid hung back. "That's it?" he hissed. "The whole plan?"

"Trust me. It'll be the last thing they're expecting. By the time they know what's going on I'll be out of that door and back in the saddle."

And with that, Gisburne pulled up his hood, and plunged in.

XLIX

AT THE PRECISE moment the heavy door crashed shut behind his master, Galfrid heard a voice call his name. A female voice. Instantly familiar.

"Squire Galfrid!"

Galfrid turned, and looked. His heart leapt – and sank. "Oh... balls."

It was, perhaps, the least likely sight Galfrid could have imagined on this grim street – for there, on a richly decorated litter carried aloft by four strong servants, was Mélisande de Champagne. She beamed her irresistible smile at him. "What a piece of luck finding you here!"

There was an indistinct shout from inside the tavern. Galfrid smiled weakly – torn between joy at seeing her and a desperate urge to get her as far from this place as possible. "Indeed..." he said. "But... You should leave, my lady. This is not a good place to be."

Mélisande looked askance at him, then gave a laugh. "If you're in London and seeking passage on a ship to France, I'd say it was the perfect place to be..."

Galfrid glanced nervously towards the tavern door, his hands gripping the reins tighter. "You misunderstand... Please. You should get away. As fast as you can. The streets... They're not safe." To his own surprise, he found himself trying to shoo the litter-bearers as he spoke the words.

"What's the matter, Galfrid?" she said with an amused smile. "D'you think I can't handle myself?"

Few people in Galfrid's wide experience could handle themselves quite as well as Mélisande de Champagne. But she had no idea what she was walking into. Above the raucous buzz of the tavern's interior came a sudden crash. Galfrid started and turned at the sound.

"Is Sir Guy with you?" she said, hopefully. Then she followed his gaze back to the tavern. From within came raised voices – harsh, Germanic oaths. Something smashed against the door, almost shaking it off its hinges.

The door was hauled open roughly. Shouting, and heat, and the smell of burnt fat, stale beer and sweat erupted – and with them came Gisburne, flung bodily into the street. He rolled to a halt at Galfrid's feet, as an angry rabble of cursing, Teutonic roughs swarmed into the narrow thoroughfare, armed with every kind of implement: knives, stools, an earthenware jug dripping beer, a poker still smoking from the fire.

They flowed about them – more than he could have imagined the place could hold – the litter swaying and tipping like a ship in a storm as it was swept out of sight by the angry throng. Before Galfrid knew it, he, Gisburne and their horses were staring at a solid wall of scowling, grim faces upon every side. For a moment, nobody moved.

"So," said Galfrid as his master struggled to his feet. "How did that go for you?"

"Not so well. You?"

"I'm still here. Did you get your precious knife?"

"Yes."

"Well, that's something. What was it you said again – that we absolutely must not allow to happen?"

"Forget that."

"So what's the plan now?"

"Not dying."

It was then that the crowd parted, and Günther von Köln stepped into the arena. At his shoulder staggered the hulking figure of Otto – now, somewhat inexplicably, with a two-headed eagle imprinted on his forehead.

Günther looked Gisburne up and down, shook his head, then began to laugh. "You are either one of the bravest men I ever met, or one of the most stupid."

"Opinions differ on that score," said Gisburne, glancing at Galfrid.

"The question is," said Günther, "what to do with you now." His eye moved to Nyght. He looked the stallion up and down admiringly. "Yours?"

Gisburne nodded, and Günther stepped closer. "Your legendary black charger!" he said. "Quite beautiful." Nyght shook his head and stamped. "Well, I am a merchant. So here is my proposition to you: your life, in exchange for this fine horse." He put an arm about Nyght's neck and patted it.

Galfrid saw Gisburne tense. His fists clenched. Then he heard him mutter under his breath. "Remember Carcassonne?"

"Of course," said Galfrid. "High up. Lots of walls."

"I mean the donkey."

"The don – ? No... You mean?"

"Yes. Get ready."

Galfrid gripped his trusty pilgrim staff tighter.

"When you ladies are quite finished..." said Günther irritably. "Do we have a deal? Or do I let Otto loose on you?" Otto growled.

Then Gisburne leaned forward, bared his teeth, and snapped his jaw together three times.

Günther stared in bemusement. "What in Hell is that suppo –" He was cut short by Nyght's teeth clamping onto Günther's right ear, and tossing his head so hard that the German was almost pulled off his feet. Gisburne drew both sword and seax and booted Otto in the stomach, sending him staggering backwards and taking two more with him. "Heads!" shouted Galfrid, and Gisburne dropped to his knee as the squire swung his staff about him in great swooping arcs, cracking a new head with each revolution. One after another, its victims fell at their comrades' feet.

A trio of mariners, thinking taking a prize better than fighting – or perhaps to deny their enemy a means of escape – went to grab the horses. Nyght broke the leader's jaw with a flying hoof, then bucked and kicked two more behind him, sending them hurtling backwards into their comrades. No one troubled the horses after that.

Gisburne, meanwhile – crouched low beneath the booming staff – was also kept busy. Those behind the decimated front rank, frustrated at being denied the fight, had begun to hurl a barrage of objects at the pair: ale mugs, parts of a chair, plates, a boot, a heaved-up cobble. A wooden bowl caught Galfrid a glancing blow on the temple. An earthenware jug smacked into Gisburne's chest and smashed on the cobbles, spraying the squire with beer. Gisburne batted them aside with both blades as if it were some frenzied childhood game. In each lull he struck out, cracking a knee of one with the back of his seax, lashing another across the face with the flat of his sword. Out of nowhere, between two bodies, a polearm was thrust at him. Gisburne dodged it, knocked it down with his sword and stepped on the shaft, pitching its owner into the arena on all fours, his face just inches from Gisburne's. The pommel of Gisburne's sword put him down for the remainder of the fight.

Galfrid realised that the Germans' one advantage – greater numbers – had been almost neutralised when they'd surrounded their opponents. He even began to see the real possibility of escape. Then, in his moment of greatest hope, the staff stopped against a bar mace with a jarring crack. He stumbled, and before he could recover, they closed in like a pack of wolves.

The fight was messy. There was grabbing, scratching, smashing of fists. Galfrid and Gisburne gave as good as they got, but sheer numbers were going to get the better of them.

Suddenly, there came a shout from beyond the fray. Then another. Men cried in pain, and surprise. Günther's men turned in shock. Someone was coming to the Englishmen's aid. Grabbing what advantage they could, Gisburne and Galfrid felled those nearest them with a series of ferocious blows. Their attackers stepped back, suddenly unsure what they were facing. A space cleared – and a huge German was sent skidding across the muddy street towards Gisburne and Galfrid.

All stopped dead, and Günther – lost in the fray once the mêlée had begun – was once again revealed. He and his men stared in amazement. Standing in the space, sword in one hand and mace in the other, her hair wild, was Mélisande, bloodied men sprawled all about her.

"Well, there goes the secret identity," muttered Galfrid.

GISBURNE LOOKED ON in wonderment and horror, his heart thumping in his chest. This was the best and worst thing he could have imagined.

By now he had imagined her to be hundreds of miles distant. He told himself that if he could transport her there with a wish, he would. Yet when he looked on her face, burning with fearless and irresistible passion, all selfless resolve faltered.

"Good to see you," he called.

"You too," responded Mélisande, eyes fixed on her wary opponents.

"What brings you here?"

"I was just passing through."

"To where?"

"France."

Günther, meanwhile, burst into astonished laughter, shaking his head in disbelief. "You two know each other?" Half his ear was now missing, blood coursing down the side of his head, yet his face registered a curious kind of joy. He clapped his hands as he guffawed. "Well, this just got more interesting than even I could have imagined..." He put his hand across his breast, and bowed. "Madam, I am no slave to custom. I embrace new ideas and bold endeavours of all kinds. And so I must salute the manner in which you have overcome the disadvantage of your sex."

"Disadvantage?" said Mélisande. At that, she whipped around and buried the point of her right boot in the nearest German's groin. The whole assembled company winced at the impact. Incapable of exclamation, the man crumpled, a sound like a broken bellows issuing from him as he hit the ground. She glared back at Günther. "What disadvantage?"

Günther chuckled in delight and turned to address his men, arms spread wide. "You see? This is why I love London! Just when you think you've seen it all, up pops something you could not possibly have expected."

Some laughed gruffly with him.

He turned back to her. "My lady, you are truly a revelation, if a short-lived one..." His laughter suddenly faded. "But it is time to move on from this play-acting."

"Play-acting? You think I do this for entertainment?"

Günther looked Mélisande up and down, then turned his gaze upon Gisburne, a sly smile upon his lips. "I think, perhaps, yes..." Then the smile also dwindled. "But I have no argument with you. This business is between me and Sir Guy. Be on your way. Back to your woman's things."

Gisburne had noted no signal, no instruction, yet as Günther had been speaking, his men had begun to shift and reconfigure. Bit by bit, he now realised, the Germans were surrounding them once again. He could see Mélisande sensed it too.

"Go," he breathed. "Go quickly..."

She looked at him, and flashed a sweet smile. Then turning back to Günther, she raised her sword point. "If you fight Gisburne, you fight me."

Günther's eyes remained fixed upon Gisburne, his voice like cold steel on stone. "My lady... You have only to walk away. I suggest you do so. Consider this my last warning."

Gisburne looked at Mélisande, his eyes pleading for her to do so.

"And you listen to my warning," she said through clenched teeth. "No one has yet died today. Until now, each side has spared the other the blade. But if you think I will hold back once you take this next step, you are mistaken. If you fight me, you will have to kill me."

Gisburne winced at the words. They were meant as an ultimatum, to force Günther to back down. But in the few minutes he had known Günther, he had learned that such a tactic was folly. He also knew that in the month that had passed since her encounter with the Red Hand her wounds would not have completely healed, that her strength would be reduced, her responses slowed, her movements restricted. And yet here she was, about to throw herself into the wolf pit.

The German shrugged. "Have it your way." And he turned to signal to his men. Gisburne tightened his grip on sword and seax. Galfrid released the hidden blade from his staff.

"Do you have any idea what that will bring down upon your head?" she said, now with a note of desperation in her voice.

"But of course. How silly of me." Günther's tone was harsh, mocking. He had tired of this amusement. "Your father is the Count of Boulogne. And that is supposed to intimidate me, is it not? Well, my lady, a new age is coming. In twenty years we'll own him – along with the Holy Roman Emperor and the King of England." He nodded to his men to close in for the kill.

"*Enough!*"

The voice boomed from outside the circle. An English voice. Yet at its sound, Günther held his men back.

For the third time, the rabble parted, and into the ring stepped a hooded figure. He was lean-faced, a thin scar across one eye, with the manner and physique of a soldier. And from his left hand were missing the first two fingers.

"Ranulph Le Fort..." muttered Gisburne.

Ranulph stepped forward to face Gisburne. He had no trace of fear about him.

"You say this man's name is Gisburne?" he said. He addressed Günther as an equal.

Günther frowned. "It is. What of it?"

Ranulph frowned, and studied Gisburne's face. "I knew his father. And he has been striving to prevent my death these past few weeks, as he tried to prevent Baylesford's." His voice dropped. "And all the others..." There was pain behind his eyes. "He has done this with little thought for his own safety, as you see plainly."

Günther looked about at the carnage. "You are saying I should spare him? After all this?"

"It's what Baylesford would have wished," said Ranulph.

That struck home. Günther looked hard at Gisburne. "You are using up your many lives with amazing rapidity, my friend. You should take more care." He turned to his men, and his icy demeanour suddenly shifted to that of an affable host. "Well, then – we have no more business to discuss. Perhaps, after all, the world is more interesting with Guy of Gisburne still in it." He turned to Mélisande with a bow. "And you, too, my lady. My apologies for inconveniencing you. And my best regards to your father." And with that, he and his men melted away.

The trio were left standing in a deserted street, Ranulph facing Gisburne.

"Well, here we all are, then," said Galfrid.

"It's time we talked, you and I," said Ranulph. "Alone."

L

Eastchepe
22 June, 1193

WIDOW FLEET HARDLY knew what to do with herself. As they had crashed
through the front door, she had beetled out in her nightdress, her hair awry,
eyes like muddy puddles, fully prepared to berate her tenants for bursting
in upon the house so late with no thought for those already abed. Doubtless
she had expected to find Gisburne and Galfrid the worse for drink, and
ripe for moral censure. What she actually saw in the light of her flickering
candle, however, threw her into total confusion: the two men muddy,
beaten and bruised, and with them – in a no less disordered state – a lady
of noble bearing. As the trio fell into the hall and towards the stairs, she
gaped, open-mouthed.

"It's all right, madam," Galfrid had said. "We're all right. Just cuts and
bruises and trampled English pride."

Then she had looked from her gentlemen tenants to the fine but dishevelled
lady who now stood in the hall – her hall – and back once again to Gisburne
and Galfrid. When neither spoke, Mélisande herself took the initiative.

"I am Mélisande de Champagne," she said. "A pleasure to meet you."

"Lady Mélisande is the daughter of the Count of Boulogne," added
Galfrid. At this, Widow Fleet gave an intake of breath, then flushed, passed
the candle from hand to hand, then bowed, then ran out of things to do
entirely.

"I must apologise for disturbing you at this late hour," said Mélisande.
"Some trouble upon the streets, as you can plainly see."

"Oh, my lady, it has been terrible these past days!" The Widow looked
upon Gisburne and Galfrid with infinite admiration. "And these good
gentlemen came to your aid?"

"Something like that," said Mélisande with a wry smile. "But all is well.
And we must to our beds. Ready for the morrow." She caught Gisburne's
eye, her smile fading.

"It is late to venture again into these troubled streets," said a troubled Widow Fleet. "One of these gentlemen must see you safely back, or..."

"Or I could just stay here," said Mélisande sweetly, her hands spread apart. She turned to Gisburne. "If you'll have me."

Widow Fleet, who had never seen or heard the like in all her born days, stood like a shrunken effigy of a woman, impossibly torn between scandalised outrage and overwhelming pride at having such a person under her roof. She finally gave in entirely to the latter, and broke into embarrassed laughter like a madwoman.

"Well, it's decided, then," said Mélisande, smiling warmly, and grasped her hand. "You are most kind."

Widow Fleet blushed scarlet. Then as they turned toward the cramped stair, their long shadows cast before them, she bowed again, and laughed, and put her hand over her face, then, still tittering like a hysteric, scuttled away back to her bed.

"I DIDN'T THINK to see you again so soon," said Gisburne. He stroked his fingers down her cheek, along the length of her slender neck and across her naked shoulder, sweeping aside the cascade of red-gold hair as he did so.

Mélisande shifted in the bed, propped her head upon her right hand, and made a show of scowling at him. "You know, those are the first actual words you have spoken since we got here?"

"Sorry about that," said Gisburne. "But I am glad to see you."

Mélisande's scowl turned once again to a smile. "I could tell."

He reached his hand behind her head, and kissed her upon her lips. She tasted of roses and spiced wine.

"I've missed you," he said.

She looked around at the crazed inscriptions covering every inch of wall. "I could tell that too." She turned her gaze back to him. "Not just because of the drawings." And suddenly, she was not smiling – her expression instead turned to something deeper, strangely sad – something that made Gisburne wish to clasp her to him as tight as he knew how.

All at once, a loud snort made them start. It was Galfrid, in the neighbouring room, snoring. Gisburne and Mélisande simultaneously broke into stifled, adolescent giggles. The moment they had reached the top of the stairs, Galfrid had yawned very deliberately and immediately made himself scarce – an act, for which Gisburne would be eternally grateful.

"Well, at least we didn't keep the poor fellow awake," she said.

His hand traced a line across her breast, and down further still to where her waist dipped. The skin across her ribs was still discoloured from her injury. It looked grey in the moonlight. He stroked his fingers across it. "Does it hurt?"

"Only when I breathe deeply," she said. "Or fast. Or when I exert myself."

"Ah," said Gisburne. "Sorry again."

She touched his cheek. "Stop apologising. I said it hurt; I didn't say I minded. But what about you? Are you hurting?"

"Just a few cuts and bruises," he said. "An average night."

"I didn't mean that," she said.

He stared at her for a moment, uncertain just what she did mean. There were many types of pain. But which was she referring to now?

"That shoulder of yours," she said, poking the left side of his collarbone. Then she stroked it gently. "Your souvenir from Hattin. How is it?"

"It comes and goes. With the weather. With the phases of the moon. The tides. Who knows?" He have a half-shrug. "I have been training with the bow again. It has helped."

She raised an eyebrow. "Gisburne the bowman. Is there no end to your talents?"

Gisburne gave a weak smile. There was an end, a limit. He just hoped, this time, he had not reached it.

She turned, and lay on her front, one leg kicked in the air, her hair strewn across her pale back. "That man," she said, "Ranulph Le Fort. What did he say to you?"

Gisburne had changed after talking with Ranulph. Both Mélisande and Galfrid had seen it, he knew, but neither – until now – had asked. And now that someone had, he found it was too big, and struck to deep, for him to explain.

"A long story," he said.

Mélisande lifted herself up onto her knees, studying the wall by the bed. "Is it to do with this?" Pinned immediately above where they lay was the parchment relating the altercation between Ranulph and the Irish lord.

"Yes," said Gisburne. "How did you guess?"

She shrugged, and tossed her hair. "It wasn't a guess. Ranulph's name is upon it. And John's. And it relates to Ireland."

"But when did you read it?"

Mélisande smiled. "Don't worry your head about that..." And she ruffled his hair. Then she leaned in, squinting at the parchment in the gloom, and placed a finger upon it. "But what is this name? *La...?*"

"Liadan," said Gisburne. His voice was flat, without emotion. "The Red Hand's mother."

"My God. You found his name? Who he is?"

"Yes," said Gisburne. "Finally."

"This must help your task," said Mélisande.

Gisburne said nothing. He turned on his back and gazed for some time at the dark beams above. "Ranulph leaves tomorrow on a ship bound for Calais," he said at length. "It belongs to one Thomas of Baylesford, and sits at the wharf at Byllynsgate. Baylesford is dead, but he laid plans in advance – for himself and Ranulph to escape the Red Hand. I have arranged for you to take Baylesford's place."

"But I..."

"It is arranged," insisted Gisburne.

Mélisande leaned over him, resting upon his chest, and moved a strand of hair from his forehead with her finger. "You are trying to keep me safe..." For once, she seemed to accept her lot. "So it is to be like before. A single night together before one of us departs on a ship... But what of you?"

"Tomorrow we prepare. The Red Hand will come. He will find a way into the Tower, no matter what anyone does. And then he will try to take his revenge. It's there we will make our stand."

"Revenge for what?"

"For his family," said Gisburne.

Mélisande's expression saddened as she gazed off into the distance. "It is terrible when one is condemned to be so full of hatred."

Gisburne sat up, and with one hand on her cheek, kissed her on the forehead. "Goodbye, Mélisande," he said.

She frowned at him as he drew back. "Goodbye?" The remaining warmth drained from her face. He glimpsed something in her he had rarely seen. She was frightened. But not for herself – never for herself.

Gisburne smiled a reassuring smile. "I'm saying it to you now because I know when I awake in the morning you will be gone."

"It's a long time until dawn," she said. "Surely you can do better than just 'goodbye'?"

He put his lips to hers, wrapped an arm about her waist and pulled her towards him.

LI

HE WAS NOT sure how long he had dozed, but the moment he opened his eyes all trace if drowsiness fled. It was still dark, the moon shining through the half open shutter. Mélisande was still there, her arms entwined about him, her soft breaths against his cheek.

With infinite care he extricated himself from her sleeping embrace and stood.

THE NIGHT WAS supernaturally still. It seemed impossible to believe that this was a city in turmoil, in a kingdom on the edge of chaos. For a moment he paused, listening to the soft sounds of Mélisande as she slept. He gazed back at her willowy, naked form, her tousled hair spread across the white linen of the sheet – her beauty rendered ethereal by the moonlight. He did not know when he would see her again.

Scrabbling in his bag at the foot of the bed, he drew out an irregularly shaped scale of metal, then threw his nightshirt over his head and pulled on his boots.

Creeping across the creaking boards, he took the longbow and quiver from the corner of Galfrid's chamber, and, as he headed back to the stairs, grabbed the plump leg of ham that had sat upon the table awaiting their return that evening, and which had, until now, been entirely ignored.

GISBURNE DREW A bodkin point arrow from the quiver at his back, and took aim. At the far end of the yard, the ham hung from the crudely repaired post, and upon it – its dark surface glinting in the pale light – the plate of armour that the Red Hand had lost.

He drew. Loosed the arrow. It glanced off the metal, sailing high across the yards. He nocked another, heaved on the great bow and released. With a sharp crack the shaft shattered, splinters flying in the night air. He took a step forward, and shot again. Again, it went spinning, and did not bite. Another step forward. Another arrow loosed. Time and again he shot and advanced, shot and advanced, each sent towards its mark with increasing fury. Arrows bounced off, sent in all directions, until finally he stopped less than three yards from his target. His last arrow, and that alone, was embedded in it.

He pulled the arrow from the joint of meat. The metal scale came with it. Nearly half the bodkin point arrows were now lost or destroyed. But the last of them had penetrated the battered, deformed plate by almost an inch.

V

JUDGEMENT

LII

The Forest of Sherwood
February, 1193

HEREWARD STAMPED HIS numb, crudely swaddled feet upon the frozen earth and looked about him at the assembled company. Two hundred – maybe more. An army. That was how Hood had encouraged his followers to think of themselves. But today, in the weak winter light of this bleak and frosted glade, they seemed an army of the damned.

Shivering, grey-faced as ghosts, wrapped in rags and dwarfed into insignificance by the towering, creaking black shapes of age-old trees, they were an army not merely in retreat, but on the verge of collapse – beaten not in battle, but by the merciless daily grind of their bleak, meagre existence. As he took in the lifeless eyes and foggy breaths, Hereward shuddered. It wasn't just the cold. He felt himself in the company of wraiths. He had known things were bad, but this supposed rally had hammered home the scale of that creeping disaster. They stood, now, empty of purpose. Leaderless, directionless. Lost.

Today may yet change all that. Today, if the monk Took had his way, they might leave this spot with new fire in their bellies. An army once more. It was not too late – the fire had not entirely gone out.

But Hereward did not want to think about that.

Took was the one point of fierce energy in the small, circular clearing. Clad plainly in his monk's habit, with a conical helm upon his head and a sword strapped about him, he strode tirelessly back and forth, one hand upon the sword's pommel. Every few paces he would stop and – thrusting out his chin, his black beard grown full these past few weeks – throw a challenging glance towards the men. And, as if by sorcery, every man upon whom this gaze fell tensed, as if awoken from a frozen slumber, and stood more upright – their defiance and boldness, perhaps, a little greater. It was a rare gift Took had. A different kind of inspiration from that which Hood had provided, to be sure, but Took remained a real danger, nonetheless.

Only three times before had he seen the whole band gathered together in this place – and the last of these had dealt them a shattering blow. That had been the occasion John Lyttel had informed them of the loss of their beloved leader. Today, however, was different. This was no mere gathering to pass on a piece of news or decide upon some matter of internal politics. It was something that had never been attempted before. A meeting; an alliance, perhaps. None knew for sure. All they did know was that it was a parley with others from outside of their close-knit and jealously-guarded group – that it meant admitting strangers to the secret realm they had carved out for themselves in these ancient woods. It was an act that, likely as not, Hood himself would never have contemplated.

Even Hereward did not know for sure who their guest was. Took had kept that information close. But there had been rumours. They had filled the assembled company with trepidation. So feared was the man's name that few even dared utter it. But if the rumours proved true, and they survived the encounter, Hereward would have the greatest prize his master could wish for. Then he could return to his old life – his real life – and be Hereward no longer.

It was, now, the only name to which he answered. That part – growing accustomed to a new name – had been easy. Stopping himself from turning his head whenever he heard the old one, the real one... That had proved far harder. Fear of discovery and death had ultimately provided motivation. But now he vaguely wondered how long it would take to fully divest himself of his new name.

It had been carefully chosen. It was commonplace, so would not draw attention; it was Saxon, and so aligned him with the oppressed classes. It was also the name of the rebel who had resisted the Norman yoke after the Conqueror's invasion. Little wonder the story's currency had grown of late. It was an insider – a monk – who had finally brought about that troublesome rebel's defeat, revealing a safe path through the Fens to the pursuing Norman army. That was the part the new Hereward – Hereward of Sherwood – liked the most. It was the part from which he drew strength – the part which he judged Sherwood's outlaws to have forgotten, and its lesson with it. Well, they would remember it soon enough.

It was painfully clear, today, that numbers were severely depleted. And anyone could see in the gaunt, half-starved faces that their mettle was dwindling, too. Merry men. That's what folk called them: *Robin Hood and his Merry Men*. Now there was no Hood, and as for them being merry... Hereward fought to suppress a laugh. Spirits crushed, bodies withered and weak. Fingertips turning blue – or, in some cases, black. The dead of plague and famine looked merrier.

They had been no less cold and hungry when Hood had been here, of course. But somehow, then, that had looked like tenacity. Like the driving hunger of the lean wolf in winter. A hunger for action, for change. Now, they merely looked defeated – no longer predator, but prey. Hereward almost felt sorry for them. Almost. But even if they did recover – even if they found their fighting spirit again – they would all hang by St John's Day. He would see to that.

Many had cut loose around Yuletide. Those who joined the previous summer had been first to go. It was easy to be a noble outlaw when the sun shone; with warm feet and a full belly, one could follow any cause, no matter how slight. Come winter, the natural hardships of the forest had begun to take their toll. Then came the hammerblow of Hood's capture, and the baffling silence that followed. It was this, finally, that had crushed their resolve. At first, the capture had sparked outrage. For a day or two, it had even looked like this outlaw rabble – accustomed, until now, to the measured guerrilla tactics of the forest – might turn into a rebel force, and march on Nottingham. There had been many who roared terrifying oaths to that effect. Small as their numbers were, Hereward feared the smouldering flame could yet spread. If it did, many hundreds of others – the disaffected, the hungry, the wronged – would flock to their banner, and set this land afire.

But no word came. Not of execution. Not of burial in a grave, unmarked or otherwise. Nor of burning on a pyre. It was as if Hood had simply disappeared.

The big man, John Lyttel, had tried his best to rally them as the new year dawned. All liked and trusted him – even Hereward. But, respected though he was, John Lyttel was no leader. Hereward had seen it before, at other times, in other battles. Contrary to what many believed, the common fighting man did not want thoughtfulness and consideration from his general. He wanted strength – and something more. Something decisive – even cruel. That, he would follow – far easier than he would follow a good man. On the battlefield, empathy was an unwelcome companion. And that was John Lyttel's deficiency. He offered milk, when what they craved was blood.

Things had shifted with the rise of the monk Took. He had ideas. He was a man of reading, versed in philosophy, yet not afraid to act. He was good with a sword – that fact had won him respect within the first week of his arrival. But whilst John Lyttel for the most part lay dormant – awaiting either imminent threat, or orders – Took had a fire behind him. He had that same, grim determination common to so many of Hood's die-hard followers, but advantage in life had also given him ambition, and the means to further it.

His swift ascendance had been a surprise to Hereward – something for which he had not been prepared. The spur that Took promised was not something Hereward welcomed. It threatened to give them new hope, new purpose; make them dangerous again. It was everything Hereward was sworn to resist. And yet, in spite of himself, he had felt a curious thrill at the possibility of the outlaws' renewed energy. It was, perhaps, a mood to which even he was not immune after so long amongst them.

But there was another, more basic emotion. Relief. The relief of a soldier for whom the wait was finally over. For good or ill, they would make their move, and this, finally, would be the culmination of all his efforts.

Hereward looked about again, searching for the big Irishman. Even with his characteristic stoop, that shaggy figure should be easy enough to spot, rivalled in height only by John Lyttel. But there was no sign.

Somehow, it had been he who had inspired all this. The one they called the Red Hand. It had taken an iron will and extraordinary fire for the Irishman to seek them out. And he had done it not once, but twice. The first time had been just days before the archery tournament at Clippestone. Hood had been preoccupied with the contest – some might say obsessed – determined to take part and win in spite of Lyttel's warnings. It was clearly a trap – any fool could see it, and Hood was no fool – but it drew him, nonetheless, as a flame did a moth. Hood saw no danger, for him or his men – or, if he did, chose to disregard it. He saw only challenge. And opportunity – for something more, Hereward had come to believe, than the simple glory of winning. But Hood had never revealed his full intention, and none questioned him on it.

This was the circumstance into which the Red Hand had blundered. Despite his clear delight at the man's tenacity, Hood had sent the Irishman packing, telling him to return when he was ready. Hereward had wondered at that. Far less worthy men had come seeking to join Hood's band and been welcomed into the fold. Why reject this one? At first, Hereward wondered if that had the problem. Perhaps this man had been *too* good. Perhaps, in him, Hood saw a potential threat. If that was the case – even if it wasn't – Hereward was also curious why Hood had not simply had him killed. No outsider had come here and left alive before.

Then, when they were at their lowest ebb, just weeks ago, the Red Hand had appeared again. He was a sullen and strangely intimidating figure. Speaking to no one, he would sit for hours on end, hooded, staring into the ground, or the flames of the fire. Took conversed with him from time to time, in private, but there was something in his near-mute melancholy that made everyone else keep their distance.

Finally, realisation had dawned. Hood had not rejected the Red Hand at all. In telling him to return "when he was ready," he was enacting a plan – but what that plan was, and how it had become entangled with Hood's capture, was not entirely clear.

There had been a time, not long ago, when gathering information had been easy. Took had seen something in Hereward, and for a while he had been close to the heart of the band. But somehow, of late, that connection had withered and dwindled. Took had become distant, and Hereward had been reluctant to push. Nothing revealed one's hand like excessive eagerness.

There was sudden movement in the crowd beyond Hereward's line of sight, and men shuffled and parted. A familiar figure appeared before the throng, and advanced to join Took. All had grown accustomed to her now, but nothing could change the startling, almost absurd incongruity of her presence here. She, too, was dressed plainly, almost in the manner of a nun, her head and hair respectfully covered. But such youth, beauty and bearing could not be so easily disguised – could hardly have been more at odds with her grim, filthy surroundings. *A rose amongst thorns,* mused Hereward. But in truth, the contrast was far greater than that. These were not things grown from the same root. Her presence here was not only incongruous – it seemed almost dangerous, as if she should be ushered in all possible haste away from these gaunt, desperate peasants with their hungry looks and rusty blades to a place of warmth and safety. To her own kind.

At her approach, Took turned. He smiled warmly, and, grasping her hands in each of his, breathed her name with an almost paternal tenderness. "*Marian!*"

Lady Marian Fitzwalter had been Took's other great surprise – and a clear indication of the authority he had built up in recent days. Not that she was the only woman here; there were many – and children too. At times, over the past year, whole families had flocked to Hood's cause, believing him their saviour. But Marian was something quite different. Had any other man brought a beautiful young noblewoman into their midst – monk or not – there would have been no end of crude jibes at his expense. And protest too. But none challenged Took.

At the sound of hurried, soft-booted feet upon the frosty ground, men all around Hereward tensed. Spears and axes were gripped more tightly. Took turned and raised a hand, indicating that he wished no weapons to be drawn. From a narrow path though the spiked tangle of bough and shrub hurtled a gangling figure, crossbow slung low, his long hood flying behind him. There was sweat on his brow, his red, watery eyes bulging. He had evidently been running.

"They're coming," panted the newcomer, approaching Took on heavy feet. The monk gave the man a clap on the shoulder, and the exhausted lookout plodded on, melting into the throng.

Took turned and exchanged some hasty words with Marian – too softly for Hereward to catch. She seemed to protest. Took's response this time – gentle, but firm – was audible. It was not safe for her to be here while the meeting was taking place, he said. He made it seem utterly reasonable – caring – but Hereward suspected other motives. Perhaps the monk wished to avoid her being seen by their guest; perhaps, also, to shield her eyes. A lady of her standing might prove crucial to their cause – that, Took understood well – but, committed though she was, Hereward doubted she had the stomach for all they were prepared to do.

Marian glanced nervously the way the lookout had come – her face flushed, her eyes as wide and alert as a doe's – and without further question was led away beneath the large, protective arm of John Lyttel.

Took turned and braced himself. They could hear horses: at least a dozen. Took had taken a great risk, exposing them in such a way. None of Hood's party were mounted. Great though their numbers were, twenty knights could cut them down at such close quarters. Hereward had seen that happen, in other lands, under a different banner. Those with bows might get off a shot if they were lucky. But by then the horsemen would be upon them. This was meant to be a peaceful parley, of course, but there could be none here who were not thinking the same thoughts.

No one spoke as the pounding of hooves on hard earth neared. Suddenly, they were there. Grim-faced, hard eyes glinting beneath battle-scarred helms, the twisted braids of their beards and hair falling over blackened mail and thick studded leather. Hanging about the broad backs of their short, stocky ponies were swords, axes and rounded wooden shields with battered iron bosses, their boards painted blood red – some bearing symbols: a raven, a great hammer, a skull – one, a fantastical image of a horned god upon a nine-legged horse.

Norsemen. Pagans.

This was not what was expected. Hereward felt the man next to him take an involuntary step back; several more did the same. Took glared at them. They held, but only just. Someone made a strange, constricted sound, as if the air had grown too thick to breathe. Hereward was thrust back to a dreadful day in Aquitaine, when he had stood amongst men paralysed by the certainty of their imminent death – by a fear so immediate and tangible that men had choked upon it.

The Norsemen spread out as they advanced, rearranging into a tight horseshoe facing Took's men. And then, into the midst of them, emerging like a ghost from the black gloom of the forest upon a moon-white destrier, came their guest.

At the sight of him, there were gasps. One man whimpered. Somewhere, a child wailed in terror and was hastily whisked away.

The figure sat a full head higher than his guards. He was tall and thin, a long dark cloak hanging about him, its hood framing his face. Or at least, what should have been a face. For within the cowl there were no features of flesh – just a blank, eyeless face of metal.

The mask was simple and functional: a straight slit for the mouth, two circular holes for eyes, two smaller holes beneath the slight bump of the nose. It was a face that neither smiled nor frowned – devoid of expression, doggedly resisting all attempts to read within it some intimation of humanity.

There could be no doubting his identity now. The White Devil. Tancred de Mercheval.

As one, the Norsemen dismounted. They moved ahead of their mounts as Tancred slithered from his saddle, their stone-grey eyes fixed on their ragged hosts. Hereward had heard that Tancred's views were now so extreme – heretical, most would say – that he trusted Christians least of all. In his twisted world, Christians were simply further down the path of corruption. Heathens were closer to God. And so Tancred had drawn his personal guard from the remote islands where the Norse – renowned for their boldness and savagery in battle – remained resistant to Christian ways.

Hanging back at the mouth of the path, still mounted, were three more knights, their faces hidden within dark cowls. Knights of Tancred's new order. What these men had been required to do – or sacrifice – to earn a place in this warped brotherhood, and how any survived in such poisonous, life-sapping company, Hereward could not imagine.

The Norsemen stopped, Tancred within their defensive circle, his blank face turning slowly. Finally, it fixed on Took.

"I am here."

From any other mouth the words would have seemed absurd. But none laughed. The sound of Tancred's voice, like steel against stone, chilled Hereward to the marrow.

Took smiled with the same warmth he had given Marian, and spread his arms, his eyes glinting with irrepressible zeal. "Welcome... Welcome! This is indeed a great honour. A *great* honour..." He almost chuckled with delight. "I have long admired the boldness of your ideas. They proved an inspiration to me when I was a lost soul. But I wish you to know that in addition –"

Tancred's raised hand silenced him. "Save your flattery."

Took, mouth still hanging open, stared at him, waiting for what utterance was to follow. But nothing came. He looked flustered, his prepared speech in ruins, his hero showing not the slightest interest in him. But Took remained the most pragmatic of men, not afflicted by an excess of self-doubt. And so he nodded, straightened, took a deep breath, and got down to business.

"A man came to our company, calling himself the Red Hand," he said. "He risked much to find us. But he sought information. He had also heard of certain... events... with which you were involved. He wishes to learn from them."

"What is this man's education to me?" said Tancred. His voice, muffled by the mask, was a low hiss – barely more than a whisper. Yet it touched every ear like an icy wind.

"The Red Hand wishes destruction upon someone. This also suits our purpose. And, I believe, yours too, my lord..."

"I am no one's lord," snapped Tancred. "There is only one worthy of that title."

But Took, the wind now in his sails, ignored the rebuke. "This enemy is common to us all – a pest we would all rejoice to be rid of. Certain information that only you can supply will give our ally an advantage in his quest. Our quest... Such is the reason I contrived this meeting between us."

The monk thrust his hand beneath his cloak, then, and drew out a small, yellowed, tube, barely larger than a child's little finger. He held it out, taking a step forward as he did so. The Norsemen tensed, their hands going to their weapons. Took stopped, his arm outstretched. "I will not speak the name openly," he continued. "It is writ upon this parchment."

For a moment, there was only the snorting and stamping of the horses. This, Hereward sensed, was the moment in which Took's fortunes – perhaps the fortunes of all within this lonely glade – would be made or lost. In the long silence, as Hereward's eyes roved about Tancred's Norse warband, he noticed that warrior nearest Took wore a necklace of small bones, just visible between the braids of his beard. They were human finger bones.

"You dress as a man of God," said Tancred, finally.

"Yes," said Took, holding his head up.

"And yet you choose to fight amongst these... people." Tancred looked about him at those gathered there.

Took rose to the challenge. "Eat, sleep and fight," he said. "And proudly so." He raised his voice and gave a glance about as he proclaimed this. But none were bold enough to respond.

"If you wish to fight for God, why did you not join one of the military orders? The Hospitallers? The Templars?"

"Their fight is not my fight. And this battle they take to foreign lands is mere distraction, a diversion from what is most pressing to us all. And an affront to the Almighty."

"You are aware that I was accepted into the Order of the Temple, and have been their fiercest advocate?"

"I am," said Took, still confident. "As I am aware that you outgrew them. That you left them behind. And you were right to do so." He hesitated for a moment, as if uncertain whether to continue. "They have lost touch with the true meaning of Christ's message. Become corrupted, rotten. Slaves to material wealth and earthly power."

Silence. Took stood, his confidence now seeming to waver every bit as much as his still-outstretched hand before the implacable, unreadable steel visage. Then, from within the mask, came a weird sound. It cut the cold air: a dry, rasping croak, like a death-rattle. Hereward shuddered involuntarily. It was a moment before he realised it was laughter.

"You answer well, monk," said Tancred. "So tell me – who do you fight? Princes? Barons? Bishops?"

"All," said Took.

For a moment, Tancred stood motionless, silent, the expressionless holes of his eyes fixed upon his host. From beneath the mask was uttered a word Hereward did not understand, and the Norseman with the bone necklace took the parchment, and passed it to his master.

Tancred held it aloft, and regarded it between thumb and forefinger. "Before I read this," he said. "I would have you know the nature of this alliance you now seek to forge."

Hereward, puzzled by the words, did not see Tancred's free hand pull at his hood. He was aware only of the dark fabric sliding off smooth metal. What was revealed was more than a mask. It was an iron skull – solid plates, shaped and joined by rows of rivets, covering the whole of Tancred's head. Down the left side – the side Hereward could most clearly see – were catches, to allow the faceplate to be opened or removed.

Then he saw Tancred's left hand go to the side of his head, and with a shudder realised what the rebel Templar meant to do.

There was a sharp click. Then another. The whole of the expressionless face jolted, then with a grating squeak of metal against metal, swung open.

"Look into the face of Death," said Tancred.

The assembled company gasped. Took's eyes bulged. Hereward heard himself utter a plea to God.

Within the metal helm was a living skull, its dark flesh burned and withered until it barely covered the bone, its lips drawn back across blackened teeth, its lidless eyes staring. But even this was not the limit of the horror. The two sides were somehow misaligned, as if a giant had taken hold of the head – palms upon its ears, thumbs upon its cheeks – and made a crude attempt to twist the two halves apart.

Hereward had seen hundreds, perhaps thousands of corpses in his time. He had seen mutilation from the battlefield that had so distorted and disfigured the victim as to render them unrecognisable to their own kin – at times, hardly recognisable as human. But he had never witnessed anything like this. It seemed inconceivable that life could continue behind such a shattered visage. It was a face that belonged in the grave. In Hell.

"Many men have tried to destroy me. All have failed. I now stand as embodiment of a truth that cannot be denied. This is the reality of our material existence: pain, defilement, decay. All else is illusion. Know that I have no interest in your petty politics, your childish arguments, your pointless quests for what you call *justice*. These things are meaningless to me, as one day, they shall be to all. They merely prolong the death-throes of this irredeemably corrupted world – a world whose end I wish only to hasten." Tancred turned his head slowly, so all present could see. "This is the one whose help you now seek. Do you still desire it?"

Hereward detected fear in Took's eye. But the monk fought it down. He clenched his fists and pushed out his bearded chin. "We do."

Whether that was the wish of all here, Hereward seriously doubted. But there was no going back now. Tancred's thin fingers unwrapped the tiny scrap of thin parchment. The glassy, staring orbs of his eyes scanned its mottled surface.

A crow called, distantly. Tancred's eyes seemed suddenly to blaze with a cold fire, and for a moment, Hereward thought he could detect some mockery of a smile upon those devastated lips. Tancred crushed the scrap in his palm, and looked up once more. "I will help you."

A palpable sense of relief swept the crowd. Took himself clapped his hands together, and almost laughed.

Hereward's relief, however, was far greater than any there that day. In that one moment, with a sense of finality that almost made him weep, he realised his mission really was at an end. In recent days, he had ascertained what Took wished to achieve by using the Red Hand, and when it was to occur. He now knew of Tancred's involvement, and if he was swift could bring about the rebel Templar's capture whilst he was still in England. He did not have the name that was writ upon the parchment, true, but it was a mere detail. He would not wait for that. The first moment he was able, he would go directly to the Sheriff in Nottingham with his information. He would leave Sherwood and all these months of lies and restraint in this borrowed life behind him, and be Hereward no longer. He would see the wife who thought he was dead. And – praise God! – he would have a bath. His heart thumped and his head swam at the thought.

"There is one matter that must be dealt with first," said Tancred. Hereward looked up as a hush fell over the throng. Took was nodding slowly, his head downcast. Hereward looked around, and saw that others were as baffled as he.

"We must thank you for the information you've given us," said Took. The monk's voice was grave, but it almost seemed there was a note of sadness in it. Took breathed deeply, lifting his head and his voice, then, as if to banish his suddenly sombre mood. "It shall be dealt with here. Now."

With that, Took turned towards his men. His eyes, glittering in the cool light, moved methodically from face to face, scanning each in turn. Men shifted nervously as the gaze passed. Some began to mutter. Took's eyes drew closer – met with Hereward's. Hereward stood straight, defiant, determined to hold the monk's piercing gaze until it had moved on.

But it did not.

Took, staring fixedly at Hereward, raised his right arm, his finger pointing, his expression cold. "Him," he said.

All eyes turned upon the object of his gaze. Space cleared as those closest to it backed away.

And then Hereward knew he was dead.

LIII

The Tower of London
23 June, 1193

LATE UPON ST John's Eve, Guy of Gisburne and his squire Galfrid presented themselves at the gates of the Tower of London. The guards at the gatehouse – several of whom now knew Gisburne by sight, and who greeted him genially – were just as reticent as ever to admit them. Now, at least, they had the courtesy to obstruct him with apology and regret, and Gisburne understood, finally, that their hands were tied – that it was Fitz Thomas, and no other, who determined to make his life difficult. Finally, the gates creaked open, and Gisburne – longbow over one shoulder, quiver hanging at his saddle – rode into the castle ward with his squire at his side.

And thus it was that the great longbow returned to the Tower.

Within the castle, all was the same as ever. Grooms and servants went about their business as if this day were no different from any other. It seemed impossible to Gisburne that life here could carry on in a state of such total oblivion.

There was, however, one deviation from normality. At the centre of yard, before the keep's west wall, a scaffold was under construction. Hood's scaffold. Before it stood a beaming Fitz Thomas, admiring the work as if it were all his own idea, and his own sweat. So low had the man now fallen in Gisburne's opinion that he found himself unable to believe the Lieutenant capable of admiring things in any other way. It was his – in fact, or by some imagined right – or it was nothing.

"Magnificent beast, isn't it?" he called across to Gisburne with a smile. The hearty relish with which he regarded this instrument of execution made Gisburne feel sick. He and Galfrid dismounted, and the squire led the horses away to the stable. "I imagine you have come to see that all preparations are in order for tomorrow?" said Fitz Thomas. "The big day! Well, I can assure you they are. And what is more –"

"I have no interest in what is happening tomorrow," interrupted Gisburne. "Only in ensuring we reach it."

Fitz Thomas guffawed as if Gisburne had made some unintelligible theological pronouncement of dubious scholarship, pulled a face at one of the workmen, who laughed dutifully, then looked back at Gisburne. "Well, God willing," he chortled.

"It'll take more than God," said Gisburne. "We need men. Armed and ready. For tonight he will come."

Fitz Thomas stared at him with what Gisburne finally realised was a kind of pity. The Lieutenant laughed as one might laugh at a deluded infant, or a particularly dim dog. "Are you still fretting about this Red Hand of yours?" Gisburne half expected to receive a pat on the head as he said it. "This is the Tower of London!" As if this, and this alone, were the entire answer to the problem, Fitz Thomas spread his hands wide and chuckled ever more heartily, catching the eye of one of the carpenters upon the scaffold as he did so. The man joined his laughter, and one by one, his fellows joined him.

Gisburne's patience was gone. Today was the last day. Perhaps the final time he would ever see the Lieutenant of the Tower. He would not be missed – and Gisburne no longer cared much whether he offended him. But he did need his co-operation until this thing was done.

That morning, as predicted, Mélisande was gone. How, he would never know – years of practice creeping past armed guards, he supposed. Then he had gathered his things, ensured that money was left for Widow Fleet should he not return, and as much for his own sake as his host's, he had washed his walls clean. All of those obsessive marks – all the words, numbers, pictures and plans – were now meaningless. Now, there was only action.

"I need your help," said Gisburne. "We must work together to prevent this catastrophe – to safeguard the life of the Prince, and to bring the Red Hand's reign of terror to an end. And for that, I need your men at my disposal. To distribute around the fortress. There are things that we can do. Traps that we can lay. I know this enemy – how he will try to trick us, how he will attack. This way, we have the best chance of bringing him to justice."

Fitz Thomas frowned and nodded sagely. It was clear he had barely listened to half of what Gisburne had said. "But you see, the problems are not within these walls, but out there." He gestured to the city beyond. "The people are in a state of turmoil. They are afraid – whipped up, may I say, by stories such as the one you continue to spin!" He laughed, and looked to the workmen again for support. This time, they studiously avoided his gaze. "These poor folk look to us to help them in their hour of need. And for that reason, the Tower garrison has been put at the disposal of the City to help keep the peace – a gesture to the Lord Mayor, Henry Fitz Ailwyn." He smiled a patronising smile. "You see, there are more important collaborations, Sir Guy. It is not all about you and your needs."

Gisburne fumed. He wished, there and then, to dash out Fitz Thomas's brains. "Are you telling me that at a time of threat, the foremost royal palace in England is without a garrison? Whose idiotic idea was that?"

Fitz Thomas's sickly smile curdled, but the Lieutenant recovered. "You talk of threat..." he said, smiling again. "But it is one man! Let him come, I say. Let him be broken against these walls!" He sighed, and smiled again, and then explained as if to a deaf old woman. "Relations between the Lord Mayor and the Crown are delicate. It will be good for the city. Good for us all."

"Well, that's something," said Gisburne. "Next morning, when they find you, your men, your dog and the king's own brother slaughtered and the Tower put to the torch, we will at least have good relations with the Lord Mayor to fall back on."

At that, Fitz Thomas's mask of affability fell away completely, and Gisburne found himself staring at the face of a bitter, hateful old man, his eyes devoid of sympathy or care. With a reddening face, Fitz Thomas stepped towards him. "I give you my permission to move freely within these walls," he rasped, spit hitting Gisburne's chest. "But should you interfere with the running of my castle, or attempt to foist your orders upon my men, you will be cast out of those gates!"

"You can't do that," said Gisburne.

"I'll do as I like!" snapped Fitz Thomas. He was shaking with fury. Gisburne watched as the Lieutenant fought it down, then plastered another false smirk across his face. "Well... Now that is understood, I'm sure we can continue to be friends." And with that he turned and walked away, exchanging a joke with the watchman as he went.

"THAT LOOKED LIKE fun," said Galfrid, weighed down with their gear.

"He threatened to have us thrown out," said Gisburne.

Galfrid looked around. "D'you think there are enough here to do that?"

Gisburne gave a humourless snort. "I said he couldn't. I think he misunderstood. So how's it looking?"

"Not good. We have a fair army of cooks, scullions, stable lads and pages, but beyond that..."

"How many guards do you count?"

Galfrid puffed out his cheeks. "Four on the gate. A few on the Towers. A couple loitering over by the stable. In all, I'd say no more than a dozen."

"The heart of England, presided over by that oaf and a dozen men... And them not even the pick of the crop."

Gisburne sighed, and looked westward towards the city. The evening sun was setting beyond the wall, its deep shadow creeping across the yard. "Prepare the weapons," he said.

LIV

It was close to midnight when Gisburne and his squire stood upon the battlements of the White Tower, watching for whatever might come. John had been forewarned, and was secured within. There was little more they could do now but wait.

Gisburne leaned on the stone parapet and faced into the steady breeze, gazing towards the glinting water of the river.

Galfrid looked across at the two Tower guards upon the battlement, who had at least afforded them the courtesy of keeping their distance. "You haven't yet asked what Ranulph Le Fort told me," he said.

"You'll tell me in your own time," said Galfrid with a shrug. "If you need to."

"I need to," said Gisburne. "Want to. You deserve to know."

Galfrid nodded slowly. "Was he able to fill the gaps in our knowledge?"

"Yes. And more." Gisburne sighed. "It transpires that Ranulph was one of the men my father trusted most in the world. Everyone trusted Ranulph, it seems. Well, you've seen him... He's a force to be reckoned with. And uncompromising. One of the reasons, I suspect, why he never became rich. So much did my father have faith in Ranulph, that he charged him with carrying out one of his last wishes – delivering a casket in the event of his death. To Ireland. To a woman named Liadan."

"Liadan?" said Galfrid. "Is that...?"

"Yes," said Gisburne. "The name upon the parchment. The one we could not read. Whether my father had obscured it deliberately, or through some impulse of which even he was not aware, we will never know. But Liadan was the widow of the chieftain Faelan Ua Dubhghail. It was my father Ua Dubhghail had been coming to kill that night – the night Ranulph intercepted and killed him, and lost his fingers. There was a word I occasionally heard my father mutter in his sleep. I never understood it.

But now I do. I understand it all. It was Liadan's name he uttered. The name of the woman he had met that first time in Ireland. Who he met again when he returned with John, when her jealous husband sought him out, out of revenge, or for fear that their love may be rekindled."

Only when he spoke these words, the matters behind them being made more real, did Gisburne realise how hard it was to accept this truth – to face the fact of his own father's infidelity. There was pain in pushing them out – but, like a bad wound, it felt good, and right, to get rid of the poison.

"She must have meant a good deal to him," he continued, steadily. "Or perhaps he was wrestling with his guilt. Either way, he left her what little wealth he had left. Not much. Ranulph did not know what was in the casket – and being a man of trust, did not look. But it seemed that, alongside the small quantity of silver, it contained documents from the Irish expedition – including the third copy of the Milford Roll – and a letter to Liadan, penned by my father. Perhaps he hoped to make amends by it. If so, it did not have the desired effect. In fact, it was the spark that lit the inferno which now threatens to engulf us." He turned his face away from the squire.

"My father did not think beyond Liadan being a widow. But she'd had the good to fortune to have remarried, and into a noble Irish household. Her husband discovered the letter, learned the truth. Liadan and her two sons were cast out – disgraced and disinherited. Ranulph later learned, to his horror, that Liadan had died by her own hand." He sighed heavily once again, and bowed his head.

"And so to the final detail... The younger of Liadan's two sons – thirteen in the year of John's expedition – had been of prodigious size and strength. He looked, by all accounts, very different from his brother. There had always been cruel whispers about his parentage. When driven out, penniless, he had been forced to find a trade. He did so – as a blacksmith and tinsmith. That boy would now be twenty-one." Gisburne paused, took a deep breath, then continued. "When my father went to Ireland the first time, for King Henry, it was the spring of the year 1171."

Galfrid frowned at this information. "Spring of 1171. That would have been –"

Gisburne anticipated him. "Twenty-two years ago. Nine months before the boy's birth."

For a time, they stood in silence, then Gisburne spoke again. "Through all of this, as we have crept closer to this truth, there is one fundamental error that we have made. It has been with us right from the very start, nudging us off course." He turned to Galfrid. "He's not coming for John. He's coming for me."

*   *   *

GISBURNE TURNED BACK towards the river, and as he did so, a patch of pale white caught his eye. There, in the moonlight, he could make out the sail of a ship: Baylesford's, leaving upon the tide. Somewhere on it was Ranulph Le Fort – and Mélisande. It was coming closer, sailing past them to the sea, and on to France. His heart was heavy at the sight of it. He would have done anything – paid any price – to have her with him now. But he knew it had been right to send her away, to safety. This was his fight alone. It had always been so.

It was, he now knew, the revenge of a son upon a son. What the Red Hand had always known was that wherever John was under threat, there would Gisburne be. He had known John would come to the Tower. He had known Gisburne would come to protect him. He had known too that Gisburne would torture himself almost to madness chasing the murdering phantom around the city. Gisburne had done everything the Red Hand had wanted – unwittingly, and unaware that he himself was the focus of all his hatred.

As Gisburne stared towards the steadily approaching ship, half in a dream, it seemed a weird light flickered. He blinked, thought he had imagined it. But there it was again, seemingly upon the ship itself. In a great burst, the whole sail seemed to light up, as if it somehow had the sun behind it. A shout went up from one of the guards upon the battlement. Then Gisburne saw the flames.

"Mélisande..." The name caught in his constricted throat.

Cries broke out on the shore far below. Bright with flame, but still with a head of speed from the brisk wind, the ship suddenly veered to port. He heard a great creak and a crack of timbers as it turned sharply towards the one weak point in the Tower's outer curtain wall: the wide inlet that cut through from the river – a half-completed moat abandoned by Longchamp. There was a horrid familiarity about the scene now unfolding. This had been Gisburne's point of entry to the Tower complex over a year earlier. And he, too, had set a ship afire.

The entire vessel shuddered as it smashed through the staves bristling the mouth of the inlet. Cries of alarm echoed all about the shore. Driving deep inland, the ship struck the bank, rose halfway up it with a great groan of timbers, and keeled to one side, flames leaping high into the night sky.

Gisburne stared, sick to his heart.

"It's begun," he said.

LV

It was as if the sun had risen in the castle ward. Even as Gisburne emerged from the keep, he could feel the heat from the flaming wreck. "Get more men on this door!" he bellowed at the guard, and ran down the stone steps to the castle ward.

All about it, dark silhouettes of panic-stricken servants flitted, fetching water and hurling it wherever they could reach. Some drenched the nearest buildings and trees as proof against the fire spreading, whilst the meagre remains of the garrison dodged about in response to Fitz Thomas's orders, barked above the crackle and roar of the flames – some gripping spears and crossbows, others helping to move water, but almost all without clear direction, and to little effect.

"He's here," said Gisburne looking about him.

"How can you be sure?" says Galfrid.

"Because it's what I did. The same trick. *The most important thing of all is happening while everyone is looking somewhere else* – that's what Hood said."

"But what is the most important thing?" said Galfrid. "Where is he headed? The keep? Or there?" The squire pointed to the far tower in which Hood was held prisoner. Gisburne looked at it, then back to the keep. It was an impossible choice. But there were only two of them. They could not cover it all.

"The keep," he said. "It has to be the keep. If we could only get more men..." He ran to Fitz Thomas, and caught hold his arm.

"Leave the ship to burn," he shouted. "There's nothing more to be done here. We must secure the Tower."

Fitz Thomas turned to him, his face red and sweating from the heat. "Are you mad? A fire is raging at the very heart of the kingdom, and you tell me to simply ignore it?"

Gisburne almost laughed aloud at his words. "The heart of the kingdom..." Only now did the Lieutenant show concern. "The fire is not the issue," insisted Gisburne.

Fitz Thomas gave a sarcastic laugh and held out his hands towards the inferno. "You think this is not an issue?"

"It's a distraction to keep you busy while the Red Hand makes his way in there!" He pointed towards the gaunt edifice of the White Tower.

"Good luck to him!" scoffed Fitz Thomas. "He'll be banging his head against the most secure walls in England." But Gisburne could see he was close to panic.

"You're doing exactly what he wants." said Gisburne.

"I am doing exactly what *I* want!" snapped Fitz Thomas. "Instead you would have me do what *you* want, but what do you know of it?"

"More than you! I have tracked this man for six weeks – have faced him in combat."

"And yet still he runs free! Not a resounding success, is it Sir Guy? Well, this is my domain. Mine! I am the commander of this garrison and custodian of this castle. Me! Not you. And I will do as I like."

Gisburne turned to any member of the Tower garrison who were near enough to hear. "We must search the Tower wards for an intruder," he shouted above the din. "Someone who may have jumped from the ship as it ran aground. He is a big man –"

"Ignore that command!" interrupted Fitz Thomas. "He has no authority here!"

"This intruder threatens the life of Prince John! Your King if Richard should not return!" At that, the guards hedged and hesitated. Several looked at Fitz Thomas not just with concern, but with challenge in their eyes.

"Ignore him!" bellowed Fitz Thomas. "None shall take orders from this man! The first to do so will be flogged! I will do it myself!"

None chose to defy him.

In disgust, Gisburne turned back towards the keep, but as he did so Galfrid rushed towards him.

"Something's happening at the gate," he said. "I don't know what. The guard is shouting, but there's no one to hear him."

The pair broke into a run towards the gatehouse.

"Christ Almighty," said Gisburne as they approached. "One guard on the battlements! With the Tower under attack! An idiot could take this castle." He stood beneath the gatehouse battlement and cupped his hands around his mouth. "Hey up there!" he called, craning his neck. "What's happening?"

A face appeared above – the skinny young guard who had welcomed him here a month before. "I need the porter!" he cried. At the same moment, another guard – an old lag, who Gisburne knew well by sight, and who was acting as porter – emerged from the gatehouse hauling up his drawers. Behind him, the red face of a maid peered round the door, then hastily retreated. "What's all this?" he grumbled wearily.

"For God's sake, man, are you deaf as well as blind?" said Gisburne. "The place is collapsing around your ears!"

"I was told to stay at my post and at my post I stay," he protested.

"We can see well enough what you're doing with your post," spat Galfrid.

Gisburne wanted to slap him. "What use are you if you don't even listen to your damned watchman?"

The old guard merely harumphed and looked up to the battlement. "What's going on, boy?"

"People at the gate," called the lad.

"Who?" demanded Gisburne.

The guard looked from the old guard to Gisburne, uncertain whether to respond.

"Come on, man, you know me well enough," called Gisburne. "A knight in the service of Prince John. And I'm only asking what your porter should. So, out with it!"

The old guard looked Gisburne up and down. "Better do as he asks, boy," he called. "Quickly now, or I'll have your guts for sausage skins."

"Armed men," called the young guard. "A dozen or so. Half of them Hospitallers. They say they're here to offer help."

Gisburne looked at Galfrid. "Hospitallers?" When he looked back, the guard was gone. There were further cries beyond the gate – words between the guard and the knights that Gisburne could not make out above the clamour of the fire. Suddenly the guard reappeared.

"And there's a woman with them," he said. "She says she's the daughter of the Count of Boulogne."

"A likely bloody story," mumbled the old guard.

But Gisburne was no longer listening. "She's alive..." he breathed Then he turned and grabbed Galfrid by the shoulders, his face beaming. "She's alive!" Galfrid laughed and hurrahed with joy as Gisburne turned on the gatehouse guard. "Half a dozen knights of the Order of Hospitallers and the daughter of a count," he said. "Do you intend to keep *them* waiting?" The guard hesitated. Gisburne took a step forward. "Open this gate or by God I'll open it myself!"

"All right, all right," grumbled the guard. "Keep yer hose on."

"Maybe you should try keeping yours on next time," shot Galfrid.

Ignoring him utterly – as he seemed to ignore most everything – he set to the task at his own pace, refusing to be rushed. Keen, it seemed, to show that the gate, and the opening of it, was his duty, and his alone. Gisburne did not blame him, but cursed Fitz Thomas for setting such an example to his men.

THE GATE CLANKED and creaked open. The party of armed knights and serjeants marched in, swords rattling, mailcoats glinting – at their head, armed and dressed half like a Byzantine knight, half like a *hashashin*, was Mélisande. Gisburne threw his arms about her.

"I couldn't leave you wanting," she whispered. Then she drew back, held his face between black-gloved hands, and, looking deep into his eyes, said: "You do realise my career as a spy is over..." Gisburne could only smile stupidly in return, grateful to the Fates, or God, or whatever it was had delivered her. Had he learned then it was the Devil's work, he would have shaken that old gentleman by the hand.

As she peered past him now, she stared aghast at the great burning hulk. "My God..."

"Ranulph's ship," he said. "I thought you were on it... Though what became of him..." he shook his head in despair at the thought.

She stood back then, seeming to hold back a smile. "I brought some friends," she said.

There were six Knights Hospitallers – instantly identifiable by their black surcoats bearing the white cross; straight-backed and grave-faced beneath their gleaming helms. Their leader – a steel-grey-bearded man approaching fifty, but who looked more than a match for any guard here – immediately stepped forward. "I am Theobald of Acre," he announced. "We come to avenge the murder of our brother, Jocelyn de Gaillard." Gisburne grasped his gauntleted hand. Theobald lowered his voice. "And because we were told *you* were here..."

Gisburne frowned at his words. The Hospitaller smiled and leaned towards him. "You are Guy of Gisburne. You outwitted the Templars at Marseille. Made them look like idiots. For that alone, you shall ever be the Order's friend." He stepped back and raised his head. "It is St John's Eve and we are the Knights of St John," he said. "It is fitting that the earth be cleansed of this foul creature before the dawn."

The others who accompanied the Hospitallers – every one of them a giant next to Mélisande – were richly clothed and armed, but bore no livery that Gisburne could recognise. He did know the face of their leader, however, for it still bore the eagle-shaped bruise he had inflicted upon it the previous night: Otto. He was now dressed in a surcoat of rich black velvet, picked out with rivets of pure silver. Gisburne could not imagine the cost of such a garment. Gisburne also recognised the fork-bearded rough who had stood against the door in the Hansa tavern – now every inch a knight. At the sight of Gisburne, he stepped forward and bowed his head. The silver details on his surcoat glinted in the firelight like stars in a night sky. "I come from Günther von Köln," he said, his voice deep, his accent heavy. "He gives me a message: 'No solid feelings.'" Gisburne smiled and shook his hand as heartily as he knew how.

"How did you manage all this?" he said to Mélisande.

"My womanly wiles," she said, then shrugged. "But Sir Ranulph also helped."

And then, from behind the main group, stepped Ranulph Le Fort. His mail had clearly seen better days, his red surcoat was worn and his sword was battered, but Gisburne could not have been more glad to see him. Ranulph grasped Gisburne's hand with both of his.

"We must put this right," he said. "Do not judge your father too harshly. I am here today out of love for him."

Gisburne bowed his head. "You are most welcome," he said.

From behind him came a deafening crack, and he turned to see the ship's mast collapse in a great shower of sparks.

"We must move quickly," said Gisburne. "He is here already."

"You are our captain today," said Ranulph. "What are your orders?"

"Answer well, Gisburne..." said Mélisande.

Gisburne clutched the strap of the quiver at his back, alongside which hung the great longbow. He turned to the Hospitaller. "Theobald – do you see that eight-sided tower to the far south-west corner? It has only one door. Put two of your men on it, and let none pass – in or out. None! All know your livery. None will challenge it." Theobald nodded, and immediately dispatched two of his knights. "As for the rest of us," said Gisburne, gazing towards the great, square stone keep, "our business is with the White Tower. Follow me." And as one they strode away across the castle ward.

"OUR FOE IS heavily armoured," said Gisburne as they went. "Swords and crossbows are nothing to him. Do not rely on them. His main weapon is a heavy hammer. Against that there is no defence, not even from your helms. And he has Greek Fire, which he shoots to a distance of up to ten yards. Do not get close. Do not engage him hand-to-hand."

"Then how are we to fight him?" said a bemused Ranulph.

"Tire him. Trip him. Keep him down if he falls, and call upon the others. If he charges, dodge him. Strike from behind, or at any weak point you see. But do not face him." The assembled army exchanged troubled looks at these words.

"And you?" said Mélisande. "What will you do?"

"I must get to Prince John before the Red Hand does."

"But he is depending on you doing that," muttered Galfrid.

"There's nothing else I can do," said Gisburne.

As they approached the keep, Gisburne caught the eye of a boy carrying a basket of bread towards the garrison – a half-familiar face. Immediately, the boy dropped his gaze to the ground and hurried off. Gisburne looked back at the assembled band. It was hardly surprising, he supposed, that it should inspire such fear in the lad. In the past hour his forces had grown from two to fifteen – hardened fighters, every one. But he still was not sure it would be enough.

"No one to challenge us," said Galfrid as they marched towards the forebuilding that protected the keep. As they rounded it, Gisburne looked up the stone steps to the keep's entrance.

"And still only one guard upon the door," muttered Gisburne.

"A disgrace!" said Theobald.

"But predictable," said Galfrid.

They clattered up the steps towards him. The guard – apparently without fear – stepped across the door to bar their way.

"There is an intruder in the Tower," said Gisburne. "Step away, in the name of Prince John."

"And the Count of Boulogne," chipped in Mélisande.

"And God," added Theobald.

Otto simply loomed over the man. "Move," he growled.

The guard straightened his back and looked at Gisburne. "You may pass, sire, for I know your face well," he said. "And if you vouch for those with you, they too. But I will not step away from my post. I am charged with guarding this door, no matter what."

"What's your name?" said Gisburne.

"Gilbert, sire," said the guard.

"A good name," said Gisburne, and clapped him on the shoulder. "Then you can help us, Gilbert. We must clear the keep. Get everyone out. Servants and staff."

"They're all out, fighting the fire." He looked embarrassed. "And the guard is... depleted. There are just two, upon the battlement."

And John... thought Gisburne. By now it barely came as a surprise to discover that Fitz Thomas had so abandoned the Prince. "Then we must secure this door," he said.

"It will be easy enough to hold," said Ranulph. "With men inside and out."

Gisburne turned to Otto. "I need three of your men on this door with Gilbert here." Otto bowed his head and barked the orders, then turned back to Gisburne. "No man will get in."

"You're not keeping him from getting in," said Gisburne. "You're keeping him from getting out."

"A trap..." said Theobald.

Gisburne glanced back in the direction of Hood's octagonal tower. "It's as good at containing men as it is excluding them."

"But if we have blocked the one entrance..." began Ranulph.

Mélisande nodded slowly. "You think he's in there already..."

Gisburne said nothing, but simply gazed up at the great expanse of stone.

Gilbert frowned. "Sire, no one has passed this door who I did not recognise, and then only to leave."

"And if the door is now barred," said Ranulph, struggling to make sense of Gisburne's strategy, "how is he to enter this trap?"

"This one doesn't always use the door," said Gisburne.

Theobald stared up at the hundred-foot-high stone wall. "It's not possible..." he muttered.

"Trust me," said Gisburne. "It is."

All at once, Gisburne heard a sound from above, and several of the men looked up. Something was whirling through the air towards them. He drew back, dragging Mélisande with him. The object bounced on the roof of the forebuilding, somersaulted, then plunged into the darkness of the yard below. From its sound, it was a long length of wood. As it spun past, a spiked steel tip had gleamed briefly in the light of the fire: a guard's polearm. Before any could speak, a light flared upon the battlements, and a bright object hurtled down from the parapet. As it roared past leaving a trail of flame, they heard the shriek and saw the flailing limbs of the burning guard. His body struck the ground with a thump. There were shouts from the yard – screams.

"Now we know," said Galfrid.

"And I suppose now you're going in there," said Mélisande.

"I must," said Gisburne.

"Before you even ask," said Galfrid. "Yes, I'm bloody coming. I've swum through every shade of shit with my head on fire for you – this'll be luxury by comparison." Theobald looked askance at the strange little squire.

Gisburne nodded. "I'll need seven more men with me," he said.

"Six men," said Mélisande. "One woman."

"You'd better make the choice, Gisburne," said Ranulph, "because there's not one of us who will not volunteer."

Gisburne turned to the youngest of the Hospitaller knights. "Search the perimeter of the keep. Look for a rope on the north wall." He saw the knight's disappointment, and put a hand on his shoulder. "This task is no less honourable, nor any less important."

"If I find this rope?" said the knight.

"Burn it. And look for a crossbow. A large one. Something with which he may have shot a grapple over the battlements."

"How do you know the rope will be on that wall?"

"Because it's the shortest section and easiest to climb. Because it's overlooked less than other parts of the keep. And because it's what I did." With a bow, the knight turned and hurried down the steps into the darkness.

Gisburne looked up towards the parapet. Nothing stirred, but he knew what waited there.

"We know he is above us. We will move up floor by floor in three groups of three. Upon the first floor there is but one stair to the next level, in the north-west tower. But from there, each group will take one tower each."

"Three towers?" said Ranulph with a frown.

"There is no stair in the south-east tower, for it is over the chapel," said Gisburne. "On the third floor we make contact, and if all is clear, move on up to the battlements. Theobald – you and your men take the south-west tower. Ranulph, Otto, and his man take the north-west. The north-east will be for me, Galfrid and Mélisande."

All nodded. As they turned, Gilbert opened the thick wooden door, and one by one the small army entered the dark interior. Only Gisburne hesitated.

"What is it?" said Mélisande.

"Something I must do first..." he said. And he threw off the longbow and quiver and unbuckled his belt.

"Now?" said Mélisande coquettishly. "In front of strangers...?"

Without a word he removed his horsehide surcoat, then lifted the long coat of mail over his head and let it fall in a heap upon the stone flags. It had been his father's – one of the few things left him when the old man died, along with his sword, and his horse. He pulled his black coat back on, and buckled his sword belt.

"You go without armour?" said Mélisande with a frown. "Today of all days?"

"It offers no protection," said Gisburne. "It's dead weight." Then he bent the great longbow to nock the string, slung the quiver across his back once more, and strode into the keep.

LVI

THE INTERIOR OF the White Tower was like a tomb. Many times Gisburne had passed through the long hall into which they now stepped, but never had it possessed such an air of abandonment. There was no sound, no movement. Half the flambeaux had burnt out, casting most of the echoing space into deep shadow. The hearth was empty and cold, and if candles had been lit at all that day, they had long since guttered and died. The fire had all but gone out in the heart of England.

The temperature dropped perceptibly when they entered. In the extreme quiet, Gisburne heard Mélisande shudder. All drew their weapons as they crept into the gloom, their movements tense and cautious, as if watched by the silence – or something in it.

As he advanced, Gisburne felt something crack under his boot. The company tensed and froze at the sharp sound. He bent, poked at it with the stave of his bow. A chicken bone. How it got there, he could not guess. He flicked it away, and pressed on.

The whitewashed chamber was austere. Its purpose was clearly military, but it offered few other clues as to what lives had been lived or lost within it – just a few pieces of plain, functional furniture, mostly pushed back against the walls. Along the left side were deep recesses, cutting through a dozen or more feet of stone, each leading to a small arched window. Two rows of stout posts ran the full length of the chamber, and filling half the opposite wall was a long wooden rack stuffed with pole weapons. Beyond it, four archways opened onto the smaller, north-eastern chamber.

In the daily life of the castle, this great hall was presided over by the Lieutenant of the Tower, William Fitz Thomas, and mainly used by members of the now-absent Tower garrison. It did not seem a living space at all. At first glance, there were no decorations of any kind: no wall hangings, no tapestries – nothing, in fact, to signal that this was the entrance to a royal palace. As their eyes adjusted, however, a thick, darkly patterned curtain could be made out in the far north-west corner. It hung from a timber frame, completely concealing whatever lay within.

The Hospitallers advanced towards it. Theobald stood ready with his sword as another gripped the curtain and thrust it back. Dust rose. Inside was a broad but disordered pallet bed, a table, a chair – and nothing more.

They moved on.

Ranulph and the Germans were first into the eastern chamber. It was from the corner of this room – the personal chamber of the Constable, Walter de Coutances – that the single stair rose. The room was as plain and practical as that which came before, but small touches of ostentation – gaudy covers upon the bed, an elaborate iron perch intended for a hawk, a mirror made of glass – suggested that in de Coutances's absence, Fitz Thomas had made it his own. Now, it was as devoid of life as its neighbour – except in one respect. On the table sat a goblet half-filled with wine, on a platter a fowl half eaten, and next to it an eating knife, as if only just laid down. A beeswax candle had melted to a pool in its dish, a feeble flame barely clinging to its wick.

Through both of these rooms all had to pass in order to reach the north-east stair. But at the far end of de Coutances's quarters lay another chamber, closed behind a blackened wooden door.

Gisburne shouldered his great bow, took up a fresh candle from a box on the wall, and lit it from the half-dead flame. He turned to his companions. "Wait here," he said, then, ignoring Mélisande's furrowed brow, advanced towards the closed chamber, one hand curled about the flame, its vast, spidery shadow sliding across the ceiling.

The door opened with a squeal of dry iron, the sound echoing about the dark space and grating his nerves. He held the candle before him, pushing it into the pitch black, shadows dancing around arches and angles of stone as he turned. Here and there, empty eyes and stone faces stared back. But there was nothing human here. Not alive, anyway.

For a moment he paused, staring towards the chamber's eastern end, and listened.

"What is this place?" said a hushed voice behind him. Gisburne looked back. It was Otto – a black ghost in the gloom, his eyes and the silver rivets of his surcoat glinting in the candle flame.

"The crypt," said Gisburne. Otto frowned at the word. "A place for bones," he explained. "Of saints. And sinners."

Otto's expression shifted. He looked about and crossed himself, taking a step back into the doorway as he did so.

Gisburne had seen enough, but no sooner had he turned back towards the door then there came a shuffling from deep within the shadows. Then an odd sound – almost a whimper. The sounds were muffled, as if buried behind feet of stone.

"You hear something?" said Otto, raising his sword.

"No," said Gisburne. He did not turn back into the crypt, nor did he allow space for Otto to pass. "It's nothing."

Otto looked at him for a moment. "Rat, maybe?"

"Yes," said Gisburne. "Just a rat." And he herded Otto ahead of him, out of the dark chamber. Otto stepped forward, as if to close the door behind them – to shut that cold space and whatever it contained.

"Leave it," said Gisburne, and moved on.

THE NARROW SPIRAL stair had one flambeau still lit near the foot of it. Above it, all disappeared into black. Gisburne extinguished and discarded his candle, retrieved three unlit torches from the empty hall, then lit them one at a time. He passed one to Theobald and one to Ranulph, and kept the third. Then he led the way on up the stairway towards the second floor. Weird, shifting shadows cast about the curved stone wall as they climbed.

It was cramped – so much so they were forced to ascend in single file. If anything came at them here, wielding a sword would be difficult – the bow would be impossible. A single armed man at the door to the next floor would have no difficulty holding them back.

But the doorway was empty.

With tentative step, every sound magnified by the night, they crept into the still air of the first chamber.

Although a near duplicate of de Coutances's room below, the court chamber had a very different aspect. Within it were long benches, at the far end a low wooden dais with a heavy, elaborately carved throne, and behind it, hanging so as to cover almost the entire wall, the banner of the King. A gold lion as big as a horse rose rampant upon a field of red. The symbol of Henry II, to signify his kingship over England.

Despite having passed this chamber on numerous occasions, on only a handful of those had Gisburne set foot further within it – and only once had he passed through the small door in the far right corner of the back wall. It was in an identical position to that which opened into the crypt on the floor below, and was built of the same blackened wood. Gisburne stared at it in silence, then turned his flambeau around the room, putting the closed door at his back, and moved instead towards the arches that opened into the great banqueting hall.

On the first floor, they had communicated only in hushed tones; on the echoing stair, in whispers. Now, none spoke. Gisburne gestured to Theobald and Ranulph to spread out, each entering the hall through a different archway.

From here, if all was well, Theobald would continue on up the yet more confined stair of the south-west tower. Ranulph and the Germans would move up the north-west, whilst Gisburne would return with Galfrid and Mélisande to the remaining stairway in the corner of the court chamber.

But first came the banqueting hall itself.

Gisburne had been here twice before – once, to dine in the company of Prince John. Then, it had echoed with the sounds of joyous chatter and music, the air filled with the aromas of roasted meats and spices, a crackling blaze in the hearth keeping the winter chill at bay. Now, forsaken, it was dark and damp and heavy with the creeping smell of mildew, whose relentless march the midsummer air outside had failed to impede. On the walls were dark, Flemish tapestries from the time of Henry – their tops now festooned with cobwebs. Behind the dais where England's absent monarch should have sat – but never had – was a newer addition: the red banner of the Lionheart. Much like his father's, it bore not one, but two gold lions. Richard could never resist going one better – it was what drove him. Gisburne fully expected a third lion to join them should Richard ever return from imprisonment.

The banner was poor quality – hastily prepared when Richard had rushed to England after his father's death, eager to be crowned. It now had a torn, ragged hole in its top left corner, where it had been badly nailed to its timber spar. A tangled skein of old web, thick with black dust, hung across the head of the uppermost lion like a dirty crown.

The groups fanned out to check each nook and recess. Otto took the furthest. As he drew close, a shrill screech tore the air. From behind one of the tapestries, something flew at his head. He shouted and ducked, and Theobald raised his sword.

The chattering bird fluttered off into the rafters, where, finding no way out, it eventually settled. Ranulph smiled and clapped Otto on his enormous shoulder. They breathed again. There was nothing in the hall – nothing but a terrified sparrow for a monarch, and a company of spiders for his court.

There was one more place to check before moving on. It lay beyond the arch at the furthest end of the hall. This doorway led into the same chamber as the small black door – the Chapel of St John. It was open, and from it, a dim light glowed.

Gisburne moved towards it, gathering pace as he did so. The others fell into step behind him.

None – not even Gisburne – were prepared for what they found. In the chapel – dominated by massive Norman columns, above which, bounding the overlooking gallery, was a second row of stone arches – dozens of candles burned. It was not, in itself, a strange sight. But after all they had seen thus far – or, rather, all this place had been lacking – the sight of it chilled Gisburne to the bone.

For a moment, all stood transfixed. Then Ranulph stepped forward, and examined the tops of the candles, poking one with his finger. "These were lit not half an hour ago," he whispered.

Theobald looked from Ranulph to Gisburne to Otto.

"John?" whispered Mélisande by Gisburne's ear.

"Not John," said Gisburne. Quite apart from anything else, a chapel was the very last place one would find the Prince.

"Tell me," whispered Otto. "Are there ghosts in this place?" This big man, who Gisburne had judged to be afraid of nothing, had a tremor in his voice.

"No ghosts," said Gisburne. "None but the human kind."

"Then what is that?" said Otto. And he pointed up to the gallery.

Framed in one of the archways was a dark shape, massive, yet weirdly without depth – like a shadow. And it had the horned shape of a demon.

All stared at the motionless thing, striving to make sense of it. Still it refused to move.

"It's just an illusion," said Theobald. "A trick of the light. Nothing more." One by one, the others – baffled by the eerily still shape – lowered their weapons. Even Otto turned, and wiped a hand across his forehead. He looked sheepish – embarrassed. Gisburne, too, was ready to look away.

Only then did it move.

With almost supernatural speed, it darted away, across the next opening, and there merged completely into the shadows. Mélisande saw Gisburne tense, and turned back to the gallery. All followed her gaze – and gripped their weapons tighter. Almost without thought, Gisburne had whipped an arrow from his quiver and set it on his bow. Now, his eyes strained to see – to find a target. To detect some movement. But there was nothing.

Then he heard it, echoing above. The rhythmic chink of metal.

"It's him," he said.

The sound receded. The shadow had been heading towards the north-east stair – directly through Prince John's bedchamber. Realisation struck. "He will fail to find John up there," said Gisburne. "He will come looking. Try to move down. But we must contain him – drive him back up to the roof if we can."

"But where is John?" said Mélisande.

Gisburne was already at the small black door leading to the court chamber. He wrenched it open. "Go!" he hissed to Ranulph and Theobald. "Guard the stairways. Call out if you see him – but do not move from them. We must not let him pass." They ran back into the banqueting hall with their men to take the remaining towers up to the next level, while Mélisande and Galfrid hurried after Gisburne towards the main stair.

THE SOUNDS THAT erupted and echoed through the north-east tower as they ascended were those of wanton destruction. Above them, furniture crashed and splintered. Objects were hurled across the room. Metal clattered. Pottery smashed.

It stopped abruptly. When Gisburne, Galfrid and Mélisande emerged from the stairway door, the dust still hung in the air.

This floor followed the now familiar pattern of three distinct chambers: a large hall to the west, a smaller room to the north-east, and a level of the chapel to the south-east. But it differed from the others in one important respect: around all of these chambers ran a continuous passageway set into the fifteen-foot-thick walls, part of which formed the gallery around the Chapel.

From the doorway at the top of the stair they could not see directly into John's bedchamber. Instead, they were faced with a solid corner of stone, and stretching from it, at right angles to one another, corridors running the length of the north and east walls. From this, some yards distant in each direction, dark arched doorways opened into the chamber.

Gisburne looked to the nearest – the bedchamber's north entrance – then unslung his bow, and nocked an arrow upon the string. "Stay by this door," he whispered. "Let nothing past."

"I didn't come this far to guard a damned door," said Mélisande. But behind the indignation, Gisburne sensed something else. Fear for his safety? Perhaps he flattered himself.

"You must stay," he said, looking her in the eye. "No matter what you hear." Mélisande knew as well as he that it was a necessary tactic. She gave a reluctant nod. "If he comes, keep him here. By any means. Distraction, diversion. Anything."

"May we kill him?" said Galfrid.

"Please do," said Gisburne. "Just don't kill yourselves." Then he turned, padded silently to the chamber door, peered around its edge, and slipped in.

It was as if a wild animal had been let loose. Everything was wrecked and strewn about. Prince John's fine clothes were torn to shreds, his possessions broken and scattered, a barrel of wine – smelled before it was seen – burst open, its contents splattered and now flooding the wooden floor. Even the bed had been destroyed, its spilt straw guts – now stained deep red, in parts – transforming the royal chamber into a disordered stable.

He picked his way through the wreckage. Moving silently proved all but impossible – doubtless part of the Red Hand's strategy. So be it. It was time to come out of the shadows. He levelled his bow, his eye to the arrow.

"Ranulph?" His voice rang though the silent spaces. "Speak!"

"Here!" came Ranulph's echoing voice from the council chamber beyond.

"Theobald?"

"Here!" called the Hospitaller, his voice more distant than the first.

"Niall Ua Dubhghail!" bellowed Gisburne. It sounded like a challenge – and it was meant as one.

Before its echo had died, a huge figure burst forth from the furthest archway, roaring as it came. Gisburne drew and loosed his arrow at the great, misshapen head. There was a clang like a bell as it struck. The Red Hand reeled at the impact, the floor shaking under him. Gisburne loosed another at his chest. Then another.

None bit. But they hurt him. A fourth shattered to splinters on his midriff. The roar turned to a cry of pain, and he turned and fled into the third archway through to the council chamber.

He was limping. This, and the debris that cluttered the chamber floor, were all that had protected Gisburne from death. As he darted through the nearest arch, he set another arrow upon his bow – but the Red Hand was nowhere to be seen in the great hall.

For a moment, it seemed some act of magic. Then a crash within the bedchamber told Gisburne that his foe had wrong-footed him, and doubled back through the archway. He glimpsed the dark shape as it ran into the shadows of the corridor on the bedchamber's far side – the corridor leading directly to the stair which Mélisande and Galfrid now guarded. Gisburne ran headlong to the other corridor, meaning to head him off.

He stepped into it with an arrow at full draw – and there, at the corridor's end, standing before his arrow's point, was Mélisande. He lowered the weapon. She looked along the adjoining corridor, then back at him, and shook her head. But Gisburne could hear heavy footfalls, and the clank of metal.

After a moment of disorientation, he understood. They were receding. The Red Hand had turned the other way, and was running along the passageway that circled the entire floor, and from which he could strike anywhere.

A cry went up from Theobald. Gisburne dashed back into the dark council chamber and towards the south-west stair. Another shout of alarm. A cry of pain, and a clatter of weapons, as if some great struggle were taking place. As Gisburne approached, he was dimly aware of Ranulph – the indefatigable fighter – rushing to the aid of the Hospitallers, both Germans hard on his tail.

"No!" cried Gisburne. "Stand fast!"

But Ranulph did not hear, or – with thoughts of revenge for Baylesford burning in his mind – chose not to. There was no time to argue now. Gisburne threw himself through the arch, arrow drawn – and there saw the Red Hand, two knights hanging off him, crashing against the walls of the corridor, and Theobald beyond, striking merciless blows with his sword. Gisburne aimed, but could not shoot without risking the Hospitallers' lives. Then Otto and Ranulph charged past and flung themselves into the fray. They gripped him all around, Ranulph clawing at his helm, and for a moment it looked as if they may wrestle him to the ground – but the Red Hand, suddenly possessed of renewed strength, crashed back and forth between the stone walls – once, twice, three times – then flung all of his assailants off as if they were stalks of grass.

Two of the Hospitallers tumbled and crashed down the stone steps, and Otto and Ranulph fell in a heap, blocking the corridor. With astonishing agility, the Red Hand leapt over them, slammed Otto's fork-bearded comrade against the wall and sent Gisburne flying.

Gisburne gathered his wits and looked the length of the corridor stretching towards the now unguarded north-west stair. No sign. A flare of light – unaccountably bright – caught his eye from within the council chamber. Scrambling back to his feet, he ran towards it.

The unoccupied throne had been set ablaze, thick, choking smoke billowing from its upholstered seat with the sickly smell of burning horsehair. The others ran into the chamber – all, by some miracle, alive and walking.

Otto went to fight the fire, but Gisburne held him back. "Leave it," he said. "Let it burn..." Then, frowning at the familiarity of the words, cursing his own stupidity, he turned and ran to the north-west stair. The Red Hand had long since passed, but from somewhere – he could not tell whether up or down – came the echoing clink of his armour.

Gisburne withdrew to the council chamber, his head bowed. "Mélisande?" he called. "Galfrid?" They came running. "We lost him," said Gisburne. "We must regroup. Start again."

"But what of that?" said Mélisande, pointing to the end wall.

The fire – which had seemed more a provocation than a serious attempt at destruction – was already dying. Now visible beyond it, illuminated by the flames, was a message. On the whitewashed wall of the Council Chamber, in smudged black charcoal, were scrawled three words:

NUNC IOANNES HABEO

Now I have John.

Gisburne stared in disbelief. "That's impossible..." he muttered.

"It would appear not," said Ranulph gravely.

"But John was never here," said Gisburne. It was a bluff. It had to be. But the terrible possibility gripped him, nonetheless. "I must go," he said. "Find John. Get him out."

"What of *him* – the Red Hand?" said Theobald. "Has he moved back up to the battlements?"

Gisburne gazed upward. "That is where he means to draw us. I'm certain of it."

"And if he has moved further down?" said Mélisande.

"Then my mission is all the more urgent," said Gisburne, and turned towards the north-east stair. "Drop back to the second floor. From there you have only one staircase to defend. I will continue down to the first. Keep him in as best you can, but do not engage him if it can be avoided. It's me he wants."

"And if he does have John?" called Ranulph.

Gisburne shook his head. It was not possible. But even as he thought it, he was beset with doubts. "We'll know soon enough."

He turned into the stair and hurried down into the darkness.

GISBURNE DESCENDED ALONE to the first floor. Where the Red Hand now was, none could be sure. The possibility that he had overtaken them all – that he had somehow slipped past and even now was here – flashed through his mind. He dismissed it. For a moment he stood in semi-darkness, looking across de Coutances's chamber to the open door of the crypt. There was no sound. On the table – against all expectation – the puddled candle still somehow clung to life, its feeble flame barely more than a glow. Gisburne took another candle, lit it, and hurried to the far side of the chamber.

Pausing for one last look around him, he turned and plunged into the crypt. He turned left and walked almost to the end, where, upon the side wall, was a motheaten arras depicting scenes from the story of The Three Living and the Three Dead. He drew it back to reveal another arched door, looked back to the crypt entrance once more, then heaved the door open.

Inside, cowering in a dark, stone space not even wide enough for him to sit, was the huddled figure of the Prince.

"I'm sorry I ever dragged you into this," said Gisburne, holding out his hand. "But now I mean to get you out. Come on." He hauled him fully to his feet – then saw his eyes widen with terror in the candlelight.

Gisburne did not have time to turn. The last thing he heard before blackness fell was the clank of metal.

COLD STONE GRATING against the edge of his teeth.

A ringing in his head.

His left eye burning. Stinging.

Echoing shouts.

His toes moving in his boots, sweaty and stiff.

A cry of pain like none he had ever heard – which suddenly ceased.

Then blackness once again.

SOMETHING WAS SHAKING him. His eyes opened to points of light, and faces like skulls. His eyes cleared, the images resolved. Candles around him. The faces of his comrades. Then he remembered.

He sat up, feeling a rush to his head. His left temple throbbed. When he put his hand to his forehead, it met flesh sooner that expected – and it was sticky. A swollen gash above his left eye – just above the other old scar. Well, at least it wouldn't be lonely now. He laughed, and found himself looking up into Mélisande's face.

"You think this is funny?" she said.

It wasn't. Not at all. And it was coming back to him now. His face fell. "He's taken him..." he croaked, and stood unsteadily. He was back in de Coutances's chamber, though he had no memory of having been moved. Across from him, Ranulph lay half slumped on the bed, his left arm soaked in blood, his face pale as death. And one of their number was missing. A Hospitaller. "What happened?" he said.

"That's better," said Mélisande, satisfied. "It's no good you being alive if you've lost your mind."

He took a swaying step towards Ranulph. Mélisande reached out to support him. "I'm all right," he said, waving her away. It wasn't true, but it would be, soon enough. "How long was I gone?"

"Not long," said Galfrid.

"Long enough," said Theobald, despondently.

Gisburne's head was clearing. He could see now that Ranulph's arm was badly broken. His sleeve was pulled back, the wound partly bound – but yellow-white bone protruded from the exposed flesh of his forearm.

"Someone tell me what happened," said Gisburne.

"The Red Hand hit us hard," said Ranulph. "No mercy this time."

"My fellow Hospitaller, Sir Robert of Oglethorpe, lies dead upon the stair," said Theobald. "Smashed beyond recognition. We could not even move him." He shook his head in disbelief. "I have never seen such complete destruction of a man with a single blow."

"I was the lucky one," said Ranulph. He looked downcast. "But he dragged John with him."

Gisburne clenched his fist and slammed it against the stone wall. "I'm a *fool*," he said. "*Now I have John.* Well, now he has. Because I led him here." It was one of the oldest tricks there was: to draw your enemy out, to weaken them by threatening something they valued, and for which they were prepared to take risks. It was how Richard had taken Taillebourg, ignoring its unassailable walls and instead ravaging the villages around until the army within could take no more, and rode out to their villagers' defence. It was their doom. In his eagerness to protect a man's life, Gisburne had committed the same blunder – and condemned him.

"I should've seen it," he said. "Trusted my instincts. Trusted that he was safe."

Mélisande placed a hand on his shoulder. "It's not over yet," she said. He looked her in the eye. It was just the kind of thing de Gaillon would have said. Just what he needed now.

"There's blood here and on the stairs," said Galfrid. "And it leads up."

"We think it may be John's," said Mélisande.

Galfrid shrugged. "Whoever it belongs to, it's left a good trail."

"That is unlucky for him, then," said Ranulph, as if trying to rise above his injury.

Gisburne shook his head slowly. "It's not luck. He means for us to follow. He is clever, and he fears nothing. I do not believe he even expects to get out of this alive."

"Do you think John still alive?" said Mélisande.

Gisburne nodded and stared at the floor, stained with blood. "For now."

Theobald jabbed his sword point at the thick wooden post in frustration. "What kind of enemy is this? You said he had come for you. But he has had two chances to kill you."

"Three," said Gisburne. "And you've seen what he can do. He wasn't fighting us before. He was toying with us. Herding us. Making sure we did exactly what he wanted. Just like he made sure I was here tonight." He looked up above. "There is no question he means to kill me. But there's something he wishes to show me first. Up there. On the battlements. That's where I must go."

"But if that is what he wishes..." said Theobald.

"The time for wishes and choices is past," said Gisburne. "That's where this will end."

"Well, what're we waiting for?" said Ranulph. He struggled to his feet, looking as determined and battle-ready as ever – but it was clear his fight was over.

"You must stay," said Gisburne. "We'll come back for you when this is done."

"I will *not* stay," growled Ranulph. "I still have one good arm – and I learned to fight with both!"

Gisburne put a hand on his shoulder. "Too many men have died already," he said. "Too many I failed to protect. Let me say I saved one, at least."

Ranulph tried to protest.

"Please," interrupted Gisburne. "For my father's sake. You saved his life. Let me repay that debt."

Ranulph held his gaze for what seemed an age, then sighed and nodded slowly. "Give him Hell," he said. "And give them reason to remember the name Gisburne."

Gisburne turned to the others. "We move up to the battlements in three groups." He turned to Mélisande. "Take Ranulph's place with Otto."

She pulled him to one side. "Why me?" she whispered.

"I need someone there I can trust. Someone with a strategic mind."

"Are you sure you're not trying to get me out of harm's way? Trying to protect me? I don't need that."

He moved closer to her. "Nowhere will be out of harm's way up there," he said. "And when he comes, I don't want you behind me. I want you behind *him*. Ready to take him. Because I know you can."

He turned to the others. "Are we ready?" All nodded in acknowledgement. "Then we go."

LVII

GISBURNE AND GALFRID emerged from the tower to find the Red Hand waiting. He stood mid-way along the north wall, stock still, like some monstrous pagan effigy, his black scales gleaming in the weak moonlight. About his neck, Gisburne now saw, was a necklace of severed human hands.

His hammer stood idle upon the flagstones, next to his right foot. One great, steel-clad arm – his left – was folded across the chest of a quivering figure in fine blue robes, now torn. The other hand held a sword, taken from the dead Hospitaller, its blade across his prisoner's throat. Prince John.

The remainder of Gisburne's army – Mélisande and Theobald, Otto and Forkbeard – had also emerged onto the battlements from the other towers. None dared move.

Gisburne put his bow down upon the stone walkway and held up his hands to show they were empty. "Please," he said. "Spare him. It's me you want. Take me. My life for his."

Mélisande, standing on the walkway on the far side of the monster, gasped in horror.

"Please," he implored. "I beg –"

But before he could complete the sentence, the Red Hand drew the full length of the blade across the Prince's throat. Steaming blood cascaded from the gaping wound, splattering upon the stones. Clutching at his neck in a horrid, convulsive gesture, a thick gurgle bubbling from his glistening throat, the Prince collapsed to his knees, then keeled over, his head hitting the stones with a sickening crack.

"No!" cried Gisburne, lunging forward. But as he did so the Red Hand took up his hammer, then plucked up the body of the Prince as if it were a doll, and with it raised over his head and charged towards Mélisande.

She threw herself down against the parapet as he thundered straight past, and with a roar hurled the body of the Prince from the west wall. Blood spattered as it spun in the air and plunged the hundred feet to the earth below.

All set about him without restraint. Theobald's brother Hospitaller was the first to him, sword raised ready for a crushing blow – but the Red Hand's hammer was already on the move. It swung, struck and demolished the knight's head, flattening his helm. He collapsed, instantly dead, blood pumping from the ruptured, misshapen metal. Forkbeard, meanwhile, had rushed forward with astonishing speed, and looked about to leap upon his foe when the hammer swung back again. With amazing agility, Forkbeard dodged the blow, and dropped against the parapet, one hand upon the crenel. Continuing on its course, the huge hammer smashed into the stonework – and crushed the German knight's hand. He howled in agony, rolling on the walkway, as on one side, Mélisande and Galfrid, and on the other, Theobald and Otto, closed in.

Gisburne, now the furthest from the fight, gathered his wits and laid an arrow upon his bow. A blinding light lit up the battlements as fire shot from the Red Hand's left arm and set Theobald ablaze. Gisburne took aim and loosed his arrow at the Red Hand's eye slit. The great monster turned as the screaming Theobald charged past him, and the arrow clanged against his helm, glancing off and sending him momentarily reeling.

Theobald collapsed to knees at Gisburne's feet. Gisburne pushed him to the ground and rolled him over and over until the flames had ceased, but it was too late. Theobald of Acre was now no more than a smoking corpse.

Gisburne heard the clatter of great impacts, and looked up to see Galfrid raining blows upon the beast's helm with his pilgrim staff. Breaking through that thick helm was a forlorn hope – but Gisburne could see Galfrid's plan. As the Red Hand staggered, dazed by the ferocious impacts, Otto and Mélisande were closing in on either side.

Otto, advancing from behind in the Red Hand's blind spot, swung his great two-handed sword at the killer's neck, striking with shuddering force. The Red Hand roared in pain – but stood as firm as a tree. In a rage, he swung wildly, his hammer battering Otto about the shoulder, smashing the bone. Then he grabbed the big German, flinging him onto the roof of the chamber below, and in the process knocking Galfrid almost off the parapet and sending Mélisande sprawling past him on the opposite side.

Gisburne was racing to their aid around the narrow stone walkway when the Red Hand turned and advanced on Mélisande. Gisburne, flying past her, threw down his bow and dropped into a ball. The big man stumbled over him and came crashing face down upon the stones – narrowly missing Mélisande. In a moment, she was on him, knife drawn, heaving up the metal plates and stabbing between them. He wailed and hurled her off; she staggered and fell, and was knocked senseless against the parapet.

Gisburne took up his bow and turned to see the Red Hand already advancing on the unconscious Mélisande, his left arm raised. He meant to burn her. Two thoughts flashed through Gisburne's mind: that he was tiring, for he was not using his hammer; and that Gisburne would never reach her in time. He drew an arrow, heaved the heavy bow, and shot at the Red Hand's broad back. It shattered against the armour and the Red Hand was knocked almost off balance. The big man turned to face him. He shot another. Then another. With each he advanced, and with each the Red Hand staggered and cried out from the impacts. One stuck fast in his shoulder.

But still the Red Hand did not stop.

And now he raised his left arm again, ready to incinerate Gisburne. Suddenly Gisburne saw the weakness – and the opportunity. He loaded an arrow, aimed it at the copper siphon, and let go.

From a distance of mere handful of yards, the arrow hit its mark. The arm jolted – a jet of bluish flame leaping from the pierced container and striking the Red Hand in the face. He roared, momentarily blinded, one of his weapons now useless.

Gisburne had only seconds before the other was brought to bear. Their earlier encounter in that muddy lane came back to him – and he charged at the towering figure.

Launching himself, he flung his arms about the metal giant, forcing him backwards towards the parapet, the tongue of flame still licking from the ruptured siphon. The big man crashed against the stonework and swayed dangerously over the precipice, his breaths – inches from Gisburne's face – coming fast and loud inside his helm. For an instant, Gisburne glimpsed an eye glinting within the metal shell.

He could no longer swing the hammer. But that was not the end of him.

WITH A SUDDEN sense of panic, Gisburne felt himself being lifted. There was crushing pain as the great hands gripped him, and as he fought to free himself, the Red Hand heaved his whole body above his head. Fighting for breath, Gisburne swayed upon the Red Hand's extended arms, and gazed down at the straight drop from the battlement to the earth below.

He blinked, strangely calm, staring into the abyss, the hiss of the Red Hand's sulphurous flame in his ears.

Then a small object, no bigger than a finger, fell out of the pouch on his belt. It bounced upon the Red Hand's helm and lodged between its spikes.

As the Red Hand's arms flexed, Gisburne reached down, took up the small, papery tube, lit it from the siphon's flame, and thrust it into the helm's eye slit.

There was a brief moment in which the Red Hand exclaimed wordlessly, sparks fizzing from the eye-hole. Then a dull boom, like a clap of thunder inside a barrel, shook his every bone.

The Red Hand staggered, trails of smoke issuing from the eyes and nostrils of the dragon helm. He let his burden drop the wrong way, and Gisburne bounced on the stone parapet and twisted over the edge. As he fell, his left arm flailed and hooked around the merlon, and there he hung, a hundred feet up, legs flailing, suspended by his bad shoulder.

Above him, in the gap of the crenel, he saw the Red Hand swaying, still stunned by the explosion. With his last ounce of strength, Gisburne reached up with his right hand, wrapped his fingers about one of the metal scales at the small of the Red Hand's back, and heaved for all he was worth.

The big man tottered backwards, stopped momentarily against the stonework, then began to tip. He tried desperately to right himself. But all that weight was now on the move, and would not be stopped.

Gisburne watched in a kind of detached horror. The huge figure tumbled over, past Gisburne – then, inexplicably, swung and dangled there. The great hammer was hooked over the crenel like a grappling hook, only the strip of leather looped about the man's wrist – stretched to its limit by that huge weight – keeping him from oblivion.

Gisburne heard an entirely new sound from the terrifying figure: a human sound. The sound of fear. In response to some instinct beyond his understanding, Gisburne reached out his free hand – to what end, he did not know.

Then the strap gave.

The Red Hand plunged over the west wall and into the night, leaving a glowing trail of blue-white flame in his wake. Gisburne, swinging a hundred feet from death, watched as the flame grew smaller in the darkness, only dimly aware of the hands reaching out to him in aid.

Then came the sickening, crashing thud, and the light was extinguished.

LVIII

THE SURVIVORS OF the Battle of the White Tower stood beneath the west wall of the keep, gazing at the shattered, ironclad body of the Red Hand. None spoke.

He was face up, his limbs neatly splayed, as if he had just laid down to rest. Fragments of his armour lay about him, flickering with the reflected flames of the fire ship and the torch that Gisburne held in his hand. The copper siphon upon his arm was now crushed beyond recognition – the sharp smell of fuel pervading the air, its slick sheen covering portions of his metal shell. Four yards away, his great hammer – which had tumbled after him – was embedded in the earth. His dragon helm had come loose in the fall and was lost in the night. The face was as so many had described – bearded and shaggy-haired – but it was not at all as Gisburne had imagined. Not the face of a monster, but of a young man. Features that in Gisburne's mind had been brutal were soft and open, almost child-like. But for the smudge upon his cheek where Llewellyn's black powder had left its mark, and a trickle of blood from his mouth, one could believe him in a peaceful slumber.

At the sight of it, Gisburne – utterly drained – dropped to his knees upon the damp earth. As he looked into that face – hauntingly familiar, though seen for the first time – he wondered why so many of his victories filled him with such bitter sorrow.

SOME DISTANCE AWAY, a small group of people was gathering, at least half of them Tower guards. All stared down in disbelief, paralysed by what they saw. A woman wailed and sobbed uncontrollably.

Gisburne stood and moved to join them. Galfrid and Mélisande followed his flame.

This body contrasted in every way with the other. It was face down – broken and contorted and covered in blood. Gisburne nudged the body with his foot and rolled it over, to a collective gasp of horror. As the head lolled back, the slashed neck wound yawned open like a lipless mouth. The woman's sobs pierced the air.

Gisburne drew his torch closer to the face. As he did so, Galfrid frowned. Here were John's clothes, John's hair and complexion, John's stature. Even, somewhere behind the terrible injuries, John's face. Yet as they looked upon him now, in the full light, all began to understand.

It was not John.

"Behold, Edric, son of Ælfric," said Gisburne. "A weaver from Pocklington who had the dubious honour of looking every inch like our noble Prince." This was the man who had taken John's place with his entourage on the journey from Nottingham, who had caused Gisburne and the real Prince to be kept waiting outside the Tower gates. As the truth was revealed, a murmur gradually rose. None now knew whether to rejoice or to continue mourning.

"Then where is Prince John?" said Galfrid.

"Hidden with Llewellyn in the bowels of the castle," said Gisburne, "accompanied by the last two members of his bodyguard. It is a place none but a handful of people know. I had thought it prudent to consider additional precautions should our defences be breached." He sighed heavily as he looked upon the battered body. "I gave him the choice. At least, I hope I did. He knew of the dangers. Yet he accepted the task without question." This man – this humble weaver, who had cowered in his wagon from Nottingham to London – was, Gisburne thought, one of the bravest men he had ever met. He only wished he could have saved his life, instead of hastening its end.

"Misdirection..." he muttered, to no one but himself.

THE SPELL WAS broken by the jovial tones of Fitz Thomas, as he bustled over in a state of self-important jubilation, his hands held aloft in triumph. Behind him scuttled a hunched servant bearing a tray of cups and a flagon.

"A great day!" Fitz Thomas proclaimed, rubbing his hands in glee. "The fire is contained, the Red Hand vanquished and I hear now that the Prince yet lives! A great day indeed!"

"A great day?" said Gisburne, barely able to conceal his disgust. "Six men lay dead. One of them at your feet."

"Ah, yes, of course," huffed Fitz Thomas. "Very sad. Tragic. Yes." He grinned once more, his token grieving completed. "But a victory! Still a victory! And so here..." Turning to the servant, he took up the flagon and filled a cup with wine. He thrust it into Gisburne's hand, then proceeded to fill another. "I think you have earned this, my friend. So let us drink to success, and –"

Fitz Thomas never completed the sentence. When he looked back on it, Gisburne would recall a distinct sound which, had he not been distracted, he might have identified. But all he knew at the time was that sudden stop, and a weird look of surprise upon Fitz Thomas's face. The flagon tipped in his hand, splattering wine upon the earth, then both flagon and cup were dropped. He staggered forward a step, blood appearing from nowhere on his white surcoat, and spreading from the centre of his breastbone. There were screams. His eyes bulged. His throat gurgled. More blood frothed and cascaded from his contorting mouth, and with a sickening crunch, the gory spike of a polearm burst from his chest.

The crowd scattered, but Gisburne stood rooted to the spot as Fitz Thomas's body began to rise into the air before him, hoisted on the polearm's point until it was flailing like a beetle on a pin. Behind him – roaring, now, with the effort – was the Red Hand, smashed, bloody, but alive, his eyes wild. How he lived – how he had survived such a fall – Gisburne could not comprehend, but before he could move, the body of Fitz Thomas was flung away, crumpling upon the ground like a doll, and the Red Hand lurched unsteadily towards him. He swatted Galfrid aside, grasping at Gisburne with outstretched hands.

Falling back, stumbling on uneven ground, Gisburne thrust at his attacker with the torch. Sparks flew at the impact – and the Red Hand burst into a fierce column of flame.

With a great howl he ran headlong, the heat near roasting Gisburne as he passed. Running blindly, he plunged off the steep edge of the half-constructed moat, and with great spray of water and a hiss of steam was sucked into its dark, weedy depths by the weight of his own armour.

LIX

It was some time before the assembled company gathered their wits and allowed themselves to believe the danger was past. Mélisande hauled Galfrid to his feet, and together they crept to edge of the black water. There Gisburne stood, staring at the still-rippling surface of the moat.

Mélisande stood beside him. "I have never seen a human body cling so determinedly to life," she said. "It took all the elements to kill him: air, earth, fire and water."

"Who was he?" asked one of the Tower guards.

"Niall Ua Dubhghail," says Gisburne. Then added: "My brother."

Gisburne turned his back on the dark water then. "We're done," he said to Galfrid.

"Not quite," said Galfrid, and looked up at the sky, already beginning to redden with the returning sun. "There's an execution come dawn."

"I've no taste for it," said Gisburne. Galfrid simply nodded.

Wearily, Gisburne looked up at the White Tower. Within, the injured were having their wounds tended by the still able-bodied Hospitallers. Some, he knew, would not survive. But Ranulph would live to fight another day – or to spend it in quiet contemplation. Gisburne would suggest the latter.

As he turned, he gazed back towards the octagonal tower at the far south-west corner of the outer wall – thankfully far from the night's chaos. There, he could see, the two Hospitaller knights still stood guard over the outer door. "We must remember to relieve our Hospitaller friends before we go," he said, gesturing towards the tower. "I think the prisoner is now safe up there without their presence. Or ours."

At that, a member of the garrison – one who Gisburne recognised as having regularly guarded Hood's cell – frowned, and stepped forward.

"Pardon me, sire," he said, hesitantly. "But you don't mean to refer to Hood?"

"Yes," said Gisburne. "Why?"

"He's not in that tower, sire. Hasn't been all night." Gisburne's blood froze in his veins. "He was moved, earlier today – I mean, yesterday. Before all this. I took him across myself."

"Across? Across where?"

"The stables," said the guard. "Over yonder." He pointed towards the stable block, a stone's throw from the main gate.

"What idiot ordered that?" fumed Gisburne.

"The stables are attached to the garrison," observed Mélisande. "There may be some logic in it."

"But the garrison is empty," said Gisburne. He turned again on the guard. "Hood was the prisoner of the Sheriff of Nottinghamshire and Derbyshire," he fumed. "On whose authority was he moved?"

"The Sheriff himself," said the guard. "Sir William de Wendenal."

Gisburne and Galfrid stared at each other. "That is not possible," said Gisburne.

"But I saw the order," protested the guard. His manner was nervous. "It bore his seal. There was no question. It said he was to be moved in the light of the threat from the Red Hand."

"Who brought this order?" demanded Gisburne.

"A young lady," said the guard. "Nobility. She was not expected, but Sir William welcomed her."

"Of course he bloody did..." muttered Galfrid.

"Name, man!" demanded Gisburne. "What was her name?"

The guard looked from face to face, and swallowed hard. "Lady Marian Fitzwalter."

Gisburne felt his world collapse around him. Marian. His Marian. Daughter of one of the most respected knights in the land, last seen associating with a sympathiser of Hood. And carrying the orders of a dead man – stamped by the seal ring that had been upon his severed right hand. Pieces of the mosaic – until now, meaningless shards – clicked together, the pattern suddenly becoming clear. The Red Hand had given Hood's men that ring. In return, they had given him the information he needed to enact his revenge – had even brought him to Tancred – and used the attack as a diversion from their own rescue. As a final insult, they had tricked the Tower's own guard into moving Hood – to a place a child could break out of. A child...

The final piece of the picture fell into place. The face of a boy, in a tavern outside Nottingham, who had raved about Hood. And the same face, just hours before, here within the Tower, carrying bread towards an empty garrison.

Without a word, Gisburne turned and raced towards the stable block.

LX

MICEL LOOKED DOWN in numb silence at the knife in his hand, and the dead, bloody body of the boy – the same age as him, more or less. His first kill.

"You bunch of rogues took your damned time!" laughed Hood, and clapped his arms around them in hearty greeting. He stood now, unbound and beaming, surrounded by the principal members of his loyal band, Took and John Lyttel – dressed as Tower guards – and in her finest gown, Marian. Beyond the door, the crackling fire ship – whose arrival moments before had been their signal to move – bathed the stable's interior in orange light.

Micel supposed it the greatest of honours to be included among this select company, and to be witness to this momentous deed. He had long anticipated this moment – had looked forward to it, and worked towards it with every ounce of his being. Yet he found that he felt nothing at all. Perhaps it was necessary. Perhaps this was the price you paid for becoming inured to death.

Hood was exactly where they said he would be – where Marian had made sure he would be. He had been tied like a hog, but the guard had been minimal, enacting their plan was absurdly easy.

Three guards and a stable lad now lay dead upon the straw. The stable lad had been his; they had saved that kill for him. Micel stared at the still-warm corpses – slabs of meat that only moments before had been living, breathing beings, with dread and sorrow and regret in their eyes. Time and again he went over the violence of the past few minutes, but he could make nothing of them. What lay at his feet now was utterly without meaning.

He glanced up and saw Marian staring, hollow-eyed, at the same butchery. Yet what went on behind those eyes seemed just as distant, just as unfathomable.

Hood rubbed his wrists, and – laughing heartily – stepped forward and caught hold her arm. She snapped out of her weird reverie and smiled weakly.

"It's all right," she said. "I'm all right." Her voice cracked slightly even as she tried to reassure him.

"But of course you are!" laughed Hood. "We're all together again!"

Micel saw her fists clench and her back straighten, as if she were steeling herself.

"I know this was necessary," she said. "For the greater good."

Hood regarded her as one regards a child speaking charming but meaningless babble, then threw his great arms about her. "My sweet Rose!" he chuckled.

"We must hurry," said Took. "They won't be distracted forever. If the gatehouse guards get wind of what's afoot..."

"They'll let us pass," said Lyttel. "I'll make sure of it."

Then Micel saw Hood's eyes upon him. It was the first time his idol had stood before him as a free man. The moment had fuelled a thousand fantasies, but now it was real. Somehow the man appeared not as indestructible, the scene not as composed, the colours not as bright as in all his imaginings. And yet, there was that spark lighting up the man's face – something he could not have imagined before meeting him – that rooted him to the spot. The outlaw king stepped past Marian, and nudged Micel upon the arm. "And this is the fine fellow who made it all possible! Where'd you find him?"

"Starving and half-dead in the forest," said Lyttel. "He'd killed one of the king's deer, but didn't look like he had much idea what to do with it next. He'd come looking to join us. I took him under my wing."

Hood placed his hands upon his knees and bent towards the boy. "Every day you brought me food," he said, his beaming face and white teeth looming down at him. "Yet still I do not even know your name."

"Micel." He had meant it to sound strong and fearless, but what he heard coming from his mouth was the voice of a nervous child.

Hood roared with laughter at that. He gestured to the big man – "So, you are Little" – and then to the boy – "and he is Much! Well, there is no better, or bigger, wing to be under than that of John the Miller."

An anxious Took looked out into the castle ward, then dodged back in. "We must go."

But Hood, refusing to be hurried, bent down, dipped his finger in the blood of the dead stable boy, and smeared a red mark upon Micel's forehead. "Now you are truly one of us."

"Please," said Took, "God is with us, but even His patience is not infinite."

Hood ruffled Micel's hair and turned. "So, how do we make our escape from this wretched place? Plunging into the river? Leaping from the battlements?"

"We walk out," said Took. "In plain sight, through the main gate, with you as our prisoner. Lady Marian is known; she carries the seal of the Sheriff. And we have a familiar face..." He gestured to John Lyttel. Micel had learned the big man was once a guard within these very walls. It was his knowledge that had furnished the Red Hand, and provided the means for the plan, but it was Took had given it shape.

The rebel monk shoved a page's hat upon Micel's head, then wrapped rope around Hood's wrists so they once again appeared bound. "God will make them blind," he said. And, taking up positions either side of him, with Micel walking alongside Marian, Took and Lyttel closed the stable door behind them and led Robin Hood to freedom.

LXI

THE STABLE STALL lay open and empty, the straw soaked with the blood of the dead.

Exhausted, beaten, his shoulder feeling like it had been wrenched from its socket, Gisburne contemplated the disaster. And in the face of it all – even in the presence of this slaughter – he found himself laughing. How could he have been so stupid? *Every day the boy brings the bread and potage.* Hood had said it to his face. And still, he had not seen it – how Hood had got information from outside. It was the boy. All along, it was the boy – the least regarded. He was just the lad who fetched and carried – and they had checked everything he fetched, everything he carried. For blades. For messages. But none had spared a thought for what the boy himself might whisper in those fleeting moments. *The most important thing of all is happening while everyone is busy looking somewhere else.* Hood himself had said it. *The answers to your questions are far closer than you think...*

As he stood there, a figure appeared in the doorway, silhouetted against the glow of the blazing ship. Gisburne half turned to face Prince John – the real Prince John. He gazed about in horror.

"What in God's name...?"

"He's gone," said Gisburne.

"What?"

"Hood. Gone. Whilst we chased after our killer – as they knew we would – they took him. From here, where they had made sure he had been moved. And it was Marian who did it." He laughed again. "Marian!"

"We must alert the guard!" cried John, turning for the door. Gisburne now saw that two of his own men – the very last remaining to him – were positioned outside.

"It's too late," he said.

"But if we move swiftly..."

"It's too late!" snapped Gisburne. "He will have disappeared into the city as surely as if it were a forest. Another rat in a city of rats."

"Surely we must try to..."

"No!" shouted Gisburne. "No more."

John's guards looked in on the stable, hands on their swords; the Prince signalled for them to leave. He and Gisburne stood in silence.

"Very well," John nodded. "You are tired. I know that. These past months have taken their toll. But we must not let this setback defeat us."

Gisburne stared at the ground, his jaw clenched, every bone in his body aching. "You knew..." he muttered. "About my father. About *this*..." He gestured towards the fire, the Tower, the swirling, green-black water into which the Red Hand had plunged. "What hope have we when our enemies work together, and we cannot?"

"I suspected," said John, defensively. "I knew of the scandal, yes. Seen a possible connection. But I was trying to protect you from..."

Before he could finish, Gisburne had grabbed the Prince by fistfuls of his tunic and lifted him onto his toes. "You *knew!*" he roared, and flung him across the stable, sending him sprawling amongst the bodies and straw. What would come of it, Gisburne neither knew nor cared. He was done.

As he turned to leave the stable, a page from John's entourage, breathless from running, careered into him, then pushed on past, fit to burst with the tidings he carried.

He stopped and stared in astonishment at finding his Prince sitting upon the ground with straw and blood in his hair – so much so, he forgot to bow.

"What is it, boy?" barked John, shaking his head. The boy looked at the lingering figure of Gisburne, then back to the Prince.

"Speak, boy, speak!" John roared, his face reddening.

"There is word from Queen Eleanor, my lord," panted the boy. "King Richard is free of his prison. Even now he returns to England!"

John's face turned ashen, and as Gisburne turned to walk away, he heard him mutter: "The Devil is loose..."

LXII

The Forest of Sherwood
1 July, 1193

THE MAN WAS brought in blindfolded. John Lyttel and two others led him in, emerging from the forest like hunters with prey, their sudden appearance from the unbroken wall of green setting the whole place abuzz. A newcomer was a great event here. No roads led to this village.

The man looked rough – not poor or needy, but weatherworn. Used to a life of extremes. If anything, he reminded Micel of the man he had seen at the Ferry Inn near Nottingham a lifetime ago – the one who had ranted about Hood, and the King, and rebellion. The man he had since come to know as Guy of Gisburne. Micel had barely begun to pay the bastard back for that insult. But there would be other opportunities. This one had the same defiant demeanour, the same strong, wiry limbs, the same dark look. Micel could tell as much even with the man's eyes covered.

Micel had stopped feeding the fire. It could wait. People stopped and stared, arrows unfletched, blades unsharpened, turnips for the pot, for the moment, left unpeeled. The arrival of an outsider meant an audience with Robin. What happened next would depend entirely on the mood of their leader. Life with Hood could be unpredictable, but one could never claim it was dull. Over near the forge, a huddle of men were already placing bets on the man's chances.

His hands were bound in front of him, and as he neared, Micel saw that about his belt hung scabbards for a knife and a sword – both empty. The naked sword now tucked into Lyttel's belt had doubtless been taken from him. It was exactly the kind of sword Micel expected such a man to have: old and a little notched, but a good blade. Not made for show, but well-cared-for. A tool of his trade. But as the stranger drew closer still – uncertain where to place his feet – Micel saw something he did not expect. Across the man's back was a musical instrument with a long neck and broad, flat, pear-shaped body. Micel almost laughed.

As the stranger staggered into the broad clearing, he stopped, and for a moment seemed to turn his blind gaze upon Micel. There was something uncanny about that look. Micel shuddered, and felt his grip tighten about the faggot of firewood in his fist. Then the man turned again, swivelling his head this way and that, taking in the sounds of people and industry into whose midst he had now been brought. It was as if he was trying to build an image of the sprawling encampment – the secret village to which no path led, and which had, thus far, eluded all who set themselves against it. Only a select few found this place and lived.

John Lyttel shoved the man forward. From the heart of the camp, where Hood's great hall clung about the trunk of a great oak, Took was now striding, habit flapping, beard jutting ahead of him. Others came at his heels. If Robin was monarch of this forest, then Took was his chancellor. For reasons Micel could not begin to understand, he had taken to calling himself *Friar* of late. John Lytell had told him that just meant "brother". It was some monkish thing, he supposed – though who he was supposed to be brother to, now he was so far beyond the reaches of any monastery or order, was anyone's guess.

John Lyttel was the closet thing Micel had to a friend. The big man – miller, soldier, Tower guard, and now outlaw – had taken young Micel under his wing from the very first, and so close had the attachment become that Lyttel's comrades had jokingly referred to Micel as "The Miller's Son". The name had stuck.

It amused everybody greatly, the contrast of "little" and "much". As a result of it, even John Lyttel himself seemed to grow fond of his long-detested epithet. He was a good man, and kind. There had been tragedies in his life, Micel knew, though he also knew better than to ask about them. Somewhere, he believed, John had a wife, though what had become of her he never found out. His dismissal from the Tower guard clearly rankled with him, and it was only in relation to this that Micel saw him occasionally boil with anger. It had meant him quitting London, for his own good. Perhaps that was where his wife still was, Yet within the man's being was to be found not a trace of bitterness, no hint of resentment towards those of better fortune.

There were few like him in the band. Every once in a while, Micel tried to imagine what John Lyttel's life would have been like had he never left his father's mill, watching the water turn the millstone, heaving sacks of grain off a wagon two at a time, just because he could – wanting for little, questioning nothing. Contented. In his quieter moments, Micel too questioned what *his* life here was for. Back home, it had seemed a wonderful dream, but now it was real. Too real, sometimes. Then he looked upon the face of Robin Hood, and all doubts melted away. He knew he would die for Robin.

And when he turned, there was Hood – advancing rapidly, a great crowd gathering around him, on his face the irrepressible smile of a man for whom death, hardship and pain meant nothing.

Bodies jostled past, pressing around the newcomer and obscuring his view. He abandoned his fire entirely, and pushed between them, just in time to see Took whip off the blindfold and cut the man's bonds. The stranger blinked and looked about, apparently shocked to see so many here. But there was a hard look in his eye. He held Took's gaze without fear.

"It says much for you that you got this far," said Took. "But that in itself does not make you worthy." Micel had heard of the spy who had infiltrated the band. It had stung Took deeply. The monk would not be fooled again.

As Took turned, the crowd parted, and Hood – as green from head to toe as an unripe corn stalk – stepped before the stranger. A hush fell as the pair eyed each other. Took stood to one side of his master. Behind Hood's other shoulder hovered the ghostly figure of the woman known as Rose.

Micel had heard she was a nobleman's daughter, and that it was partly this that had made Hood's rescue possible – but then, everyone here had concocted some outlandish story for themselves. Certainly her clothes were fine, if now a little ragged. But they also seemed to hang off her. Either they had belonged to someone else, or she had grown thin since coming here. She edged towards Took, who patted her slender hand discreetly with a fatherly gesture. But no smile disrupted her oddly vacant expression, or brought light to those shadowed, haunted eyes. Today, a purple bruise also extended down her left cheek. Micel had known her first as Marian – but Hood now never referred to her as anything other than Rose. Names changed in Sherwood. Histories too. Here, Robin would often say, there were no rules. One could do, and be, whatever one wanted. For a fleeting instant, Rose-Marian's sad eyes met with Micel's, shaking him from his reverie. He briefly wondered whether she had found as much difficulty realising the dream as he.

Hood stood, feet apart, planted his fists on his hips and looked the newcomer up and down. "Well, what's this?" he said. "A minstrel?" His great, hearty guffaw ignited the crowd, spreading laughter like a fire, and with it went a strange thrill. Of danger – of sudden, infinite possibilities; it was the thrill that accompanied Hood's every move, and swept all before it. So bursting with good cheer was Hood that he almost seemed a caricature. Something beyond real – a character from a story or a ballad, somehow dropped into the ordinary world. It was not merely strange. It was mad, impossible. But it was also irresistible.

He leaned forward. "Tell me, minstrel, what can Robin Hood do for you?"

"Let me join you," said the man. His voice was stern. He had an accent Micel could not place. Hood cocked his head on one side, never once breaking eye contact with their unexpected guest – not even to blink.

"An Irishman?"

The man gave a curt nod.

"We've had one or two of those before, though never a minstrel. I hear your country's rich with songs."

"We have our share," said the Irishman.

"And do they sing of me there?"

"No," said the Irishman. Then, after a moment, added: "Not yet."

Hood chuckled to himself. "A good answer! So, tell me, minstrel, why do you want to join us? Do you think we lack entertainment?" There was a loud chuckle from the back – but the Irishman did not smile.

"Because Prince John and his cronies insulted my people. I would see him rot in Hell – and sooner, rather than later."

Several muttered in agreement. One gave a muted cheer. Only Hood and those around him remained unmoved. Hood – still smiling his inexhaustible smile – narrowed his eyes.

"That's why you *should* join us," he said. "What I asked was why you *want* to join us – why you risked your life for it..."

The Irishman stared back at him for a moment, as if uncertain or unwilling to explain. But before he could speak – if he ever meant to – Hood's attention was suddenly distracted. He took a sudden step forward.

"This instrument you carry," Hood said. "I seem to have seen its like before."

"I doubt that."

Hood's face fell into a childish pout, but the smile broke out again an instant later. "No, no – I am certain..." He wagged a finger. "It's Saracen, is it not? What they call *al-'ud*. Or something like one?"

"With a few improvements of my own," said the Irishman.

"And you do actually play it, do you?"

A few men sniggered.

"I do," said the Irishman. But I doubt you want to hear the music this makes."

"Really? Are you that bad?" There was more laughter at that.

"No, I'm good." There was no humour in his voice. Without taking his eyes off Robin's, the Irishman slung the instrument off his back. Hood grinned and clapped his hands in anticipation. But instead of putting the instrument across his chest to pluck at the strings, as Micel had seen other minstrels do, the Irishman held it straight out before him, lengthways, strings uppermost, the body extended towards Hood, the headstock tucked into his shoulder.

Hood looked down at the instrument in bewilderment, uncertain whether the Irishman meant for him to take it, or was awaiting some kind of benediction. He extended his hand – to what end, Micel, and perhaps Hood himself, did not know. In one swift move, the Irishman flipped the instrument over.

There was a collective gasp, and a shout of outrage. All around Micel, knives were drawn, muscles tensed. Only Hood's raised hand kept them in check. Between the jostling men, Micel saw the source of their shock. Built into the back of the instrument, and almost completely concealed from the front and sides, was a crossbow – its steel-reinforced stock running the full length of the neck, its bow almost the full width of the body. The bow was drawn and cocked; a bolt aimed directly at Hood's chest.

"Do you still want to hear its music?" said the Irishman. His thumb, Micel now saw, hovered over a trigger set into the instrument's neck.

Hood smiled. Then laughed. And then he clapped his hands, as if at some entertainment. "Well done," he said. "A winning performance!" He dropped his eyes to the crossbow, and raised his eyebrows in approval. "Compound bow. Also Saracen, I think. Good choice. Their crossbows are the envy of the West – famed for their power and accuracy." He spread his arms wide. "Well, you have me. Finish me here and now and you can sing to your countrymen of how you killed Robin Hood!" He looked around at the dozens of weapon points now directed at their guest, each a tongue thirsty for blood. "I fear it would be a short song. But your fame would be assured."

The Irishman stared at him, unblinking. For what seemed an age there was no sound but the wind in the tress and the crackle of the fire. "It's the last thing I want," he muttered, then swung the bow about and shot its bolt into the trunk of the lookout tree. Micel felt the mob lurch around him.

"Hold!" bellowed Hood. All froze on the spot.

"I meant only to show my worth. Now you see what kind of minstrel I am. What kind of music I bring. I can be of use to you, or not; do with me as you will." And, quite unexpectedly, he dropped to one knee, his head bowed.

Hood studied him crouched there for some time, then again began to chuckle quietly. "I like you, Irishman," he said. His eyes narrowed again. "But before we go further, let us return to your reasons for coming here..."

The Irishman hesitated and looked around, as if, for the first time, uncertain of his position. Then he looked Hood in the eye. "Niall Ua Dubhghail – the one you knew as the Red Hand..." he began. "He was my brother." There was a murmur. Took leaned in and whispered something in Hood's ear. Hood smiled, but waved him away. "I come to add my sword to yours, and to take revenge on his killer. John Lackland's lackey. Sir Guy of Gisburne."

The murmur grew into a rumble. There was not a man here who did not know that name.

"Don't you know, Irishman?" said John Lyttel. "Robin has forbidden any man from laying a hand on Gisburne. Those are the rules."

Hood closed his eyes and shook his head. "No rules, John," he said. "Not if we decide otherwise."

John Lyttel looked down at the mud, chastened.

"You are set against him and his Prince," the Irishman said. "Bent on their destruction. To help you in that goal would be enough."

Hood frowned a playful frown. "*Am* I bent on their destruction?" he said. Then he turned to his men, and bellowed: "Well, am I?"

They roared their affirmation back at him, fists and weapons raised. Micel, caught up in the frenzy, cried out with them. As the tumult died down, Hood turned back, his even white teeth bared in a broad, predatory smile. He shrugged, nonchalantly. "It would appear that I am." The next instant, he turned away again. "Will?" he called. "Will! Get your scrawny arse out here!"

There was a shuffling. Directly opposite Micel, the men stood back, and into the space slid Will Gamewell. He turned a half circle around the Irishman, his black, beady eyes upon him, toying with a notched and rusty knife as he did so.

He was called Will the Scarlet – but none said it to his face, or none but Robin. It did not do to upset William Gamewell. Those who did were liable to wake up with their throats cut. Even in this select company – which had attracted many of the vilest villains in the land – he was regarded with caution, and near universal hatred. Some was the result of pure envy – Robin favoured this lank-haired wretch above all others – but there was no shortage of reasons for hating William Gamewell.

"Will?" said Hood. "You're an excellent judge of character. What do you make of him?"

Will grabbed a handful of the Irishman's tunic and pulled him to his feet. He looked the stranger up and down, poked him in the chest with a bony finger, tapped his knife against the purse on the man's belt, then flicked him on the nose. Those about him tittered. The Irishman's eye's blazed, but he did not respond.

Picking dirt from under his fingernails with the point of his blade, Will turned to his master. "He's a keeper," he said. Hood grinned broadly and extended his hand.

"Welcome, minstrel," he said. The Irishman grasped Hood's hand as those all about cheered and clapped, his face breaking into a smile for the first time.

"There are great things ahead of us," said Hood, with a wild glint in his eye. "So, now you know our names. Will the Scarlet. Friar Took. John Lytell there at your shoulder" – Hood scanned the surrounding throng – "and where there is Lytell, we must also find Much..." The men laughed. Several stood aside and turned to Micel, who reddened as Hood's eyes fell upon him. "Hail to you, miller's son!" Hood said, with a bow and an exaggerated wave. "But you have not given us *your* name, friend? The one you were born with or the one you wish to be known by, I don't care which."

"Ailin Ua Dubhghail," said the Irishman. Hood frowned fleetingly at the unfamiliar syllables, then his smile returned. He shook the newcomer's hand with unrestrained vigour.

"Welcome to our merry band, Alan O'Doyle," he said.

LXIII

The Village of Gisburne
4 July, 1193

"THIS WATER'S TURNING green..." said Gisburne, staring down at the stone trough. Galfrid wiped the sweat from his forehead, and sniffed and nodded. Across the paddock, Nyght tossed his head and neighed in disapproval.

With a sigh, Gisburne knelt and plunged his hand into the slimy water, scrabbling around for the bung. He'd drunk worse in his time – but he wouldn't wish it on his horse. His fingers found the wooden stopper and tried to get a grip. They slid off the slimy surface, scum and rotting wood scraping under his fingernails. "Damn it," he said, withdrawing his arm and flicking the drips from his fingers. "Help me turn this over, will you?"

Galfrid gripped one end of the trough, and together they heaved it onto its side. Water cascaded out, soaking their feet and flooding across the dry earth. The warm, damp smell filled Gisburne's nostrils. An upturned black beetle, legs flailing, sailed off on the deluge like a coracle.

Gisburne's hand went to his left shoulder and rubbed it. It had ached like Hell since the desperate encounter on the Tower battlements – like it had been wrenched from its socket and stuck back in again. Which, he supposed, was more or less what had happened at Hattin. Except that it felt like the wound had been inflicted only yesterday.

"You all right?" said Galfrid.

"I'll live," said Gisburne. He thanked God he hadn't worn his mail coat that night upon the Tower battlement. The outcome may have been very different. "Come on..." He slid his fingers under the rough stone again, and together they righted the trough upon its weathered plinths, woodlice and earwigs fleeing in all directions.

"Now what?" said Galfrid.

Gisburne shrugged. "We fill it up again."

Galfrid sighed and nodded. "It's at times like these," he said, "that I wish Sir Robert had put the paddock closer to the stream." And with that he sighed heavily and trudged off through the open gate, back down towards the manor house and the stream beyond.

"I'll be along..." called Gisburne after him. But Galfrid was already out of sight.

He looked up at the place in the Tall Tree where the wasps' nest had once hung, a lifetime ago. It did not seem so tall now. That whole time felt like a dream. But the evidence was right there before him; his arrow – the one which, as a headstrong boy, he had used to shoot the nest down – still embedded in its trunk where it had struck, though now twisted about with ivy.

He sighed and looked about him. The day was still. No wind; no sound but the calls of birds and the lazy drone of insects. A dragonfly – encrusted in blue like an Egyptian jewel – swooped, hovered over the wet earth for a moment, then darted off, wings rattling. Beyond, Nyght was cavorting like a young colt. Gisburne smiled at the sight – the pure, unrestrained joy. But an uneasy, restless melancholy stirred in the pit of his stomach. *Make the most of it, boy,* he thought, and breathed deep. The midsummer sun was hot on his face – but with the passing of the Feast of St John, the days would now only be getting shorter. What, he wondered, would the dwindling days ahead bring? The rise of Hood? The return of the King?

It was some time before he realised he had barely considered his own position in all of this. There had been too many revelations – too many distractions – for him to grasp the full implications of events as they were happening. Now, he only wished to forget them.

He had found a brother, and lost him – been responsible for his death. Had been hated by him, with an intensity that had shaken him. He tried not to think of that. Niall Ua Dubhghail – the Red Hand – was dead. That was the plain fact. But there were matters still unresolved. Loose ends that nagged.

One such matter was the arbalest. It had been found beneath the north wall of the White Tower by the young Hospitaller knight, just as Gisburne had predicted. It was not the presence of the great crossbow that troubled him; logic dictated that if the Red Hand had got a grapple and rope over the north battlement, the arbalest – or something like it – must be there. What troubled him was how the Red Hand came by it. Gisburne recalled the Welsh enginer's words: *Barons may bend the rules, but you'll not find a banned siege weapon knocking about London streets...*

Gisburne had at first believed that the Red Hand – the most self-contained, self-reliant fighter he had ever encountered – had equipped himself. But now he had reason to doubt that. There were elements in the arbalest's design that echoed the Red Hand's fire siphon – but neither of these, Gisburne had come to realise, matched the crude workmanship evident in the armour. Someone had made them – had helped him. Not Hood, not Tancred. So, who?

He had also lost Marian. The loss was somehow worse than bereavement. The Marian he had known and loved – the happy, carefree child; the beautiful, principled woman into which she had grown – had died. Yet still she walked, a decaying effigy – a mockery of what she once was. A shadow. A ghost.

He had let Mélisande slip through his fingers once again – and not through neglect, but out of love for her. It was, after all, her independence of spirit that so enraptured him. But how did one lay claim to such a thing, without also destroying it?

He had heard nothing from John. No apology, no death warrant. He supposed that was something. He would have to face that matter soon, and put things right – if it were still possible to do so. No matter what, John's fortunes and his own were entwined. But what chance was there for John now, with Richard making ready to return? What chance for England?

Thinking of these things, it sometimes seemed the whole of England was being rocked about him, like a boat tossed on a storm. The mere thought made him queasy. But at least here, at its centre, the upheaval was distant. Perhaps he might even forget about it for a while. He should try to master that trick. To concern himself only with what was within his grasp – the soil at his feet, the animals within his domain. At this moment, the life of a simple farmer did not seem such a bad thing. Except that somewhere out there, battered by the growing storm, was Mélisande. Elsewhere – drowning – was Marian. Looking on – now grown stronger than ever – was Hood. And he was laughing.

"Not that I wish to disturb your repose," said a voice. Gisburne snapped back to the present. Galfrid, red-faced, was toiling back up the path, a slopping water bucket hanging from each hand. "There's another pair of pails lying idle back there, if you're interested," he said. Gisburne smiled at his squire. Honest work; that was the thing. He laughed, and slapped Galfrid upon his shoulder as he passed, then turned his attention towards the stream.

He had barely taken a step when the sound made him stop. A hiss, barely audible, yet cutting through everything, and the dull thud of an impact.

Gisburne heard rather than saw Galfrid's pails drop to the ground –

felt the cold water splash about their already wet feet. Gisburne eyes darted about as he turned, scanning for any movement, any anomaly. There was only one, and he saw it almost immediately.

Embedded at head height in the trunk of the Tall Tree was a second arrow.

In the time it had taken him to do this, Galfrid – who would not so much as go to the privy unarmed – already had his shortsword drawn, and had swung around towards the trees, ready to rush the bowman.

Gisburne gripped his arm. Galfrid's response was a futile one. Any archer worth his salt could get off two more arrows before either of them made cover. His eyes flicked to the dense foliage from which the arrow had come, but there was no movement. No sound. Nothing to follow, nothing to aim at – even if they'd had the means. "If he'd meant to kill us, we'd be dead already," he said.

Galfrid frowned at the odd familiarity in the words – at the subtle emphasis on the *he*. But he needed only to follow his master's gaze for an answer.

The arrow in the tree was fletched with green goose feathers, tied about with green thread. Hood's arrow.

Gisburne, his movements slow and precise, stepped towards it. He held his left hand out low, towards his squire, indicating that he should stay where he was.

Galfrid did not move. "This is something new," he muttered, as if conscious of being overheard. There was a fire of outrage in his voice. "He's never this far north. Are we supposed to feel honoured?"

Gisburne was certain they were. That was the way Hood's mind worked. But he only felt a tightening in his chest – girding himself in response to what he understood was the opening move of a new game.

"What is it?" said Galfrid. "A warning?"

Gisburne stopped by the tree. "A message," he said. Not far behind the point, tied tight around the shaft with the same green linen thread, was a tiny parchment. Gisburne pulled on the arrow, but it was sunk so deep it would not shift. Hood was close. Perhaps still watching. He put both hands to the task, bending the arrow until it snapped.

Galfrid crept closer as Gisburne drew his knife and cut the parchment free. Gisburne's eyes widened at the unfurled scrap. "It appears there is no honour amongst thieves," he said, and looked up at his squire. "All those months he was in captivity, Hood gave us nothing. Now he is free, it seems he has information for us after all."

Gisburne turned the parchment so Galfrid could see. On it, in a neat hand – a rebel monk's hand, perhaps – were three words. Gisburne recognised them as a Gael place name, but one he did not know:

And above it – in heavier strokes, as if to imbue it with greater urgency – a word he knew only too well:

TANCRED

About the Author

TOBY VENABLES is a novelist, screenwriter and journalist who also lectures in Cambridge, England. He inhabits various time periods and occasionally writes about zombies. A descendant of the Counts of Blois and Champagne, he numbers the slayer of the Moston dragon among his ancestors, but despite being given a longbow at the age of twelve has so far managed not to kill anyone. In 2001 he won the Keats-Shelley Memorial Prize, and squandered the proceeds. *The Red Hand* is his third novel.

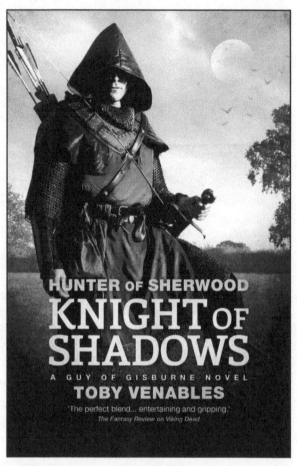

HUNTER OF SHERWOOD

KNIGHT OF SHADOWS

A GUY OF GISBURNE NOVEL

TOBY VENABLES

'The perfect blend... entertaining and gripping.'
The Fantasy Review on *Viking Dead*

England, 1191. Richard Lionheart has left the realm bankrupt and leaderless in his quest for glory. Only Prince John seems willing to fight back the tide of chaos threatening England – embodied by the traitorous 'Hood.'

But John has a secret weapon: Guy of Gisburne, outcast, mercenary, and now knight. His first mission: to intercept the jewel-encrusted skull of John the Baptist, sent by the Templars to Philip, King of France. Gisburne's quest takes him, his world-weary squire Galfrid in tow, from the Tower of London to the hectic crusader port of Marseilles – and into increasingly bloody encounters with 'The White Devil': the fanatical Templar de Mercheval.

Relentlessly pursued back to England, and aided by the beautiful and secretive Mélisande, Gisburne battles his way with sword, lance and bow to a bitter confrontation at the Castel de Mercheval. But beyond it – if he survives – lies an even more unpredictable adversary.

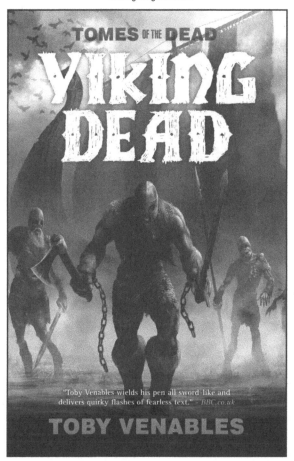

UK ISBN: 978 1 907519 68 0 • US ISBN: 978 1 907519 69 7 • £7.99/$9.99

Northern Europe, 976 AD. Bjólf and the viking crew of the ship *Hrafn* flee up an unknown river after a bitter battle, only to find themselves in a bleak land of pestilence. The dead don't lie down, but become draugr – the undead – returning to feed on the flesh of their kin. Terrible stories are told of a dark castle in a hidden fjord, and of black ships that come raiding with invincible draugr berserkers. And no sooner has Bjólf resolved to leave, than the black ships appear...

Now stranded, his men cursed by the contagion of walking death, Bjólf has one choice: fight his way through a forest teeming with zombies, invade the castle and find the secret of the horrific condition – or submit to an eternity of shambling, soulless undeath!